Advance

This is a novel about baseball, best friends, and boyhood. It's also a nostalgic, conversational trip down one man's memory lane: one imagines a friend relaying a tale in a warm, familiar bar.

Stay for the gorgeous descriptions: 'With heightened expectation each day, packs {of baseball cards} were sorted through in concentrated abandon, as the scent of cardboard drifted toward our nostrils; as the chalky and broken taste of cheap chewing gum splintered in our mouths,' and especially 'Baseball and Spring – two words more synonymous have never been uttered in American English.'

This novel is a meditation on loss and jealously, but above all, it's a celebration of life – and, central to that life, the enduring role of fandom.

-Robert Yune, author of *Eighty Days of Sunlight*

between the innings

Dan J. Kirk

Pocol Press

DEAR JOY,
Good NEIGHBORS ARE A
TREASURE. I HOPE YOU
ENJOY THE STORY.

Peace,
Dan J. Kirk

iii

9/29/17

POCOL PRESS
Published in the United States of America
by Pocol Press
6023 Pocol Drive
Clifton, VA 20124
www.pocolpress.com

Publisher's Cataloguing-in-Publication

Names: Kirk, Dan, 1970-, author.
Title: Between the innings / Dan J. Kirk.
Description: Clifton, VA: Pocol Press, 2017.
Identifiers: ISBN 978-1-929763-75-7 | LCCN 2017939499
Subjects: LCSH Baseball--Fiction. | Friendship--Fiction. | Cooperstown (N.Y.)--Fiction. | BISAC FICTION / General.
Classification: LCC PS3611 .I745 B48 2017 | DDC 813.6--dc23

Library of Congress Control Number: 2017939499

Cover art created by Michelle Kirk.

Table of Contents

To Michelle
and for the late
Professor Mark J. DelMaramo, Ph.D. (1959-2017) of
Thiel College, Greenville, PA -
Teacher, friend and baseball fan...
Because I said I would write one.

Prologue: The Drowning

Silence. Of all the universe contains, it was only the silent, rolling wonderment of Nothing that overwhelmed me as the water poured inward. The surface disappeared above, along with all I had ever known. Nothing afterward would ever measure up to such sensations. But, still, that stillness. That peace, that swallowing incubation. How calm the surrounding blue, the surrendering tranquility. How utterly warm and pacific.

Drowning. A shrieking, violent, fearful suffocation. And then...the most serene somnambulant sensation. *This isn't like they show it in the movies at all.* From where had such a thought arisen? Numbness took hold. I sauntered downward. The surface tension gave penance to the night. Nothing around me stirred. It was as if the lake itself had succumbed to death and had fallen along the way. *Is this death then? Is this sleepy darkness? To that end, I welcomed it, as if I had been born for just this final moment of clarity. When everything makes sense.* If it were to become a defining moment of life, surely it must be worth surviving.

Upward! The icy awakening. Precious time remained. This peace will lure one toward death, but time will not allow it. In moments, the swallowing water would overtake me and bring about the end. I had no knowledge of how long I had been enveloped under the calm realm of surrender, but it was beginning to register that brain damage could not be far behind. Time now to act or to not, to either live or die.

Upward!

The pleasurable, giddy lightlessness that moments ago had cradled me in comfort was of little help for no footing could be found.

Swim.

Push through!

Move out of the darkness.

My lungs squeezed against weakened oxygen molecules and pushed their last ounce of energy into my limp body.

Swim.

Swim! Goddamit, swim!

Push. Push against the thin water.

Propel toward the surface.

The car teetered along the icy shore, a wrecked, smoking, blinking reminder of the moments just before. I sprang through the surface, bobbing up once and sinking into the water again, but revitalized by that first stroke of new air. Balance resumed in the buoyed bounce of gentleness that rocked me atop tiny ripples. Again my head peered out from the gloomy depth, again air was inhaled. A chill skittered along my forehead. A throb of agony pulsated from a punctured leg. Exhaustion tantalized, luring me back toward the depths. But nothing could compare to this resurgence...life offered anew.

After the ordeal and throughout my life I would be asked once then twice then a thousand times again how it felt to nearly drown, to be so close to death. *Serenity,* I would answer. *Serenity, and simple euphoria, followed by fear and panic and hope and...*

1 Baseball Wishes

Trips. Sometimes life is all about making trips. Some significant, some inconsequential. From varying points on a map we depart and to varying destinations we direct our intentions. If life is indeed a journey, then that journey is the culmination of experience gained during trips taken, trips remembered, and those we choose not to take.

My life has largely been defined by two separate trips taken years apart that merged to form a single point of understanding. The more recent of these trips, not so long ago in the summer of 1998, was to visit a friend who was dying. He was a man I had gone to school with as a boy; a lanky kid who had always adored comedy but couldn't help the fact that he just wasn't funny. And the other trip, much longer ago in 1978, changed what I had known about life and ultimately brought me to a place I would call home.

As for my friend, we buried him late in that summer of 1998 in an unassuming grave in North Carolina near the plot where his parents lie. The funeral itself was small and quiet, somber and filled with remembrance. That had become his way. In a quiet that did not grace him as a youth, Kevin Bentworth spent his latter years in a quick descent from enthusiasm and mischief. He was only twenty-nine years old, hardly ever given the chance to escape youth before life escaped him. I can only think of how peculiar it was each time he attempted to raise a laugh from anyone we met in the nineteen years I was fortunate enough to have known him. On such an occasion when he was able to get near a punch line (one that in the hands of a comedian would send an audience into fits of laughter), Kevin would somehow botch the ending by delivering it incorrectly, stressing the wrong syllable or mistaking the true "umph" of the joke. Time and time again he tried, but no matter — he just wasn't funny. His life story isn't all that funny either. In fact, it is quite sad.

I am indebted to Kevin Bentworth endlessly and graciously, for what he has taught me and what he has meant to me. His humanity exceeded what any philanthropist could ever hope to achieve, and it is with utter reverence for him that I speak, and in his memory that I write. After all, he was my best friend. And every year, as spring returns and baseball games fill the calendar, I am reminded of him; and in that reminder I understand what it means to be a son.

That first trip, in 1978, is what sets this story in motion. That voyage was taken when my mother, a Lutheran Pastor, accepted assignment at a new church and our family was relocated from Pittsburgh, Pennsylvania, to mid-central New York State. Both Kevin and I were young children when that trip was taken — I, an only child of two loving parents, and Kevin, the eldest son of a widower who raised him and his sister to be determined, strong-willed people of dignity. Neither Kevin, nor his father, nor many of the inhabitants of their town (save one or two parishioners who had met mom before she had accepted her position at the church), knew anything of the trip I was about to take. I would like to think in retrospect that my trip had meant as much to Kevin as it has to me. After all, it was because of this trip that we met and embarked upon our journeys into adulthood.

I am, above all, a baseball fan. I have loved the game since I was a boy and would have played it until they dragged me from the field an old, washed up semi-pro retread, had I been the one to decide. Today, I can no longer play the game at a level to which I was once accustomed. I am a broadcaster. I call baseball games for local radio and occasionally for television. Sure, it is a step removed from playing, but at least I'm near the game.

I was transported away from Pittsburgh, an exodus from which I have never permanently returned (though I have visited often) over these twenty-plus years, yet the Pittsburgh Pirates were, still are, and will always be, my favorite team. If things had happened as I had hoped, I would have played an illustrious thirteen-year-career for the Pirates. Apparently, life had other plans for me.

If life were truly fair, I would have seen my first baseball game at Forbes Field in the Oakland section of Pittsburgh. But, alas! By the time I was old enough to attend a professional baseball game, Forbes Field had long since been demolished and it was at Three Rivers Stadium that I first saw my beloved Pirates take the field. And oh what a misery it was as that! Despite their numerous successes throughout the 1970's, the Pirates took a proverbial nose dive during the eighties, a downfall foreshadowed (at least in my young eyes) on the night that I was to catch my first game on Pittsburgh's Northside where there now sits a parking lot. While I can say for certain that the Pirates lost by a score of 4-2 to the Los Angeles Dodgers that July night in 1976, I can hardly describe my excitement at having witnessed my favorite team on the field in front of me for the first time. Nor can I convey the sorrow I felt as the home team wallowed in mediocrity during the decade when I would pass into and through my teenage years. Even harder still would it be for me to express the agony I felt when my parents uprooted our family from Pittsburgh in the early days of autumn, 1978 – a single season before the Pirates would capture the World Series, the only one thus far in my lifetime.

It was somehow ironic that I wasn't excited about moving to Cooperstown, NY. Despite its lack of a major league team (particularly the Pirates), Cooperstown holds what baseball immortalizes, not what serves its motion. But, at the young age of ten, when I first called Cooperstown home, I was more interested in the games and stats of contemporary players than in history. Mom's new position would assure her a secure future for our family: a promotion, a higher salary, and the possibility of better schools for me than Pittsburgh could offer. Big deal. This was baseball that was being sacrificed.

So in the fall of 1978, the house in Pittsburgh was packed up – the only house I had ever known – and the family trudged across Pennsylvania, heading into the vast stretches of woodland that define mid-central New York. The sight of the Monroes, including myself, August, loading ourselves and our miscellaneous belongings into the family station wagon must not have been very sad for the neighbors. No one came out to say farewell as we left silently – the driveway disappearing first, then the larger scenery of the old neighborhood following away; and last, the panoramic stretch of a city skyline belching smoke into the air, and one empty stadium which I longed to visit.

The prospect of living so close to New York City and the Yankees (or Mets for that matter) itched like a rash. And as Pittsburgh's Golden Triangle disappeared behind me, I sensed my childhood disappearing too. However, as life would go on to prove time and repetition again, not all that I imagined would manifest itself. My young mind could hardly then have imagined the many opportunities the ensuing years would offer. Ahead lay my formative years in a new town and a new school, engulfed in an atmosphere of baseball and passing the days with the best friend a guy could have.

At the end of 1979, the Pirates captured that aforementioned and seemingly ever-elusive prize of a World Series Championship. In Pittsburgh, on October 17, 1979, when the city celebrated its championship team's come-from-behind victory over the Baltimore Orioles, I imagined that former neighbors, classmates and friends, enemies and strangers alike were celebrating together. What should have been the most joyous days of youth provided me my first experience of regret. The Pirates had won the World Series! And where was I, August Wilson Monroe? Marooned in Cooperstown, NY, the birthplace of baseball itself.

2 A New Friend

Judging from History's peculiar timing, I must have developed my love for sports during that winter when 1979 dissolved and 1980 was born. Between October, when the Pirates were crowned World Series Champions, and late February, when the United States hockey team shocked the Olympic world by beating the Soviet Union and later capturing the gold medal in the Games at Lake Placid, NY, the Super Bowl trophy returned to the Pittsburgh Steelers for a fourth time in six years. Is it any wonder that I am a sports fan who is convinced of my favorite teams' superiority? Still, I felt removed from the celebrations. I was not in Pittsburgh, so I rebelled my first winter in Cooperstown. Instead of perusing the halls and chambers of the Baseball Hall of Fame, I avoided baseball's history and my new home's pride all together (though I have spent every winter since spending hours combing the building). Eventually, I would come to recognize that the grandeur and pageantry all around me was not just a tribute to baseball but a celebration of America herself; a symbol of our dreams and our disappointments.

As every year, that winter passed and nature gave beautiful pause to boredom when spring returned and baseball followed. It dawned on me that April that there was perhaps no better place for a baseball fan to be than Cooperstown. The first trickle of seasonal pilgrims visited the baseball museum, and before long the Hall was abuzz daily. It became apparent to me that Cooperstown meant Americana — as much as spring break, Easter and the first car wash all rolled into one.

No matter the miles between Pittsburgh's home plate and my whereabouts, the team I rooted for would begin the season as defending World Series Champs. The words evoke fine wine, romance and destiny. Even to this day, my chest swells with pride when I don a fading black and gold ball cap, knowing that a silk World Series banner will wave above Pittsburgh for as long as baseball is played.

While the 70's may have been a tumultuous time of social upheaval, civic unrest and fear for the future, I was just a kid in 1980. My only concern was waiting for the first day of baseball. It had not yet occurred to me that a finer portion of the population was blossoming, and in four to six years take me into uncharted waters wherein I would learn to swim anew. That girls were ready

5

to meet me and my friends was not even a thought that crossed our pre-adolescent minds in 1980. To us, girls were the chatter boxes in the cafeteria, the sassy, smart kids in school who did nothing more than wreck the grading curve and sing in the chorus.

For Christmas in the winter of 1979 I received a single gift, a gray tee-shirt that read simply: "Pittsburgh Pirates — 1979 World Series Champions!" I wore the shirt indoors all winter, cleaning it and putting it away each week, folding it properly and treating it like refined silk. It was the closest thing I had to a Pirates jersey, and I could hardly wait for spring to wear it outside and unmasked from beneath the heavy parka that betrayed my loyalty. After the first day of spring that shirt was all I wore, and whether mom diligently washed it every night or became tired of the chore and set me off in dirty clothes I do not know. I strutted the tiny villa of Cooperstown to proclaim myself part of a special legion of fans dedicated to the team that had finished on top – at least for that one season. It was on that day I met the greatest friend I would ever know.

Three blocks from home, deep in a journey to nowhere really – just a kid kicking around, trying to show-off a cotton shirt – I met Kevin Bentworth. Kevin was a scraggly kid, quite the opposite of my usual tidy appearance (even if my shirt may or may not have been soiled), and a lankier fellow compared to my stocky frame. He was standing in front of the convenience store on Main Street, head down, sorting through the first release of that year's Topps Baseball Cards.

"Are the new cards out already?" I asked the stranger.

Looking up in surprise, he caught me with a nasty glance. "You talking to me?"

"Yeah. Are those the new Topps cards?"

"Of course they are. I would never buy Fleer or Donruss."

Right then I realized how unconnected myself and this stranger might be. Oh, not because of the baseball cards, certainly not. I as well would not have bought anything other than the revered Topps brand. Donruss and Fleer were simple rip-offs of the classic Topps in those days and hardly the established trading cards they have become. I had no problem with the cards. It was his own tee-shirt apparel that set me back. While I was busy showing off my pride in the Pirates, this kid was suffering an ignominy I seldom knew that year: The Cincinnati Reds.

In 1979, the Pirates not only bested the powerful Orioles and their amazing pitching staff to win the Series – they also had to get

6

past the 70's most dominant team to advance to the Fall Classic in the first place. Of course they won the 1979 National League Championship Series, thus setting the stage for my bitter-sweet destiny as an expatriate. The team that had stood between the National League East crown and a trip to the World Series in 1979 were the same Cincinnati Reds represented by this kid.

"You root for the Reds?" I asked, as unassuming as I could. I covered my Pirates victory shirt with my arms crossed. It was then that I learned one of my first lessons in both life and baseball.

"Yeah, I grew up near Cincy. Tough loss last year in the play-offs. I guess Pittsburgh was just too solid. The Reds never could get their hitters figured out. Besides, the Big Red Machine is just getting old."

Sportsmanship. What reason had I to brag after that? We shared a common respect for the game, and that seemed better than any cocky bragging rights.

"Well," I answered, still covering my shirt, "before I admit that I'm a Pirates fan I suppose I should introduce myself. I'm August. August Monroe."

"August?" he asked, a bit too condescendingly I thought. "Isn't that a month?"

"Hey, listen. I've heard all the jokes before. I don't need it from anyone else. If you are gonna be that way, then I'll leave and we don't ever have to be friends. Got it?"

A seriousness crept across his face, not quite an apologetic glance but more of an embarrassed grin.

He looked me over. "Yeah, sure," he said. "That sounds fair. Sorry. I'm Kevin. Kevin Bentworth. And that's okay if you like the Pirates – but I got one question."

"Sure," I said. "What is it?"

"How long you lived here?"

"What, here in Cooperstown?"

"Yeah."

"About a year. I grew up in Pittsburgh. Honest, I'm a real fan. I didn't just become a fan when they started winning."

"Oh, yeah. Who was their manager before Chuck Tanner?"

Not one to stand down from a challenge, I answered proudly, "Danny Murtaugh – any real Pirates fan knows that. Tanner was actually part of a trade with the White Sox."

He looked me over again. "I guess you're an okay guy," he said. "You wanna go inside and get some cards?"

"Yeah. I just got my allowance. Who did you get?"

"So far I got a Mike Schmidt and a Carl Yastrzemski."

"Not bad for the first pack of the season."

"Yeah, I suppose so. The rest are all commons. I did get one of this guy named Rickey Henderson, though."

"Who?" I asked.

"Henderson. Do you think he will ever be a big player?"

"Who's to say? Who does he play with?"

"The A's."

"Awe, they stink anyway. They had their glory years in the early 70's."

We carried our conversation into the store and left the sidewalk unaware then that either of us had just met our best friend. Also unable to predict just how good Henderson and his later A's teammates of the 1990's would become.

Buying the first pack of cards each year is a rite of passage, a ritual of spring – at least in those days it was. That was before the market explosion of the 1990's when the business took over and the beauty of baseball trading cards was veneered behind a corporate image attempting to capitalize upon a child's wishes. But for me and Kevin, and an entire generation of boys like us, it symbolized the combination of hope and expectation not unlike that which is felt as spring training offers the possibility of a pennant-clinching season ahead. Within each cheaply wrapped pack of wax paper rested the possibility that an all-star would be found; or that a favorite player would pop into our hands. With heightened expectation each day, packs were shuffled through in concentrated abandon, as the scent of cardboard drifted toward our nostrils; as the chalky and broken taste of cheap chewing gum splintered in our mouths. A true collector could be spotted in any room just by how the pack was approached. The final goal was either 792 – the number of cards in a complete Topps set; or anywhere from 24-28 – the number it took to complete a favorite team. An amateur might be distracted by the statistics printed on the reverse side, or would scan each card considering momentarily whether or not that card already sat in a shoe box at home. But a true collector sorted the cards like handling prey with a silent murmur. Imagine a pack of 15 cards. From the top card to the final one in each stack, be the card a checklist, a manager, a team photo or a record breaker from the previous year, "Need it, got it, got it, need it, got it," was uttered half-aloud until the pack was examined.

Each pack was special, and later, either in math class or after bedtime when mom and dad thought we were asleep, myself, my friends and even the occasional girl would study each card, or file it in its proper place along with doubles and triples and so on; but each was revered.

Kevin and I eventually made our way out of the store, and as each sorted through our separate packs – an especially rewarding day for me personally as it usually wasn't until pack number six or seven before I would have to utter "got it" for the first time – we got on about doing what boys do best; being boys.

"Hey, there's a game tomorrow over at the International League Field. You wanna go watch?" Kevin asked me outside the store.

"Sure. I got nothing else to do. Who's playing?"

"The fierce Cooperstown Owls and the Rochester Americans in the most anticipated rivalry of the season – the International League First Pitch Game. A contest matching the heavily favored Owls and their crafty right-hander, Neil Tomlins, against the visiting cross-staters whose showcase talent includes; well, no one actually. A stunning duel, no doubt."

I sensed that Kevin liked to talk, a trait I found to be appealing after having lived with so many city kids who had answered and spoken equally in *huhs* and *yeahs* and *I dunnos*. As well, I was able to detect a humorous respect for the game. After all, while baseball was good on any level, the games we would spend our summers watching together in Cooperstown were certainly not on the same level as the Pirates and Reds, or even the Texas Rangers and Milwaukee Brewers for that matter. Those teams are the Majors, the big time; this was semi-pro ball. But any baseball, even minor league baseball, was better than none at all.

"So, you wanna catch the game?" he asked.

"Sure, why not?" I answered. "I mean, it sounds fun."

"You think so? Well, don't get your hopes up. There's not much else around, so we might as well take in the only game in town."

"Okay," I answered. "So it's a deal, then?"

"Deal. Be here at 10:00. The gates open at 11:00. First pitch is at 12:35."

"Okay, see ya then," I added with an enthusiasm that masked my waning interest in the baseball prospects of 1980.

9

"Oh, and one more thing," Kevin added (as if a kid our age had so many concerns that merited a list), "Little league sign-ups are next week."

"Cool," I answered with true enthusiasm.

"Do you play?" he asked.

"Are you kidding? Is Dave Concepcion the best shortstop of all time?"

"He was," my new friend answered, having not yet grasped the concept of the rhetorical question. "Until that Ozzie Smith guy came along. You should keep an eye on him, Augie, he is gonna be something amazing to watch."

"What position do you play?" I asked.

"What else?" He answered as he straddled his bike, "Pitcher!"

Kevin was up on his bike and down the street quicker than a Nolan Ryan fastball. *Augie?* I pondered. No one had ever called me Augie before.

3 Game Time

That evening, long after my new cards were alphabetized and stored in team order, I drifted off to a solid sleep. I remember dreaming of game six of the 1994 World Series. By then, baseball would no doubt be at its finest level of sportsmanship and collaboration. Kevin was on the mound and I stood nearby defending second base. We were teammates, one out away from our own championship glory. For reasons that only make sense in the world of dreams, we were sporting the uniform of the Montreal Expos and our opponents, the Cleveland Indians, stood before us as worthy adversaries. I could not tell the score nor recall who was leading the series, but as Kevin hurled in toward home, the roar of the crowd pulled me from slumber. I awoke, solemn with the realization that it was only a dream and that I would have to wait a long time before ever realizing the possibility of playing in the 1994 World Series.

Morning came filled with an excitement and promise I had lacked since leaving Pittsburgh. I dressed quickly, gulped down a quick breakfast and told mom I was off to the ballpark for the season opener. Her wishes for good luck and being careful faded behind me as I stole the porch like Jackie Robinson taking home plate.

The local International League franchise had the potential for a solid team that season, and all of the Cooperstown faithful considered them a legitimate contender for capturing the East Coast Championship. The start of the season was nothing short of a town event. While the highlight of each season arrives at mid-summer when the world turns its historic eyes to Cooperstown to welcome the newest class of inductees into its Hall of Fame and Museum in August, opening day is tantamount to a grand opening. The start of each season, regardless of whether the level of play is high school or pro, represents more than baseball – it signals spring. Winters in upstate and mid-central New York come harsh and hazardous. Who in their right mind would not welcome Spring? It is on these days that even the baseball naysayers take up the charge and join Cooperstown in its yearly renewal with the outdoors. Those less interested in the game are the ones to sell raffle tickets or run the refreshment stand, and might be seen burning a few hot dogs hardly even aware of the action on the field, but they too embody a shared community.

11

How fitting that this sleepy province tucked in the shades of maples and the solitude of oaks would be the immortal resting place of memory – as if the tired, aged superstars of our collective youth found solace in their enshrinement, a spot where winners and losers, players and coaches stand on equal ground. And in that place the two meld together in a beautiful symphony of rebirth. Baseball and Spring – two words more synonymous have never been uttered in American English.

At best, the International League is a launching ground for the big leagues, and many a player hopes as much to earn his way out of that league as he does into the Majors. But to the locals, it is all about the home team. "The Coopies took one on the chin last night," an old-timer might be heard saying. "This year's boys of summer look promising," a newcomer to the game might offer. "Seems their pitching staff is weak again," an ardent skeptic might add. The echoes can still be heard today as clearly as the folks in the local diner or tavern have been speaking them daily for decades. For Cooperstown is the Mecca of baseball.

I met Kevin at the same store and off we pedaled toward the ball field, he atop a red Schwinn and I aboard a silver Huffy. What a carnival it was that awaited us for my first full season of baseball in Cooperstown. As the players warmed up on the field, the townsfolk meddled about in a flurry of activity. There was so much hype and fanfare that one might believe baseball was the furthest thing from their minds rather than the point of their day. Rides and amusements blotted the parking lot. Candy vendors, soda hawkers and game tents filled the scenery like something imagined from the World's Fair. It was the largest gathering of people and events I had ever seen assembled. Broadcast across the park's entrance in a banner typically reserved for Fourth of July celebrations all across America was a sign that read, "Baseball Season Annual Kick-Off, April 1, 1980."

Amidst the hoopla and revelry, the finishing touches were being applied to the playing surface by a grounds crew busier than any usher in the stands. Managers exchanged line-up cards, players were introduced and the game itself eventually got underway. The Star Spangled Banner drifted away in disappearing melody over the outfield wall and the umpire's guttural shrill called out the hearty phrase, "Play Ball!"

The Rochester Americans had in the previous season captured the North Eastern Conference pennant only to lose in the

12

championship to a team from Maryland. This was to be their year, and a true test for the improving Owls on opening day.

The game proceeded with a slow, uneventful pace as the innings waned on into the warming afternoon. Despite the absence of any real excitement, the very joy of baseball's yearly pilgrimage back to our hearts had begun. By inning number eight the home team was behind 2 to 1, but within minutes (though little did we know), our lives were about to change.

4 The Tent

To claim that the game itself was monumental would be an outright lie. To even pretend that either of us understood the implications of the next few hours at that very moment would be perjury, contempt, hearsay and blasphemy combined. Still, searching through the years that have made up my life and putting together the ever-changing puzzle that has altered my view of the world, it all traces back to that day. A day when spring had slowly rolled its way into town and a baseball game had been played – just as had occurred ever year.

With two down in the top of the eighth and a runner on second, a batter for the Americans – a name so lost to time: Jones? McMillan? Hendrickson? Who knows? – lobbed a foul ball over the third base stands and out across the parking lot. Skyward it flew toward the empty alleys of games and food carts left abandoned hours before when vendors and customers alike had flocked to their seats. The ball bounced daringly toward a red tent left opened yet unoccupied.

Boys being boys, and no matter how devout we may have been to our team, we took to flight for the wanted souvenir. Even at the risk of missing an eye-witness account of the next home run or amazing play in left field, we were off to the races – in search of that most precious of grails: the foul ball. The fact that it wasn't a real Major League ball mattered little. Some who had caught them over the years did not even keep them as mementos but rather knocked them about in practice the next day. Many great artifacts have been lost to the boys of Cooperstown. Who would have known which player might have gone on to become the next Robin Yount or Cal Ripken, or that the pitcher might have been the next Tom Seaver or Nolan Ryan? Hardly were we concerned, for our quest was of greater importance – a free baseball!

Kevin and I were both fleet of foot, and before long the race came down to our own two-man challenge. As the older kids lagged behind (the ones who should have easily smelted us in the race had they not taken up the then cool habit of smoking), we pulled up to catch our breath.

Kevin panted. "Let's make it a fair race from here," he said.

"What do ya mean?" I asked. I puffed for air. (The guy had hit the ball a ton and there were a lot of bleachers to navigate on the way out of the stands.)

He looked ahead. "On the count of three, we race for it," he said. "You against me and we both win but one gets bragging rights. Deal?" He extended his left arm and said, "Let's shake only with our left hand but never tell anyone else why – best friends for life."

"Deal," I said. "Best friends for life – that sounds cool." A pact had been signed.

"Ready?" he asked.

"Ready," I answered as we continued in unison: "One. Two. Three." Across the lot we skimmed.

Oh, how I see it now, as if a dream. I was Roberto Clemente legging out a triple in game five of the 1971 World Series. Kevin was the die-hard Pete Rose making a final, hustling rush around first, heading hopefully toward the Hall of Fame awaiting him at second base. The race was on. Kevin held a slight lead and I barely kept up at his heals. We turned the corner of Gunman's Alley, a row containing shooting ranges and other target games. Half way down the alley, and just as a few boys who had long been dusted had gained ground while we made our pact – adding insult to their slower pace – came around the corner, we realized quickly that the ball was out of sight. As for its position, we were certain it had careened off the light post after leaving the batsman's swing; and all in the crowd saw it shoot toward Gunman's Alley. From there, I saw it ricochet down the center of the avenue. Interested more in the outcome of the game, most of the other boys had returned to the stadium, defeated. But Kevin and I had entered into a pact and already the first test to a lifelong friendship was upon us. The acquisition of that ball was not so much in the spirit of competition, but in the completion of a task. We were determined to find that baseball.

The weather had been pleasant that day with clouds swaying quickly about in the sky and periodically revealing a bright sun countered with periods of unwelcome shade. The air was not quite warm enough on its own to keep spectators outside on a normal day. The townsfolk had sworn allegiance to baseball, and whether embattled by miserable gray or dazzled by splendorous blue, they had come in flocks only to watch the game and not worry about the weather.

We strolled the Alley, eyeing each tiny corner and focusing on each spark of white that might lay hidden out of view or under a shadow. The air turned eerie and loose. The clouds spun tightly and the wind howled a slight foreboding echo, barely heard. I glanced back to the park – as lonely as saying goodbye to Pittsburgh. The clouds sprang angular shafts of warm sun onto the playing field and all those wrapped under its blanket of spring. Above us and the alley of games lingered a threatening mass of gray, twirling slightly left to right. As a subtle cheer lit up from the crowd, behind us arose a laughter; barely audible.

"Did you hear that?" Kevin asked.

"Yeah," I answered, hiding my fear. "Sounds like we got a runner into scoring position."

"No," he answered, probably sensing I too had heard the laugh, "A noise – like a laugh – from under that tent over there?"

"You mean you heard it, too?" I inquired.

"Yeah." He paused. "We gotta go." Kevin turned up the lane.

"No way, Kevin. We made a promise."

"Come on, this is creepy. It's just a ball. We'll still be friends."

"No. We gotta find that ball – together!"

Kevin stared down both lengths of empty asphalt. "Alright already. Let's go," he said. We stood still, not sure how brave either of us really was.

"You ready?" I pleaded.

"Yeah. Which way should we go?"

"The sound came from near that tent," I said. I pointed to a lopsided teepee with its flaps rolled down at the far-left side of the alley, a distance that seemed miles from home plate.

"Okay," Kevin said. "Let's go. On three, right?"

"Right," I confirmed.

"One. Two. Three," we repeated in unison. We stepped forward. A loud rumble leapt into the atmosphere and fireworks exploded into the afternoon sky. We sighed, relieved.

"Owls must have pulled off a victory in their final at bat," I said. "Let's just find the ball, okay?" I was nearing the end of my bravado.

"Yeah," Kevin added. He completed our count again: "Three!"

We reached the tent at the end of the alley. Our walk down the corridor of mesh-over-wooden-framed tents allied us with James Bond or The Lone Ranger, or even better Luke Skywalker and Han Solo. We were warriors – together on a mission. A few feet from the tent we stopped short.

"Maybe we were just hearing things," Kevin said.

16

"Yeah, that was no laugh, just an echo from the ball game," I replied.

"Go ahead. Check under the tent," he directed.

"Why me?"

"Because I have to stand guard. That's what Ben Kenobi did in Star Wars when Luke and Han and the others needed to get out, remember? He kept Darth Vader out of sight as they boarded the Millennium Falcon."

"So?" I pleaded, to no avail.

How I had suddenly been abandoned by my comrade was a mystery, but to the task I was set! I reached a trembling left hand toward the flap and made ready to pull at the canvas, but fell short of even touching the weathered surface. My reach was too short. I took a deep breath and plunged a full step forward. I grabbed the tent's lining. I peered in, fearful of the unknown. A shock ran along my spine when the haunting laughter filled the air again. I sprang back only to find my new "friend" rolling with laughter as he echoed again the voice he had created, mimicking the laughter he had managed to cast along the corridor.

"You jerk! You scared me half to death."

"Oh, but I got you good, Augie. I did. I really did," he said. He wiped tears of laughter from his cheek. "You gotta admit, I got ya good."

"Well, it isn't funny," I declared, a bit embarrassed for having been duped. My pulse slowed and I was able to realize the hilarity of the situation. "Yeah. I guess you got me," I said. I chuckled and pretended to be a good sport.

"You boys there! What are you doing?" a voice clamored through the air.

We spun in quick, alternating circles around each other and searched the empty street for the sound too mature to be any voice Kevin could have mimicked, and one too rasped with anger to be either of our dads. An old man hobbled toward us, adorned with a thick, salt-and-pepper beard and a checkered flannel shirt. He waved a fading blue ball cap in the open air.

"I said, what are ya doing there?" He spoke loudly, though we were no more than two feet from him. We stood still, too startled to flee, perhaps too stunned to answer.

And perhaps too young to be rebellious. The thought of bolting never seemed to cross our minds. Instead, we stood there, two morons lamenting the honor code that our parents had taught us: when an adult asks a question, you answer it. Just how akin we

17

were to each other began to clarify itself. Certainly, either of us could have outrun the old man. Besides, after the fear of the foreboding tent, the anger I felt from my friend's shenanigans, and the pesky respect for elders, there was still the question of finding that damn baseball. Kevin drew courage enough to speak first.

"Uh, nothing sir. We were just looking for a foul ball that came this way."

The man pondered. "Foul ball, eh?" He was dusty, and not in a good way. He hadn't the stench of a vagabond but rather the withered, disheveled dullness of disuse. As if someone had just dragged him from an old closet and put him on for the first time in decades. "Oh, from that insipid game over there, I suppose," he complained.

"Yes sir," I joined in so as to not abandon Kevin in the inquisition. "Don't you care for baseball, sir?"

"A ball you say?" The man said, ignoring me entirely. "What do ya want with a ball, precisely?"

"To keep it, Sir?" Kevin answered.

A gruff voice replied from somewhere under the man's chest, his mouth hardly moving, "But it's not yours."

I stared at him. "In baseball, Sir," I said. "The fans keep the ball when it leaves the playing surface." He stared at me. "As a souvenir," I dumbly added.

"I know that!" he barked. "But why do you want to keep it, boys? That is the question, is it not? To hoard it? To sell it in a pawn shop? To remember this day forever? Or for the love of the game?" He paused. I was about to answer when he added, "What is your need to keep this so-called souvenir?"

Being the ever-wise student, I answered to appeal to the man's sense of history and right fellowship. "To honor the game, Sir. Of course."

"Bullocks!" he shouted. "No. You are wrong, Sonny. To gloat!" His gruff voice had disappeared and in its place rose the cheery lilt of an Irish songster telling tales of lore. "If you find that ball, every kid for three counties in each direction ought to know that you have it! It's a bragging right, don't ya know! Now, which way did it go off?" he concluded before he scampered absent-mindedly.

Kevin pointed toward the tent. "We think it might actually be inside that tent," he said.

The worn-out man dragged on his beard. "Ohhh," he said. "Well, there is a dandy, then, ain't it boys? It went into *that* tent did it, eh? Well, we will have to see about that, I reckon." The grizzled old-timer stepped determinedly to the right of the tent and, reaching for a length of sisal rope, rolled the front flap up to reveal the game within. With one flashing switchblade flick of his wrist the tent flap launched upward and coiled itself into place above our heads. The deft motion with which the man swung the awning up and tied it off – so imperceptible as to appear motionless – was as if he had been a carnival master all his life. It was impressive, if not perplexing.

He hobbled under the weight of age. "No, boys, I am not thinking you will find any baseballs in there. At least not the kind you're looking for. This here is a special tent!" He turned his eyes to us with a gleam of mystery and a twinkle of childhood. He bade us forward. "Come closer, boys. Come, take a look."

We stepped forward and peered into the tent. Kevin hesitated, but I leaned further in.

The race of my heart was equally disproportionate to the pace by which my eyes adjusted to the darkness. Against the shadowy glare of the sun masked behind the rolling clouds above and the dark interior beyond where light could reach into the tent, I squinted to look within. I couldn't see much at all, save a few glimmers of color sparkling through the murky shade, and it seemed Kevin was equally unable to perceive the interior. My eyes focused, and the imagination must have danced to life with images and ideas. The trick of the emerging light tripped and scampered into vivid consciousness as ghosts of heroes emerged, demons appeared, medieval landscapes opened before me and mystical realms played out in conquest. I was too heightened with ultra-fantasy to take notice of any true surroundings. Before me circled all the wonderment of books I had read and movies I had seen. The artifacts within the tent appeared like those of any carnival game of skill. Rows reached away from the front like shelves in a supermarket; boards ran left to right and stretched back ten or more aisles into the deep, undefined space. The farthest reaches were out of sight and would have been so even to a trained military reconnaissance expert. A grassy moss covered what passed for wood; a timber painted carnival-red faded under its weathering, cracked surface. Throughout there lingered the smell of freshly cut grass. Intermixed in the green and cross-stitched shades of black were tiny speckles of color – not white but dapple tints of beige with pale tans or fading browns, like aging leather.

Kevin leaned in closer, and as quickly as the old man had opened the tent and tied it fast, the release cord was yanked and downward slapped shut the opening. I thought I heard the sound of a brass band echoing from the deepest enclaves of the tent as I stared unsuspectingly at the now closed flap before me.

"What'd ya do that for?" I begged.

The gruffness returned to his voice. "The ball you're looking for ain't in there."

"It has to be! I saw it go near there," I whined.

"Yeah, me too," Kevin added. "Open it back up."

He held tight to his tethered rope. "You boys are pesky," he said. "I like that in a young fella." And with that the tent whirled open again. "Go on. Peer in there and get a good look while I fish your ball out."

Such stories may do nothing to prove or disavow ghost tales as told throughout the county, but at no point then or throughout our lives did either of us take the temptation of denying or corroborating what happened next.

While we both witnessed it, it went unspoken until now, left for each to discern, never to be shared and left to pass with each of us in our own mind as a product of mere fancy. As sure as we were part of a new-found adventure, I swear that the old man extended his short, rough arm into the open air of the tent, and in a wisp the air swooshed away and was calmed. And suddenly in his hand was none other than the foul ball we had been after. Yet he barely moved a fingertip.

"How'd you do that?" I asked, swallowing the words even as the unspeakable approached my lips.

He held the ball aloft between three dirty fingers. "Is this what you're looking for?" he asked.

"Yeah," Kevin answered. He snapped the ball into his own hands.

Not too quick to excite, I assumed the role of a skeptic and took the ball from Kevin to observe it myself. Sure enough and as plain as the leap in my heart, stamped into the cowhide outer surface were the words: "1980 Cooperstown Owls Season Opener."

"Do you boys believe in wishes?" the old man asked. He peered upon us, one eye closing.

"What?" Kevin asked. "You mean like when we blow out the candles on our birthday cakes?"

"Yeah, sort of like that, only bigger. Stronger, staggering, more important wishes. The kinds that make dreams come true." The man was possessed with an energy and enthusiasm he had not shown prior.

"Yeah," Kevin answered. "Sure we do."

The old-timer lifted a scraggly finger in my direction, his eyes fixed on Kevin. "What about your friend there? He looks like he isn't so sure," he said.

Kevin cajoled me into siding with him in the old man's gimmick. "Come on, Augie. Tell him you do. I know you do. You believe in wishes, don't you?"

"Yeah," I said. "Sure. I mean, who doesn't? Wishes make dreams come true, right?" I answered too quietly to be entirely convincing.

The old man looked us over once thoroughly and rubbed his graying beard, it appeared to be growing an inch as each stroke caressed the scraggly mop. A minute passed before he spoke again, the beard threatening to trip him should he step away for further contemplation.

"Well, boys. Let me tell you a little something about this tent. You see, this is no ordinary game of skill like your typical shooting and target games along the way here. This ain't no knocking over milk bottles and it isn't no b-b gun breaking a balloon neither. This is a tent of wishes and wishes do bring dreams as you both so astutely mentioned.

"I won't lie to you boys. This is not the only tent of its kind. There are many of them all over the world, but each is different, you see. Now what kind of wishes and dreams is dependent entirely on the tent itself. Some are for riches, others for love, some for power. One might even be for toys somewhere. But this one here is all about baseball. And you boys like your baseball, don't ya?" We nodded as he caressed his beard further.

"See, the rules to this game are simple but not so obvious, learnable but the outcome unforeseen. The game is a paradox and an enigma. See, ya toss a baseball in there into the darkness and make a wish as you let it fly. Wherever the ball lands determines the outcome of your wish. Now there just happens to be two tricks involved. One, you cannot see where the ball lands – ever. And two, you have to be very careful what you wish for because the wish may or may not come true in the way you imagine it; depending, like I said, on where the ball lands. Most importantly, and this is the only rule – once you toss the ball in there and make

21

your wish, the ball can never come back out again...not once, not ever. Understand?"

"So we lost a wish since this ball came out," Kevin demanded.

"No, not exactly. See that ball just happened to bounce its way in there and was not willfully submitted as a wish. That ball has to come back out. Perhaps it is the fulfillment of someone else's wish that it went in there for just that moment, but we will never know that one way or the other. All we do know is that the ball was not willfully wished into the tent. Got it?"

He must have interpreted our glazed stares and absent-minded nods as affirmations to his inquiry. He went on without either of us encouraging further discussion. "So, do you boys want to take your shot and make a wish for yourselves?"

"How much does it cost?" I asked, certain we were about to be shammed. I figured I had only eighty cents in my back pocket, along with a pack of cards I had bought on the way to the park that morning. The cards had exhausted most of my three dollars, as well as a few Cokes and a hot dog at the game.

"Oh there isn't a cost, boy. Dreams may come with a price but wishes are free."

Kevin nodded sharply. "Not in a wishing well they ain't," he said.

"That is a different sort of wish, young man. Do you want to toss a ball in or not?" The old timer was growing ill-tempered and impatient. We had a decision to make. Not one to stand down from confrontation, I looked my friend in the eye and said nothing. It was, after all, painfully obvious that my skepticism had gotten us nowhere and he was the more daring.

"Let's do it, Augie. What can it hurt? It'll be fun."

"Sure," I stammered. "You wanna go first or should I?"

"How old are you?" Kevin asked unexpectedly.

"Eleven, why?"

"Me too. When is your birthday?"

"July. Why?"

"Of what year?"

"1969. Get to the point," I pleaded.

"Yeah, kid," the man added, "What's all this about birthdays? Are ya gonna make a wish or aren't ya?"

"I just thought it would be fair to let the older one go first. My birthday is in January of 1970, so you're older. You get to go first. Deal?" We shook with our left hands.

The wish-granter smirked. "Sounds fair. Okay, kid. You're up," he told me. From under the side of the tent he produced three baseballs and juggled them rhythmically above his shoulders. Without so much as a flinch or a warning, one ball shot toward each of us, and one seemed to just disappear back into the tent.

Kevin caught his in the breadbasket, as the baseball term indicates the area just below the ribcage and above the belt line. I dropped mine and scampered to pick it up from the loose gravel, hoping equally that Kevin hadn't noticed and that the ball had not been scuffed. He did and it was.

I sized up the distance from where we stood and guessed it was probably a good three feet to the service line of the moss-covered wood. I positioned myself in the proper pitcher's stance and began an imbalanced, undeveloped wind up.

"Whoa! Hold it there, boy!" The old fellow bellowed. I lumbered out of my wind-up and nearly fell, dropping the ball a second time. "Do you want to throw it clear to Ohio, boy? All ya got to do is toss it in there. Heck you're winding up so hard it will go straight through the back of the tent. You only got about ten feet back inside there. So toss it, softly. Ease it up there. This ain't the ball park, kid."

I had gathered the baseball again and examined its added scuffs. *What kind of wish could a scuffed ball offer?* I wondered. With the power of motion toward an imaginary home plate dwindled by the rules of physics, I set my mind more to concentrating upon my wish than pretending a game scenario. Any self-respecting kid would have envisioned a game scenario during a wind-up. But not for this moment. And what would that wish be? How infinite the possibility. To wish for anything in the world – even the universe! The very thought of just how far reaching the imagination could stretch was beyond what my juvenile mind could create. Somewhere between a chance to walk on the moon alongside Chewbacca and the more worldly hope of managing a team to a World Series title one day, I ran the gamut of hope and possibility, ultimately deciding upon a wish.

And with stern concentration, I lobbed the ball inward toward the great unknown.

The ball did not take flight like a long home run, nor did it bounce about in directions every which way. Rather, it took a solid plop, then a roll to the right and landed with a reduced shudder, embedded upon a heap of moss and fantasy. And that was it. The ball just laid there, all but unseen amidst the landscape of baseballs dotting a canvas of possibility.

"Your turn," I told Kevin. He too seemed to be disappointed in the uneventful discharge of the wish and all its quick hopes.

"Yeah, I guess I'm up, so to speak." With concentration greater than mine, he reared deep into thought. His face registered the determination of a serious child who knew precisely the wish he would choose. It was as if he had always waited for such a chance and knew without hesitation what it was that he might wish for had just such an opportunity ever arisen. Sure enough it had, and one could never doubt that the wish he had waited for would be launched into a mystery game of chance.

His throw was also more definite; as if he had chosen a tight corner of a strike zone within the darkness to set down the would-be power hitter facing him. He placed it perfectly into the upper left hand corner of the second row from the top, into a space no wider than four inches. And his ball stuck. No roll, no lunge and certainly no bounce. His wish had a purpose and it was set that very moment. Mine had simply not lived up to his drama. I was glad that I had gone first – the thought of having to follow him would have derailed my spirit.

"What did you wish for, Kevin?" I blurted impatiently. "I wished for –" The old man's burly hand clasped tight my lips. The smell of cigars and leather mingled into my nostrils.

"Don't say it!" he demanded. I saw in his eyes the seriousness with which he parlayed his game to dreamers and wishers alike. He knew something I did not, and Kevin shared in the knowledge, my younger partner adding explanation to what should have been obvious. The old man uncovered my mouth slowly. "Shhhhhhhh," he said. A moment lingered.

Kevin spoke. "A wish never comes true if you tell someone else what it is, dummy!" he said. "Don't you know anything?"

"Yeah, but," I stammered, "I, how...I mean...How do we know when they come true for each other? I mean, if I don't know your wish, then how can I know if it ever comes true?"

The old man nodded. "You are best friends, aren't you?"

"Sure, I guess," I added pathetically, not sure that I liked my new best friend all that much considering his siding with the strange old man.

"You'll know," the tent man said. "One day, you'll know for sure."

24

So that was it. The single most crucial experience of our young lives that would prove to define our time on the Earth. That one day would come to be the predominant set of events in a life filled with moments and happenings, all of which were a direct ancestor to simple wishes thrown into the mix of hope. And it would not be until nearly twenty years later that any of it made any sense at all. I, of course, had no more understanding then of its significance than I did of mine and Kevin's lifelong fates, but it would stand to be a single moment captured like a photograph that later explained so much to a perplexed jury.

My new friend and I spent a minute sort of just waiting for what was to happen next, not sure if The Old Man (whose name we never learned) was going to direct our next movement or if we should just simply stroll away and await the fate of wishes.

"Well," the unnamed dusty older gent uttered, "What are ya standing there for? Go on. Go home or wherever it is you boys should be off to. That's it."

Kevin's patience broke. "That's it!?" He shouted. "This isn't even anti-climactic, it's no climax at all. Nothing happened."

"What did you expect? You didn't even pay a buck!" the man offered. With a flick of the rope, the tent was closed again and he was off on his way, disappearing down the silent avenue and muttering something inaudible.

"Now what?" I asked.

"We wait," Kevin said. "Until either of our wishes come true or we forget them entirely, I guess." He took a breath and looked around.

We walked back to where we had parked our bikes. "What do you want to do now?" Kevin asked.

"I don't know. I guess I should be getting home."

"Do you have to?" he asked.

"Yeah, how about you?"

"I'm in no hurry." He added absently, "No place to go really."

"Well, I should probably get home either way. I'll see you tomorrow?"

"Sure. That'd be great." As I turned to go, Kevin's voice caught my attention one last time. "Hey, Augie!" he proclaimed.

"Yeah?"

"How much did you see inside that tent?"

"Not much really. A couple of baseballs. Not much else. Why?"

25

"Just wondering." Kevin said. He eyed the tent. "See ya." He was off in the direction of the ballpark, opposite the direction of his home.

"Hey, you wanna toss some pitches to me so we can hit around tomorrow?" I piped up.

"Sure. Meet me here at 9:00 AM," he answered, not stopping but rather turning on his heels while maintaining an equal pace afoot in reverse stride.

I waited a moment. "Okay, great. But where? Where can we play? What fields do you want to play on? I saw there was a new set of bases put in up at Jenkins Park across from the tennis courts."

"No, we'll play here," he added. He thumbed his hand in the direction of the Owls' ballpark.

"What do you mean, here? We can't play here. The team will be practicing."

"They never practice the day after a game unless they play that night."

"Do they let kids on the field?"

"No," he answered. His voice grew louder as he continued walking away, still backwards. "My dad's the groundskeeper and he always lets me on while he mows the grass."

"What?" This was the most exciting thing a kid could possibly dream up. To play on a professional field! "You're kidding, right?" I ran toward him. "Are you kidding me? No way! We can really run the bases and play on the mound?"

"Yeah. Calm down. It's not like we got a contract with the team, and it sure ain't Fenway Park but it's fun."

"Oh, wow! Wait till I tell my parents. Your dad has the coolest job in the world. Okay, I'll see ya tomorrow then." I hopped on my bike and pedaled home.

His voice dwindled further with each stroke of my pedals and I heard him utter, "Yeah, I guess it is real cool."

5 The List

We couldn't play baseball the next day, nor did I have a chance to meet Kevin's dad. The day awoke with the kind of rain that spoils Spring's greatest pleasure while giving cause to itself for nourishment and refreshment. Instead of dry bases and the chance of hitting the ball around the field for hours, there came the dull pitter-patter of rain. Even making our way to the ballpark would have been depressing, as if to see the wondrous field aglow with mud and trenches of rainwater would emphasize the humility of a washed out day. Being it was a Sunday, I resigned myself to the long wait through another school week before being able to pick up the glove and bat again. The curse of childhood – the wait. The waiting until school let out before every day could be played about on the fields of summer was like standing in line for tickets to a sold-out game.

To pass the day, Kevin and I headed to the last place "normal" kids might have ventured – the library. Our other means of brushing away boredom was to read. We had not even seen cable television yet! Often, we pretended to read as we searched the shelves of the library for a title that would attract our attention. While many of the titles were baseball-related, or at least about football or hockey or basketball, there was the occasional experiment with literature. By then, I had already read the entire *Lord of the Rings* Trilogy twice and my palette tasted for something new. Traditional fair was inviting and for Kevin anything readable was worthy. He read magazines, newspapers, brochures, great novels, text books – anything and everything. He was a good student, and a better one than me by far.

On this particular morning, though, Kevin introduced me to an entire new realm of reading: research.

"Research?" I asked after he had mentioned he would like to spend a few hours *doing research*. "What's research?"

"It's a way of finding stuff out," he answered. "See, everything there is to know about the world is in this library somewhere. We just have to know how to get to what we want to know about. And we do that through research. Let's say that I have an idea, a topic that I want to learn more about. I learn about it by looking for books, articles and what-not in search of this information. I research my topic, come back with conclusions and presto! I have learned. Neat, huh?"

"Great, so what are you gonna research about?"

"That's a surprise. Let's say we meet back here at three o'clock and I will show you what I have learned. Deal?"

"Deal," I answered, awkwardly checking the watch on my left wrist that was now tucked under our friend-pact handshake. It was 11:30. I wondered how anyone could plan to spend three and a half hours "doing research."

"Okay," he added. "We will meet at the table near the window at three. See ya," and off he went.

I went to the stacks, shelves of books piled neatly in order. I picked out a few books to peruse and set to reading, and to waiting. I, of course, then proceeded to do what is expected of a bored kid in the library. I fell asleep. Three hours may be a relatively short time, but in a library on a rainy afternoon when a kid has ideas of playing baseball on his mind, it is a death knell to perseverance. I wasn't but five or six pages into *Encyclopedia Brown Carries On* before the comfort and warmth set in and off to sleep I went; a sleep sound and secure – no doubt equally embarrassing as passersby witnessed a sleep filled with drool and snoring. I dreamed I was the crack sleuth hired to assist the young genius Brown unfurl his latest knotted neighborhood secrets of the missing shopping cart, or to discover the whereabouts of Miss Pumpernill's unleashed cocker spaniel. I was brought awake from slumber with the sound of books being dashed upon a table. And what to my tired eyes did appear, but Kevin with a stack of books, his purpose unclear.

"Wow, you're back early," I grumbled. "How'd you gather all those books so quickly?"

"I didn't. You were sound asleep and I was gone fifteen minutes longer than we planned. Spread some room out and move over so I can show you what I got."

"How can I see what you got if I don't even know what you were looking for?"

"I'll tell ya," he said. "Here, read this." He produced a sheet of paper from his pocket. It contained some sort of list. He began to sift through the first of his few books.

I unfolded the crumpled mass. "What is it?" I tried to make sense of his handwriting.

"It's a list. Read the first item."

"I can see that it's a list. What kind of list?"

"A list of what we're looking for. Just read."

"Okay, let's see," I spread the sheet flat on the table. "From top to bottom: 'Philadelphia Athletics, 1928; Carl Hubbel, 1934; Dean Brothers, 1934; Johnny Vander Meer, 1938; Bob Gibson, 1968; Denny McLain, 1968; Tom Seaver, 1970; and Roberto Clemente, 1972-3.' I don't get it. What is it?"

"They are all baseball players."

"I know that!"

"Each of them did something famous, right?"

"Well, yeah. But what's that got to do with anything? They're mostly lumped together by years close to each other but none of them were on the same team."

"But each were in that tent."

I stopped and stared. "What?" I asked. "You mean the tent at the fairgrounds yesterday? How so? What do you mean, in the tent?"

Kevin appraised his book collection and smiled. "Calm down," he answered and sat in the chair opposite mine.

"You're lying," I accused. "No one was in that tent. That old man has you under his spell. He's wacky and so are you. You've got some sort of weird old man voodoo curse in your head or something."

"Of course they were not in the tent. I mean, their names were there."

"Where? I didn't see any list like this."

"The names were on the baseballs," Kevin stated.

"You're making this up. We couldn't even see the baseballs."

"You could not but I could. I have great vision – Eagle Eye Vision even."

I held back a laugh. "Okay, Kevin," I said. "Whatever you say. But what's it got to do with this list?"

"You don't believe me, do you?"

"I don't care. Tell me what it has to do with your research."

"No. You have to believe me entirely. If we are going to be friends forever we always have to trust each other. Here, take this book," he said.

He thrust a heavy edition into my hand, on the history of airplanes that I had grabbed but hadn't opened before falling asleep. "Take this over there and open to any page."

"Over where?"

"I don't know. Over there." He pointed to a nearby couch. "That looks about as far as we were from the baseballs that were in the back of the tent."

"Yeah, but it was darker in the tent than it is in here," I argued, not even sure what I was arguing against.

"Fine, then go on the other side of the couch to make up for it." He was up for a challenge and I had to give in. I grabbed the book and crossed to the other side of a couch where I opened the book. I leaned over it to cast a shadow across whatever page I opened upon. Kevin then proceeded to bark orders from the table, like some sort of a general.

"Okay, open it up to anywhere." I did. "Pick a spot I should read." I did. And, like that he began reading. At first, I just rolled my eyes thinking he was making up the words. Content to simply allow him his little charade, I feigned indifference. But as I listened, the "made up" version sounded awfully well-informed for a non-expert on the history of aircraft in England during World War I. Glancing down to where my finger lay at rest on the page, I read along and heard the very familiar, very recent echo of the words that were on the page beneath my eyes. Surely enough, he was reading word for word from as much as six feet away. What a display! I finished the sentence he had reached and slammed the book shut.

"That was pretty neat. How do you do that?"

"Don't know. I've just always been able to read really small things from far away." He tapped the area just above his right temple. "Great eyesight. Anyway, let's get to this list."

I committed the list to memory, folded the paper closed and placed it as a book mark where I had fallen asleep on Encyclopedia Brown.

Kevin reached out for the paper. "What are you doing?" he said. "Give me my list."

"I've got it memorized."

"No you don't. How could you?"

"Listen, if you have a skill for Eagle Eye, I may just have a skill of my own. Like Super Memory. All the super heroes have their own powers, so why shouldn't we?"

"That sounds fair," he said. "Ya know, between us we can go far together." As I would learn in the years since, Kevin wasn't one to dwell too much on the possibility of things, nor one to savor a moment. Rather, he set himself to task. His next words surprised me. I hoped he might say we would become master spies and travel the world as James Bond's sidekicks or hold the helm with Dr. Spock aboard the Enterprise.

He snapped the fingers on both hands. "Alright, give me a name from the list." He didn't even challenge my memory. I directly put him to test claiming disbelief in his visionary skill and he accepted immediately the strength of my memory. I could only hope it wouldn't fail.

"Philadelphia Athletics, 1928," I said.

"Okay, I will look up the old A's and see what 1928 is all about. Who is next on the list?"

"Does it need to be in order?" I asked.

"I think so. Since we aren't sure yet just what we are looking for, let's keep it that way for organizational reasons. It will make it easier. I don't know if there will be a pattern since the years and the players seem so out of line with each other, but who knows."

"Carl Hubbel, 1934."

"Great. You start looking up Hubbel and see what happened in 1934 that might answer our question."

I shrugged and plopped onto the couch. "What question? There is no question. How can we look for things when we don't know what they are and what we're even looking for."

"Our question is, why were these names written on the baseballs that I saw in that tent?"

"Oh," I answered, half certain I understood.

So, off we were. In quest of something, anything, perhaps nothing that might link these names and the years ascribed to them as they were supposedly inscribed on tarnished baseballs in a tent in Cooperstown that my friend with Eagle Eye Vision had been able to read – from at least six feet away.

We split the list evenly with four assignments each, two from the modern era and two from the old days long before both of us were born. There it was that I applied for the first time the things I had learned in Library Class. Library Class? I could hear the echoes now of my mother as I asked every school year with a whining plea why I had to take a library class. For the previous six years in school, we all had to spend two hours a week in the library as part of our education. *Doing what?* I always asked, *looking at a stack of books?* Well, somewhere tucked in there were lessons about filing and how books were printed and where we could look up all the state capitals or how to use a card catalog. Boring! Little had I known then just how vital such information would become. The index actually was useful. What a revelation for a young man!

Without offering much to vindicate my library teacher, I located a chapter on none other than Carl Hubbel, professional baseball pitcher, who pitched in the 1934 All-Star Game. Being a natural born reader, I started at the beginning and found myself wrapped in his life story. Nothing quite spectacular really, just a story of a young boy with dreams of playing baseball. Before long, I switched to Seaver, lured by the instant recognition of his name as a player still active at that time. About five pages into Seaver's history, I was once again startled by my over-anxious friend. I swear he never savored a moment of anything. How could this guy be a baseball fan?

He yelled, "Bingo! There it is. B. I. N. G. O. And give the dog a bone. Kevin has found it!"

"Shhh! Quiet down. We're in a library. What did you find?"

"1928, Philadelphia Athletics. It's right there in black and white. "Get this," he proclaimed. "This is incredible. How many Hall of Famers do you think ever played for the same team?"

"That's easy," I answered, "the Yankees."

"No, not a franchise. One team, the same team in the same year."

"Oh, cool. I see. Uh, maybe the Big Red Machine. By the time their careers are over, Joe Morgan, Johnny Bench, Pete Rose, maybe Perez and Concepcion, will all be inducted. Who would have more? The 1961 Yankees, maybe?"

"Nope," Kevin refuted. "How about the 1928 Philadelphia Athletics?"

"Oh," I said, dejected. "I guess I should have figured that since they were on the list. But how? Jimmy Foxx is the only member from the A's I know of in the Hall."

"Not all of these players played their whole career in Philadelphia," Kevin added. "Get a load of this team. When the 1928 season began, the Philadelphia Athletics had on their team," he stopped and looked up. "Are you sure you're ready for this?"

"Yeah," I answered. "Come on."

"On their team were: Jimmy Foxx, Connie Mack, Jimmy Cochran, Al Simmons, Lefty Grove, Ty Cobb, Tris Speaker and Eddie Collins. The last three playing their final major league seasons that year."

As he read off the names, my amazement stretched far into the past to envision the aura of immortality that must have shone from the clubhouse on opening day in Philadelphia in 1928, even though the team went on to finish in second place behind the Yankees as further research indicated.

"Eight future Hall of Famers?" I calculated. "That is amazing. But what has that got to do, I ask again, with the tent?"

"We don't know yet," Kevin answered. "Go on. What have you learned?"

"Well, I think I might have gotten a bit away from our goal. I sort of got interested in Seaver's life and didn't learn much."

"That's cool. Hey, we got all day. Try to keep focused, though. We'll take the books home for reading but let's use our time now to get some facts together. Who's next on my list?"

"Dean Brothers, 1934."

"Okay. I'm on it," he said. "Let me know what you learn about Seaver."

It only took a few minutes of research to come across what was arguably the most outstanding day in Tom Seaver's career, and it happened in 1970. "Here it is," I shouted a bit too loudly myself. "In 1970, Seaver struck out, you'll never guess how many Padres in a row!"

"In a row? I don't know, six," Kevin guessed.

"Ten!" I announced, stunned at the discovery myself.

"Ten? He struck out ten batters in straight at bats? Wow! That had to cover four innings."

"Yep. The last batter in the fourth, all three in the fifth and sixth and all three in the seventh again. He even went on after that to strike out four of the next six!"

Kevin shook his head. "Unbelievable. Best game ever!"

We went on to discover that each year listed on the baseballs from my memorized list and Kevin's visionary recollection signified a unique event in each player's life. The mystery still sat as an unsolved enigma, however, since not all the events pertained directly to one another, though each greatly affected the players and their individual careers. Had the events all centered around activities on the baseball field that affected each separate moment only then our riddle would have been answered. Since they seemed to also include larger events outside of the game, things involving their lives, we were onto a real mystery. Detective Brown would have to wait for my services as an assistant, even if it had only been a dream. I was on a real case.

The most obvious name on the short list that suggested that baseball was not the only element involved was "Clemente, 1972-

3." This was the year he died. Clemente was killed in a plane crash on December 31, 1972 and I of all people did not need a book to tell me that. Aside from being famous lore around Pittsburgh, Clemente's story is retold like ancient tales of gladiators or tribal oral history passed down from one generation to the next. I had grown up in the shadow of Pittsburgh's greatest pride – not their famous son but most certainly their most important adopted citizen. Even as the football Steelers were wrapping up their then-unprecedented Super Bowl run, Pittsburghers talked about Clemente and the feats he performed on the field as if it were mythology. With every season came the tales; some true and some, well, perhaps the product of longer imaginations: "I once saw him throw out a runner at first base from right field on what should have been a single easily." Or "Clemente nailed so and so at the plate on a bee-line from deep right; and that was back in the day when the fence was way out there." Some were so exaggerated they became a joke: "Clemente threw the ball so hard that he was playing in Chicago one day and threw a guy out running to third in a game played the next day in St Louis!"

As for the rest of the list, the events unraveled before us like a tapestry of America's great game. I learned that Carl Hubbel had struck out perhaps the greatest line-up ever assembled in baseball history, and he did it in 1934. At the All-Star Game that year, he fanned five superstars to start off the game, those being Babe Ruth, Lou Gehrig, Jimmy Foxx, Al Simmons and Joe Cronin. We thought at first that the list having both Simmons and Foxx included twice might mean something, but as far as we could discover there was nothing else linking the pair.

Kevin discovered that Dizzy and Paul Dean, the Dean brothers, combined to register forty-nine wins in 1934, thirty by Dizzy and nineteen for Paul; a single season feat for siblings never since matched. Chronologically, we continued to learn that Johnnie Vander Meer accomplished the improbable by throwing two no-hitters in consecutive outings. Throughout the game's history, we learned of a few pitchers who had thrown no-hitters twice in one season, but when Vander Meer no-hit the Braves and the Dodgers June 11th and 15th, respectively, of that year, there existed another feat perhaps never to be bested.

1968, it seems, left history to know that it was a pitcher's year. Our list from that summer season had not one but two pitchers left to be researched. McLain and Gibson, from what I could recall of my own knowledge of the game, had faced each other in the 1968 World Series. That fact would have to be verified first. But it seemed too obvious, a short shelf-life answer to a bigger question, a veritable red herring of a mystery. This would require investigation that only a superior master sleuth could handle. This was no job for Mr. Encyclopedia Brown. I needed to learn the tricks of a far wiser detective. I would need to call on the talents of Sherlock Holmes if this riddle were to be figured out.

With our list compiled, we left the library full in the knowledge that we were well on our way to an adventure. With nothing to prove save our starving curiosity, the world of wondrous imagination appeared before us. Without sharing each other's ideas about what all this might mean, we were armed with a list of eight names and years, a wild theory about how they might link together and, lest we forget, the very serious possibility of uncovering just where and how our own wishes played into this tale. After all, we too had lobbed baseballs into the tent and had to wonder what ours read.

6 Mysteries

The first question to our mystery was this: Did the players whose names compiled our list actually throw the baseballs into that tent themselves? If so, when? If not, then who did? And if someone else did, then who and when? Adding to the intrigue was whether or not our names were visible yet on the balls we had just tossed in, or would our names be added later if they ever appeared at all? I dared not raise the issue with Kevin, but I had already convinced myself that, no matter what, I would not go back to the tent to see what my ball might read. Though I could pick it out form a thousand baseballs that might be lying under all that bushy moss, there was no way I would risk ruining my own wish. Besides, this was an adventure! Why take the chance of having it proven as a cheap hoax when so much fun (a whole summer even) could be made of it? While my conviction was strong, I wondered with each passing day what Kevin might be thinking. Luckily, about three days later he answered that inquiry.

"I think we should go to the tent and see what our baseballs might say," he offered as we were walking home from school. He had waited until Davey Myerson had left our group and turned left at Crinklow Street before saying it, which assured me he had shared our adventure with no one else. "What do you think?"

I stopped in my tracks. "No way, Kevin!" I protested. "You heard the old man. There are rules."

"What, that old guy? He was a traveling carnival hawker. He probably conjured up the whole thing to scare kids. I bet he does it everywhere he goes."

"What? You don't think the baseballs mean anything?"

"Who knows? Maybe he just scribbled the names himself and made it all up," my ever-skeptical friend theorized.

"No way," I said, "and I can prove it."

"How?"

"It just so happens that I caught glimpse of a baseball myself and I have been waiting to tell you about it."

Kevin popped me lightly on the shoulder. "What?" He seemed miffed; which was good for him – a little taste of his own medicine. "Are you holding out on me?"

"No. You wrote the list, so I committed something to memory myself. I wrote it down when I got home and sealed it in an envelope. I gave it to my mom and told her not to give it back to me until after the Major League All-Star Game – no matter what!"

"That's a lie," he said, as if barely convinced. He seemed to be thinking it through. "You did not," he finally added.

"I did too. You can ask my mom. And if the name I read, which specified All-Star Game, 1980, does anything super spectacular, then we'll know that all of the tent stuff is for real."

"And if it doesn't?"

"Then we will go and see our baseballs," I stated with determined seriousness.

With the look of a much older man, he drew some thoughts together and slowly relented at what must have appeared to be a fair and logical arrangement. After all, I was eleven and had seen plenty in the world to afford the luxury of offering a fair and logical arrangement.

. He walked forward. "Okay, sounds fair to me," he agreed, extending his left hand. "Deal?"

"Deal," I followed suit. "You want to ask my mom today or tomorrow before school?"

He shrugged. "No, I trust you," he said. "No need to ask her."

With a patience akin to wisdom far beyond our years, we simply waited. Before long, summer came and school was let out and the usual frolicking ensued. While other kids ran to the swimming pools and lakes or went off on family vacations, Kevin and I headed day after day to the field of the Cooperstown Owls and played the game we loved more than fresh air itself. Baseball was our daily bread and neither hunger nor thirst could spell us of its nourishment. Our schedule rotated around the Owls' season. On their days on the road, the field was ours to hit, run, catch, pitch, slide and create every sort of game scenario we wished. When the Owls were in town, we were spectators to the level of play which we hoped ourselves to one day ascend. For out beyond semi-pro was the Big Leagues, and most, if not all, of the players whose names we knew and whose stats we could repeat with daily revision already calculated, made their way to The Show with at least one stop along the way in the International League.

Kevin's dad granted us practically unlimited access to the field, and we were fortunate enough to watch batting practice every day that the Owls played at home. Before long, we were welcome on the field itself; taking tips from coaches, playing catch with the players and even hitting on days when the batting coach wasn't around. Names like Jerry Digsby and Paul Autlin; Rusty Davis and Buddy Greer; Harold Lerner and Galloping Joe Winston became our friends, our heroes and teachers for one magical summer. Hardly baseball immortals, though they were a welcome substitute for the Willie Randolphs, Rollie Fingers, Dale Murphys and George Bretts of the world. And to whom was I to thank for it all? A man I hadn't even met. Kevin's dad, Mr. Bentworth to me, if ever I were to meet him. Ridley Joseph Bentworth to others, the adults, I suppose, who recognized his name (if they had ever read it at all) as it was listed in the Owls' souvenir programs under the position of "Head Groundskeeper."

On a day in late June, after a romping west coast road trip where the Owls went 7 and 1 to move into a first place tie with Erie, the team was especially welcoming and jubilant on the field during batting practice. Besides their fortunate wins on the road, the Owls had taken to the sunny coast at the right time as a week's worth of heavy summer rain pelted Cooperstown during their absence. The storms had saturated the field beyond playable conditions, so it was good that the team was abroad. In another season, perhaps one when the Owls were to be at home for those nine days, there would have been eight rain-outs and all games rescheduled until August. It rained that heavily. As it was, the team improved their standing by six games. And the only citizen in town busy with concern about the Owls, was the one person who would suffer the most when such weather turned sour. Mr. Bentworth had tended to the field in the team's absence and was not concerned with notions of mid-summer on top of the local baseball world.

As the team came out to take swings before the night game against Scranton, Kevin's dad was on the field for his tenth hour of patching up holes and dredging the grass. His staff was narrow that season as he had only one full-time and two part-time assistants. Diligently they raked fresh sand onto the dirt, patching up the area around home plate and tossing new sod on the outfield. Their work was harmonious as they provided a safe and glorious field for the home town boys' enthusiastic return. It was the first time in eight seasons that the Owls had been in first place, and the town was alight with the fun. Despite the hoopla and the excitement, Mr. Bentworth stayed close to his duties. A tireless man, he worked hard at keeping the field its best. It was on this day that it occurred to me just how little Kevin talked about his dad. Also, I realized I had never heard mention of his mother, a Mrs. Bentworth who would had married Mr. Bentworth or at least birthed Kevin. In our idyllic childhood the conversation had simply never come up. How odd. In my own family, mom was such a standard in the house and the community that I fear I may have overlooked her at times, taken her for granted as children tend to do. As for a Mrs. Bentworth, well, I just never thought anything of her. We had invited Kevin over for Memorial Day but he declined. He had never even been to my house, and I drew the obvious though stunning realization that I had never been to his. In Pittsburgh as a boy it was but a nightly summer ritual to spend sleep-overs at friends' houses. We held a practical rotating yet unofficial schedule: one night at the Muelten's, one at The Monroe's, one at the Watson's, and so on. But not here. Not in this hollow. I wondered if any of the other kids did. At any rate, I set myself to a new assignment that night – I would introduce myself to Kevin's dad.

"Hey, Kevin," I asked as we watched BP. "How about sneaking up to concessions and seeing if Willie could score us a couple of dogs and Cokes?" Willie was a high school kid we knew who, unlike all the other high-schoolers, still worked at the ballpark and who, even more unlike his peers, was nice to us younger kids. He had offered us an arrangement where we obtained free food in exchange for a service we were all too happy to provide. Since he could not watch the games from his vantage point, either Kevin or I were to swing by his station every other inning with an update, and in return we would never have to buy soda or dogs all season. What a deal! So, each night we alternated: I got innings 2 and 6; Kevin got 4 and 8; and after that the vendors all shut down and got to watch the ninth as part of their job. Willie was no baseball novice, however, and we had to work for our free goods. Willie insisted on details. A score to him was useless. He could ask any old fan the score. "Hey buddy, who's ahead?" "Owls are down 6-2, kid." If that were the case, who needed us? And without our knowledge, no free food. So it was with utter pleasure that we held strong to our agreement. With each trip, Willie Fontaine, a White Sox fan since relocated to Chicago, got a full account of every at bat. If the outcome called for it, the exact pitch that made the difference too.

A typical mid-inning update might be as simple as: "Henderson struck out the side; Garcia and Rhodes swinging; McMillan caught looking. In the bottom frame, the Owls scored on a bunt single by Jacobs, a sacrifice fly by Lerner; Wilson flied out; Rinex doubled home the run..." and so on for the top and bottom of the fifth. What a steal for a skill that came naturally. On some nights if the team was winning and Willie's girlfriend, Veronica, had shown up, he might throw in some fries or popcorn to impress her with his good will. What a guy!

"So," I mentioned to Kevin, hoping he would depart. "What do ya think?"

"It ain't game time yet," Kevin reminded me. "We've got nothing to report."

"Tell him that Owens is sitting out tonight's game and that the Kings are starting a new guy at short – that news is worth some food. Besides, remind him that his manager was on duty before the road trip and he couldn't get us any dogs in the last half of the game against Peoria."

"Hey, you're right," Kevin recalled. "Okay. I'll be back in a flash."

I waited until he was well out of sight before moving toward Mr. Bentworth. The average trip up to Willie's station, including waiting in line, ordering and pretending to pay while gabbing about the game, took between six and eight minutes. However, accounting for the fact that this early in the evening there would likely be no fans in line, a longer walk since we were not in our usual seats but atop the dugout watching BP, and the time Kevin might have to spend arguing our side of the story, I gauged I had only had an extra minute to lay out my plan.

Watching Mr. Bentworth's routine was easy. He was mid-way down the line in right, adding a layer of chalk to mark the lines of play. When he finished that task, it would be to the bases for dusting and tightening of the straps that hold the leather pads in place. This meant that within two or three minutes he would walk past the Owls' dugout where I could address him directly. I had played my window of opportunity just right so that as Kevin was consenting to my pillaging of Willie's good nature, Mr. Bentworth was on his way toward home plate, passing by me only moments after Kevin had ducked into the underbelly of the bleachers and out of sight. Perfect, like a called third strike.

I jumped to the soft dirt track. "Hey, Mr. Bentworth," I hollered. "I'm August, Kevin's friend. His new best friend."

"Yeah, what do you need?"

"Oh, yes, Sir. I just wanted to introduce myself, sir. That's all. Kevin calls me Augie."

"Well, thanks," he said.

That was it. He went about his business as if meeting me had meant absolutely nothing to him. I mean, I had expected a *Nice to meet you kid but I have work to do* reply, not a complete shutdown. I stood dumbfounded in my tracks, not certain what to do as Mr. Bentworth went about his duties. Had Kevin even mentioned me as his new friend? My parents had heard all about Kevin and our days at the ball field. But Mr. Bentworth passed me off as if I was just another kid asking him who the Owls were playing that night. I watched closely as he continued toward home, dusted off the house-shaped plate and kicked the dirt solid around it, waiting to witness whether he would return a gaze my way in some sort of acknowledgment. Not a flinch. He seemed entirely unaware that he had just met another human being. Denny Owens, the Owls' young stand-out pitcher, finally broke my awkward stare.

"You okay, August?"

"Yeah, sure, Denny, everything's fine," I answered, resigned to the fact that my plan had failed. "How's the sore elbow?"

"Doing good, kid. Thanks for asking. I'll sit tonight but pitch against St. Cloud again next week."

"Good," I added in a half-tone. "Glad to hear it."

"Hey, ya might want to hop off the field. Murray's pretty angry today. Seems his wife wrecked the car – again."

"Okay, thanks. Good luck with the arm." Murray was the team's manager, George Murray, and his wife had a bad reputation of having fender benders in his cars, all of them. Any time this happened, many team privileges were temporarily suspended; most off all his tolerance for kids being on the field for batting practice. It usually only lasted a game, maybe two, so it was a small price to pay for a fifty-game home schedule of free access to all points on the field.

I climbed back atop my dugout perch, an area immune to Murray's suspension, as Kevin made his way back empty-handed.

"Where's our grub?" I asked?

"Willie and that dumb old Veronica are fighting," he answered. "I couldn't get a word in. I sure hope they aren't at it all night. I might starve." My friend often exaggerated.

I hung my head and calculated my next move. "Darn." I added my own exaggeration and drooped my head for effect. "I didn't bring even a dollar. How about you?"

"Nope." He reached deep into his pockets, as if perhaps a quarter might suddenly materialize. "I don't have a dime for time or a nickel for a pickle."

41

"How about your dad?" I asked, hoping maybe he'd introduce me if I were to work the angle of my dejection.

Kevin gazed out onto the field a moment, searching for an answer, perhaps a fabrication. "No," he said. "Dad figures since he comes here to work he shouldn't give back to where he gets his money. He doesn't even know why I spend so much time here."

"He stays for the games, doesn't he?"

"Oh yeah, every single one. I don't know if he ever misses any. But it's just work to him. He doesn't want us spending our money here. Don't ask me what it means. I can't figure it."

And then, perhaps the most telling thing happened, or rather the unravelling of all that was to happen that summer. As Mr. Bentworth rounded the base path in his low, rhythmical step after he had completed his appointed rounds, he made his way toward the pitching mound. On that perch no kid was allowed. When we threw and played ball, we were relegated to the grass surrounding the magical circle of dirt. Only a player, a coach or the grounds man himself was allowed on the slope that leans toward home plate and centers the diamond; and to that only a pitcher could toe the rubber atop its crest.

We were allowed to kick at the dirt but place no more than one foot on the mound. That was the goal if ever a dream was to become reality. Kevin was the pitcher and I the second baseman on our little league team. How often that summer did we dream of one day taking the field as teammates for the Owls and holding conference on the mound (along with a catcher to-be-named later) to discuss our strategy during a critical moment. Knowing how to handle a possible bunt situation or a runner edging off second was what separated kids who played ball for recreation from the real ballplayers. But to no avail for now. We were kids, and per regulations the mound was off limits. To us it was hallowed ground, an edict we honored with as much reverence as we would the sacristy in church.

Mr. Bentworth dusted the strip of rubber and prepared the fresh brown soil. Murray, who at some moment unseen by me had picked up a bat and made his way toward home plate, hollered out, "Come on, Ridley. Let's see that Old Bentworth Steamer once for old time's sake." Surrounded by a few pockets of laughter, the sort of laugh that registers recognition of an inside joke, a few players stopped and watched the action at the center of the infield. Kevin turned quickly at the sound of "Bentworth Steamer" and held fast his glare on Murray.

42

The few players who were making their way off the field and into the locker room stopped short in their paths and turned to watch. Even a few ushers took a moment to keep an eye on the field. Mr. Bentworth looked in at Murray and gave a shake of the head. A definite, inaudible sign of "No" to whatever it was that Murray was requesting. Then a voice from deep in the visitor's dugout, a voice older and unfamiliar, further encouraged Murray's request. "Come on, Bentworth. Let's see if ya still got it!"

Kevin's dad took one long look at a stranded baseball left along the third base side of the mound. It must have been missed after pre-game warm-ups when the equipment manager was to gather up all the balls. Whatever it was Murray had offered, Mr. Bentworth was considering it – or at least calculating a way out. A hesitation showed in his step as he moved from the mound. And, just as the lights were beginning to blaze in the scaffolds above, he bent over and picked up a rake and bucket and headed off the field – out toward his fenced-in work area beyond the left field wall. The baseball remained untouched in silent protest to whatever had transpired.

Murray trotted out to the field to scoop up the ball that Mr. Bentworth had ignored. "Alright, Steamer, maybe next time," he said. An umpire patted Mr. Bentworth on the shoulder as he passed him near the third base line deep in left field. The players, ushers and other team's voices went back to their routine, muttering softly to themselves as if some chance had just slipped pass. Some answered questions, some pointed; others just shook their heads and made their way to the dugout or into the clubhouse. I turned to ask Kevin what it had all been about. He was gone.

A quick scan of the bleachers confirmed his disappearance, and I had no idea where – *or why!* – he had taken off. And what of Mr. Bentworth? No need to express just how peculiar his actions had been. I could only wonder what it was all about, and ponder further about a "Bentworth Steamer."

The game was a disappointment, one of those days when all goes wrong on the field but the agony eventually ends in a 7-1 or 12-2 defeat. It is times like those that I am grateful that baseball is a part of life rather than the other way around. In so much as baseball is a benevolent and wondrous event, it is but a simple pleasure in a life filled with complicated virtues and voices. It is quite simply a release. Without it we would be worse off, but because of it we have pause. Were it the larger scale and life its simpler counterpart, I don't know that I would survive such days

43

when my favorite team drops just such a loss onto the tarmac of my imagination. How fortunate that it really is just a game!

I didn't see Kevin at all that night, and was quite disheartened that he was not on-hand for the team's photo shoot the following day. It was a rare off-day within a two-game series and the team had planned to use the time for publicity. The free time provided an opportunity to introduce the fans to some of the newer players, and to offer the local press a chance to investigate them on a personal level absent the interrogation of why they had won or lost their last game, or why a pitcher had chosen a certain pitch to a certain hitter at a certain juncture in a certain recent game. The less obtrusive engagement usually brought the team and its fans and press corps closer together.

Kevin had expressed a deeper interest in the photo day than I had and I was surprised by his absence. His father was at work as usual and went about his non-game day chores as if nothing had happened the previous night. Odd, again, that man. Entirely un-phased when his son's friend had popped on the field and said, "Hey, Mr. Bentworth. I'm August - Kevin's friend." The same demeanor he had portrayed when challenged to pick up the ball and toss it toward the plate; still unwavering when his son neither watched the game the previous night nor made himself present the following afternoon. After all, photo day is a unique chance to spend time with the players, something Kevin and I enjoyed.

Searching the channels of memory, one begins to comprehend how such an event exemplifies just how different two friends are. My father, while certainly not a baseball fan beyond tolerant observance, was a scientist at heart, and an engineer by trade. Though I never quite understood his passion for details and schematics, I appreciated his efforts to raise me to try to do what's right, as well as his acceptance of my own aspirations. Somewhere between these two lessons I learned to treat people for who they were, to try and understand where they might have been and how they might feel.

But then there was Kevin, who in his heart and his words carried a discontent towards his dad which was unexplainable but very present. I would not have categorized it as shame nor as disappointment, but something about Kevin's relationship with his dad segmented the bond between us when it came to conversation. It was not by first appearance to have been Mr. Bentworth's chosen profession as a groundskeeper that separated father from son, for certainly no one should feel shame or guilt for making an honest living. But whatever the distance or distraction was, it held onto Kevin as a token of things not to be broached between us, as if it was the only boundary in a seamless friendship. And in many ways it affected our friendship at times when dad and I would participate in a father and son picnic or join the bowling league together while Kevin and his father remained constant outsiders, quiet observers and non-participants. It would take years before I had the conviction of maturity to bring up the matter with Kevin. For then, we were young boys and the subject remained as silent as the baseballs holding our wishes inside that mythical tent.

Mr. Bentworth's ill-fated trip to the mound during the previous night's pre-game was obviously some attempt by Murray to take a pitch from Bentworth. But why? What kind of story was hidden there? What was a "Bentworth Steamer?" And why had both Kevin and his dad acted, or better put, reacted, so strangely?

With the loss the night before, the Owls had fallen out of their first place tie with Erie. They dropped the second game to Scranton, 5-4, and just like that the buzz was gone from town. The team's eight-year absence from first place had raised interest to a new height; and like a newlywed catching his wife with another man, the fans gave up on the Owls after a two-game slide returned the team to second best. Such is the way of baseball.

So, here it was mid-summer already and I was the possessor of several mysteries: Namely, the baseball legends written and tossed into the mysterious tent; the looking forward to the All-Star game to either give merit to the tent or refute it entirely; the question of a Bentworth Steamer; the actions of Mr. Bentworth and the further, more compelling reactions of his son, my friend, the suddenly missing, Kevin Bentworth. All the while, there lingered that outside prospect that maybe the Owls might still make a run for the pennant.

7 The Steamer

I made it to the park early to watch batting practice the next day. If there was anything to be gained from a day at the park, then it was something I wanted to witness. The possibilities ranged from watching the rotation of the ball as it left a pitcher's hand to learning how to speak to the news people. All were tips I considered valuable, and everything in between was made possible throughout the season.

The park opened early and the day's events were in full swing by 10:30 AM. It was a near perfect day for baseball. The sun was high and warm, not the blistering heat that would follow in the latter stages of summer. The few clouds jumping around the sky provided sparse but occasional comfort between that sun and the suffering of exposed skin. The starting players had already taken their practice swings at the batting cage and Coach Murray was busy counseling the younger players, encouraging them with each swing, as he provided pointers and suggestions. While most of the commentary went unheard by the current players I did my best to make mental notes, logging Murray's comments as he reacted to each scenario. "Your stance is off. Square your shoulders, balance your weight to your knees. Swing through the soft ones, they make nice singles. Keep your eyes level with the playing field." These and other pieces of advice were lumped upon men who would most likely never make it out of the International League rosters, though they could hope for an invitation to a big league camp at Spring Training. At best, they might see their name on the International League All-Star roster. Years beyond his talents and energy for the game, Murray barked out his advice like a ridiculed scientist in the pre-industrial age before reason and theory were welcome. Had he had better luck in his younger years he might have been seen toasting a World Series Championship in San Diego or Philadelphia or Boston or Chicago. He was that good – a solid baseball man with a genius for the game and a passion for excellence. At first he was a teacher, and perhaps that alone kept him from leaping to the next level. He was to prepare players for their shot at the pros, that was his job. Maybe he cared about them too much as men and wagered their chances against a pro career of his own in the exchange.

Between swings Murray would routinely spit into the soft earth and methodically rub away the saliva and tobacco mixture with the back of his heel; hiding the habit that would go on to kill him later in life as mouth cancer crept downward into an esophageal ailment from which he would never survive. Taking a break, he instructed a coach to watch the hitters.

Murray spoke with authority. "Kip," he said to a red-headed assistant. "Take over. I'm gonna get a drink of water."

"Yes, Sir," the over-enthused Kip responded, sprinting across the short infield, unaware of the possibility that a ball could strike him in the skull any time he darted in such a manner without looking, which he did constantly.

"And Kip!"

"Yes, Sir," the man asked, halted in mid-sprint.

"Don't get too excited. You're not getting my job. You're just covering for a few minutes."

"Of course, Coach. You got it," he added, almost as if he was wondering how Murray had read his thoughts. Springing to duty behind the cage, he tipped his cap.

"Don't let them go soft on you," Murray added. "If they think they can walk on you they will. And tell Henderson to keep his damn feet from moving. He looks like he's trying to jitterbug out there." His comment was lost in the crack of a bat sending a home run practice swing into the empty bleachers out in deep left-center.

I bolted toward Murray. "Coach?" I asked with a pinched screech of puberty. Murray gulped at the water pouring up in a bow from the fountain and either ignored me or heard me not. "Coach, ya got a minute?"

He wiped the back of his hand across a wet mustache. "August," he declared. "What can I do for you? Say, how's the pitching arm, kid?"

"Good, Coach. Real good. Say, can I ask you a question?"

"Sure, Kid. Say, you been practicing your grounders?"

"Yep. You bet," I answered. The guy never quit coaching.

"Good. Good for you. Remember the basics, kid, and you'll always play ball real well. Even a good pitcher needs solid defensive skills. These guys, sometimes, they forget how to cover a bag on a bunt." His attention to his team distracted him momentarily as he addressed a sorry effort from his second baseman fielding grounders. "Awh! Come on, Stannings. Get in front of the ball. Hell, this kid here can do it better than that."

Stannings' response, a challenge to see me actually get the chance to stand up to Murray's words, went unheard by all but his

47

own ears and mine as Murray returned his attention in my direction.

"I swear, these guys," the coach sighed. "Aw, never mind. What was it you needed, August?"

"Well, Sir. What is it about Mr. Bentworth? Last night. You asked him to pitch to you, remember?"

"Yeah, what's there to it?"

"Why'd you ask him to do that?"

"I had a bat in my hand. I needed a pitched ball."

"You said, 'let's see the old stuff.' What did that mean? Did he used to pitch?"

He glared across the field. "That's none of my business, kid," he said. "Nice swing, Matthews. Keep it level, swing through. That a boy."

"Coach?"

"Yeah," he answered, still watching the field.

"What's The Steamer?"

Murray shot me a stare that would stop a ninth inning rally with a runner on second. "That's none of my business either, kid," he said sternly. "Let's keep it at that."

"Yeah, but you asked him to toss you a Steamer. What is that?"

He stepped deeper into the dugout and plopped down on the bench. "Listen, kid," he added, "That was a long time ago. I don't think Mr. Bentworth would appreciate me talking to anybody about it, most of all his son's best buddy."

"But I got to know. Kevin won't tell me anything."

"August!" Murray barked without a movement other than the strength of his voice. "I told you. I can't say anything. I'm sorry, son. I really am."

"But, sir," I persisted. "Just tell me it if it was a pitch that he threw or if it's something else or someone else's pitch. That's all I need to know."

He wiped his brow and sat upright. With a heavy sigh, he brushed his hands across his knees and looked me straight in the face. "I will tell you only this," he answered. "That pitch may be part of baseball lore around here but it is a source of difficulty for Mr. Bentworth. He and I are old friends and I should not have kidded him about that." He paused, spat again and rubbed away the spittle. "Yes. It's a pitch," he continued. "Or was. I am not telling you anything more about it. There are plenty of people who will tell you what they think. That doesn't always make it true."

Murray rose from the bench and headed for the field, patting me firmly on the shoulder. At the top step, just as the sun reached his proud face he turned again toward the bench, half in shadow, his hulking shoulders framed in sunlight.

"And one more thing, young man," he demanded.

"Yes, Sir?"

"Don't go bothering Mr. Bentworth about any of this. He doesn't need to hear anything more about it from you or anyone else, not even me. Do you understand me?"

"Yes, Sir," I answered.

"Good. Now get outta here. The players are gonna start to think I'm taking advice from our number one fan."

"Sure thing, Coach. Thanks." I turned to leave.

"Say," Murray asked. "How do you like our chances tonight?"

"Oh, you can whoop Davenport," I assured him. "Their bullpen is weak, so get a lead on them early and the Owls take the W."

"Ya think so?"

"It's a sure thing. Besides," I added, "They'll be tired from the bus trip. It's a long ride from Iowa!"

I sat for a while, deliberating whether to hang around the park to catch the game or making for town to find out about the Steamer and whatever it was that made it such a hushed topic. With the mind of a reporter beginning to take shape, I rationalized that while Murray hadn't offered any information and had insisted that I keep my questioning to a limit, he gave no specific instructions either for or against talking with his players. Thus, I reasoned, it was fair to assume that I had every right to interview the Owls' squad for any information they may have about the pitch. Murray had not only confirmed its existence but had also verified the pitch's mysterious name, "The Steamer."

I headed to the most logical of places – The Nest. Where better to discuss pitching than in the bullpen? In the great tradition of the Cooperstown Owls, the pen, as it is commonly known in most ballparks, was a place all its own and referred to symbolically as, The Nest, The Owls' Nest. While the locker room and clubhouse were collectively christened The Roost, it was the bullpen's moniker that had gained notoriety throughout baseball. Like the flag-topped scoreboard at Wrigley or the Green Monster in Fenway, The Nest was a revered place filled with lore and intrigue.

Baseball pitchers are a unique and strange breed all to themselves, and perhaps nowhere else were they so rare than in The Nest. To say that The Owls' pitching staff were their own species of bird was no understatement. Position players seldom entered The Nest, both out of fear for its oddity and respect for its reverence. The Nest was paradigmatically a pitcher's haven, and all hitters, fielders and many coaches steered clear of it entirely. Even the catchers who were relegated in its direction for assignment to warm-up a hurler or to loosen up a relief pitcher went there hesitantly. Not that it was haunted, but just because the pitchers were different, odd, and separate from the other players. They had their rituals and routines, such as a showering rotation directly equal to the team's pitching rotation. The starter always showered first, followed by any potential long relievers, then the closer who was succeeded by the next game's starter, and then through the rotation until the previous game's starter showered last, usually suffering through cold water. This oddity was equaled by their irreverence toward the press corps who were not welcome into The Nest. The pitchers, when addressing any member of the media, always referred to themselves as "We" and never as individuals. "We left a high one over the plate that got away from the strike zone." Or "We are developing a two-seam fastball." Never were they individuals, always a unit. Perhaps it was good chemistry or solidified teamwork. Mostly it was odd. But on this day, I needed to speak with pitchers, so I took my chances in The Nest.

I jogged down the third base line and came upon a utility infielder making his way toward the dugout.

"Hey, Benji."

"August. What's up?" The fielder sliced a high five into the air, to which I responded with a solid slap.

"Anyone down in The Nest?"

"I don't know, my man. I never go in there."

"But I got to talk to a pitcher about something."

"I saw Bigsby heading that way about a half an hour ago. He might still be in there."

"Cool. Thanks."

"No problem, Kid." Benji picked up a slow trot. "You ever been in there before?" he asked me.

"Where, in The Nest? Sure. Why?"

"Just curious. You think it's...I don't know. You know, normal in there?"

"It's okay. The guys just talk about different stuff, that's all."

"Oh, okay. Sure. Listen, I gotta get going. I'll see ya." He jogged into a warm-up routine and took a lap.

Left alone, my feet ground firmly into the soft cinder that formed a ring around the field, I felt the distance between myself and the park emerge, cavernous and solitary. Unsure why the mystery of The Nest kept other players away, I headed in that direction and unlatched the gate to the bullpen. Inside it looked normal, two mounds with two plates 60 feet 6 inches away; a double-tiered bench for players to sit on; a cubby hole like a miniature dugout for players to stand under in the rain; a few charts on the wall, a drinking fountain, and a phone. Maybe it wasn't The Nest itself, I gathered, that made it special but rather the people who resided there.

The silence of the bullpen was the only oddity that separated me from any other awareness in the park. So far removed from the playing area of the infield, it seemed quiet, lonely and distant, with a serenity usually reserved for a church or a morgue. The sound of bats hitting balls and players and coaches making chatter faded to a din. I wondered if there really wasn't something else about the place that scared people a bit.

"Hey, Kid. You ain't allowed in here," a voice rose from the shadowy depths around me. I didn't recognize the voice but searched the bullpen for a sighting. I saw no one. I looked up into the seats where fans taunted the Owls' pitchers endlessly, still no one loomed.

"Kid, are you listening to me?" the voice bellowed a second time.

I turned sharply and saw Paul Spellminster near the gate. The young, aggressive right-hander had an ability to control the game that would lead him to the majors but whose attitude might land him a return trip to his native South Carolina and back to his previous occupation of building bridges. I knew most of the Owls' players, but Paul had only joined the team in recent weeks and had not been introduced to the freedoms to which Kevin and I were accustomed.

I ignored his warning. "Yeah, I heard ya," I answered. "I was looking for some of the guys."

"The guys? Kid, how old are you?"

"Twelve, almost."

51

"Almost twelve? And you hang out with 'the guys,' do ya?"
He chuckled. "You should probably get out of here. I think the
boys play over in Hatsfield Little League."

"Hey, listen, Mister –," I began but was cut short by an even
stronger voice overtaking mine.

"Spellminster!" the voice boomed. Both I and the brash
young pitcher turned upward and toward the sound, coming from
the stands where we looked up to see Matt Sypress, the pitching
coach. "Allow me to introduce you to our friend, Mr. Monroe,"
Sypress said. "August, this is Paul Spellminster. He was just called
up from the Carolina League and you will love his fastball when
you see it."

"Pleased to meet you," I offered.

"Yeah. Same," he replied.

"August here is a good young man, Paul. You'll see that he
and his friend Kevin are the best fans we have around here,"
Sypress claimed. "He is welcome anywhere and everywhere the
Owls go. Except during game time, right August?"

"Yes, Sir," I answered.

"Paul, why don't you go throw some warm-up tosses."

"Alright, Coach. Will do," he answered, and made his way
to a warm-up mound.

"What can we do for you, August?" Sypress asked. "It's not
often you make your way out here to The Nest."

"Just had a couple of questions, that's all."

"Well, shoot. I have a few minutes. What do you need, some
pitching advice?"

"No, it's a little more complicated and may take a few
minutes. It's about The Steamer."

"The Steamer?" the coach responded. "What do you want to
know about that for?"

"Murray mentioned it but wouldn't say anything else when I
asked him what it was. I just want to know what it was, that's all."

Sypress thought a moment, chewed a sunflower seed, spat
out the shell. "It was a pitch of some sort if I recall," he said.
"Before my time, though." He gazed across the park.

I waited before continuing. "I know it might have been a
pitch," I said, "but what makes it so special that no one talks about
it anymore?"

"I reckon I don't know. Feel free to ask around, though."

"Thanks, I think I will."

"I need to get to my office. Enjoy the game. And keep an eye on Spellminster. He is starting tonight and is a thrill to watch."

I learned little if anything else that day about the pitch that was etching itself into my consciousness as a folkloric icon. I left The Nest with the promise from several pitchers that they would keep an ear out and even ask around themselves, reporting anything they might learn. As usual, I stayed to watch the ball game and witnessed Spellminster indeed throw a thrilling game. In his Owls' debut, he struck out eight batters, walked none and only surrendered two hits in a two-to-nothing victory. The crowd was sizeable but hardly enthusiastic for such a performance. A collective representation of their time, and despite claiming to be baseball fans, they could not help but hope each night for offense, offense and more offense. A game in which home runs soared and the runs were amassed in quantities so heavy as to threaten the burden of numbers a scoreboard could hold, was somehow more appealing than a masterful control of the game by a young, southern boy journeyed north to stake his claim among baseball's elite.

Not ones to underscore the finer appreciation of a pitcher's duel or a defensive gem, Kevin and I often took heart in all of the game's intricacies. Even a finely choreographed double play that might have squelched an Owls' rally was typically applauded. Much to the dislike of fellow attendees, we would cheer in approval for the opposing players when their feats were deserving of praise and when their plays went unjustly unnoticed in the predominantly Owl-infested stadium. To make up for it, we would hoot and holler louder than anyone to show allegiance to our hometown team.

I made my way back to the field after the game and caught up with Spellminster.

"Great game, Paul," I said as the pitcher broke away from the sparse group of writers who had covered the game.

"Thanks, kid. It's August, right?"

"Yeah," I nodded.

"Hey, sorry I was rough on ya earlier," he offered in a voice different from our earlier introductions. "I didn't want to be mean. It's just that I get pretty psyched up before a game and really hate to be distracted. I guess I was nervous with tonight being my first start with the team and all. You just surprised me out there, that's all."

"Hey, no sweat. If you pitch that well, I can bother you before every game."

He laughed and adjusted his hat. "No, thanks. I'll take my chances otherwise. You seem like a pretty smart kid. You like the game a lot, do ya?"

"Oh, yeah. I'll play some day. I know I will."

"Well. Good. Here." He tossed a ball. I caught it and admired it momentarily, as if it were crystal.

"Wow! A game ball. Thanks!"

"No problem."

"I can't keep this, Paul," I protested. "It's your first game as an Owl. You should have it."

"Don't worry about it, kid. I keep the first pitch from every game I start. That's what is important to me, knowing I started something. I sure won't finish 'em all. Not even Nolan Ryan did. But I account for each one that I start. At least I made it that far each week."

"Are ya sure? Because my dad will make me give it back. I just know he will."

He smiled. "Yeah, I'm sure. If your dad has a problem, tell him to come by and I'll let him know it's okay. Maybe I'll give him one, too," he laughed. "If he's jealous that you got one and he didn't."

"Great. Thanks again. Wait till Kevin sees this." I left without saying good night.

I raced off the field with speed only a kid could muster, forgetting entirely the questions I had intended to ask Paul. I had hoped to practice a mock post-game interview I had planned.

8 A Night at the Library

I spent the next few days searching for any and all information I could about the fabled Steamer. From the barber I learned that it was a curveball with spittle. Whatever spittle was I wasn't sure, but the old-timers spoke of it with authority so it must have meant something. The lady who worked the phones at the fire station said she thought it might be a sandwich. This was corroborated with a story from a fisherman who agreed, though it was served with rice as he recalled. The mailman wasn't sure he had ever heard of such a thing, and the grocer knew nothing about touchdowns either, so he shouldn't be bothered. I didn't take the time to explain to him that this had nothing to do with football; instead, I thanked the man and went on my way. All over the town square, from construction workers to one of the town's only two cab drivers, and from shopkeepers to elected council leaders, I received many opinions but nothing that seemed to be true. Joe, the soda shop owner, thought it sounded illegal and the third grade school teacher, Madelyne Alston, commented that perhaps she should ask my parents if they were aware what I was up to. No one ever suggested the library, until Mr. Highsmith, the librarian's husband who worked at the mill, found himself unable to answer the inquiry to any sound degree and told me that he would ask Ellen, his wife, and report back to me what she had to say.

The logic of the matter had not yet occurred to me either. Not even Kevin's ability to turn our previous research experience into an adventure had suggested that the answers might be found somewhere in the halls of the library – the same entrails of paper I had never before perused and would now call upon a second time in a few months for answers to the questions of life's greater mysteries (or at least those pertaining to baseball). So it was also that a larger, perhaps more profound, revelation struck me en route to the library. Here I was in the cradle of the American Pastime, with the largest collection of baseball memorabilia and facts at my beckon call, and it hadn't occurred to me to check the Hall of Fame itself for information. I'll admit I never was the quickest to consider the most logical solution to a problem. Thus, a second adventure began. This time, however, it appeared I would go it alone and set out absent my quick-minded friend to find my answers.

Entering the Hall of Fame and Museum, I had expected to be met with a plethora of details through which to search for the mythical Steamer. Instead, I found nothing. The archives were sealed and only allowed investigation by employees of Major League Baseball. I had been through the hall so many times that there was no need to search amongst its artifacts and treasures for any mention of a Steamer as a pitch, or a sandwich for that matter. I could probably quote from memory (and almost in order from floor-to-floor) every memento the Hall possessed. Finally, the curator reminded me that the majority of the Museum's heirlooms were from the Major Leagues, with but a few from the Negro Leagues and even fewer from minor league organizations, such as the Owls and other local teams.

Dejected, I made my way out of the Hall and onto the stoop of the great museum. The Owls were on a short road trip, and those few patrons who had remained in town were busy pursuing other means of entertainment and business. Echoes of history whispered as I sat outside, and I thought I had heard laughter. Ty Cobb ridiculed: *Kid searching for a Steamer, huh!* And Jimmie Foxx admonished: *Who cares about minor league myths anyway?* It was the cool wisdom of Lou Gehrig that acclaimed my right as a fan: *Go on, all of you and hush up! Let the boy pursue what he believes.* The ghosts are a part of the spirituality of Cooperstown that maybe no one else had ever heard. I didn't care; it was time to ponder. The colorful voices of the past that give baseball its greatness, as well as its greatest moments, were as much a part of me as summer itself was part of the game. Each off-season, during numerous visits to the Hall of Fame, I had sat alone outside the museum on warmer days and just inside the vast lobby on cooler ones, and listened to the voices as they emanated from the corridors and portals of the grand building, speaking to a legacy which all shared but few truly cherished.

The library would remain open only another hour or so, and I needed to move quickly to accomplish much of anything for the day. I would have had all of the next day to research, but the curiosity would wager too strong a leverage until then. I sprinted the three blocks to the library and splintered through the main door with an hour left before closing. Mrs. Highsmith greeted me generously, in response to which I offered a flick of a wave. A quick glance through the card catalogue directed me toward the periodicals, and corresponding signs pointed me downstairs. I canvassed the steps in multiple leaps and was in the research area

56

within moments. No one else was present in the dim expanse before me. Black steel shelves stretched out in length across the uninhabited floor. The retrieval system the library had in that day was slow and tedious. The advent of the computer had only recently taken place and had not yet made its way into all areas of society, especially into library studies. I headed straight for the periodicals directory and began a search. Ruling out *Sports Illustrated* and the other frequently read newsstand magazines, I flipped through the index cards that registered the collection of sports publications. In the older libraries, one was required to search via one of three headings: author, title or subject. Having no idea of where to begin, and having no way of knowing who might have written an article nor in which magazine it may have appeared, I praised the meticulous ability of an unnamed librarian who had some time ago painstakingly chronicled the catalogue into its appropriate order. I began with the subject cards.

Out of the corner of my eye I saw another person approaching, and I lifted my eyes in that direction. I discerned a shadowy figure perusing the magazines across the narrow hall that separated the metal shelves. I had not heard the person enter the room, and I thought from the frame that it could be a man. He seemed to be in a struggle to manipulate the magazines he was pulling from the shelves with only his left arm. His right hung unseen and unused as some four or five magazines rustled imbalanced in the crook of his left arm.

"Can I help you out there, Sir?" I asked. "Maybe carry a few of those for you?"

The man reacted with a sharp pause, glancing in my direction as if he had been caught red-handed looting coins from the library's copier funds. With sudden spasms of the neck in directions east and west, he took off toward the stairs, dropping the magazines to the floor as he scampered out of the room. I stepped into the aisle to call after him, and distinctly noticed that his right arm was missing entirely! No wonder he had such trouble with the stack of magazines. But he was gone, up the stairs so quickly there was no point in following after him.

I interrupted my search to gather up the magazines he had dropped and began to replace them on the vacant shelf. The topics were different from one journal to the next, and it appeared as if he had been searching at random rather than actually tracking down materials on one specific subject. *Was he watching me?* I pondered. I shook the possibility off to an over-indulgent imagination, reset the chronicles as best as I could on their shelves and went back to my task. Throughout the evening, though, the mysterious appearance and actions of the man lingered in my thoughts.

The first and perhaps most tedious task was searching through all the possible interpretations of "steamer." Certainly the word "baseball" as a cross-reference in a more sophisticated system would hasten the search, but with impatience a necessary emissary I forged on. I combed through references to steamers, a list that was comprised of ships, carpet cleaners, heavy blast furnaces, geysers, motorized vehicles, geological tools, ancient trains, endless theories and even a self-generated heating unit designed to warm a house in the 18th century. I was ready to give up. *It's no use*, I uttered to the increasing shadows taking employment around me, themselves going to work for the evening as the sun's light faded from the few available windows. It seemed I was wasting my time. With one last push, I filed through the final group of index cards, and in bleary discouragement nearly passed my goal, completely unaware that I had stumbled upon a lead. "Steamer, Base / Military" rolled into "Steamer, Base / Occupations," to "Steamer, Baseball / Pitch" and in a daze I flipped onward through "Steamer / Bass Fish" and "Steamer/ Bass Guitar," when a noise disrupted my catatonic rhythm.

"Attention, please," a voice cracked from a loudspeaker in the corner. "The library will be closing in fifteen minutes. Please prepare your materials for check-out before 9:00 PM. Thank you." The voice disappeared into the dry air as the outdated public address system hummed even after an unseen microphone had been clicked off somewhere in the offices above.

I returned my focus to the yellowing cards laid out in a brick-like row before me and flicked backwards through a few of the cards, realizing that my attention had waned over the previous cards and that I was quite unsure of what I had read. Flipping through the short repetition of cards, I stopped on "Steamer, Baseball / Pitch." There it was! Something, perhaps someone, had given cause for hope. I jotted down the location numbers for the periodical, which included all of one article, and slid the card tray back into place just as a bank of lights flickered along the ceiling and shut off with a slumbering buzz. Left in eerie half-darkness, I peered around the suddenly smaller area and listened to another announcement through the loudspeaker. "Your attention, please. The library will be closing early. If there are any patrons who wish to check out books, please do so now. Due to the apparent low volume of readers in the library, I am going to close up early this evening. Please make your way to the front desk for check-out. Thank you."

I located what I needed for the evening, though time would hold my search up for the night. I considered the day to be victorious and strolled up the stairs toward the lobby. The Librarian (who split responsibilities at school as the only one in all of Cooperstown) was busy at her desk, face down and checking out the only other reader of the evening. Recalling that she had only a half an hour earlier addressed me directly with "Hello, August," I skipped through the exit with stealth and ease. Once outside, I considered momentarily heading back inside to wish her a good night but instead strode down the steps and out into the night, knowingly sending her on a search through every stack in the library – all four floors – calling out my name before feeling secure enough to close the library against the chance of leaving someone locked in the building overnight. And, thus, rendering her plan of closing up early as having been thwarted.

9 A Trip to a Summer Past

Perhaps the true beauty of research is the ability to tie two ends of time together – to, in essence, accomplish time travel as writers and dreamers have hoped for centuries. As I lie awake in bed that evening, the visions of HG Wells' fictional time machine came whirling in and out of my thoughts. The next day was to be an adventure into the past, wherein the mystery of the Steamer was to be discovered and the true purpose of my ordeal began, that being the uniting of Kevin and his dad. For as little as I knew at that moment, one thing was certain. Whatever the Steamer was, Mr. Bentworth was not fond of its existence.

I returned early the next morning to find a surly Mrs. Highsmith sitting at the library's front desk.

"Good morning, August," she said.

"Hello, Mrs. Highsmith," I replied.

"Back so soon?"

"Ma'am?" I asked, wondering what trouble I might be into.

"I missed you last night when you left. Did you leave early?"

"Uh, yes, Ma'am. I suppose I did." I suppressed a chuckle as I turned and headed back toward the periodicals.

The room seemed to be more detached in the morning light that crawled through tiny corner windows. I found a switch at the base of the steps, flicked it and waited for light to emerge. A distant hum awakened the slumbering electrodes and resonated through the room, casting a faint pale-green tint throughout. The lights blinked to life and sharpened in quick, spasmodic flashes before glowing permanently, casting a brightness of artificial sustenance across the shelves and down the corridors of the catacombs.

I scanned left to right and made my way through the shelves that ran along the room like high-backed pews in my mother's church. I searched the shelves with a near swooning rush of head movements back and forth. I was mildly dizzy by the time I arrived at the number I had jotted down the night before. I checked my scribbled note of catalogue numbers, and confirmed then found the correct row. A sense of accomplishment overwhelmed as I ran a finger along the central shelf, searching for the journal that would answer my questions. I was looking for *Sport*, an edition from May of 1954, Volume 33, Issue 5. Finding the particular bound book of multiple magazines was easy. Adjusting to the weight of the tome, however, proved another matter. Its heft was cumbersome and, lifting it from its place upon the shelf with a hearty grunt, I pushed back a layer of dust and moved toward the nearest table to search the collection.

I sifted through reams of fading paper, located the May issue and quickly read through the table of contents. The yellowed pages offered a glimpse of just how exciting the sports world might have been for spring of 1954, including news about baseball's early-season leaders, hockey and basketball's crowned champions and other events. Nothing about the Steamer anywhere. A bold-typed heading read **Features** and underneath it, in the "Across America" section, I found my quest's end: "'Baseball Pioneer Hurls "Steamer": Semi-Pro Pitcher Reinvents the Fastball,' By Stanley Whitaker, pg. 94."

I flipped through the magazine's frail and dusty pages. The scent of musty, withering paper wafted toward my nostrils. Amidst advertisements for old cars, funny-looking suits and archaic razors and aftershave, the numbered pages counted upward towards the goal: 89, 90, 91, 92...97, 98, 99.

"What? Where are the other pages?" I asked to no one, save the characters of lost articles silently at rest upon the shelves.

I retraced the pages, hoping to have stumbled across those that must have stuck together, I tried again in vain to find the article: 91, 92...97, 98.

"No! This can't be," I uttered in disbelief, dropping into a chair behind me. Despite my solo protest, I had no choice but to believe it. Where pages 93 through 96 might have stood, and where certainly the answer to those inquiries must have once been written, were only stumped pages, torn loosely from the magazine – how long ago, no one knew.

I left the library (and avoided Mrs. Highsmith) in abject disappointment. I had treated her unfairly the night before and knew I deserved a smug response, but considering my recent failure I couldn't stand facing that. She was a kindly woman, indeed, but how would I have known to trust grown civility at that moment, the first and saddest defeat of my life?

Undaunted, I continued to search for answers. Surely, someone, somewhere knew something or everything about the Steamer. And if Mr. Bentworth would not talk about it, that only strengthened my resolve. I was set to figure this out, whether it drove me batty or not.

My quest continued fruitlessly for a number of days. Neither the Cooperstown Library, nor the one at nearby Roth College or any of the other universities and colleges in the area were able to produce results as I labored to find the slightest clue about the ever-increasing mystery. But then a break finally came my way on a rainy Wednesday in mid-July.

A visit to Lincoln College had provided equal disappointment, but the day was still long. The trip was more than I could handle by bicycle, so mom had offered to ride me up in the car, provided we return within a few hours. Afterward, instead of facing the dull quiet of home where I would lazily contemplate the fact that I was getting nowhere in my quest, I had asked her to drop me off at Watson's Deli where its proprietor, Mr. Dewey, offered companionship as welcome as his food.

Passing Mr. Johnson, the grocer, on the way out of the deli, I tipped my Pirates' hat and asked him if he would be at the game over the weekend. He replied with his stock answer: "Always there if the Owls are." I switched places with him and entered the diner. The door pounded shut with its usual thud, a nuisance to customers, an unfixed hinge that tested the frame's endurance. The owner, who had named the place after his favorite golfer, Tom Watson, had never fixed the door. It was the one spot of laziness in an otherwise pristine diner. The owner had his own dream that someday, somehow, someone who passed through the tiny hamlet might get word to the legendary golfer about the restaurant which bore his name. And in that hope rested Bill Dewey's only chance of meeting his lifelong idol.

Mr. Dewey greeted me with a welcoming smile as the door clamored shut behind my entrance. "Hey, August!"

There were no other customers in the antiquated eatery, and I think Dewey may have been glad for the company. He rustled up the newspaper he had spread on the counter and had probably read twice already throughout the slow afternoon, and set about his usual cordial manner as host. Despite the habit of carelessness pervasive in the times, he personally wiped the seat of each customer before they sat. "Have a seat. What can I get for ya, the usual?"

"No. I think I'll take a burger and fries today, Mr. Dewey," I answered, eyeing the menu board above his head and refusing my standard lunch.

"What? No grilled cheese? Are you growing up on us, kid?"

"I guess so," I replied softly.

62

"Good enough for me," he answered.

He spun back to the grill and busied himself to cooking me a burger, never asking how I wanted it prepared. I think everyone in Cooperstown eats it well done anyway, so I would take whatever he offered.

"The Owls won again last night," I said.

"Yeah. I saw the paper. Good road trip they are having out west. Is that three in a row over Peoria?"

"Two so far," I answered, holding back a smile. Dewey had a reputation for being the type of fan who had some idea of the team's success but never quite knowing much about baseball as a whole. In fact, it seemed he had passing knowledge of every topic that he pretended to know fully. Often enough to label it as a trait, I witnessed him in conversations about knitting, steam-pipe fitting and churchgoing with whomever happened to practice each trade or hobby. Kevin put it best one day when he quipped, "He must live in a world where the Owls always win, the cops always get the bad guy and the weather is always fine - a real *Leave it to Beaver* kind of life that Dewey has." I saw little reason to doubt my friend's humorous observation. It was a stock greeting for Dewey when he served a baseball fan: "The Owls won again, hey?" he would ask, allowing the guest to offer the facts he knew little about. This time he happened to be right.

"What's got ya down, August?" he asked, turning away from my burger, minding little how scorched the tender meat was quickly becoming.

"Sir?" I asked, feigning comprehension.

"You don't seem yourself today. The team is playing well and you're moping around like an old lady who lost her bonnet in a wind storm. Heck, for an Owls' fan to be as blue as you are, something must be in your head. What's up?" I could offer less than a half-hearted shrug as a reaction to his kindness. "Well, let me get to your burger," the underweight man offered. His smile bulged through the freckles of his younger appearance.

"Hey, Mr. Dewey, why'd you open this restaurant for?"

"That's kind of an odd question, August." He turned back before touching the burger. "I've told ya that story before, haven't I?" he continued. "As I've told just about everyone come through that door. I hope to meet Tom Watson this way. I figure someday, someone –"

"Excuse me for interrupting, Sir. But that isn't what I meant. And pardon me for saying, but if your idol is a golfer, why not open a place down in Augusta, Georgia, near where they play The Masters? Or somewhere like that?"

He stared long at me and twirled his upper lip in thought...and his smile drifted away. I had shamed him. I was such a jerk. In a matter of twelve hours I had cruelly acted out against two of the nicest people in the world, people I had no right to accost: Mrs. Highsmith over at the library and now Mr. Dewey in his own establishment. He wiped his hands slowly on a towel and raised his chin a little when he spoke again.

"I guess I never thought about leaving my home, is why. You make a good point though. Say, this burger of yours will be ready any minute now. Ketchup?" he added, turning to find a small plume of smoke billowing from the grill.

"Sure, ketchup will be fine." I wondered if there was enough in stock to soften the bitter taste of charcoal that awaited my pallet. "Sounds great."

His smile returned. "I know. Just kidding with ya. Never heard of a boy who didn't like ketchup."

"Food has a lot of great flavor all its own. Maybe some people see no need to goop it all up with extra stuff."

"I suppose ya make a good point there, too. You're an all right smart kid, August."

"Well, Miss Hollencheck wouldn't think so. I don't do so well in my classes all the time."

He carried the plate to the counter. "Miss Hollencheck, you say?" He provided a heaping, if not burnt, pile of French fries along with the searing burger. "Don't think I know her. Is she a new teacher over at the elementary school?"

I bit into a fry. "Come on, Mr. Dewey," I said. "I ain't no dummy. I see how nice you polish the joint up when she comes in for lunch on Tuesdays. You kinda like her, don't you?"

"Oh, you mean Laurie?" He blundered through an embarrassed attempt to cover his crush on the teacher. "She won't let me call her Miss Hollencheck, on account it makes her feel old. Yeah, I know her now that you mention it. Nice enough lady," he added. "Say, how about an ice cream float instead of that Pepsi?"

I accepted the float, giggling at my server who fumbled through its preparation like an excited school boy pre-occupied as he was with thoughts of "The Lovely" Miss Hollencheck. I ate my lunch in silence and he busied himself with cleaning an invisible spot on the mixer, forgetting to add a few ingredients to make the shake, namely the ice cream.

"She'll be at the game Sunday when the Owls are back in town," I mentioned between bites.

"What's that?" he asked.

"Miss Hollencheck. She'll be at the game this Sunday."

"Oh, is that so?" he asked, looking out the window; barely hiding the smile I could see creeping across his face. "Say, I haven't been to a ball game yet this year. Maybe I'll think about going over. Just cause you mentioned it, of course."

"Sure, Mr. Dewey. I mean, of course. What other reason would there be?"

"Right you are. Just a good night at the ballpark."

"Day," I corrected.

"Hmm?" he asked.

"It's on Sunday, Sir. It'll be an afternoon game."

"Oh, sure, yeah. Right," he added, gleaming. "Afternoon, you say?"

"Uh-huh, at one o'clock."

"Sure will be warm, too. I suppose I could get a haircut on Saturday. To keep the heat off, ya know?"

I swallowed instead of laughing. "Sure, good idea," I said.

He wiped down the ice machine and said, "Well, I got some cleaning to do so holler if you need anything."

"She sits in section 232, along the left field line," I added as the man's nimble frame bumped the counter in a stammer step towards the back.

"Two - three - two, you say. Well, maybe I'll stop by to say hello or something." His voice trailed off into the back, and I distinctly heard the scratching sound of pen on paper at what was no doubt the number 232 being jotted down to support the man's memory.

I continued to eat lunch in quiet solitude, absorbing the calm of the diner as its home-cooked hospitality and somber familiarity shrouded around me. As much as Mr. Dewey made me laugh, I was grateful for the conversation. If for nothing save the company, it took my mind off the quest for a while. Miserable with defeat after several dead ends, I had joined that list of unnamed sea voyagers who had sailed the oceans for a seemingly eternal time span with nothing to show except their tattered brow and dusty elbows from the searching. My boyish imagination had fancied me a great commander at the onset of a quest; but now I envisioned myself a bitter sea captain aboard a plank-worn pirate ship with only candles and lace to be stored where gold and jewels belonged.

65

Little did I know in my then youthful misunderstanding of the value of goods that there was a time when lace was worth its weight in coinage and candles brought the same bounty as oil.

Either way, I felt better and enjoyed lunch with little other thoughts until a shadow crept across the wall of the diner above the menu board. In a quick glance, I caught the shadow sprawling in elongated arches across the booths along the south wall, stretched out like a phantom aboard deck. A return glance raised my suspicion that the shadow was casting itself over my shoulder. Spinning on my stool, I saw the door slide peacefully shut, a sound distinctly different than the familiar thud of the door. The shadow glided along the glass storefront and out of sight toward the alley. I jumped to my feet and headed for the doorway, hoping to catch a glimpse of the shadowed figure. The street outside was as busy as Cooperstown might be on any day and nothing peculiar caught my eye. I recognized no one who might stand out as a stranger. Despite what folklore might suggest, there are no towns left in America that can boast with absolute truth that every single person knows every other person by sight. Cooperstown was no exception. While I recognized a few friend's parents and a store clerk or two, no one else was present.

I returned inside and was greeted by Mr. Dewey. "Where ya going, pal?"

"Nowhere," I answered. I held the door ajar with my right hand, peering over the same shoulder and out into the street. "Just thought I saw someone I know walk by outside. Say, Mr. Dewey, when'd you get the door fixed?"

"I didn't have it fixed. I prefer that thud over a bell – that way I know when anyone enters."

"But," I continued, still watching the street as I let go the grip on the wood-framed door. "It used to –" My words were cut short by the familiar heavy crash of the door smacking into its frame, rattling to a stop and shuttering once, then twice with a bouncing thud before resting silently closed. I gave the proprietor a slightly embarrassed grimace. "Never mind."

"Who was it you thought you saw?"

"No one important, really," I lied with no reason to conceal that I had no clue.

"Say, it wasn't your teacher, was it?" my companion asked hopefully. "That Miss Hollencheck? Is that her name?"

"Yeah Laurie, remember?"

"Oh, yeah," he answered, absent-mindedly. He glanced through the window, no doubt hoping to catch her walking past. "Laurie. Yes, that would be her name, wouldn't it?"

"No. I didn't see her. But I'll be sure to tell you if I do."

"Oh, no bother. How's that lunch of yours?"

"It's good," I answered and turned back to the line of stools along the counter.

What I saw was a different layout than I had seen when I was eating my lunch moments before. To the left of my plate sat a book, though I had entered empty-handed as much as empty of heart. I slowly returned to my seat so as to not disturb the set-up and eyed the book suspiciously. It wasn't there when I sat down, that I knew for certain. Mr. Dewey had hardly left the front of the counter space and was in view the entire time he cooked my lunch. Yet there it was – immediately to the left of the plate I had been using just moments before. Tilted at a slight angle away from the half-eaten burger, the book's title was not new to me but it was an edition I had never seen before, at least not that I could recall. It had been published long before I was born: *Who's Who in Baseball, 1947.*

The red cover was dappled from time and wore a border of yellow edges similar to the books I had perused in the library earlier. Its spine was bent and cracked from repeated reading, as if it had been studied. Across its face was a banner celebrating the 1946 World Series Champion St. Louis Cardinals! Its pages were ear-marked, well-read. Unsure if this was a sign, or a lead, or perhaps an apparition of my fatigued and disheartened spirit, I rubbed my eyes heavily. Granted, I was a kid but the comedy of holding my eyes shut one full minute to test the book's existence in reality must have been worth a good laugh because Mr. Dewey giggled warmly as I peeled my hands away. I stared at the book a moment as the soft patter of Dewey's footfall grew closer.

He lifted the book in a deft swoop. "Where'd ya get this?" he asked, flipping its venerable pages without reading one. "It looks kind of old." He examined the cover, and the gangly fellow let out a whistle. "Wwweeeewww-weeee. 1947. Why, would ya look at that? This here book of yours is over thirty years old now."

"It isn't mine," I offered in a half-voice. "I thought it was yours."

"No. I like baseball enough, but I got no need for the likes of this kind of information. I wonder who would keep such a thing lying around all these years." He swooped the book under his elbow and turned toward the office. "I guess I'll toss it in lost and found," he said. "Maybe somebody will ask for it."

"No!" I said, a little too loudly; after all, he was only three feet away. "I just realized where I've seen that before." I made up the lie as I went. "Yeah, yeah. It's, uh, Johnson's. Marty Johnson's. I knew I recognized it, I just couldn't place it right away. He must have left it in here."

Convinced that it was no hoax I was pulling, he flopped the book on the counter. "Okay, but be sure to give it back to him when you're through with it," he said. He set himself to his chores, rubbing again the untarnished, shining counter he had rubbed over and over throughout the day. "You gonna finish that burger?"

"Yeah," I answered, finally resuming contact with the peripherals around me. I finished the burger in two bites and began flipping through the rustic pages of the softbound book. Never one to pass an opportunity to delve into baseball's glorious past, I practically consumed such texts. In fact, mother and father often argued over the matter. *He should branch out and be more well-read, more learned*, I had heard father demand on several occasions. *At least he's reading something*, mother had countered. *He'll get around to other books when he's ready*, she had theorized in my defense. *By then it might be too late*, father had returned, assuming the worse. I wonder if they are still arguing over to this day in their retirement.

Other than its tattered outer edges and well-read interior, the book was in fine condition. No pages were missing and not a single tear creased the paper; there were no stray markings and not a single notation. The only deficiency was a paperclip attached to page 618, in the upper right-hand corner.

Reaching toward the plate in search of the one remaining French fry, I dropped a north bound potato straight to the floor as it missed my agape jaw towards which it was half-heartedly aimed. With new-found exuberance, I slid off the stool and headed toward the door, offering to pay Mr. Dewey later for his lunch.

"Not to worry," the cook answered. "I'll put it on a tab." The answer I barely heard met no one's ear save the bugs of summer that flitted in through the door as I sprinted out the exit.

With the very breath of Mercury I ran, or Han Solo in a land cruiser (which could have dusted Mercury any given day), rounding corners with the lean balance of an Olympic sprinter; hushing the crush of gravel beneath my feet to a mere swoosh as I glided past in purposeful stride. I transgressed the six blocks to home in mere minutes. Mom was seated on the porch busy discussing matters of the upcoming church picnic with the neighbors as I brushed past the yard, scampered the double length driveway, catapulted all four steps at once and was into the house with hardly a hello as the door slammed shut behind me.

"You must excuse my boy, Mrs. Jamisen," I heard mom say to the chairwoman for the Social Committee who shared the porch with her. "He's been in a spirited mood this summer and tends to forego his manners. August," she hollered into the house. "I think you might want to come down here and say hello. While you're at it, you can apologize to our guest."

"Oh, that's okay, Renee," I heard the mild-mannered woman offer as I hesitated on the steps. "Boys will be boys. I know my nephews are headstrong on making their way through this world with the wrath of God in their back pocket. They take no concern as to what may break or shatter in their path." The elderly lady giggled with a shaking voice. The clamor of my footsteps grew louder as I bounded back through the house and opened the door, thrusting it aside with a whirl.

"Sorry, mom," my breathless voice ushered. "Hi, Mrs. Jamisen. Can I go now, mom?"

"Sure," she said and I was gone again. A breathless sprint across the living room, up the stairs and into my room.

"Nice boy you have there," I could hear the neighbor consent through my window above the porch. "What's got him so full of energy, other than boyhood?"

"I'm not sure to be honest with you. He's been at the library these last few days. I drove him up to Lincoln University this morning. I figure when an eleven-year old boy has that much passion for studying, regardless of the subject, there is no reason to question it."

I ignored the continuing conversation below and set myself to this new avenue on my quest. The book I received held within its pages the clue I had been seeking, and would certainly come to answer the riddle of the Steamer!

Who's Who in Baseball, 1947 was certainly no classic of the imagination, it was merely fact. Within its pages stood the first clue to solving the illustrious baseball riddle of 1980. On page 618, as marked by either the phantom gift-giving shadow or by a previous reader whose hopes rested on the chance that the St. Louis Cardinals of 1947 might have headed toward the pennant, stood a biography. It registered the life statistics, baseball accomplishments and other facts of none other than The Owls seasonal groundskeeper, Ridley Joseph Bentworth, pitcher St. Louis Cardinals.

The article on Bentworth was short, yet offered that singular reality I so desperately needed. It was real! "The Steamer" was real and Mr. Bentworth its originator. My appetite was hardly satiated, however, for the brief biography was merely enough evidence to launch a full scale investigation. It read simply:

Famed for his ingenious, and some may say bizarre,
new delivery technique, Bentworth will long be
forgotten before the foibles and pundits let loose the reigns
of his childlike dream of inventing a new pitch and
introducing to the world "The Steamer." Bentworth pitched
seven complete games in 1946 and was...

The article went on to recount the man's stats and records from the previous season, along with a brief mention that he had appeared in two innings of relief for the Cardinals two years prior during the 1944 World Series. Other than that, the piece was factual and mundane; a fact not surprising to me since I had read many such dockets before.

Having received validation of my first concern, I pieced together the remainder of the puzzle with these new bits of details, which like any good mystery seemed to yield more questions than answers.

I had received this most fortuitous yearbook, but from whom? The Steamer was a pitch, that much had been validated. But the synopsis on Bentworth's career referred to it as a "delivery technique." Perhaps the two are one in the same and I was simply caught in a game of semantics. And, most importantly, if Mr. Bentworth had had such a unique brush with fame – having pitched in the World Series even! – why were he and his pitch unknown to the common fan, why had Murray not provided me with any information, and finally, what happened to his career after 1947?

As much as my earlier trip to the Cooperstown Library had proven futile, *Sport* magazine had been my first lead, and somewhere existed three to four pages on the topic of The Steamer which to this point had gone unread by my eyes. Back to the library I sped!

Enlisting the aid of Mrs. Highsmith once again, I learned of the rigor with by the library's holdings were kept. An entire history of humanity lay buried under dust in the lower recesses of the library, or at least a comparative history of Cooperstown and Mid-central New York state.

Again, it was a nameless employee somewhere off in the world to which I owed gratitude as I continued my search. For whomever had spent the dullest of hours meticulously cross-referencing the piles of newspapers into a searchable catalogue of lists was one possessed with an organizational magnitude I could hardly fathom then and can hardly rationalize to this day. But, alas! There it was, listed and cross-listed by subject, person, date, event, major influences – everything imaginable. All I needed then was a little help.

"You look a bit dumb-founded, August," Mrs. Highsmith said.

"I think I don't understand this. How do these things work?" I held up a reel of what looked like film as it spooled out of control and dangled helplessly in the air.

"First you need a machine for reading this," she laughed, realizing I had been holding the tape-like film up to the light in attempts to read its contents. "Come with me."

We headed down a short corridor into a separate room. "What is that stuff?" I asked.

"It's called micro-film and it holds tiny records of all the library's books and articles. You view it through that machine over there." She pointed to a goliath of steel and glass positioned atop a table near the entrance. "Now, what is it you're looking for?"

"Articles on baseball from a really long time ago," I told her, a bit in awe of the machine, which to me seemed a marvel despite its relatively outdated features.

"Okay, that's a start. I think I might be able to help you. How long ago?"

"Around 1947," I answered. "A really long time ago. Heck, Pete Rose wasn't even playing then."

"That's not so long ago, you know," she answered with a vague smile. "I might remind you that both your mother and I were born *after* that time."

"Yes, ma'am," I uttered, a bit embarrassed.

"Any specific topic with baseball, perhaps?"

"Yeah, pitching. Or pitchers, for the St. Louis Cardinals."

"The Cardinals? My, you do have a plan laid out. Well, thanks to that plan we are half the way home." She paused a moment. "Home. That's a baseball term, isn't it?" She chuckled, I forced a smile.

"Yes Ma'am, it is," I answered.

Mrs. Highsmith continued to explain just how the information could be found, and after a quick tutorial on loading and viewing the microfilm, I was on my way to those depths of the library where such seldom used documents are relegated. Not to the archives, but rather to dry storage. I began yet another search.

"Thanks, Mrs. Highsmith. You've been a great help." I paused. "I need to apologize for that night I snuck out on you –"

"Never mind, August. You're a good boy and I must admit I enjoyed the hunt. Good luck with your research," she finished and turned toward her duties.

"Oh, and, ma'am," I proclaimed loudly. "One last thing."

"Yes, what is it?"

"Have you ever had vandals in your library?"

"Good heavens, I hope not. Why? Did you see something?"

"No, not exactly. It's just that – well, never mind."

"August Monroe," she demanded. "What are you thinking about? Did someone tell you not to say anything about something that has been vandalized in the library?"

"Oh, no. It's not me, Mrs. Highsmith. Honest. It's just that when I was here earlier I found some magazines downstairs that had pages torn out. That's all. I thought you might want to know so you can replace them."

"Well, I'm afraid they are probably not replaceable. Magazines, you say?"

"Yes, ma'am."

"Hhhmm. It certainly is not the first time. I have found sheets torn out in plenty of places myself. Any one in particular that you recall?"

"Yes, ma'am." I affirmed. "It was *Sport*. I know for sure. In fact, it was from the same year I am looking for now. I have the volume number written down at home and if you'd like I could get it to you."

"No, that won't be necessary. That magazine went out of circulation years ago. There would be no way of getting back issues. It's a pity, really. Unfortunate when others wreck the good will for the common reader. Thank you for reporting this to me, August. Now if you will excuse me, I do have a lot of work to do."

Finding the materials was easy enough. After all, Mrs. Highsmith had done the leg work for me. Her example of how to search the reference chart and then track down the microfilm had produced a volume of samples from which to read. The microfilm, however, produced only a few resources, but they too were cross-referenced to the older relics, the bound newspaper books downstairs.

Again, the research started out slowly, as such tedium must, but quickly gained pace as I sorted through spring training previews, mid-season recaps and pennant chase highlights. It was clear that what I was looking for would not be headline material so I scanned all the columns of the newspaper's pages. It was somewhere around late June of 1944 that Bentworth's name first appeared. "Bentworth was strong in his first professional start, despite losing to the Giants 5-3," it read; telling briefly of the man's call-up from Triple A the previous week. The Cardinals had been plagued with injuries and a depleted pitching staff that season. Thus, Bentworth's chance. The next mention of Kevin's dad appeared two weeks later, announcing that Bentworth had pitched with control in a heartbreaker, taking his second big league loss to the old Boston Braves, 2-1. Again, almost two weeks went by before another chance when he was racked for five runs on eight hits in inning one: "Bentworth benched and may head back to Carolina League as Pittsburgh ripped the St. Louis boys 12-0." Such a setback was evident as Bentworth's name did not appear again for all of 1944.

The 1944 spring training guide listed him as an invitee to camp with little hope of making the club. The April 10th issue included the Cardinals' opening day roster without Bentworth on it. It was his second call up in May, again due to injury, that gave Bentworth another chance and boy did he make his presence known. Striking out a then-Cardinals' record of twelve batters, he threw six innings of no-hit ball as the team rattled the Cubs 7-1. Five days later, he was on the mound again, this time winning 6-4 and fanning nine. The streak hit three wins in early June as the Cardinals traveled east to play the Pirates where Bentworth picked up two wins over five days, appearing on short rest. He was suddenly the team's number one pitcher!

The pattern went on for the remainder of that season, though not quite as spectacular. He finished with 9 wins and only 2 losses, including two no-decisions where the Cardinals failed to score enough runs to aid his victory total. By late September, Cookie

Stephens, the team's ace starter, had recovered fully from a bad back and Bentworth was moved to the bullpen. Cruising to the National League Pennant, the Cardinals went on to face their cross-city rivals, the St. Louis Browns in the series, going on to win in six games.

Bentworth had seen two seasons of experience in the Majors, and still I had found no mention of The Steamer. I pressed on, thirsty from the dry air in the library but eager to quench a deeper desire.

1946 newspapers heralded the start of the new season as "The Year the Cardinals Take the Series Again." Expectations were high and the team coasted throughout the summer, winning an average of four out of every five games, thus distancing themselves from the lowly Dodgers who were fading in the standings by the Fourth of July. And there was Bentworth, posting impressive numbers all along and consistently building a respect among the league as one of its bright new talents. Still not the number one guy, he gained his starting spot in the rotation when Syd Johnston was traded to Cincinnati for a shortstop. Bentworth made the most of the opportunity. He was 12-3 by mid-season and was well on his way to setting a new single-season strikeout record. But then disaster struck.

In a July Fourth showdown at home against the Cubs, Bentworth was slated to start game two of a double-header. The game was to be broadcast on WGN all across America as part of the continuing celebration of America's preserved freedom just two years after the end of WWII, and a Chicago journalist in attendance thought enough of the event to recount the day's affairs. Lucky for me, or else my quest might have gone unsolved.

Game one went to the Cubbies in an unprecedented display of offensive power for the last-place team. They scored in all but two innings, thrashing St. Louis 17-3. When Bentworth took the mound for game two, the home crowd was abuzz with impatience and discomfort. The sun was rising high in the afternoon sky and even the ice intended to cool the lemonade and Coca-Cola gave way under nature's oppressive demands. If the fans were to remain for the afternoon, the Cardinals would need to command the game from the opening pitch. And that pressure fell on Ridley Bentworth.

I traversed history. Reading the article in the cramped, dimly-lit library, I felt part of the spectators in attendance that day from the mid-40s. I pressed onward through the journalistic heat that launched into what must have been a worthwhile series of events. I too sat in the outfield bleachers, along with working men and grizzled war veterans, waiting with anticipation to see if the Cards could take back the win in the standings against the hapless Cubs. The story unfolded in the paper, written like a good crime novel.

Bentworth strode to the mound, ignoring his usual pre-game chatter with the press and many of the fans along the dugout. He raised his open glove in the direction of the home plate umpire, received the game ball with a stout determination and circled to the back of the mound. The second game, absent the festivities which preceded game one, was to get underway with much less fanfare. Bentworth rubbed the ball with grave seriousness as the umpire hollered the opening words, "Play Ball!"

A veteran left-handed batter stood in to take the first pitch, warming himself up with nimble swings, viewing the mound and awaiting Bentworth's delivery. Bentworth stepped to the top of the hill and eyed his opponent. His steadfast stare hushed the abating crowd; the catcher dropped into his crouched and tired position, knees cracking in protest (himself wondering why the fans were complaining – a least they're in the shade and did not have to catch both ends of this inferno of a doubleheader). Bentworth toed the rubber, set into his wind up and what followed stunned the crowd, the umpire, both teams, even the catcher himself who watched the ball sail into his unsuspecting chest where it thudded the padded leather protecting his ribs.

Deep into his wind-up – as if one could slow it down to each tenth of a moment – Bentworth gyrated into a strange spasm of the most unorthodox behavior a baseball had ever experienced. Midway through his delivery, his throwing arm, the right, spun down under his hip and bounced into a two-step position wherein the arm ran parallel to his torso, much like a steam engine or turbine piston, the ball at his ear, where everything paused. For just the shortest breath, the baseball world itself stopped breathing, and in that pause all eyes took notice of Bentworth's action. Following, his arm was thrust in an upward trajectory, straight into the air; releasing the ball into the atmosphere above him where it soared upwards of six to seven feet, then hesitated and paused, and dumbly returned in a descent accelerating with gravity toward the ground. Simultaneously, as the ball ascended and turned an about face in mid-air, the pitcher continued to swing his arm through its regular wind-up, lowering it under the hip again and then circling it upwards in a counter clockwise motion where it sprawled upward toward the descending orb. And, as if strung together, the rotating arm jockeying for position reached its exterior top height just at the very instant that the ball was within reach – and both converged with the most perfect grip, hurling the ball with velocity and accuracy in the direction of home plate. The pitcher landed in his customary stance, both feet off the mound, nearly on the grass with his right arm hanging limp, relaxed in anticipation of the umpire's call.

Sensing that no one else had made a sound and not quite knowing what to do exactly, the umpire peered in each direction awaiting any sign of reaction from one of the benches. He then realized that it was his duty to call the pitch a ball or a strike. In the lower path of his vision, he saw the ball lying lonely in the dirt beneath the catcher's left ankle, where it had fallen after striking the catcher's chest.

"Ball?" he ushered, only half-assured of his answer.

A resounding murmur of questions, giggles, confusion and disbelief ran through the large and sweltering crowd. From somewhere in one of the dugouts rose a voice asking the question perched on each witnesses' mind: "What the hell was that?" No one was certain whether it came spoken from the home or visitor's dugout but most certainly the sprinting manager in dispute arose from the Cubs' holding area. An argument ensued for nearly ten minutes, eventually being joined into by the Cardinals' skipper and both full coaching staffs as each man barked at the umpiring crew. If one were to imagine that the conversation centered around the legality of what had just happened, then surely the Cardinals argued that if the kid could get the ball across the plate and into the strike zone, who could refute the innovation? Whereas the Cubs' charges attempted to oust the "crazy, gyrating motion" at first, ending with an all-out banishment of Bentworth from the game. All the while, Bentworth stood in mild amusement of the ruse which he had caused. He doffed his hat to a few screaming kids chiding him on as a new legend, rolled his eyes at the ribbing his teammates tossed at him and ignored the ridicule the opponents lobbed in his direction. It was the catcher who ultimately braved the situation and made his way out to the mound. Later recounting the conversation to the newsman who brought the world the story (and the very same which I was reading) he asked, "Say, uh, Bents, what was that? Some kinda joke?"

"No. It's a delivery I've been working on. It gives better speed with tighter rotation as the centrifugal force of the ball is brushed through the wind, it's kind of like a thoroughbred horse gaining speed heading to the wire."

The catcher glanced out to centerfield, cracked his gum and spit into the dirt. He stood with a mitt locked into his hip. "Uh-huh. I guess so" was all he could suggest in his confused state. "All right, then. Let's play ball, hey?"

But the officiating crew would have none of it. In a reasonable and unanimous vote, a concession to which both manager's agreed, the umpiring crew had decided it would be best to tell the kid not to throw "that pitch" again. Making his way to the mound, the crew chief, Larry Malmansteen, a name apparently lost to all other history save that one moment, brought himself to the verge of laughter and empathy as the fiery-eyed youngster gazed at him.

"Listen, uh, Rid, is it?"

"Ridley, sir."

"Right, Ridley. Ah, listen, as far as we know there ain't nothing wrong with your wind-up, but seeing as we never saw nothing the likes of it before we kind of voted – and your skipper, he agreed to the vote – that you better not use that style of pitch in the game. At least not until we approve it with league officials. Fair enough?"

"Fair enough," a dejected Bentworth answered. "Fair enough."

The game went on as a usual game might and the crowd soon put the experience of the moment in the backs of their minds, though they would not soon forget what they had seen. The Cardinals did win the game, collecting all their runs in the seventh and claiming victory, 4-2. Bentworth pitched effectively through the fifth when either the heat or the embarrassment (perhaps both) got the best of him and his control began to unravel. Lifted for a relief pitcher, he descended from the mound a changed man, unaware of the destiny which lay before him.

As he packed up his personals to head home, a reporter tracked him down.

"Hey, kid. Bentworth?"

"Yeah, Chip" he answered, recognizing the newsman from the clubhouse post-game interviews after the previous year's World Series where extra attention was given to every aspect of the game.

"Say, uh. About that pitch of yours."

"What about it?"

"It's different."

"Glad you noticed."

"Yeah, sure. No problem. The thing is, I was going to write about it but wasn't quite sure what to call it. Ya got a name for that thing?"

"A name?"

"Yeah, a name to identify it. You know, we've got the curveball, the spitter. Your pitch, it needs a name."

"Never thought of it as needing a name. Just an idea I came up with."

"Kind of looks like you're a steam engine out there with your arm pumping and going up and down, all over everywhere."

"Well, that's it then. Name it Steam Engine."

"Steam Engine? Huh, I like that. I might just call it that." His mind raced to find the creative spark which so often alluded him. "Maybe Steam-up? No. Steamship or Steam whistle; or just whistle." I know, he emphasized, snapping his fingers tersely. "Steamer! Yeah, just Steamer. I like that. Do you like that, kid?" he concluded.

Bentworth leaned toward the exit. "Suit yourself," he answered.

Thus, the fabled pitch was dubbed, "The Steamer" and, much to his dismay, the label would bear a heavy burden on Bentworth's remaining life, even if its memory faded and his persistence to recall what might have been stung as bitter as a frozen wind.

I searched the remaining papers but found little else to learn about Bentworth's career, with hardly a mention of the success or failure that followed that summer day. He did not appear in the roster for spring training in either 1948 or 1949 and by then the Cardinals had dissolved into yearly also-rans in the standings.

One last lead I had to track I had found in a by-line upon going back over the article of the Steamer's introduction, christening and apparent dissolution. The author, who dubbed the pitch, had a credit which lead me onward to the next phase of my investigation: "Mr. Chip Carnustle contributes regularly to *Sport View* Magazine."

10 Mrs. Denton

Summer wore on. My plans included loafing, taking life easy, playing ball and letting each day come as it may. My parents, however, had other notions. Instead of playing ball and lounging throughout the summer as I had expected, they arranged that I would be available for some light yard work, painting and miscellaneous chores for an elderly lady in the community, Mrs. Rose Marie Denton. She was a widow whose husband had died way back in World War II and who had never married again. She had become something of a fixture in Cooperstown and all the townsfolk knew her as a lady of quiet kindness. Despite her sorrow of losing a husband and having no children of her own, Mrs. Denton was a sweet, endearing old lady. Her neighbor, Maye Belle Winthrop, was another story. Where one went the other followed. And Miss Winthrop was quite simply the pest of all pests, always insisting on how low her bushes should be cut or how close to the curb the grass could be cut before a weed-whacker had to be used. Fortunate for me, the older boys flocked to her house offering their services each summer since it was rumored that Miss Winthrop paid handsomely for their efforts. My series of chores for Mrs. Denton were simple, routine and always without pay. My parents felt I ought to lend a hand to the elderly and do so without asking a penny for my effort and time. Typical. I gained valuable, "character building" life experiences while the other kids raked in real cash.

I had begun my chores at Mrs. Denton's on the same day of the photo shoot, and had promised to head there at least once a week. I rode to her house on Chestnut Street and always enjoyed the swift ride along quick turns. Secretly, I had planned to spend as little time as possible with Mrs. Denton and as much as I could at the ballpark. But by 3:30 on most afternoons my time with the Owls would be delayed and Mrs. Denton would be directing me from her porch with Miss Winthrop at her side. Miss Winthrop often brought a pitcher of lemonade and wanted Mrs. Denton to share it with her hard-working helper, me. If Mrs. Denton was well known and the Owls were the town's darlings, the only thing more famous in Cooperstown was Miss Winthrop's lemonade – and how awful it tasted.

"Hi, there, August," Mrs. Denton hollered with a big, old-fashioned here-I-am-on-the-porch-in-case-you-can't-see-me sort of wave.

"Hello, Mrs. Denton; good afternoon, Miss Winthrop," I replied. I set my bike down on the gravel driveway and noticed that Miss Winthrop's yard was meticulously trimmed to her specifications. I wasn't even sure who she had hired that summer, but the laborer had done well.

Miss Winthrop delivered an order. "Give the boy some lemonade, Rose Marie! He must be dying of thirst."

"No, thank you, Ladies. I had a whole pitcher of water over at the stadium. I think I'll get straight to work on the backyard. Thank you but I'll pass for now." How I had dodged the drink all summer up to that point was the work of minor miracles, and I was intent on keeping my winning streak alive for as long as I could. What a fool! To be spent of energy out there in the back yard a full hour later, wanting quenched by water or *good* lemonade or anything; and refreshment, while meager, was awaiting me out front, and still the suffering constituted a better option than the one placed before me. Oh, to youth!

I finished my chores and made my way up the side yard to begin clearing some debris that had been kicked up from the road. I heard the fading voice of Miss Winthrop heading toward her own porch, shouting that her own helper had apparently missed the precise trimming of a mulberry bush by all of a half an inch. At the same time, Mrs. Denton produced a pitcher of her homemade iced tea. Now there was refreshment, a drink worth the wait. I seldom had to ask for such a treat since Mrs. Denton often had a pitcher ready for the offering, so long as Miss Winthrop was not in sight.

"Where is Miss Winthrop?" I inquired.

"Oh, those dogs of hers are acting up again. It seems her summer help forgot to lock the basement door. She ran over in a huff to stop them from killing one another."

Laughing at the old lady wasn't fair, but it was welcome release from her company to know she was busy separating her dogs from one another. Her dogs, one either a Sharpe or a Shih Tzu or maybe a Pomeranian (How the hell could I tell the difference?); and the other, a sizable bull mastiff, absolutely hated each other. The funny thing was that the smaller dog, the unidentified breed she called Mopsy, was a mean, feisty, terrible dog who thwarted and attacked the massive fellow dog named Poppy. Miss Winthrop had no cognizance for naming her dogs and had less understanding that getting rid of one would have solved every problem imaginable. Still, she kept them both, and each time they found their way to each other Mopsy managed to beat the stuffing out of Poppy.

"How about some tea, August?" Mrs. Denton said as Miss Winthrop disappeared behind the far eastern edge of the house. "Why not take a load off? It's a hot day and you've been at work a long time."

"Thank you, Ma'am. I think I will."

Mrs. Denton pointed to a chair. "No need to thank me," she said. "As long as you don't take Miss Winthrop's lemonade, I can get out of it myself. I'm glad you're around to make the excuses for me against drinking it; it's better for both of us. Just horrible what that woman does to water and sugar, don't you think?"

Mrs. D. sure had charm. Here I was, her obedient servant, the young respectful lad playing the part of the thirsty, though determined kid, who chose not to insult her neighbor; and all along she saw straight through me and agreed with my actions.

"Yes, Ma'am. To be honest, I agree."

She sat and sipped at her tea. In the hot, waning day, she seemed content, as if things more important than chores and weather filled her spirit with joy.

"So, what are your plans now that you are growing up, August?"

"Plans, Ma'am?"

"Yes. What are you going to do in high school? In college?"

"I haven't really thought much of it, Ma'am. I'm only eleven this year."

"Oh, I forget how young you boys are. Well, you be sure to get yourself a good education," she insisted. Her way was absent the authoritative *I know it better than you do* attitude kids so often get from elders. She gave advice, simple and plain, when speaking to me; though at that age I saw it only as idle prattle, an old woman making conversation. In her wisdom, she was planting the seeds of my future.

"I want to play ball," I said, sipping at the cool refreshment she had offered.

"All you boys do, and even some of the girls these days too I suppose. My dead husband, Walter, God rest his soul, loved all sports but never played a minute of one, he only observed as a spectator." She sat another moment and reflected further on ideas that were unreadable by her expression or manner. I was prepared

81

to charge back to work should she start on with crying over Walter, her dead husband, God rest his soul. Instead, she continued talking as if we were of the same peer group. She sure didn't treat me like a kid. "What do you suppose you will you do if you can't play ball?" she asked.

I downed my tea. "I don't know. I never thought much about it," I answered.

"Well," she said, automatically filling my glass when I set it down, "you're young so don't spend too much time worrying about it. Just be sure to keep it in your thoughts so that it pops up now and then. You'll eventually figure out where you want to go and what it takes to make you happy."

"Yes Ma'am, I'll be sure to do just that," I lied, wondering how anything in the world would ever take place of what I was doing those very days. I was not the least bit concerned about what I would "do" if I couldn't play ball. And that was all she said about it. No nagging, no preachy episode about kids today or what I "should" do with my life. Just the comment, and that was enough. Over the years, she would occasionally come back to the topic, offering a subtle reminder that I should still be keeping it in mind. And she always seemed to know to do so at junctures when I was moving onward into maturity, at moments when her subtle reminders began to leave their greatest impact. Later, she would mention it casually when I showed up in mom's car after I received my driver's license; again when I had earned extra money at the summer fair by working the Ferris wheel; and a host of other moments when rites of passage intersected with opportunity. She was a wise woman, that woman was.

"Where is your friend, Kevin?" she inquired. "I've seen the two of you around so much lately I thought he'd be joining you today."

"I ain't seen him since last night."

"Do I need to correct your grammar, August?" She would have been a kind school teacher if she had lived at a time when it was more common for young wives to join the work force.

"No, Ma'am," I assured her, correcting myself. "I haven't seen him much recently."

"Better. Is he okay?"

I wondered silently for a moment. "I was thinking of heading over to his house to see if he is around," I said.

"Are they still over on Twelfth Street, he and his dad?"

"Yeah, I think so," I answered. "I haven't been to his house yet."

Picture it: Here I was, a sweaty young kid enjoying a nice, cool glass of iced tea with a lady who had lived in Cooperstown for longer than I could imagine forever itself being, wondering on one level what was up with Kevin and his dad, yet it took me at least three minutes before the logic of that moment came together. Mrs. Denton could be a town historian for all I knew. Surely anyone so well liked had had her turn of evenings chatting with everyone around town. She must have known something, and could have probably answered a few of my questions.

"Mrs. Denton," I asked, about as casual as an elephant through a funeral, "do you know who Kevin's mother is?"

"Well, August," she answered with a knowing pause. "I think he's your friend and if he wants you to know that, he would tell you himself."

"But Kevin doesn't talk much. I was just thinking that if I knew what happened with his mom, then maybe I could get him to start talking about other stuff."

"What makes you think something happened to her?" Her voice warned me while she scolded with her eyes. For all I knew, there actually never was a Mrs. Kevin's mom. Maybe he'd been adopted by Mr. Bentworth, or found at a bus depot, or had fallen from the stars. Who could tell?

I waited for the stare to dissolve. "But, she's never around," I said. "I mean, at least I never see her and he never talks about her." Between the silences, I juggled whether the next thought that had been mingling around in my head was the proper thing to ask. Finally, after a deep breath and a moment of decision, I asked her. "Is she dead?" The look of indignation I had expected never surfaced, and, again, in her wisdom she somehow knew how to answer the question without answering it at all.

"Well, there are some things young people don't understand. It's part of growing up. You just have to experience these things." She contemplated her next words carefully before speaking again. "I really think you should ask him yourself. If he wishes to share it with you, he will. Otherwise, you'll just have to wait until he's ready to bring up the matter. Now," she added, her tone strikingly opposite her previous seriousness. "How about we get inside before Miss Winthrop comes back? I don't think I can take much more of her today."

I finished my second glass of tea. "I thought she was your friend. Don't you like her?"

"Oh yeah, sure I do. She is good for occasional company." She picked up the pitcher of tea and headed toward the front door where she paused. "She just gets on my nerves sometimes," she admitted. Laughing again, I followed her inside.

The Denton house was a preservation of that day long ago when Mrs. Denton heard the news that her husband had lost his life in service to his country. Absent the dust that might have settled through the years, the house appeared as if it hadn't been entered, touched or walked upon since late in the winter of 1944. The pictures, the frames, the drapes, the furniture, even the crystal vase with its nectar-like iced tea – everything from the wallpaper to the holiday garnishments in the photos showed the house as it was in a time long gone. Memories, along with the dust, had been swept in and out on a regular basis over the decades. Being there, one wondered how Mrs. Denton could ever have been so happy. The quiet lingered, and the many antiques on display resonated of sadness, but she had gone forward, accepted her life and found peace.

My first chore was to bring a window air conditioner unit down from the attic so Mrs. Denton could enjoy cooler air as summer heated through August. The only modern conveniences she had were a color television set and that air conditioner. The unit wasn't heavy but still Mrs. Denton insisted that she guide me down both flights of stairs. It would have been easier for me to just lift the machine and carry it straight to the window that looked over her yard.

I secured the unit in place and plugged it in. It reacted with a subtle hum. "Oh, I don't think I need that thing running all day," she said nervously. "But your parents were over last night and thought it was just too hot this year not to use it. I appreciate your work. I hate so much to be a bother and I wish your folks would let me pay you a little something."

"No bother, Mrs. Denton," I replied. What I wanted to say was: *Sure, I'll take five bucks for my effort.* Instead, I bit a lip of respect which I had been taught to show elders. "It's really no problem. I'm just glad I could help."

"You're such a nice boy," she reminded me. "Would you like another drink? How about a soda this time? You deserve a treat after so much work, and iced tea just won't hit the spot the way a nice cold soda does. I have some Pepsi in the kitchen."

"Sure, that'd be great," I answered.

I waited for the soda (or pop as it is better known where I grew up) and scanned the den. I had never been in that particular room, and its comforts proved to be intriguing. It was a nice den with a reading room encased in the corner, a nook that captured daylight often. It was a museum unto itself, really, with a sparse and diverse oddity of collections: an old ivory pipe displayed on a desk; a half-sewn dress in a corner draped over a yellowing mannequin; a chess board sat on a table absent any playing pieces; a few photos; a sizable globe mounted within a wooden stand and other miscellany. I sat at an old telephone desk and relished the mechanically forced breeze as it chased the humidity and stuffiness from the air. After all, I had lugged the thing into its place. The least I deserved was cooler air. I felt the welcome call of curiosity and examined the smaller artifacts in the glassed-in cases.

Upon one shelf sat a small ship in a glass bottle with its cork missing. Upon another stood a bowling trophy and a collection of China dolls, sprayed out behind them were a number of ornate Chinese bamboo fans. And to the left and almost behind them, a framed magazine. Above it, a museum lamp set to illuminate the frame and its singular content. The bulb had expired long ago and, judging from the layer of dust there upon, had not been replaced for many years. It seemed the only object to have accumulated any dust at all in the room, if not the whole house.

I was tempted to lift the frame and inspect its contents. I checked over my shoulder. *Am I snooping?* I wondered. *What will my hostess think if I am prying through her artifacts?*

"Go on," her soft voice uttered from the entryway, startling me. "Take a look at it. This room has a lot of treasures lying about. Most of the others grab the attention of many guests. I'm not surprised you picked that one. I think you will like it the best."

I backed away from the display case. "Pardon me, Ma'am. I didn't mean to be nosy."

"Oh, go ahead," she insisted. "You of all young ones around here I can trust. Go right ahead. I think you'll find it to your liking."

I carefully lifted the oak-stained frame from the display case. "What is it?" I asked. My imagination ran amuck with possibilities be. "A magazine?" I wondered out loud upon taking a closer look.

"Not just a magazine," Mrs. Denton answered. "*Sports View.*"

"Yeah, I've heard of it. It's not as good as *Sports Illustrated*, but I have read it now and then." I examined the cover of an athlete and a signature across the image. "Is that Jim Thorpe's real autograph?"

"Yes it is. He was Walter's favorite."

"Your husband?" I asked carefully. A smile returned to her weathered lips.

"Yes. Walter had him sign that in, oh, must have been 1941, about a month before Walter left for Europe." Her smile slid away as she sat. "He never came home, though, my Walter."

I can't excuse my reaction on just being a kid. That would be too easy. The way I see it, I was either too naive to notice *anything* or I was so enamored by the real Jim Thorpe and the legends I'd read about him, that I completely skipped past the woman's reminiscence about her husband's death. Instead, I said, "Wow, Jim Thorpe. How did he get Jim Thorpe to sign it?"

"He just asked him during the interview I suppose." She said it so matter-of-factly that it seemed unreal to me. Here was one of the greatest athletes of the twentieth century, and Mrs. Denton's husband had just met him in passing.

"Interview?" I asked. "Your husband was a reporter? A sports writer?"

"Occasionally. Mostly an editor, though," she told me. "He started that magazine with his cousin in 1936 – just after the Olympics in Berlin. It was his passion. His father had left him a lot of money. Walter bought this old house and put much of the money away for a rainy day. We spent the rest starting a magazine. Seems silly now, but it was the right thing at the time."

"Wow! I wish I could read this one." I practically squealed.

"I have an extra copy upstairs. You can read it any time you wish. That one is one of only two editions that I framed."

"What was the other?"

"The first that my name appeared in. I was a typesetter for sixteen years, and had my name in the editor's box many, many times. The first is always special, so I framed it. Just a silly girl's memories."

"Do you still own the magazine?"

"No. Certainly not. I sold it off – or, rather, my lawyers did – in 1977. I still have a subscription, though. I keep every issue."

"Wow," I uttered, a little too amazed probably. This was, after all, just a lady's collection. I mean, how big of a deal is that? "Can I see them some time?"

"Sure. Would you like to see then now?"

I checked the clock. "No, I'd better get going. I should have been home twenty minutes ago. I'll save that for a rainy day myself."

I placed the frame back on its pedestal and wandered over the possibilities that, had Mr. Denton lived and still owned and operated *Sports View,* maybe I could have a had better summer job than chores and cleaning for his widowed wife.

"Is the magazine still in town?" I asked, hopefully. "I mean the people who own it and where they work?" Maybe I could still land a job. Maybe she still had connections at the magazine. Surely, a magazine had enough errands to keep a young man busy.

"No. It was always published in New York City, but after we sold it they moved out west. San Francisco, I think. Why?" My sudden hopes had been dashed. I was ten, and already I was resigned to a life in Cooperstown.

"Oh, nothing really," I replied quickly. "I just thought I would have gone to see where they are printed. Gotta go."

I thanked Mrs. Denton once again for the iced tea and passed quietly through the door. Her voice delivered a combined you're-welcome-thank-you, primarily for the work but maybe for the company. Down the porch and back on my bike in moments, I caught a glimpse of Mrs. Denton waving goodbye as I pedaled away. I always liked Mrs. Denton, and found her company unlike that of other adults.

I pedaled up Chestnut and onto Beech, considering that maybe she saw me as the boy who could have been her own grandson, or even a reflection of the boy she might have raised had the outcome of World War II been different.

The bike ride from Mrs. Denton's house to ours was hardly a match for my and Kevin's usual speed, as we had often raced each other home along the same route. However, I was tired after a busy day. The trip was more of a coast along the familiar terrain.

There are two entrances to the street we lived on then, Wilson Ave., and both entrances met at a junction with Mrs. Denton's street, Chestnut. The options of entry, while not cumbersome, offered different challenges for the ride home. Heading north on Longview, one could take the first entrance to Wilson but that would prove a longer trip, either walking or riding, though it was mostly flat. The street wound itself through the east end in a disjointed figure eight, as if the eight had been laid on its side, like the infinity symbol, and then segmented almost evenly down the middle to resemble a wavelength though not quite so symmetrical. Thus, the end furthest to the north, while a longer walk to the entry way itself, presented a hillier path with dips and shoots. In winter, the street made for great bobsledding, provided we kids could convince our parents to avoid driving there.

I chose the farther entrance, hoping to pass by Kevin's house and see what he was up to, or if he wasn't home, learn where he might have been. The Bentworths lived on a tiny circle, not even a full cul-de-sac midway along Longview on Trappers Bend. Presumably the street had been named for a former hiding place where poachers in earlier frontier days would take hold and sit in waiting until a shepherd or a farmer passed by with his herd. They would spring upon the unsuspecting sheep herder and steal away the precious flock in quick motion. Why this deserved the honor of having a street named after it was beyond me!

I approached the entrance and stopped to look around the tiny circular avenue. One of only three houses, it was anyone's guess which was the Bentworth's. Each home was a mirror copy of the other and all three were covered in the same tacky blue that happened to match the dugouts at Owls Stadium. Having never before visited Kevin's home, I found it still curious that he had never invited me over. I applied slight pressure on the handle bars of the bike and followed suit by pushing off with my feet. I circled into Trappers Bend and proceeded to the mid-point of the semi-circular road.

Neither of the three houses held any distinguishing feature to set one apart from the other, save the size and variance of the hedges along each short driveway. And it appeared that all three were vacant, no activity to any surrounding. Even the mailboxes were identical and each house was numbered systematically 111, 222, and 333 in an attempt to make the non-circle some kind of a full street. Wishing I had with me an Owls' media guide, where all the addresses of players and employees could be found, I climbed back onto my bike and against tired weariness, pushed the pedaled machine into motion. I completed one full lap of the street and made my way to the exit from which I had entered only moments before. I looked over my shoulder and peered into each house slowly before speeding back onto Chestnut where I headed home, navigating the more difficult hills and steep angles to which I had committed myself by choosing that path.

11 Mom and Dad and Grandpa

Arriving home brought a sense of comfort after such a long day of work and a little bit of wonder. Besides feeling detached at the mystery of Kevin's family history – not to mention his current whereabouts – I took pleasure in the solitude of home. Mom and dad seldom fought, and when they did, usually made an effort to apologize to each other and to me in an over-affectionate sap fest. I am their only child and they wanted to teach me how relationships work, how people get along and even argue but still love one another. They were good parents and I never thought to consider myself lucky until I saw the possibility that not all of my friends had as good a home to return to.

I dropped on the couch. "Mom," I said, interrupting her reading. "Why don't I have any brothers or sisters?"

"What kind of a question is that, August?" She didn't actually answer, and continued reading.

"Mom?" I said, strongly.

She closed the book. "Yes, dear?"

"How come?"

"Why don't you have siblings? That's an odd question, isn't it?"

"I don't know," I said, the logic of a kid leading my thoughts. "All the kids at school do, and I was just wondering why I don't."

"I'm not sure how to answer it. What's on your mind?"

"Nothing really. Just thinking. Did you and dad stop having kids for a reason?"

"Your dad and I wanted to have more kids but it just never turned out that way. I became awfully busy in the church, and your dad's work took up a lot of his time. We weren't sure if it would have been fair to you, or to a possible brother or sister, to have even less time and energy for both of you than we had."

"Does that make you sad?"

"No. Not really. As long as we are happy I see no reason to dwell on what we don't have. I have a wonderful family with you and dad. I see no reason to wish for more."

"I would like to have a sister. She'd be neat."

"You hope so, you mean," mom reminded me. She had a way about her that made me think about what I was really saying. "But you don't know for sure. A sister would make a lot of changes around here. Like, who would watch her if you had a game you wanted to go to? Or, where would she sleep? We only have two rooms. Would you share your room with her?"

"With a girl? No way. Maybe I'd be better off with a brother."

That inquisitive motherly look still lingered across her brow. "Maybe. Are you sure you're alright?"

"Yeah, I guess so."

Mom was keenly aware of everything I said or thought, and always had been. I understand now that she probably recognized that a new phase in her boy's life was beginning; or if not beginning, taking shape in my thoughts. This seemed to move her a little, this knowing her baby was growing up. I can still see the look in her eyes – that far away glance that begins to register when one realizes the world is changing and there is nothing that can be done to protect those you love. All a parent can do is hope they have done their best. Mom also had a tendency to over-react. I wasn't quite ready to move out just then, yet she looked as if she had been informed that I was moving to Belize. I wondered if she was uncertain of her feelings, and that maybe should be expected and accepted of parents. One part was sad that her boy was maturing as the other celebrated his discovery. She easily changed the topic, however, and set to more practical matters.

"What do you say we ask dad if he wants pizza?" she offered.

I blurted out what was really on my mind: "Kevin only has his sister, no brothers and his mom is gone."

She spoke patiently. "Kevin has a different family than we do," she said. "There is no telling why his mother isn't around."

I was determined to not let this topic go until I had it figured out, or until I had exhausted all possible lines of reasoning. "Does that mean you'll be gone some day?" I asked. It just didn't make sense to me. Having to face her own mortality was one thing; having to answer her son's inquiries into the matter must have shocked her.

"August," she declared, as if forgetting to breathe. "What are you getting at? I'm not going anywhere, honey." She stood and crossed to the couch. She held my hand and asked, "Where have these ideas come from? You've been watching movies with your dad again, haven't you?" she joked.

"No. But who is Kevin's mom? If she is gone, then so can you be gone too, right?"

She rubbed my cheek. "Well, yes," she said. "Anyone is capable of going away at any time for lots of reasons. But I am not going anywhere." A reflective moment seemed to pass into and through her thoughts. "Is Kevin's mom dead?" she asked. "Is that what you're afraid of, that I will die? Or that daddy will?"

"No. I don't think you'll die. I don't even know if Kevin's mom is dead or missing or lives somewhere else. He never talks about her. Isn't that weird? Not to have a mom?"

"Not everyone is as fortunate as we have been. Some married people get divorced. Other times, people die and the rest of the family goes away from each other. Kevin, his sister and his dad, they're together. So no matter what happened to his mom, that is his family now."

I responded quickly. "Should I ask him?"

"I don't think that would be very fair. I think that if Kevin wants to tell you anything, he will in his own time. Asking could hurt his feelings."

"But I'm his best friend," I said. I started to cry but sniffed it back in quickly.

"Then, as his friend," mom assured me, "you can build trust so that someday you will be able to ask him, or he will want to tell you himself. I want you to promise me that you won't bring this up unless he does so first, okay?"

"Okay, I promise."

"Good. You're okay then?"

"I don't know. Probably. I guess you're right but I just want to know." I forced a smile. "Yeah, I'm okay."

She squeezed my hand again. "In time, August. But only when it is right for Kevin. I guarantee it. Okay?"

"Okay," I said. She then went about obligatory mom doings; kissed me softly on the forehead and probably thought of things she chose not to share, probably about how or why or when her son had started growing up on her. "It's a deal. Deal?" I added.

"What?" she asked.

"Deal. That's what Kevin and I say when we make an agreement. We say 'Deal?' and answer 'Deal' and then shake on it."

She stood and stretched out a hand. "Okay," she answered. "Deal. Now – how about that pizza?"

"Okay. Where's dad?"

"Downstairs, doing what, I have no idea."

"I'll get him," I said, and shot across the room with a renewed energy. "I get to choose the topping since I am the only one without siblings!" At the corner to the kitchen, I stopped. "Mom."

"Yes?"

"Thanks."

I bounded through the kitchen to the stairs to get dad.

"You're welcome," I heard her answer, much in the way Mrs. Denton had said, "Thank you" earlier. People have a beauty of sharing more in how they speak, though not necessarily realizing they hold such a similar perspective.

My mother was (and still is) an exceptional woman. Raised with five brothers, she had succumbed to the rigor of the classic tom-boy image, yet paid no attention to sports. She was a fine student, entered Ohio State University as a student of political science and graduated with a second degree in theology. She attended Seminary in Dayton where she met dad who was teaching engineering to what he always called "bored students who had no reason for being in college." How that meandering path through college led to Cooperstown and to my family roots is of little importance. Of some significance, however, is the diplomatic way in which she chose to raise her family. If college education has come to be the proper time in one's life for a person to "find herself" and come out of the experience a better person than she was when she began her education, then Renee (sans McConagall) Monroe was the epitome of a college woman who had made the best of her time on campus. In short, she entered a shy, determined girl and emerged a brave and confident woman.

Mom turned down the opportunity to study abroad and passed on a worldwide ministry program to become active in local government. She made the transition from seminary student to working woman with ease and efficiency. Later, she would add the moniker of working mom to her many-titled resume with equal ease and fervor. Nothing much was known that could shake my mother. Whether persuading the elders to change a church policy or defeating self-interested legislation, she was active both civically and spiritually. While it opened many interesting doors of possibility for myself, it also led for some strict living as well. The same rules and disciplines she used to solve civil matters as a leader of church and society were utilized to administer justice within her family.

Her marriage to dad was not one of difficulty nor of conflict. In fact, they got along rather well. I recall many happy memories as a child, most of which involve both my parents. They shared their dreams with intimacy and laid their plans out fairly but not necessarily rigidly. It was dad's wish to raise a child who would follow his passion for science. Mom had always wanted a boy, and neither regretted their decision to have only one, or at least that is what they told me. Upon the birth of a boy named August they were both "proud and happy." August, though, aligned an early and obvious penchant toward his maternal grandfather, mom / Renee's dad, and this soon became the first thorn in the side of my mom's marriage to her husband, my dad. I of course had no idea this was going on. I just naturally took to Grandpa. Seeing early on in her marriage that the division between her father and her husband could cause lifelong heartache, she had acted pro-actively, initiating a diplomatic procedure that would hold them together in peace, perhaps even force them to get along. Albeit cumbersome to convince him that their son needed the freedom to pursue his personality, it was with equal cunning that mom devised the scheme in which dad understood just how much baseball was a science, and that simple principles of science could be applied to its procedures and its teachings. Thus, before a dispute ever reared its complex head, mom had quelled what may have been a lifelong distraction between father and son and grandfather.

And, up until their first time teaching me the skills to play baseball, our family, including Grandpa, was content. When it came time to administer the lessons to be learned, that was when the battles ensued.

Spring, 1974: Pittsburgh, PA. Picture it! On the very same lot where my grandfather, fun-loving, hard-working, get-your-hands-into-the-muck, blue collar guy, had played ball as a youth along with the great Honus Wagner, my immediate predecessors, Grandpa and dad, gathered so they could teach me to play the game my grandfather adored, my mother tolerated, and my father simply did not understand. Quick-witted mom explained to dad just how much science there is in baseball, and her scheming had paid off. What had been a sore spot had become an opportunity for dad to bond with both son and father-in-law. Dad relished the thought of passing along his passion for science to me through a game to which I was just beginning to take a liking. After all, a man of science demands repetition, scholarly approach and most of all cleanliness, order, structure. One could not repeat the discovery of scientific inquiry in a lab soiled with grease, sand or even a dusting of earth. And that was only where the contact between dad and Grandpa had begun.

Times had changed since 1935; the year Grandpa had played sandlot ball with the future Hall of Famer. Honus Wagner, The Flying Dutchman, was a local boy made it big. He grew up in Pittsburgh under the hasty shadows of the belching steel mills of smoke and smog which had lingered in the air from the city's very livelihood. As the son of a young immigrant, it is easy to imagine Wagner had to fight off plenty of tough Irish or Italian kids over the years who crossed the Birmingham Bridge to raise ruckus as quickly as play a game of pick-up. He was a legend in Pittsburgh who had risen from the ranks of poverty to become the greatest ballplayer of his era, some argue of all time! Honus Wagner was no doubt tough – but he never forgot where he had come from. And neither did my Grandpa. After Honus' career was over, the giant slugger with a golden glove continued to reside in Pittsburgh, often playing ball in local fields with neighborhood kids, teaching them the game and enjoying the retirement years he had worked hard to obtain.

Fortunately for Grandpa, and perhaps for me as well, Honus had taught my mom's father a lot more about the game than any coach could have. And, had Grandpa not been riddled with bullets in World War II, he himself may have made the trek to the Big Leagues. Shot three times during his tour of duty, Grandpa was not incapacitated from his regular duties, though his legs were weakened enough to limit mobility. So, as is the tale of many citizens of this world, he had learned to accept the sacrifice for his country at the risk of his own personal hopes and dreams; often reminding me that he was at least lucky enough to still have his life, a gift which many fallen comrades and enemies alike had lost in the surrender to a greater cause.

But still, a lot had changed, and the same lot where my grandfather stood to teach me ball in 1974 was the same field where a vicious peace rally had taken place eight years prior, in 1966. No, my father was not a rebellious sixties youth whose ideals fired his vision and promise for the future. He was too wrapped up in chemistry debate clubs and math competitions to take notice of his peer's activities toward unraveling and rewriting social order for that turbulent decade. Instead, he was what today might be called a "geek." He was more studious than rebellious, more constrained than freedom searching. Regardless, dad was present as a spectator in 1966 when five black high school students from the near Hill District attempted to enroll in his high school. And it was on this same field that an altercation took place between five students on one side and at least twenty on the opposition. As can probably be guessed, the five new students attempting to gain entry to the public high school had recently moved into the neighborhood, the same neighborhood of those tough immigrants Grandpa had survived. And their counterparts, in society's eyes, in color of skin, in where they came from, were all white. No one apparently noticed that those black kids (two of whom were brothers who would die together in Viet Nam) were intellectually equal if not superior to my father's classmates. As well, their fathers had jobs alongside the students' parents, and they would soon be shopping in the same stores, eating from the same tables, and, perhaps, in a future too far away from the eyes of hatred and ignorance in 1966, living together in a loving family, or at least a supportive community.

If a lot had changed from the pre-WWII era when Grandpa had played ball alongside Honus Wagner (and when he managed to swat a home run over the famous shortstop's head, collected two doubles and had a perfect day in the outfield), a lot more had changed since my dad had stood along a fence and witnessed a crowd the size of a pep rally cheer on as more than twenty white kids bested the five black kids in an unfair, violent mismatch of ignorance and abuse. Dad admits openly now that his hatred of the day rests as much in his lack of action as in the display that was unleashed before him. He was much younger then, and did not know what he had allowed by not acting. He realized later that was his error, and he makes no excuses for it now.

So, when the day finally came along for dad and Grandpa to teach little me how to play baseball, the mixed feelings between the men were present in ways I could not understand then, and maybe don't even fully grasp still today. After all, I grew up in days when the only hatred (if it can even be called that in light of larger things) came from bullies who stole milk money and from families who stole parking spaces in the street. I had no introduction to differences that would cause anger or violence. The Italian kids were just kids, the black kids were just kids, the Polish kids, despite being the brunt of dumb jokes, were just kids. I guess that means I was just a kid, not a white kid.

For dad and Grandpa, there was a connection to the place, that was certain; and each had memories far stretching the spectrum of human emotion and experience. But for them to carry such misgivings into my upbringing is peculiar, or so I thought.

The field sits between Charles Street and 18th to the east, and 19th to the west with Carson running along the southern border. It is a square block that had stood as transitions for each of them, and only came to intertwine on that day when one's only son and the other's third grandson wanted to learn how to play baseball. They had no way of knowing that either had ties to the field. Perhaps, if it had been my dad and his father, then both would have known the history the place held for the other. Or if dad and mom had dated in high school, then both would have known each other's history as well. The conflict, however, arose from the sport itself, and the setting, a mere backdrop, only served to heighten the emotional investment each took in participating in my learning and my playing. Here was dad, on a lot where he had witnessed the most serious offense committed and he himself a young father who did not even understand (or enjoy) the game of baseball; all the while my grandfather was spouting off about how he used to love coming there as a teenager and tossing the ball around, paling around with the guys. It was only natural that they would eventually argue.

The afternoon started off well enough. Dad stood on the mound, litigiously lobbing easy-to-hit pitches toward Grandpa as I trotted around centerfield attempting to catch the flying spheres of our attention. Grandpa was either too good or too lousy to be consistent, and with each swing of the bat the ball caromed off in the direction opposite where I was standing. In what started as sprints I would track down one fly ball as it sputtered to a stop in the thick grass, and begin picking it up just as I heard the crack of the bat in time to turn around and see another ball zinging off toward the very spot I was standing before the previous pitch. I would drop the first ball and make for the newly launched target of my own attention. Upon arriving at the second ball and scooping it up into my hand for a throw toward home, another crack would reverberate the tiny park and yet another baseball would be sent sailing into the other side of the outfield, near where lay the first ball I had abandoned moments ago. Again, I dropped the leather treasure and headed to duty.

The cycle repeated itself over and over for sixty solid hits (we had brought a lot more baseballs than I even knew existed in the world) and not one left the ballpark in a home run swing to provide me a moment's rest. Grandpa stood with pride as each hit sailed a solid line drive into the expansive green that surrounded my tiny three-foot, seventy-pound frame of a then-five-year-old outfielder. If I had had enough and had grown tired, dad had had enough of me having enough and had grown furious. Though muted by distance, the complaints he logged were clearly audible as I stood in dead centerfield, stranded between thirty balls to the right and thirty more dotting my left, listening to my respected elders argue over their behavior.

"What the hell are you doing, Stephen?" dad hollered. He tossed his glove into the dirt.

"What? What's wrong?" Grandpa followed. "Am I going too soft on the kid?"

"Too soft! Jesus, Steve. You're wearing the kid down. He's only five, and it's hot out here. Couldn't you hit just one in his direction?"

"He needs to learn to track down fly balls, Chris. What do you want me to do about it? The kid's gotta sprint."

"This isn't try outs for the Olympic! The kid's exhausted."

It was embarrassing. The tirade went back and forth for what seemed twenty minutes or longer. I could see (or imagine) people in nearby bars and stores and their homes wondering what in the world was so serious that deserved such a ruckus. Slowly they would creep from their porches and bar stools and make their way to the field between 18th & 19th to witness two grown men arguing over how the kid was being treated. All the while I stood out there, surrounded by dead baseballs, wondering what I should do. My indecisiveness was taking root early in life, and between Grandpa and dad, I had no idea whom to side with. I didn't know how to compromise, so I just remained silent and stood in centerfield with baseballs that waited to be picked up and tossed back into play before the grass grew up around them.

Finally, the argument subsided with my father uttered something about, "Oh this is just ridiculous." He turned toward the outfield, stormed into my territory and one-by-one launched each baseball back into the batter's box with force...and rather impressive aim. Grandpa tolerated the occasional missile for the first five or six attacks, but after long he took up arms in defense of his home base and perhaps his ideals. He began lobbing baseballs *back* toward my standpoint, most of them bouncing softly just beyond the infield dirt where they rolled to a stop at a safe distance from both myself and my dad. This only irritated dad further. He was a better, perhaps younger, arm than Grandpa and, after having systematically lobbed the sixty baseballs homeward, advanced on his front between the infield dirt and shallow centerfield where Grandpa's first offensive lay in a batch of sixty that had begun to re-accumulate in my grandfather's attempted rebuttal. Dad assembled his arsenal and again launched baseball after baseball in toward home.

After tiring his arm out, Grandpa lifted the bat upon his shoulder and began his second counter-offensive. He sailed the baseballs out over dad's head while dad was still busy bending to, picking up, and throwing baseballs inward for the second of his attacks. Each increased their anger toward sheer madness. It was during Grandpa's counter-counter-offensive that I realized it was time for the innocent civilian, me, to take cover. I dropped my head and walked toward the dugout, sat hard upon the clapboard bench and hid under the cinder block cover. It was the same dugout that dad and Grandpa had worked together to build a few years earlier with other dads and grandfathers who had readied the field for a new season after a harsh and devastating winter had let the field in disarray.

Before long, it had become an all-out contest of will, a war. Baseballs were flying in and out of centerfield toward home plate and back again in a meteor shower of the game's most essential piece of equipment, the ball. Gravity and power collided in a barrage of will where neither army seemed to tire and the frontline would not be lost. The complete ridiculousness of the matter came to fruition when one of dad's throws met in mid-air with a ball that had just been sent from Grandpa's bat. The two balls smacked dead-on above second base and ricocheted into separate corners, dad's ammo falling toward first base and Grandpa's near third; both sprawling out of the contest as a casualty of war.

It wasn't until the fourth offensive that Grandpa finally tired. Mid-way through what must have been his 350th swing in a mere two hours, he had had enough. Dad was still busy scooping up baseballs, lobbing them without direction into the infield when he must have realized the other side had surrendered. Symbolically, dad stopped and surveyed the battlefield, tattered everywhere with white baseballs. One last time he scoured the entire outfield and emptied the battlements of their spent weaponry. He lethargically threw baseballs in toward the backstop, where each skipped to a slow but steady stop along the fence's lower ring, piling up into a sizeable mound of fifty-eight tiny spheres. Then he finally ceased fire. He had won the battle, but surely not the war. In his pyrrhic victory, I still loved baseball and Grandpa would go on to teach me the game.

Soaked in sweat as if he had torn up our entire yard and planted new grass in the time we were supposed to be playing baseball, dad made his way toward the dugout. Along the first base line he noticed the odd ball sitting lonely in the grass, the one he had thrown but had not seen collide with Grandpa's would-be base hit. Dad reached down, gathered up the ball, tossed it softly in the air once, then twice, allowing it to smack soundly off his palm both times. He then took one last glance around the field and resumed his stride toward where Grandpa and I were sitting. He didn't sit down though. He tossed the ball to Grandpa and continued walking, off the field, past his own parked car and down the street toward home.

Grandpa caught the ball just barely as his fatigue had slowed down his usually adept quickness. He eyed the ball and rolled it over in his burly hands before he spoke.

"You know, August," he began. "Your father and I have a lot of work to do to get along better. It think it's high time we got to be friends. What do you think about that?"

"That would be great," I answered. "Real swell."

When dad had first met Grandpa, there was no bond created and it was obvious. If the old wives' tale that declares a girl will marry a man most like her own father has any merit, its counter argument is my parents. Grandpa did not necessarily dislike dad, not hardly. He held him in sound regard. He admired dad's commitment to his family, respected the fact that he had provided Grandpa with a grandson, and envied dad's education. He just didn't know how to reach him.

"What does he do?" Grandpa had long before asked my then-love-struck mother.

"He teaches, dad," she had answered. "He's a professor at Ohio State."

"Oh, I see." Mom can attest to the wrinkled brow that had formed across Grandpa's head, the complexity of imagining how one ought to speak to a professor worrying him. "Well, what does he teach? Perhaps if I know I can make him feel more comfortable; you know, make small talk."

"Dad, you don't have to do that," mom had said. "He'll like you and he'll feel comfortable. He's very nice."

"Come on, Renee. Give me a shot. I want to try. What can he teach that is so complicated that I can't at least hold a conversation with the man? I'm pretty smart, ya know. I've read a lot. What does he teach? Math? Reading? Uh, what do you college kids call it now a days, Literature? Whatever he teaches I'm sure I can discuss."

"Well," mom had said. "He's a scientist."

"Great! That I know. I wired this whole house myself, electricity and I are like cousins. What else?"

"Dad, it's a specialized field of science, though I am sure electricity is something he knows very well. He teaches water hydraulic propulsion."

That was when Gram-mah-ma remembers having laughed out loud, just as the furrow on Grandpa's brow had twisted in mesmerized wonderment, as if he had been beaned with a fastball straight on the old noggin.

"What the hell is that?" he had asked after lengthy contemplation. "And both of you quit laughing at me!" I ain't no dummy you know! I got an education from the military when I was over at Okinawa fighting off the Japs."

"Pipe down, Stephen," Gram-mah-ma had demanded. "We're just having a laugh at your expense."

12 Bentworth

If tensions between Grandpa and dad had wavered between war and diplomacy, I soon learned that I had not had it all that bad. For right in my own circle of friends – okay, my *only* friend, I experienced a division far greater and sadder.

Mr. Bentworth's creation of the Steamer and its subsequent failure was not a matter of one blundering an error the likes of a news reporter mispronouncing a player's name or misquoting a manager in the local press. He experienced utter humiliation. Perhaps the saving grace was the lesser exposure due to the media and technology of that time – for one can only imagine how widespread the shame may have been had the moment occurred across the banner of ESPN or all over the Internet. Luckily for Mr. Bentworth, the heyday of cable television had not yet dawned. Still, Bentworth had suffered an ignominy as catastrophic as anyone could shoulder for his generation. People pointed fingers when he walked through town. They ridiculed his children, snickered behind his wife's back at the beauty salon and all but avoided the whole bunch when amassed together in church, at the local grocery store or at a ball game. He had moved to tiny Cooperstown only in the hope that a small town might allow that such reminders were non-existent. As fate determined, Cooperstown was the absolute worst place for him to reside.

And then, after what may have been years of peace on the matter, some punk (namely me) had gone and dredged the whole thing up right under the gentleman's nose. In fact, I deserved a good, wide crack across the skull for intruding on the poor man's hideous past.

With the information of the Steamer logged to memory, I attended the next Owls' home game with the hope of congratulating Mr. Bentworth on his vision, the idea of a new pitch so amazing to me that regardless of success I considered it to be an impressive accomplishment.

He stepped past me in the locker room. "Mr. Bentworth, sir," I said.

"Yes, what is it?"

I shimmied a nervous side-step. "Well, yes, uh, sir." I wondered if he recognized me at all. "I just wanted to say that I was sorry the Steamer didn't work out for you. You were a good pitcher. It's too bad that you –"

"Son" he interrupted. "I think we are done discussing that piece of history." Whether the result of my mother's position or an element of mercy, Mr. Bentworth lowered a dejected smile into a heartened frown and walked silently from the clubhouse. I turned to depart and was surprised to see Kevin sitting in the vacant locker area behind me. The look on his face was saddened and dejected.

I waited a moment. "Hey, Kev, What's up?"

He stood quickly. "Why'd you upset my dad?" he asked.

"I didn't mean to, I just –"

"Just mind your own business." He bumped past me and left the clubhouse.

That Kevin took to cover was not so much a mystery after all, but I had spent days wondering what I had done that was so bad as to alienate my friend. We had spent every minute together since we had met, including that entire summer. And then, just like a called third strike, that was it. No argument worthy of hell would change the umpire's call.

My mistake, I later learned, was not the discovery of the facts themselves, but in what I did once I had learned of Bentworth's ignoble brush with history. Had I simply filed the information to memory, all would have remained well. Instead, I pursued the matter further.

I had no way of knowing that Kevin had not even known his dad was a baseball player at all, yet alone a pitcher with a questionable past. I suppose I should have seen that one coming. Ever since our first days hanging out together, I had noticed a shy irreverence that Kevin had toward his dad. When I asked what his dad did for a living, it was with shame that Kevin answered that his dad was a groundskeeper. But the single most telling event occurred shortly after Murray had encouraged Bentworth to toss the old Steamer – the very event that sent me toward my research adventure.

Kevin's disappearing act occurred at the height of summer, and for a best friend to lose his daily companion was pretty bad. What was I going to do by myself? How would I trade cards and learn about girls without a best pal? I was eleven, a tragedy. It's not like I had a car and fifteen friends to count on. I had a bike and lived in a one-friend-per-kid town. I felt silly when all the other kids disappeared to the lake or to the bike trails.

I had to find new things to do on my own. I began to hang out at mom's church. Not my crowd, but it beat being alone. The weather was nice and there were some kids, though mostly younger, who gave me something to do. I had heard that some kids in the bigger cities were starting to play Atari, but I hadn't seen a video game myself yet. When the video game craze finally made it to Cooperstown and my mom acquiesced and bought me an Atari, I wasn't any good at the games anyway. I sucked at Pac Man! The tiny, dot-eating happy face kicked my ass all over his electronic wonderland. Perhaps the days before computers were better times. Instead of sitting in a shadowy basement racking up points on Space Invaders or whatever other game eventually came along, we were out in the open spaces, breathing fresh air and running, riding, swimming, and hiking. Well, at least that's what the kids with their friends still around must have been doing.

I was playing toss across on the front yard of the First Lutheran Church of Cooperstown with 4 and 6 year old kids, mostly giddy girls or shy boys. While aiming the tiny bean bags at a plastic square elevated on tiny legs, the goal was to hit any one of several squares that had blue X's and red O's on them. When they were hit, they would flip either to your side or your opponent's. The first to register a row of her X's or his O's won the game. Or were they red X's and blue O's? Either way, that is what I did for about two weeks in a row during July of 1980. Though it seemed like the interminable summer.

The second week wasn't as bad because it marked the start of the church's annual summer picnic. While we were setting up for the picnic, Mr. Bentworth showed up one day and asked if he could help with anything.

He tipped his hat to my mom. "Good Morning, Mrs. Monroe," he said. "How are you today?"

"Just fine, Ridley. And yourself?"

"Well, I'm getting along, thanks. Hey, August." He acknowledged my presence! He instinctively tapped a fingertip along the hat. "Ain't seen you around much lately."

"No, Sir. I've been busy here at the church helping mom."

"August has been a big help," mom told him.

"Of course he has," Mr. Bentworth answered. "He's a fine boy, your son. I often wish my boy would take a lesson from your son and learn to be a better fella."

The shock and indignation must have sounded from the expression on my face like a clock hitting midnight atop a sleepy village deep in winter. The stunned jaw hung slack, the disbelieving brain popped uncontrolled eyeballs out as wide as a

103

fastball, and the only sound that came from my lips was a strained, mournful groan.

"Well, August takes after his father," mom answered. "He works real hard to be a nice young man. And besides, your boy Kevin is just as pleasant as can be, Mr. Bentworth. If he ever gave a person in this town a sour face or a smart remark, I have never heard the likes of it."

"No, you probably wouldn't have, Ma'am. Kevin's got a way about himself, though. I don't think it does him too well. Needs some growing up, my boy does. Needs to get himself some experience. Wastes half his time at that old ball park, tossing baseballs around like he can get them somewhere. It ain't nothing but a pipe dream that boy hoping he makes it to play professional baseball. You too, August," he continued, dragging me back into a conversation I would rather not have heard. "You're a good student and an active kid, you keep that up because baseball isn't ever going to pay your bills. And that's about all you got when you grow up. Bills. Either your own or someone else's."

My mother called upon her professional elegance. "Will you be at the picnic this weekend?" she asked.

"I hope so, Ma'am."

Mr. Bentworth walked away without further comment. I couldn't help thinking that some way, in some grand matter of explaining things, he was more aware of our fates than any of us have ever been, even at the very moments in our lives when I and Kevin were most aware.

If the picnic had only been a temporary savior to my dull summer, as well as a financial success to mom's church, it would still be remembered as a wonderful event. First off, I had something to do! Secondly, the people showed up in droves to have fun, run sack races and eat all the pies and hot dogs a crowd could digest. Not a single apple pie, barrel of ice cream or pitcher of lemonade went unconsumed, and the register tapes kept ringing and ringing. Mom was bringing home a cash crop for the church. Yep, those bits alone would have been well enough, would have solidified my summer as bearable and would have been a kind and welcome adjustment. Instead, the picnic allowed one further benefit. As if it wasn't enough that our communities gathered from as far away as Smithport and Jonesville, the picnic also reunited friends.

Mid-way through Saturday I had already forgotten the woes that had beleaguered my mind. Toss Across had been put away,

104

and the shy boys and giddy girls had returned to their parents. I was having the time of my life tossing nickels down on Old Man Forester's gambling wheel...until I lost three weeks' worth of allowance. But the Pepsi was as cold as a batter left frozen by a sharp curveball high and inside. I had put all my troubles behind me. Then, to further my enjoyment, my best friend reappeared.

"Put the dime down on the ten, ya cheap curmudgeon," I heard from behind me. Even Sally Kingsley, the captain of the cheerleading squad who worked the wheel, spun her head around searching for the voice. At first I thought it was too good to be Kevin's voice. "Hey, Sally. How about spinning me a date?" he asked her. He appeared next to me. He had thrown his voice so well that time that he was able to sneak up next to me before I could scan the rest of the crowd for the voice. Sally curled her chin and neck into a not-so-impressed look of response, I laughed my head off. Kevin could imitate Bogart at the drop of a dime on the gambling wheel but could hardly spell intercourse, yet alone hope to ever one day experience it, and he was pretending to ask the prettiest girl in town for a date. I rolled with laughter. No one else seemed to think it was very funny, especially not Brian Helst. He would be her then-six-foot-two, 230 pound boyfriend of a wrestler. Luckily, Brian must have recalled what it was to be eleven and gawking at a girl because he just snarled a warning and smiled. He returned his attention to distracting his girlfriend from her primary duties, which was to see whether Kevin's prediction of a dime hitting on ten would be a pay-off. Finally, she got to spinning between bear hugs and a tiny peck on the cheek and sure enough – a winner! Ten cents paid to the dollar times the number on the wheel and I was walking out of that tent with a brand new ten dollar bill in my hand. So much for mom's cash cow. This was free gambling at its finest. Ten bucks! In 1980 for a young kid, that was a lot of cash.

I tucked my winnings into my back pocket and stepped away from the table. "Where have you been, Kev?" I asked. "What do you say I buy us burgers and we hang out a bit?"

He continued his Bogie impression. "Sure, kid. You got it!" Okay, it wasn't that great of an impression but it cracked me up every time.

"Great, let's go," I added. "I've got some more news on our list, too."

His face fell bored. "Oh, yeah. That. I almost forgot about that. What else did you learn?"

"Well, since we saw each other last, there was the All-Star game. Did you watch it?"

"Are you kidding? I never miss it."

"Yeah, me neither. But get this. Remember I told you I gave my mom that note about the game and something about next season from what I read in the tent?"

"Yeah," he answered. "Something about a prediction or a guess."

"No, a fact," I confirmed. "At least for now. The first baseball that I read was stamped with, 'Fred Lynn, Two-Run Home Run, 1980 ASG."

Apparently, the fact did not need to be explained to my fellow baseball fan.

"Wow," Kevin said, "Lynn knocked out a two-run dinger in the fifth. The ball in the tent is only short of predicting the inning. Too cool."

"The stuff in the tent is true. We'll have to wait a year for the other piece to the puzzle."

Kevin stared dumbly at me. "Huh?"

"Oh, yeah, I forgot." I winked – the sign of a true detective. I added a nod. Nothing. No reaction. I had laughed at his Bogart. I guess my gumshoe detective routine needed some work. "My note, the one my mom is holding, has another riddle, and we won't know what it means until next year."

"A riddle?" he asked. "I thought these were clues."

"Same thing really," I said. "Let's go eat."

A trailer that had been converted from a recreational vehicle was our restaurant for the weekend. On the way there, we passed the dunking machine, and this is where the point of all this picnicking and gambling and laughing off of heads is finally getting. After having not seen my best buddy for weeks, and after having won ten dollars, I was as confident as Patton and decided I could win myself a prize.

"What do you say we dunk the teacher for free posters?" I asked.

"Sure," Kevin answered. "But I bet I'll hit the target in less pitches."

"No way, softy. You may be a pitcher but I am a marksman."

"Yeah, right! A marksman for the toilet maybe. All you can do is pi–" He never finished due to the glaring warning he received from our teacher, Mr. Gladden, who was sitting perched on the bench waiting to be dunked. Amazing how powerful a clearing of the throat can be.

Kevin pointed to the booth. "Be my guest," he said. "Losers first."

"How much money you got?" I was so assured of myself after my recent string of luck, that I was willing to risk my new ten dollars.

"I have four dollars," he answered.

"Fine. Four dollars it is. Whoever knocks Mr. Gladden off in less throws wins four dollars. Deal?"

"Deal. Of course. That's easy," he added. "Batter up."

There are few things in life as true as the syllogism, "A fool and his money are soon parted." Before Mr. Gladden could even begin to dry off from being dunked on my fifth attempt, he was back in the water again from Kevin's first. There went four dollars of this fool's ten.

"The difference," Kevin proclaimed as if teaching me the finer points of the game, "is that you *threw* the ball, I *pitched* the ball."

"Yeah, yeah. You win," I whined. "Let's go get those burgers and I'll pay you with the change."

"Cool," he answered.

"But you have to pay for your own now," I answered back.

We were less than a foot from the booth when we crossed paths with Mr. Bentworth.

"Boys," he stated firm and solid. I responded first.

"Hello, Mr. B."

"Hi, dad," Kevin said.

Mr. Bentworth leaned into Kevin. "So, you cheated your friend out of a few dollars, hey Son?"

"What, you saw that?" Kevin dropped his eyes as if to check his shoelaces.

"You know I don't appreciate your behavior, Son."

"I know dad, but..."

The unfinished sentence just lingered. I waited. Kevin froze. No one else seemed to notice. Mr. Bentworth spoke.

"Don't waste your time with an excuse, Son. Tell August he doesn't have to pay you the money."

"Bad, dad. I won that money fair and square. Besides, it was August's idea for the bet, not mine."

"You know I don't like telling you things twice. The money is his."

And then, in an act that should have rang loud and true as a sheer moment of defiance and bravery and stupidity and narrow mindedness all rolled into one, Kevin said what I thought would have been the most absurd thing he could possibly have said at that particular moment.

"I can pitch better than you, dad."

Mr. Bentworth grabbed both of Kevin's shoulders and took a deep-knee bend to meet him eye to eye. He did not like being challenged. "Son," he said. "Don't talk back to me." Then he paused, a long serious pause, not releasing his grip, and looked once around the church yard, as if counting the eyes that might have been staring at him. "But in the interest of healthy competition, I accept your challenge. Sometimes becoming a man means being treated like one. What would you like to wager?"

"Sir?" Kevin asked in a tone of respect.

"A wager, Son. A bet. A man's way of deciding things, apparently. You placed a bet with your friend, didn't you?"

"Well, yeah," Kevin stammered, "sort of. I mean, he offered."

"So you accepted a bet. Just as well. You entered into a challenge of skill wherein the victor took a prize. Am I right?"

"Yes, Sir."

"Then, I ask you again. What would you like to wager?" There wasn't an answer. "Haven't a clue. So brash, so self-assured. Now look at ya. Can't take the dare to place a bet with your old man, can ya?"

"Dad, we were just having fun. I won't do it again," Kevin pleaded.

I couldn't stand to be silent any longer. "Really, Mr. B. It's no big deal. We were just having fun. We're friends. Always will be. Everything's fine. Really."

"Stay out of this, August," he demanded. "I'll take care of matters with my family."

"Yes, Sir," I swallowed humbly.

Mr. Bentworth finally released the grip on Kevin's shoulders. "Now, what shall we wager? As I recall, the original promise was that Kevin could throw better than me. Fine enough. Let us see about that." He raised his voice. "Uh, Mr. Gladden."

"Oh, Hi, Ridley."

"Yes, hello. Say, uh, when the ball hits that little target and drops you into the water, can you tell which balls are thrown harder?"

108

"A little, yeah. Just a bit, though. Usually the older kids can activate the spring a bit faster and I plunge right in. With the younger kids, though, I can tell the bench is about to let loose and can brace myself for the fall."

"Great!" Mr. Bentworth proclaimed in a celebratory manner. "That shall do well enough I think. Let's do this then, shall we?" He had taken on the pomp of a performer, belting out words in a manner of speech like a circus director. His swagger was almost embarrassing. He continued. "Mr. Gladden, if you will, please, kindly judge for yourself which ball hits the target hardest – mine or my son's. My boy here seems to think he is a bit of a firearm when it comes to throwing a baseball and I would like to know for certain just how hard he throws. Is that fair, do you think?"

"Fine with me," Mr. Gladden affirmed. If I had liked the man prior, despite his boring classroom repetitions of the multiplication tables, it was at that moment that I began to dislike him specifically and to distrust adults in general. He was the role model here! He should have ushered the event of ridiculous machismo away with a brush of his hand, arguing that it could be better settled when cooler heads had prevailed. Instead, he let it go on. If this ever went on to build character in Kevin, he never admitted it to me.

So, the contest was staged. Mr. Bentworth paid the man, took several baseballs up into his arms and handed the first to Kevin. With neither saying a word, Kevin took the ball and very sarcastically lobbed it effortlessly short of the target. A mild rumble of boos emanated from the tiny crowd of onlookers who had gathered. Without so much as a shuffling of foot into the gravel, Mr. Bentworth handed Kevin the second baseball and nodded in the direction of the target. Kevin took the ball, rubbed it in his palms and stepped a half a foot away from the booth. He turned so that his left side was facing Mr. Gladden and worked his way into his routine stance and wind-up. The ball let loose like a bullet. Mr. Gladden splunked fast into the pool and sprang back up laughing, wiping the water from his face.

"Wow! That one I felt," he said. A spattering of applause rippled through the sea that separated father and son. "There was some real zip to that one. Boy, I'll tell ya, he really does have quite an arm. Good pitch, Kevin. Good pitch!" Gladden climbed back onto his plank throne, prepared to face Mr. Bentworth's pitch.

Mr. Bentworth gestured to the crowd with a mock bow of approval, ushering his son to step aside. Surprisingly, most surprisingly, he too turned so that his left side faced Mr. Gladden and began a delivery and wind-up much the same as Kevin had done. The father was imitating the son; or perhaps, the son had already become the man his father had been. To my shock, their wind-ups were identical. The motion, the flux of movement and the flex of muscle, the transition of weight; even the leg kick that came half way up the torso was exactly the same in fluid movement that is the ritualistic wind-up. Mr. Bentworth let his pitch go and while its release was instantaneous, it is a moment of memory that to this very day folks bring up every year at the church picnic. It whizzed straight and true like a cannon ball from a Howitzer, deafening his son's mere pang of a bullet as it thundered forward. The ball contacted the target, and its force was so great that it splintered the wooden arm of the lever clear in two, separating the mass of wood into divisible fragments. The spring mechanism uncoiled with the sound that a "Spoing Machine" must make if one exists, and the echo reverberated a moment longer than sound itself.

The crowd stood in absolute awe, including myself and my beaten best friend. Mr. Gladden hung frozen a moment as the bench held fast. The spring had separated on the end nearest the target and had not activated the release for the bench, thus sparing him of one last dunk. But the dunking machine was indeed out of service.

Mr. Bentworth reset his stride, gazed momentarily at his son and walked away in the direction of the carousel, whistling a sad, melancholy tune. The crowd dissipated into tiny groups, recounting what they had just witnessed and split off into the makeshift fairgrounds that most closely resembled the front yard of a church in Cooperstown, New York.

13 Between Bentworth and His Past

For Mr. Bentworth to have acted so peculiar, something must have been up. The master sleuth was called to task once again. I had a continually compelling and escalating mystery on my hands, and the sources from which I was to draw my conclusions were becoming less and less apparent. Whatever it was that had inspired Mr. Bentworth to act as he had done was something I could only guess, but it had certainly created a rift between Kevin and his dad.

Kevin had nothing to say about the challenge at the picnic, and the few questions I had nerve enough to ask were answered with grunts and "I dunnos." What struck me as most disturbing about the situation was that neither seemed concerned that the other was distant and neither acknowledged each other's actions. Or, if they did, it was in the privacy of their own shared life in which they had further altercations.

One thing I did know for certain. After the carnival greeting, Kevin went into hiding again. It would be weeks before I saw him.

With Kevin absent I had two primary concerns – the first, perhaps the more obvious, concerned where my friend happened to be and why he had not been seen and, regardless of where he was spending his time, what was his condition; and the second, a less important though somewhat confounding question, what of the list of events still tucked in the tent?

The information I had discovered and had jotted down for review later went almost forgotten all together as the summer of 1980 passed onward. It wasn't until a year later, as the 1981 baseball season advanced, that the little trinket I had seen lodged in the recesses of the tent began to appear in realistic terms. Whether I called it a riddle or Kevin called it a clue, it came by a new definition regardless, or at least one that was new to me, in the word "strike." No longer was that word exclusive to baseball, as in the result of a given pitch. Apparently, workers could "go on strike" as well. Now, for the automobile industry to launch a strike or the teacher's union to do so was one thing, but Carlton Fisk, Tom Seaver, Mike Schmidt, Willie Stargell and their teammates weren't employees, they were ballplayers! Weren't they? When I realized baseball is a business, I began to understand just how far removed my childish vision was from reality. Likewise, I began to gain a wider perspective of athletes as human beings, in terms both honorable and detrimental, but also pragmatic. To many, it was a job.

The 1981 strike began as a threat in the early part of the season, and dad read accounts in the paper warning of an imminent labor stoppage to render the baseball season null and void. Each day was a perilous threat as we read of the impending cessation of play.

Dad shoved the newspaper aside one day. "These players are ridiculous! They make hundreds of thousands of dollars, some make a million! And they want to strike. Pure greed."

"What?" I argued. "They can't do that! They're ballplayers, dad. Strikes are for people with stupid jobs like, like..."

"Like what, August?" Dad pressed to teach me a lesson via my own theory.

"Well, like concrete layers or window cleaners. Factory workers. Those kind of people."

"'Those kind of people?' I doubt they would appreciate you talking about them like that."

"But, they're the ones who usually argue over wages and stuff. The players should just go back to work."

"What about ministers and scientists?"

"They can't strike, can they?"

"Sure. Why not? Who's to say who can and cannot strike?"

"But, dad –"

"Son," he interrupted, "maybe you're just too young to understand this but there are as many important people working regular jobs who have a right to fair wages as your baseball heroes do. It's what America was built upon." He folded the paper modestly and let out a subtle breath. He ended by stating, "Some day you will understand, but for now, let's worry about the season."

And worry we did. Though the strike was short-lived, it brought to a halt the momentum of the 1981 season. Yet, it proved to me the validity of that increasingly creepy tent and its peculiar holdings. For inscribed upon a baseball I had viewed too clearly were the words: "1981, Strike One." Next to it read an even more cryptic commentary: "1994, Strike Two." Where the history-ending strike three resided I could not discern, but somehow in my heart I knew it lurked back there amongst the moss and shadow of the odd man's carnival game. It might have read, "1998."

As much as the strike shook the foundation of my hope in baseball, I felt even further defeat when I could not locate Kevin to explain what I had read, and that it was happening! My perception of the tent's predictions was acute.

But, that is getting ahead of myself almost by an entire calendar. In 1980, I was still transfixed by the Steamer, the original list Kevin had acquired and the curiosity of putting it all together. I still had 1968 from the original list to solve! And the names Bob Gibson and Denny McLain were what sent me back into action shortly after the carnival.

I had not yet given up the hope that a lot of this information could be gained at the place where my adventure had begun in the first place, the library. Even though the events themselves, the fabled list of baseball stars and the introduction of the Steamer had occurred at or near Owls Stadium, it was at the library where I had gained access to my first answers. I avoided the library steadily for three glorious days, hoping summer would pause again and offer a rain-out to push me indoors. But to no avail. The sun continued onward and the weatherman predicted several days to follow of good weather. Taking solace in the air conditioning and passing up on the opportunity to play ball another day, I eventually headed indoors. I easily could have postponed the further research all summer, but where would that have landed me in the end? Back at school with none of my questions answered and no free time to explore the mysteries that confronted me. Homework would soon be due.

Which day it was after the picnic that I headed back to the library I recall not, but it must have been three or four days, perhaps a week, later. Regardless, it was with a student's determination that I walked the heavy concrete steps to the building, passed by Mrs. Highsmith once again (though I now offered a friendly wave) and headed back to the shelves that had been my companions weeks earlier.

The research was boring and slow as I hoped without reason that another such gem would present itself as the Steamer had done. Growing tired after only ten minutes, I walked to the water cooler, took a long, cool slip of coppery-tinted refreshment and headed back to my seat. A sound from my far left suggested that another scholar had made their way into the stacks of research crowding the basement. I listened again for a footstep or a cough, perhaps a shuffling of paper to determine whether it was a person I had heard or just my own echo muted by the dense walls around me. There was no other sound. Disappointed at my early failure (Hey, ten minutes was a long time for a kid on summer leave!) but

113

not yet daunted, I reminded myself that it had actually taken several days to begin to unravel the Steamer mystery. For me to expect the list to come together any sooner would have been ridiculous. In fact, ten items filled our list (or "my list" as it, and I, had recently been abandoned by Kevin), so it would take even greater time to decipher the iconic codes and inferences that had forged my riddles. I decided to keep at it for as long as it took, even if the process called for several hundred trips to the water cooler to ease the building exasperation of my impatience.

Five minutes into further investigation, another sound lifted up from the rows of shelves around me. I jolted my head upwards, a bit startled by the sudden, scraping sound, as if someone was dragging a pencil along the metal shelves while searching for a text. The sound stopped as quickly as I had heard it, and was not repeated again. I listened for a footfall or an exhaling whisper of a sigh, anything to confirm that someone else may have been present. *It's probably just a mouse*, I told myself. The building was already old by then, and an exterminator would have been welcome. At the very moment I lowered my head to take up reading again, the sound repeated.

"Anyone there?" I asked. My voice cracked. No reply. My mind raced with images of a library murderer stalking me.

I picked up my books and my paper and headed to the back table, near the stairwell exit, an escape route well planned should a ghost or a mugger present itself to me there in the dusty quiet of the library were no witness could be found to prove my untimely demise.

A few minutes were wasted listening to the empty silence in the room of mysterious shadows and creeping, aging space. My heart pounded at a high octane thump but slowed to a cautious rumble and finally to a regular, non-agitated level as calm was restored. It took all of my steel to return a glance to the books before me. As I did so, a figure appeared at the end of the far stacks, immediately opposite the fountain I had drunk from moments before, blocking the only hallway in that direction.

"Hi, there," I said loudly, invoking friendship as my ally. The figure was certainly a man, a not-so-large man but a squared frame with dull colors and a heavy hat upon his head. I could not make out a face through the dull shroud of shadow. "Good day for studying, huh?"

There was no reply.

The man turned once and fled up the stairs, not so much in a gallop nor in a regular walk, but in a fleeting decisiveness. Had he intended to speak to me and suddenly decided against the idea, and opted to flee instead? Or had he wished to attack me unaware that I had noticed him? Or was he just a regular guy who didn't even notice me? I rose to follow him and took cautious notice of his disfigured frame. For unless the man had played a trick of light with his sudden, jerking rotation out of the hallway and up the nearby stairs, I was certain I had seen that he was missing his right arm! Stunned remorse filtered through my torso and into the heavy soles of my feet as I remained planted in a stance both uncertain and unwavering. That is to say, uncertain as to what to do and unwavering in that there was no way I was going to pursue a one-armed man who had been staring at me, perhaps following me, in the library. I doubt the single arm had been an illusion. The man was not wearing a coat that might conceal a broken arm in a sling or a hand tucked heartily in a side pocket. He had turned over his left side, revealing to me the definite flap of an empty shirt sleeve pinned up half way between the elbow and would-be shoulder. The man did not have a right arm, of that much I was certain. It was the same man I had tried to help with magazines weeks earlier. This was no coincidence.

Moments passed for time unaccountable. Sitting became my best option as my knees vibrated and my heart again thundered the fear that alighted in my mind. I was in a torrent of indecision. Should I just get back to my studies or should I leave the place? Should I report the appearance of the madman or let it be? As I began to acquiesce towards the former and prepared myself to read further, a shadow appeared above my head from the window across the table. I looked and saw the same man staring down at me with a vexed and unwelcome smile. This time, fear was my determinant as I bolted to my feet, sprang through the escape door behind me and ran at first up three flights of stairs to the library's upper most floor. I blazed through the doorway and onto an unsuspecting young couple kissing on a nearby couch. I fled across the room to the main stairwell where I could look over the railing to see if the one-armed man had returned to the library to seek me out. By the time the couple behind me had forgotten my presence and resumed their embracing, I felt safe to wander down the three flights of steps to the building's main lobby.

At first cautious and then further convinced I was in a safe area, I walked less fearfully and calmed down once again. I reached the lowest step on the ground floor and peered carefully around the corner to see if the strange man may have returned. He was not to be seen. The only people present were standard looking library users, people I recognized from town and mom's church. Confident he was not present, I stepped into the lobby and the sweat upon my forehead, coupled with the apparently bleached look upon my face, brought suspicion from Mrs. Highsmith.

"August, my God!" she proclaimed. "What is the matter? You look ill. Are you alright?"

"Yeah. I mean, yes, Ma'am. I'm okay." I quickly surmised that she might be able to assist me in recovering my personal belongings from downstairs and covered my fears behind feigned illness. "Actually, Ma'am. No, I do not feel all that well. Could you do me a big favor?"

She came from behind the desk. "Of course, what is it?"

"Could you come down with me to help carry my books back up? I feel a bit weak and wouldn't want to drop anything." Using illness as an excuse to avoid facing the fear of going downstairs again was hardly the work of a Luke Skywalker protégée in terms of bravery, but I didn't care at that moment. I was scared out of my Jedi wits!

"Sure, let's go," she offered. "Would you rather sit and rest a moment while I go and collect your things?"

"No!" I answered a bit too excitedly. If I had done that I may never have stepped foot in a library alone again. Besides, I wanted to see if the one-armed man was still milling about either inside or outside the building.

The walk downstairs was an embarrassed escape into comfort. Mrs. Highsmith discussed getting me home for some rest and perhaps a trip to the doctor. The distraction calmed me. The thought of running through books upon books to avoid a man staring at me from a window above seemed much sillier then, and I felt ashamed for having done so. I had been taught to be brave, to face adversity, and here I was running from a mere glance. Oh, well. The kind of fear they talked about confronting was for men, for later in my life. I was only a boy, and that one-armed guy was creepy.

Mrs. Highsmith began gathering up my things, dividing two piles, one of books I would be borrowing from the library and the other my own notepad and backpack. Atop one of the closed books that I had already scanned through, lay a folded piece of paper that had not been present earlier.

My Librarian Nightingale scooped up the paper and began to unfold it. "Is this trash?

"No," I declared. "Those are notes I took on my research," I added, hoping with quickness of thought that it may have been a clue from the one-armed man. "I'll keep that with me." I grabbed the paper, creased it into a tighter square than its original fold and shoved it in a pocket.

"Well, let's go check your books out then," Mrs. Highsmith finished.

To avoid explaining to my mom that I had suddenly been ill, I told a not-so-true lie to Mrs. Highsmith so that she would let me go home without any follow-up.

"I'm feeling a lot better, Mrs. Highsmith," I said. "And I have a confession to make. I really wasn't sick at all. I had been running through the stacks upstairs, trying to see how fast I could cover all three upper stories. I hope I didn't disturb any readers and I promise I won't do it again. But I am sorry for lying to say that I was sick."

"That's okay," she smiled. "It's too nice of a day for a boy to be inside studying anyway. Why don't you take these books home and do your reading tonight after supper?"

"But I've already checked out six unreturned books this month, and they're all at home so I won't be allowed to check those four out."

Her smile broadened under her soft brown hair, long to the shoulders. "I think I can bend the rules just this once." She actually pinched my cheek! My goodness. Women! "If a student wants to read four extra books, especially in the middle of summer, who am I to stop him? Just make sure you return them all on time, okay?"

"Of course, Ma'am. Yes, I will. Hey, that's great. Thanks."

I checked out the books, left the library and headed home. The first thing to do, though, was to read that note that I had stuffed in my pocket. Scanning the street in front of the library, I saw no site of the one-armed man, though I felt certain he was still watching me from somewhere. His presence was entrenched on my mind so heavily that it took a few minutes to sit down and open the note. Each time I unfolded a crease of the paper, I scanned the entire area with a sweeping view of the streets and lawns around me to make sure he was not present. Empty. Clear. The length of time it took me to unfold the paper was some ten times longer than it took to read the entire note. It was addressed to no one, though reason insisted it was directly intended for my reading. In fact, it wasn't even a single sentence. The note read plainly:

Watson's Deli — 1:00 PM Today — Come alone

I checked my watch and saw that I had a little over thirty minutes to decide whether I would attend the scheduled meeting or not. Rationality instructed me that safety would not be a concern. After all, Watson's was sure to be filled with a lunch-time crowd busy about eating and discussing the news of the day. If I had to scream for help, or scurry for cover under the protection of concerned citizens, plenty would be found.

With a heart full of bravery, driven by a head still yearning deeply to answer some stifling questions, I decided to trek the few blocks across town to Watson's for the arranged meeting. I hadn't any money, and my already existing tab did not have the same flexibility as my library account. I would need to find some way to explain to Mr. Dewey why I was not ordering as I always did; but then again, maybe a free lunch was in it for me – maybe the one-armed man would spring for hamburgers!

When I arrived, the deli was closed solid, locked tight like a submarine buried beneath the sea. Perplexed, I wondered just how I was to have my meeting and what would happen if it were canceled. The one-armed man had left no further instructions in the original note, and there was no guarantee he would ever attempt to contact me again in the future. Furthermore, I was at a loss as to why Watson's Deli was closed in the first place. This mystery at least was answered with quick response. A note on the door read: "Off to the ball game. Don't worry, I'll be back in time to serve the crowd afterwards." And it was signed in the formal, "Thomas Gene Dewey." It appeared as if Mr. Dewey had finally found the courage to track down Laurie Hollencheck.

Just my luck. The one-armed man was cunning, for surely he had known of Mr. Dewey's plans. But how could he? No one else had been in the deli when Mr. Dewey and I discussed the matter. Or was there? Besides, that had been weeks earlier. Mr. Dewey had put off the meeting, even after the Owls had gone on a road trip.

It occurred to me while staring dumbly at the window and repeatedly reading the "Closed" announcement that I had dragged myself into this blunder originally by not attending the Owls' game that was to take place that afternoon. Had I arisen from slumber, stolen away to the park as usual, then I would not be facing the prospect of meeting the one-armed man in empty public where he might easily overtake me in a struggle. I might never be heard from again! I might become a statistic of a missing or exploited kid. I'd better run. Without further contemplation, I turned right and began to sprint toward home, hoping to avoid the one-armed man.

My brief sprint home ended abruptly when I smacked headlong into the bulging chest of a stranger standing alongside the window, perpendicular to where I had stood reading Mr. Dewey's handwritten note. I fell hard to the concrete and rose with apologies echoing my surprise and concern. My regrets greatly increased as I recognized the stranger as none other than the one-armed man himself!

My retreat attempt was equally thwarted as my back step away from him was met with a firm grip of his remaining arm, the left, clenching deeply into my biceps area. The arm stung with pain as he squeezed ever-so-tightly.

"Let me go, or I'll scream," I warned the stranger. "Let me go right now."

"Shhh," he proclaimed in a comforting, harmless manner; his voice replacing the assuring gesture one would typically produce when hushing a noisy counterpart. What his missing hand could not do to raise a finger to his lips, his eyes made up for with an alluring, hypnotic gaze that ushered the calming "Shhh."

"I mean you no harm, young man," he half-whispered. His voice was patient, like many of the teachers at school who were quick to discipline but slow to anger. "Stay calm. I only want to speak with you a while. Shall we go inside?" he asked. He pointed with the use of his chin in a soft, subtle jerking of the head in the direction of the deli.

"We can't. It's closed for the afternoon. If you're going to kill me or kidnap me, you'll have to do it right here in broad daylight where everyone can see." There was no one within eyesight in either direction that I could see, and I only hoped that he would think someone was coming up behind him and let go his hold on me long enough for my escape. His confidence suggested that no one happened to be standing anywhere behind me where I could not see. He looked over his shoulder and saw the street empty, save only a parked car facing the opposite direction.

"You think I want to kill you or kidnap you?" he asked. "What vivid imagination you have, boy. I only wish to talk with you a while. I understand you are in need of some information..." His voice disappeared behind the softening gaze of his eyes.

119

"If you don't want to kill me, then why won't you let me go?"

"Oh," he added. "Sorry." But he only lessened his grip, though it was enough to ease the throbbing pain. "If you promise you won't run away, I will let you go."

"I can't promise that unless you promise me you aren't going to kill me."

"I am not going to kill you. What makes you think that?"

"Then why have you been following me?"

"I'm not following you. I tried to talk to you in the library but didn't know how to begin. I panicked and fled the stairs. I peered into the window hoping to call you outside but you ran away. Won't you trust me?"

"I don't know. This is all pretty creepy. You'd better let me go and I'll think about it." And at that, he released his grip entirely. I pushed myself away from him, stumbling backwards upon my heels and catching my fall with a pause. I began to walk away, backwards, up the street.

"Wait," he pleaded. "Please, don't go. We must talk. There is something I need to tell you."

"Send it in a letter," I said. I turned away and, as fast as I could, pedaled my feet to a full gallop. I was fast out of there when his voice called out a sentence that stunned me in my disappearing tracks.

"My name is Bill Wigel," he declared, "perhaps you've heard of me?"

I stopped but would not turn around. "What did you say?" I asked over my shoulder.

"You have heard of me, then?" There was no emotion in his voice.

Most certainly I had heard of him, as his name had appeared in my research into Mr. Bentworth's place in baseball history. It was as if he had been peering over my shoulder as I read, and had logged into a diary the times I had come across that name. Bill Wigel. Surely, this was not the same man I had read of recently.

I turned around. There was not a demon before me, but rather a sad, deformed man who carried the burden of an unjust fate. "This isn't very funny," I warned. "Are you *really* Billy Wigel?"

"In the flesh," he giggled, "if not missing some of it." He laughed harder, pointing to his vacant arm. His demeanor, while still oddly comforting, was sickened, bordering on maniacal; as if having lived with his inherited infliction had caused a personality shift into madness. His eyes whispered of the depths to which his soul had suffered, a longing for normalcy and a wishing for a return to the past to erase the one thing that had forever changed him.

"What do you want with me?" I asked.

"Not quite," he answered without answering. "The question is: What do you, young man, want from me?"

"Hey, I wasn't chasing you through a library. I don't want anything to do with you."

He stepped toward me, his lean more obvious up close, as if the still-present left arm had begun to tip him over. "No," he hissed. He narrowed our gap by some five feet. "But you have been digging around into my life, haven't you?"

"No," I defended. "I was researching Mr. Bentworth's life and had no idea I would stumble across your story. How was I to know you even existed?"

"And you call yourself a fan of baseball," he sneered. "There was a time, let me remind you, that my tale was the most famous in all of sport. I was bigger than baseball, as big as the newspapers would make me for a short time."

"Listen," I demanded. "Just tell me what you want. I won't bother you anymore, I promise."

"I want my fame back!" He hollered. And then went silent.

We stood there a moment, I still in his grasp, before he continued. "I want credit for having suffered so dearly," he said. "Baseball and time has forgotten me. These players, long retired, now have a pension fund for their security. And what do I have? Nothing. But you can't help with that, can you? No. You don't even see it. You need me. And I can help you. In the long run, it will help me." His idle ramblings were scaring me. I lost all sense of what he was saying until he finished suddenly. "You have a puzzle to complete, do you not?"

"A puzzle?"

"Yes, a series of mysteries that needs to be unraveled." He answered so definitely as if to suggest that he had contemplated these matters time and again. "These questions about why Bentworth doesn't play baseball, what the Steamer is, which you have apparently solved. Other things, about Kevin, about my place in this allegory. Do you understand me now?"

121

"No," I affirmed. "I understand you less. What do you want with me? You still haven't told me that. I'm going to go to the police."

"Now that won't be necessary, will it? Let us just talk a while, you and me. Why don't we go for a walk, then, and I can explain?"

"Nuh-uh. No way, mister. Anything you need to say can be told right here in open view where everyone can see us."

"But," he stammered. "Fine, let us go to the park and have a seat." He pointed in the direction of the town square, to which we followed soon thereafter.

The details of Mr. Bentworth's life which Wigel chose to fill my head with did resolve certain elements of the aptly named puzzle, but he spoke of things older than me, more mature than my thinking. In fact, they made absolutely no sense at all to my growing mind. It has only been with the clarity of years that his message has formulated into meaning, and deciphering that meaning has been a curse most of my days.

14 Grandfather's Death

Staring out the window was easier. Making eye contact was just too difficult. I felt like I had slammed headlong into the outfield wall at Wrigley, crashing into the brick facade at breakneck speed and stopping straight in my tracks without so much as a bone separating. The lingering numbness of non-reality was more discomforting than the pain, and distance felt more real than the impact. The news was just unbearable. I could not accept death – it was that simple. And there I was, sixteen years old and imaging life forever in a happy state when suddenly mom and dad explained the unexplainable, breeched the unspeakable. My grandfather was dead. Looking through the window into the empty sunlight was not a distraction, it was escape. As long as I live, no matter how mature I become or how much wisdom I obtain, I swore to the endless sky that I will never understand the singular reality that one's life has to end. It is the most ridiculous bargain we are dealt. Here, build up your dreams, collect memories, make friends, grow with your family...and then one day you will die and all that will be gone: all that fun, all that person that you are. Vanished.

The funeral was especially difficult. I wished for rain, just to show signs that something else was going forward in life. Instead, the bare sun warped our day and sweltered our night; and on the morning Grandpa was lowered into the earth, not even the skies would cry with me.

Death is complicated, I know that now, and its complexities are far-reaching. Still, it seemed so unreal. Even to this day. Perhaps it is the closeness we shared, or just the fact that I miss him so dearly, but nothing was able to assuage the anger and hurt that swelled inside. I probably need counseling. Maybe this will help, by getting it all down. It isn't so much a part of this story as it is a major piece of me, so excuse the lapse as I reminisce.

The best thing about Grandpa was not his love for baseball, though certainly that stands as the defining connection between us. No, he was a much deeper man than that. My Grandpa was much better than a baseball fan, his greatest quality being his humility. The man had patience as deep as the oceans and understanding as long as the universe. He was just that way, simple, unassuming, stubborn. He once tried to teach me to fish, but I just couldn't get the hang of it. I couldn't catch the hook, so to speak. With each cast I would unravel the line too far or pull it in too fast. Most attempts wound up lodged in trees and bushes along the lakefront, some even landed square on Grandpa's hand. He never once complained or hollered. He just kept right on teaching, even foregoing his own trolling to take a minute to explain where I had gone wrong.

Long about 1977 or so, he just gave up trying. "August", he told me one day, "if you don't feel like you enjoy fishing then we won't go anymore. Ain't no sense in doing something you don't enjoy." I didn't answer but he saw the doubt in my face and the matter was dropped. Of course, he continued the most leisurely activity there is, he loved the sport of it. But he never once asked me along again. In my absence, my cousins, even Betty, tagged along and his coaching no doubt continued in that calm, expressionless manner of patience and trust.

In contradiction, he saw something in me that he would not let slack. When it came to baseball, he was determined that I learn as much as could be taught. "The basics," he promised, "will make you a success. Learn the fundamentals, remember them, and they will never let you down." He coached there as well and was pretty darn good at it.

On a day in April of 1973, a day too cold to be spent tossing a ball around, Grandpa decided it was apt time to teach little August how to play catch. Disgruntled by the idea, my dad had remained at home and mumbled about in his makeshift laboratory as Grandpa and I went to the park to play ball. I can still feel the cold racing through my veins as I dropped every single ball he hit, tossed or rolled my way. He kept at it, though. And soon enough, I was at least getting to the ball before it had stopped rolling. After a while, he decided maybe the outfield wasn't right for me, and called me all the way into home plate to discuss the matter.

"How are ya, boy?" he asked.

"I'm cold, Grandpa. Can we go home?"

A grin pierced his deep Irish face. "Not just yet, August," he said. "There is still a bit of daylight left, so let's use it to our best advantage. Let's warm up some. What do you say?"

He proceeded to lead us in jumping jacks, bouncing his aged frame up and down against the solid ground, waving his arms like a helicopter gone mad. If the exercise did not warm my bones and soothe my spirit, the laugher did. Grandpa was not the most graceful man, and in his lumbering frame there was an imbalance that was endearing as he tried his very best at calisthenics. No wonder he liked to fish.

"What are ya laughing at, boy?" he asked between leaps. "Ain't you ever seen no one doing jacks before?"

Now I had had all I could of laughter. I was on my knees, pounding the Earth's still-cold shell as my striding Grandpa leapt up and down in an effort to stay warm. *What are jacks?* I wondered. No one other person than my grandfather would call them "jacks." Everyone else called them what they are, jumping jacks.

"Jacks are what we shoot marbles with," I said, still hooting up a good laugh.

"Just keep jumping!"

After enough blood had flown into the slowly thawing body around me, the laughing and the jacking finally ceased. Grandpa returned to the batting cage and I headed back into the field. The exercise had achieved its desired effect, but its impact did not last very long. It was too cold to be playing baseball, and if Grandpa didn't know that, then he really was losing his jacks. Dad always said he was nuts, and by the way he kept playing in that cold, I began to agree. He just didn't have the heart to break his promise that he would teach me to catch before my first Little League game. Likewise, I hadn't the heart to tell him that I didn't care. What I really wanted was a portable heater or a trip to Florida, whichever would warm us up fastest.

Chilled to an immeasurable depth, I positioned myself between shortstop and second base, where grandfather began chopping frozen baseballs in my direction. If the cows that had given their hides to the baseballs were still roaming this Earth, they themselves would have sought shelter against the slow, biting wind and shimmering chill. Certainly the baseballs they died for felt the same way if they could have given voice to their dismay. As each one thudded off the frozen sand, I could hear echoes of long, groaning moans rise up from the ground. It was either the dead cows speaking from beyond, the dead baseballs begging release, or my own frozen sanity driving me mad. With each thump, Grandpa let out an inharmonious though encouraging, "Come on now, boy, concentrate!"

"Grandpa, I can't," a muffled voice registered from behind a woolen mask.

"What?" My elder screamed. Spittle flew from his lips and crusted into ice chips on his chest. "Did you say something?" His smile loomed bigger than the moon at its crescent stage. Grandpa wasn't the brightest guy to ever live, but he sure found joy in life.

I lowered the mask. "I said, 'I can't,' " I repeated.

"If you said 'I can't,' which is what I think I heard you say. Dammit, take off that mask. I can't hear you. If you said you can't then you never will. You must always say 'I can,' August. It will only make you a better player and a better man someday."

My internal warmth puffed away in tiny spirals of mist. "But, Grandpa," I whined. "It'ss ss-ssso cc-ccccold, I can hardly ff-ffffeeeel my tt-ttttoes. Why do we need to lll-lllearn ttt-oooo cc-catch to-dddd-today? Cccan't we pp-ppplay next week or the week after when it is ww-wwwarmer?"

I was to be filled in later concerning dad's whereabouts while I was out there freezing and chattering to end all chills. Per mom's recollection, dad had begun to search through a drawer for thermal socks. Like me, dad was not much of an outdoorsman. It probably took him an hour to find the socks. After sixty minutes of digging, he had found them and hurried himself to dressing in layers warm enough to replenish the coldest bones with warmth. He brewed a mug of hot chocolate for me and hot coffee for himself and Grandpa, stored each in separate thermoses, grabbed a hunter's self-warming seat cushion and headed for the park, determined to save his boy from the cold and make an effort to remain friendly with his father-in-law. Meanwhile, Grandpa and I continued to freeze.

"Take one or two more and we'll get out of here," Grandpa promised. The cold didn't even seem to bite him. His skin must have been made of leather heavier than that which wrapped the baseballs. "Here ya go." He tossed a high one into the clouds out of hand, even he finally realized it was far too cold for a bat in his bare hands. The ball lofted up into the thin clump of clouds above me and swirled in the wind toward centerfield behind second base. "Follow the ball, August!" Grandpa demanded, ever coaxing me toward that goal. "Don't lose sight of it now. There you go."

With an agility spurned only by the thought of warming up later in a heated car, a younger me broke toward second base, following the lightened orb in its trajectory toward the sky. In my tiny vision, it seemed to me that the ball continued to advance skyward for an eternity, and that, perhaps, it hadn't the weight to ever return to earth. At its pinnacle, it hesitated momentarily and continued downward opposite its ascending path. In absolutely proper concentration, I, of course, panicked.

126

Sometime earlier, apparently, dad had been back at home busily fumbling for keys in the cold chill of the driveway. His overgrown wool hat flapped in the wind. His hands, red with cold after just a moment outside, balanced the fluffy orange hunter's seat cushion (which he had seemingly not realized required an actual seat to be most useful), two separate thermoses, an extra scarf and his own tattered mitt which hadn't been used since his college days. All the while, he still fumbled for a set of keys that somewhere lingered inside either his coat or his trousers, mom could not tell which. Pulling the car out of the drive, dad heightened his pace and sped off in the wrong direction. Then, like a blue streak from NASA, he slid down the street in reverse, screeching to a stop out front of the house.

"Renee," he hollered toward the house, unaware that his wife, while shivering herself, was standing barefoot on the porch wrapped only in her own arms for warmth. "Renee!" he hollered again, hoping to avoid a return trip to the house.

"What, Christopher? What is it?"

"The park?" he pleaded in embarrassment. "Where is it that they play ball?"

"They're at Knowles School Road, make a right on Chesterland and you can't miss it."

He balanced a stack of Styrofoam cups on his lap and drove in reverse. (This mom recalled vividly.) "Right on Chesterland," he repeated. "Okay, gotta go."

"What?" the wife asked, through chilled vocal chords.

"What?" the husband replied.

"I didn't hear what you said."

"Oh, nothing. Just talking to myself. I gotta go."

"Christopher!"

"Yes," he inquired, blazingly impatient. "What is it, Dear?"

She hollered into a light snow that had begun. "It's okay that you don't know the park," she told dad. "We've never taken August there yet."

"Right. I'll, we'll be back soon I am sure."

He continued driving in reverse until the street intersected with an alley, into which he spun backwards, paused a hard moment, straightened out the car and was on his way. This time speeding forward in the correct direction.

Mom loves telling that story. Perhaps it reminds her of home, perhaps of simpler times. Maybe just our shared younger days. At any rate, dad apparently made it to the right right on Chesterland and sped for the park.

Across town, Grandpa watched in pride, recalling fondly his own first catch, as I, his eldest grandson, drew focus on the ball. I remained intent upon bringing the ball softly into the leathered glove. "Remember to squeeze it," Grandpa uttered to himself. "Grabbing at the ball will cause it to pop loose," he finished, repeating the words his dad had taught him years ago on a sandlot in the South Side. He watched the ball fall toward the ground but was momentarily distracted by the sound of a screeching tire and a door opening wide. *Dammit*, he thought, peering into the parking lot, *The boy will be distracted and miss the ball*. It was his son-in-law, standing wide-eyed along the side of the blue Buick, pointing out toward shallow centerfield behind second base. Grandpa returned his gaze in my direction and witnessed, no cherished, they went on to claim, as did dad the oncoming sphere as it tumbled toward the ground, aimed directly toward my head. Afoot with determination, I reached out a left hand adorned with a brand new Wilson glove and locked my eyes on the seams of the ball – and then promptly shut them in utter fear. With an innate awareness, I knew the ball was spinning away from me and would soon land in centerfield, a safe hit should the moment be within a real game, even worse if a batter had been standing on first. Giving an extra surge into gravity, I stretched my tiny body to its fullest length and lifted both hands toward the ball.

I remember most vividly thumping the icy terrain with such a force that my fifty pound frame bounced a full half-inch into the air and sprang upwards slightly in reverberation with just enough energy that I was catapulted head over shoes into centerfield. And in my glove, a lump like the one growing in my throat, only larger. I could feel the baseball firmly nestled around all five fingers as I squeezed with all my might, lest the ball squeak out as I repeated my thud onto the hard outfield. I had caught the ball!

They raced out to assure I was all right, and entirely intact. Grandpa and dad patted one another on each other's back. Yes, they celebrated! They were thrilled, filled with joy that they could share in this special moment. Though it was further from the Major Leagues than anyone could calculate, each man reveled in that one moment of my first step toward baseball adulthood. They could never have known how grand it was to witness my first catch.

But, that was the past. Those were better times. Grandfather's death hit me particularly hard. It was with great difficulty that I tried to comprehend the logical feelings my father was experiencing. He hardly cried. I wondered often though silently whether dad ever liked my Grandpa at all. I sat on our couch and wondered until dad joined me.

"August, look at me," he demanded.

"I hear you just fine from here, dad," I said. I stared through the window onto that terrible lonely sun.

"This isn't about hearing," he answered. "Look at me, August!"

"For what, dad? So you can make it all better? So you can see into my eyes and analyze this into a formula that explains it all and makes sense to you? It doesn't work that way."

"August!" dad seldom reached anger but had hit it then. "I know how you feel."

"No!" I reminded him, finally turning from the window. "No you don't, dad. Do not tell me you know how I feel, because you don't."

He drew in a heavy breath. "Yes, August. I do. In fact, you have no idea how *I* feel, okay? I lost my father too and I wasn't much older than you are now. I have now lost both my fathers. You may not have seen it, but Grandpa was like a father to me. That's a part of marriage that you can't understand yet, and you won't until you are married yourself. Grandpa and I may not have been best friends, but we were family."

A slow silence crept between us. I knew that I was only avoiding my sadness, a fear of letting go. I had no anger toward dad. He had stood by me on lesser times and all he wanted was to know I was okay. Still, I needed a focal point for my frustration, and he was the nearest target.

"August," he continued, his tone softened to the tender voice I had known my whole life. "Your mother is now grieving in a way you cannot even imagine. She needs you. Listen, the least you can do is support her a little. I know this hurts you. It hurts all of us. No one expected Grandpa to be gone so suddenly."

My anger spiked. "You barely knew your father, and you have always told me that. So don't come now and tell me how deeply hurt you were when he died because I won't listen to it."

He bit back. "You sit here, proclaiming to be so saddened. Let me tell you, it's selfish – pure selfishness, August. You don't think I was hoping to have your grandfather and I get closer? Did you ever once consider that I worked very, very hard at having the man like me? I could never measure up to him, could never be good enough for his daughter. But your mother loved him so much that I tried. And I would have tried forever if he had lived long enough." He paused. "Maybe you'll understand that when you're older."

I was unreachable.

Our arguments went on like this for days and I think it did more to distance us than any wrong I could have committed. Dad didn't require a perfect son, which is good because he sure didn't get one. He never pushed me over the edge to serve his own ego or to prove he was a better dad. He was a solid man with a wise heart. The fact was that I was more a grandson than my father's kid, and as sad as that may be, we both came to accept it over the years. Grandpa's death was the first step. And it would be a long bridge to cross.

His demise was sudden and alarming. He was a fairly healthy man. He had quit smoking years earlier and had even taken up exercise in his later life. He and Gram-mah-ma would take long walks together, and he never winded. His heart just gave out on him one day. We found him by the pond. Grandpa wasn't fishing, and he wasn't facing west in some symbolic pose ready to welcome death. He had sat for a moment, presumably to rest up before heading home. The coroner listed the cause of death as a pulmonary embolism, though he really felt that Grandpa had just given up. He sat down, closed his eyes and died. He never even slumped over. Mom found him before dinner. He must have been sitting there half-asleep and teetering on death for close to an hour, and not one of us had gone down to check on him. Mom watched him walk toward the pond, gather up the tarp and the ropes necessary to tie off his boat. She recalled it was just as dad had gotten a good fire going in the grill. She had seen her father sit, tiny puffs of air spiraling from his mouth much like mine had done years ago on a frozen ball field. She wondered what he was doing but passed it off. "He was just enjoying the cool early autumn," she often repeated through tears.

Mom said touching his shoulder was like dying herself. She knew he had gone the moment her skin touched his shoulder. It was a favorite gesture of hers for all the years she could recall. She often came up behind her father, rested a hand on his shoulder and either kissed him or gave him a good hug. And it always embarrassed him a little. It was so familiar an act to her that the difference felt instantly foreign. His hands rested softly on his lap, palms down, supporting the heavy weight of his overworked shoulders. And in the quiet afternoon, as winter crept benevolently northward, he had closed his eyes and died.

Gram-mah-ma asked if I would say a few words at the service, but I just couldn't do it. It was too soon. I promised myself that someday I would be interviewed by *The Sporting News* after winning the World Series, and tell the story of how my Grandpa had meant so much to me, about how he had created a passion for the game. How he had instilled in me a work ethic to always try my best, to always endure; of how he taught me to make my first catch. I looked forward to that, but the opportunity never came. I apologized to Gram-mah-ma for not wanting to eulogize Grandpa and she seemed to understand. She knew me as well as he did and knew him better than any of us. She sensed a knowledge that if I didn't want to speak that I certainly had my reasons. I would have explained to her my promise to Grandpa, but she believed in personal secrets that needn't be shared. So, this I owe to him. It's my way of finally saying goodbye.

15 One Deer Down

The stillness of morning caressed the cabins and surrounding woodlands in a late November chill. A year after Grandpa died, I took a trip with the men of the family. The campers, for we could hardly be called hunters except for Uncle Stan, huddled crouched and silent as the peaceful morn absorbed the first rays of sun. A slender snow sat across the tops of withered grass and the slightest puffs from our breath emanated the only movement other than wind. With an advance signal from Stan, we began our descent into the woods. Like troops on foot as soldiered in war, our fivesome set forth. We crept at a pace slower than morning itself and with calm and stealth crossed each field with prey-like deftness. Even the slightest sound, a cough or the crackle of gravel underfoot, would send the deer fleeing in every direction.

I did not want to be there. But tradition was tradition, and with Grandpa's passing came a void in the manly hunting pack. I was to fill it, though temporarily I warned Uncle Stan, reminding him weekly that baseball was my game.

The less experienced of us, mainly myself, watched each command that Uncle Stan offered, a litany of signals he had devised himself. He had made it a tradition to share his system only with those in his camp the night before a hunt. In the hopes of better communication, the code was silent and undetectable by the hunted, as well as other weekend sportsman who made a habit of following a more experienced hunter's paths and signals toward un-stalked prey.

My thoughts ran wild with hesitation. I had never been one to take up the hunt and wondered why I was even with these men. Neither my father nor mother approved, and keeping Grandpa from insisting had become a yearly battle. Despite our early tenure as Pennsylvanians, dad and I had never taken up the practice of hunting be it for sport or for sustenance. When Uncle Stan offered and when Grandpa all but begged, I opted out courteously with comments about studies that needed tending or an imaginary soreness in the arm that required attention. It was Kevin who insisted we go along in place of Grandpa and his mourning son, my other uncle, Jerry.

"It's every boy's right to advance into manhood having hunted at least once," Kevin proclaimed.

"Bullshit," I said. "I can find plenty of other ways to be a man, through patience, understanding, fairness." I went anyway.

Kevin and I were seventeen and on the brink of a perceived manhood. What better time to go out into the wild and cross over that threshold into manhood than at that age, my friend reasoned. *Into savagery*, I thought. Kevin's head had been full of all the pent-up energy that labels teenage boys as we were known: reckless, solid, troublesome. I, though, had remained true to myself, not passive, nor one to stray from adventure. I tried to be sensible and keep a clear mind. Perhaps my arrogance affronts me. I was no better than my contemporaries. I just hated the labels.

The fast cars were hardly enough, nor were the weekends of chasing girls and guzzling beer. Kevin was intent on living life to extreme. "You're only young now, pal," he had been heard saying too often. Apparently, all things American appealed to Kevin, be it partying or hunting. We had drifted apart. And in his eyes, Kevin held fixed the gaze of a killer. "This wasn't how it was to be," I argued. "We're ball players, not hunters." I lost the argument. And, twelve hours later, torn from a beautiful slumber warm in my bed, I was dragged half-asleep into some vacant, frozen field before the first rays of golden glare even scratched at the chilly sky. Before I knew it, I was awake, brandishing the weight of a terribly hefty rifle and trudging along to Uncle Stan's silly regiment in some cabin in Ohio I can no longer locate on a map.

The sign went up ahead of us. Stop! Deer sighted. It was a quick, gingerly motion Uncle Stan had devised. Right hand raised at a half-crocked elbow with a solid and flashy point to the right, the thumb holding down the index finger in a closed circle as the three remaining digits aligned straight in the direction of the find. It was precise, and the message followed through the troop with the intended precision Stan had desired. I swear, my mother had a lunatic for a brother. I could just picture right then that we'd all be bunched up around the fire later, freezing our asses off miles from a hotel and a hot shower, while Uncle Stan reiterated all his classic hunting tales. I couldn't wait for that.

We held steady and peered into the decreasing morning fog near a tiny lake. His rules for hunting also involved a set formation. A kill for the man is a victory for the men. What a ridiculous motto. Well, at least he had one. He hunted with no more than five and no less than three. Four was acceptable but cumbersome in that the point position was left eschewed between two men. The kill was indeed a shared communal exercise. He had no Native American blood, but this Ohio-raised man was akin to the land and to nature. While he despised violence as an end to its own means, he had the instinct and the respect to develop into a true huntsman. This was his domain. We others were his welcome, though less trusted, tourists.

It came to fall that I was flanker right, the position farthest from the point man on that side. The ranks were experience based. Stan always at the arrow-shaped helm. His brother, Lawrence, at his first right, their cousin, George, on first left. This was the trio most regularly to accompany one another into the great shrouded America around us. The flank positions were held out for men or boys whose time afield was less than average. For this trip, those posts fell to myself on right while Kevin flanked left.

All four tourists knew what to wait for – the signal as to whose position held the best shot upon the target. This was a simpler number system; not quite as complex as the rotating numbers assigned to the fielders on defense in baseball, it was devised to remove any doubt. Flank right was one, side right two and point man was three; side left was four with flank left rounding out the fifth. This too aided the necessity to travel only in fifths. It just made sense. And to Stan, out there in the wild, away from the world, everything had to be of order and logic. I could not blame him, as it did make a certain amount of sense and provided for safety during the hunt. So the remaining foursome stood ground, breathing evenly.

A deep sweat swelled up from far inside my stomach. It was obvious that either Lawrence or I would be given the order to take the target into sight. In what could only have passed as thirty seconds, my body temperature soared to a tension-induced heat that bathed my skin in salty sweat and then raced down into the lower digits as the cold air penetrated my outer clothing. The sweat froze like icicles to my skin.

Stan's judgment was counsel. The time between the sighting and the decision was never long. He knew his rifles. They had all been treated and prepared with caution throughout the years. He also knew his men. He studied us from the moment the caravan joined up at a coffee shop now miles away. He gauged our moods, our vulnerabilities, our fevers and nerves. Apparently, he misjudged me because I was bored and miserable. It was serious business for my uncle, and each trip brought about a whole new set of scenarios. With each battalion, Stan knew how every man felt and he could align his decision based on those facts. Those and the element of wind. Still, it felt a torturous hour until he raised his right hand to signal the kill. Next to the increasing boredom gnawing at my soul, I was also growing tired. I considered making a sound accidentally to scare the deer off just so I could breathe regularly again, but I knew that would really piss off my uncle. I remained as calm as I could and just watched his finger, searching for any god on duty to listen to my prayer that Lawrence would get the signal.

My heart raced like a panting dog. *Not me. Please not me. I cannot do this.* To deny was futile. Stan was never wrong. He had chosen.

The hand rose. Two fingers. My heart soared with glee, the sort of joy unfelt since my first ride on horseback. I was off the hook and, though breathing easier, remained absolutely still as Lawrence lifted the gun to sight. The moment grew tense, and the sliding, oiled movement of the gun locking into place was hardly audible, a mere whisper amongst the pines. The deer remained astride a creek – not entranced, not drinking. Just waiting. Waiting for the whizz and the thunk that would bring about its downfall. The tension drove steel rods through my legs. I could hardly stand any longer and needed movement to restore the flow of blood into my lower extremities. *Just fire the goddamn shot, Larry!* I screamed inside my head. I had been so still for mere moments but the impatience brought on by hope and fear while awaiting Uncle Stan's command had grown unbearable. I locked my eyes upon Lawrence's trigger. Once the crescent was squeezed, I would be free to twitch again and remove the numbness from my aching joints. Besides, with eyes focused taut on the rifle's firing point, I would not, could not, witness the slaughter.

A sharp crack rang in my ears and I shifted ever-so-slightly. But the blast of the rifle did not follow to proclaim its death knell. As quick as a bullet, Stan's hand shot in the air. Halt and hold. My imagination answered that it had registered the unfired bullet. Different than stop, Stan's palm was raised to the sky like a platform. I darted my eyes from the rifle's center scope and followed the muzzle out to the deer. It stood, unscathed but alert. Why had Larry not shot? I returned a gaze back to the group and was met with darting stares of anger, disappointment, rage. *What?* My eyes begged. A subtle nod from Kevin confirmed that I had screwed up. Kevin's eyes peered downward, his head not tilting, toward my ankles. I followed the circles of brown toward the ground at my feet. Beneath my heavy boots lie just the slightest measure of movement marked upon the soft gravel in a tiny half-spiral. I had shifted my weight. *Dammit! This is merciless*, I thought. I had tensed, and with just the slightest nuance of motion, had shifted my weight and had snapped a tiny twig. A distant sound certainly, but within range of a creature that survives by sound and depth, it rang out as a warning. The deer had heard my sound.

Fortunately for the hunt though opposite my fate, the creature stood fast. *Run! You stupid beast. Run for your goddamned life and save yourself!* I warned it quietly. It had tread southward a step, maybe two, and then stopped. The deer surveyed the distance but did not flee! Now it was straight ahead of me, certain to be assigned my kill in Uncle Stan's asinine system of order. What price I was to pay for such a simple shift of weight in reaction to numbing discomfort! Stan's hand still held hard the halt signal. Then it descended, into a solitary, empty digit affixed against the chilly blue sky: one. Thus, the confirmation I had feared. It was no longer the joy of Lawrence to attack and kill. The duty now fell upon August Wilson Monroe, the youngest and most inexperienced hunter on board.

I had played this silent moment out in my mind for the previous four days, all while feigning excitement amongst the guys about my first hunt. Secretly, I prepared a rebuttal that I thought would have relieved me of this most wretched task. Even as I lifted the rifle alongside my cheek, aligning the sight upon the venison standing in waiting, and feeling the cold steel brush my bare flesh, I uttered the protest over and over in my mind. *I will not do this. Listen, I know I came along for this but it is just not in me.* The deer searched the distance, looking straight into the vision of my scope, scanning the field to assure itself safety of the moment. It never moved. This was the last hope it and I held. *Please, flee. Get out of here. You are in danger!* But it stood strong, in certain peril, entirely unaware of its fate. *You stupid fucking animal!* I cried aloud inside a racing mind that was not even familiar to me any longer. My feet pulsated with an anger that thumped through my boots and deep into the terrain beneath where it echoed through to the chore of being.

Right eye locked, my left could now open to take the signal from Stan. He was so precise, so naturally in-tuned to the instinct of nature, that he alone imparted the wisdom of the moment, passing the order of exactly when to shoot. *He's a son-of-a-bitch for making me go through with this,* was my only thought. Then,

Uncle Stan's hand let go of the order of one and demanded the order to shoot. It was a solid, definitive gesture of a full fist. I watched the index finger tuck down and witnessed the fist roll into place. A mechanism not of myself, I had reached a point where refusal was senseless. It was the order of the hunt. The thump of the rifle sent me sprawling, and the cheer of the kill rose from the tiny group like a victory call, a plundering, lustful abhorrence. I lost myself and could see only the blue of the sky and the wisp of thin clouds dancing alight upon the morning. Hands reached under me, lifting from the armpits to pull me to my feet. It was Kevin and George. They were pointing, shouting, clapping upon my back. Their fingers, extended out into the world, returned consciousness of the moment as my eyes followed their direction. Crouched near the stream were Stan and Lawrence. *They must be viewing the tracks, to ascertain which direction the deer had fled,* I hoped. George scampered toward them, his rifle bouncing on his shoulder strapped behind his back, reaching into the air, as tiny puffs of air spun outward from the aging man's seething lungs. He reached the small group. Lawrence stood, and there beneath him was not the empty, soft bank of the sliding creek but rather the bleeding, gaping cadaver of a dying deer.

I spent that afternoon and evening vomiting in the empty woods, my only solace being the isolation of my vacant gut heaving and lurching in retribution. The kill itself was enough to cause puking and retching. I could not even consider the ritualistic, animalistic, tribalistic celebratory drinking of the animal's blood in which the others partook. Behind the cabin, I cowered from the men and hurled lunches I hadn't seen in days upon the ground.

16 The Streak

As 1987 wound down to its final months, the World Series pitted the St. Louis Cardinals against the Minnesota Twins. But that world was miles away from Cooperstown. While most of America and parts of the international audience watched baseball crown a new champion, the locals in Cooperstown could hardly bare thinking of baseball. In late September, the Owls had pushed toward their first pennant in team history and had fallen just short, losing in the playoffs to the expansion Birmingham Bullets. *Wait until next year!* had become a sore cry of hope for the Owls and their fans, but this year it was perhaps more dismal than ever.

It reminded me of 1980 and my first summer as a fan of the Owls. What had looked like promise had faded along with my fear of the one-armed man. Seven years later, the sad reality of the season came down to one fact – they were short a pitcher. Had they had just one more starter who could have given the team six solid innings to keep the score close until the skipper called to the bullpen, then they would have had a chance. Their offense was practically unstoppable, including three players in the top twenty-five in batting and runs-batted-in categories, as well as Carl Denkinger who lead the league in slugging percentage and tallied two less home runs to keep him off the pace of Vermont's Randall Klingler, who won the home run title again.

It was the best team Murray had fielded in his tenure as Owls' manager. In fact, it was the best team he had ever fielded anywhere. And everyone from the most ardent fan to the soda vendor knew that a missing pitcher was the weak link. The starting three were solid, McKenzie their ace, threw with precision; Henratty, the crafty left-hander, gyrated the ball in the strike zone, often baffling hitters with a seamless curveball that resembled the knuckle ball that Phil Niekro threw in the Majors; and Sanders had great stuff, tended to give up the long ball but could pitch well in two of every three starts. Then came the fourth spot in the rotation, which spelled disaster. It was an all but guaranteed loss every fourth game as the team tried seven different hurlers in the spot throughout the season. With that sole inconsistency there was hardly enough momentum to put together a legitimate contender. As for a fifth starter, the league was still too small then to afford an extra arm – and with the schedule covering a total of only 132 games, a five-man rotation was hardly necessary.

The team's rallying cry as October approached did little to assist them and they fell off the pace, losing the playoff series to the Bullets. 1988 would be different. During the off-season, ownership and management promised to develop better pitching for the next season's run at a pennant. Often, as in 1986, the problem wasn't even that the right talent could not be found, but the best pitchers were too frequently snagged by the Majors just as their pennant races were heating up. The team had two options: either pay a player a lot of money and convince him that he would have another chance at the big leagues down the road, which both sides knew was risky; or draft a kid to play while still in high school so the pros could not touch him. That hope rested upon the notion that perhaps there was a boy out there good enough to handle the job. The crucible being the discovery of a kid whose parents saw to it that his education came first and who would allow him to gain experience instead of grabbing Big League cash. Many parents would just as easily rationalize the boy's future away when the big paycheck was waved in their faces. But not in Cooperstown. Roots were too strongly encouraged, and parents maintained a respectful if not staunch control over family matters, demanding respect and instilling in their children the discernment between right and wrong. While morals and values could not be entirely blamed for the Owls' yearly woes, one must wonder whether a little unscrupulous belief now and then might have been worthwhile. If the needed pitcher were to be discovered in time for the 1988 season and that year's pennant chase, one was hard pressed to imagine who that player was and where he was to be found.

Winter came and passed and spring entered early in 1988. The folks again had had their fill of football and looked forward to spring and the return of their game. Pony Leagues got underway first, playing half-frozen and often canceled games in early March. The Owls headed south to train in the sun of Georgia and South Carolina where they remained still, as always, in the shadow of the major leaguers. Not many Owls got called to the Show that year, surprising considering the numbers that had been put up in 1987; a fact that gave Murray a revised sense of optimism as the new season approached. As well, the players themselves felt something clicking. It was, after all, the third year in a row that the nucleus of the team remained intact, unique to any club but ever rarer for an International League franchise.

Kevin and I looked forward to the new season with a rekindled excitement and sense of optimism. This was to be the first season that we were old enough to spend a summer with the Owls if Murray felt we deserved a shot to make the team. Still, long before that we had our own seasons to consider as the high school schedule pointed toward a possible berth in the state playoffs, our ultimate goal being a state championship. If graduation was to bring about a year of change, the first such encounter came earlier, in January, when Kevin made a most unusual announcement. He would be attending his last semester at, and graduating from, Worcester Academy, the all-boys private school in nearby Hunters Ridge.

"What? Are you kidding me?" I screeched upon hearing the news. "Kevin, you gotta finish school with me. We've been together since Little League for Christ's sake. Not to mention the team. You're our best pitcher. We are going to States this season, man. We need you."

"I'm sorry, but it's my shot. It's not like I want to do this. My grades are hurting. If I don't get extra science credits I am not going to Roth College. Engineering majors are required to have sixteen credits of advanced sciences before their freshman year. I only have twelve and I've taken every course Coop High offers. I had no choice."

"But I got into Roth without having to change schools," I argued.

"That's different. You're in communications and they don't have a pre-requisite. It's not like it matters all that much. We'll still hang out."

For the first time since I had arrived in Cooperstown as a fourth grader, we were going to attend separate schools, which meant playing for different teams. While I would finish out my high school career as a Cooperstown High School Coopersmith, Kevin would be pitching for the Worcester Wildcats. Assigned to different teams, we watched the schedule wearily. The schools would play each other four times; twice in each school's park.

"Besides," he added, as if it mattered, "a little friendly competition will be fun. Worcester pitches a five man rotation, so chances are I won't start against you guys anyway." His pause, though reflective, registered the thought we shared. "That sounds weird, saying 'you guys.'"

"Of course it sounds weird," I added. "Because it just ain't right. Kevin Bentworth no longer a Coop! I don't think it sounds right at all."

"Hey, listen. I gotta think of what's best for me. Right now I can play ball anywhere, but if I don't get to college, I'd be finished. I'd be stuck in Cooperstown with my only option being a chance at pitching for the Owls. Then what?"

Reason, somehow, took the best of me.

"Yeah, I understand. It's just that... Man, this totally sucks. You'd better still hang out with me after school or I will kill you out there on the mound."

"That's a fair deal."

"Deal," and again we shook with our left hands to seal the agreement.

So, Kevin became a former part of the Cooperstown High School landscape. In a way it worked out pretty well. I like to think that I "broadened my horizons" that semester, something dad had often encouraged. Rather than paling around with my teammates all the time, I began to socialize with other guys and girls in school. It was just as much fun. I gained appreciation for other activities and learned how other students spent their time, experienced new ideas and habits. There had been one kid who I had classes with almost every semester, Brian Timsdale, who I hardly ever got to know before. We started talking more and more between classes and got to respect each other. Like me, he was considering studying communications in college and took a lot of literature and communication courses. His focus was theatre and he hoped to make films someday. I often find myself reading the end credits to movies, hoping to catch his name scroll by. So far no luck, and we never kept in touch after high school. Still, he proposed a fair idea that wound up changing my perspective on things and in some way, at least for a few years, made Cooperstown High School a better place. It was sparked by me trying to get people to come to our games.

"Hey, Brian," I asked him one day on the way out of speech class. "How come you never catch any of our ball games?"

"Coach setting you up to get some new fans, Monroe?" he asked.

"No, really. I was just curious. I see a lot of guys at the games but never you. What gives?"

"Sorry, but I hate baseball," he answered directly. "This town is so obsessed with a bunch of arrogant athletes and their accomplishments. It's not for me."

"Hey, hold on. That's not really fair, is it? I mean, I try not to be arrogant and I thought we got along pretty well."

"No, not you," he defended. "But some of the other guys and definitely that pro team, the Owls. And every year there are so many damn tourists."

"Wow, I thought everyone liked having the Hall of Fame here." This was a revelation to me. I had never heard a negative word about the Hall before.

"Nope. Not everyone," he said.

"Well, anyway. As I recall, you were pretty good in Little League. Wasn't it you that nailed my pitch for a home run that bounced off the scoreboard in deep right field?"

"Wow, you actually remember that?"

"How could I forget? You had warned the league all season that if anyone ever hit one off the scoreboard, you'd play a game in your underwear."

"Yeah," he laughed along with me. "I guess the only way to get out of that was to hit it myself."

"I don't know," I joked. "A dare is a dare. I think you still owe us a game in your BVD's."

"No way," he promised. He nodded warmly. "Wow. That's funny. I guess I had a lot of fun playing as a kid. I forgot all about that. I bet it's not as much fun as a teenager."

"Oh, it's better. You actually win games now and then. Besides, we don't spend hours standing around hoping a kid will hit the ball. They actually know how to hit by this time."

Our laughter must have gotten the attention of Brian's girlfriend, Sissy Dalaneo, who had been standing at her locker pretending not to notice our conversation. I never knew if Sissy was supposed to be a nickname or her real name, but that's who she was, Sissy. She carried a huge set of books clenched tightly to her chest as if in defense against any guy who dared stare at her growing boobs.

She forced a kiss on Brian's cheek. "What are you two cracking up about?" she asked. "Hey, August. What makes you so interested in the other half these days? Missing your buddy?"

"Hey, Sissy," I answered, ignoring her comment. "Brian and I were just catching up on old times."

"Yeah," Brian added. "August remembers a bet I'm supposed to follow-up on. August, I'll tell ya what, I will make good on that bet. Only not in the same way. Do you like theatre?"

"Well, I don't go often, but I guess it's okay." I lied. Outside of the movies, I couldn't name anything put on a stage.

"I'll make a deal with you," Brian continued. "I'll come to one of your games if you come to see our show next week."

"That sounds fair enough. What are you guys putting on this semester?"

"A play called *Fences*," he answered.

I almost blurted out "Never heard of it," but said okay instead.

Sissy spoke up. "Wait, aren't you from Pittsburgh?"

"Yeah," I said. I lived there as a kid. Why?"

"The play is written by a guy from Pittsburgh."

"That's kind of cool," I said. "All right, it's a deal."

Sissy screeched in an overly excited voice. "Hey! This is a great idea. Brian, you are a genius! Just the other day, for Social Studies, we were given an assignment to find ways to make the school a better place. This is it! I will propose that we all trade one for one our separate activities, even if we don't like it. Think of how cool that would be if we all started attending each other's performances or games or whatever? Oooh! I know. I'll call it 'To Debate and Tackle.' Get it?" she asked. "It's a pun. 'Divide and Conquer'... 'Debate and Tackle.'" Our empty stares did not impede her enthusiasm. "Anyway," she continued. "I'll suggest that the football players attend a debate and that the debate team goes to a game next season. Awesome! Thanks, guys." Something tells me that Sissy Delano grew up to either become a high level marketing director for a multi-national company or never worked at all but instead volunteered for every single charitable organization imaginable. She had way too much energy for a high school student. At any rate, an arrangement had been made and I would attend a play called *Fences*.

"The show runs next week," Brian said, graciously stifling Sissy, who may have gone on until lunch. "When's a good game?"

"Next month," I suggested. "When it's a bit warmer. We'll be playing some good teams too. Maybe against Smithport, they're pretty good. Or Evans Heights. That's a sure win for us. They're not so good."

"Cool. Keep me posted," Brian said. "I'll leave four tickets at the box office for you next Friday."

"Four?"

"Yeah, you have to bring some teammates. It has to be a group thing, not just one person from each activity. It's only fair. And I'll bring Lisa Russell to your game," he hinted with an exaggerated smile. "She has the lead in the play."

"Are you kidding me? Do you think she'll come?"

Brian looped his arm around Sissy's waist and headed down the hall. "Sure," he said. "She'll love it."

Lisa Russell was the most beautiful girl in high school, in all of Cooperstown even. And, of course, she was also amazingly talented. It made people sick how great she was. She was actually a fairly nice person, a contradiction to most of the beautiful guys and girls we went to school with. Playing in front of her might make me nervous, I was thinking. I had always wanted to ask her out on a date, but she was way out my league.

The following Friday found me sitting alongside three sleeping teammates as I watched the play develop into a profound commentary on life through the story of a retired Negro League baseball player. Had Brian told me that the story involved anything about baseball, I would have gone regardless. I began to understand my father's worldview while watching Troy's story being told. While my hometown had its great moments, it too had succumbed to racial divisions yet remained proud that baseball has played its part in the changing of history. I thought about my name for the first time and wondered how I might carry dignity and respect through my actions.

Aside from making new friends at school, I still had a career of my own to consider if I wanted to make it as a baseball player at Roth College. Likewise, I paid particular attention to how Kevin was fairing in his new surroundings.

Not surprisingly, his season ran along uneventfully, except that his control over hitters was missing. Maybe it was the adjustment to a new team and a new coach or a heavier course load, but his usual command, a repertoire of his success, wasn't up to the high level to which he had been accustomed. I, on the other hand, took off on a torrent I had never imagined myself capable of accomplishing. With adjustments made to the line-up, I moved into the third spot where Kevin had always batted. He was that good, a solid player who could both hit and pitch effectively. So, here's the irony. While I hated the thought of seeing my best friend in a Worcester outfit, which reached a depth of treason as if it were a Yankee uniform, I was experiencing the best year of my life, and he was having a hell of a time adjusting to his new school and team. Before too long I found myself playing better than ever before. There I was, a lifetime .290 hitter who had only collected at best twenty to thirty hits each season and could only club a few home runs per year, and suddenly I found myself tearing up the league, belting enough hits to put together a seventeen-game hitting streak. During the streak, I had batted safely in five consecutive plate appearances twice, had more than doubled my average home run output by reaching twenty for the first time, and was toting around a .420 batting average on my cocky shoulders.

The previous record at Cooperstown High School for safely hitting in consecutive games fell like a Cubs' pennant chase in September when I reached game number six. At that time I thought nothing of the streak and was not even aware of a new high school record until I collected a hit in a tenth straight game. A local journalist researched the record books to determine where ten put me on the list. Shortly thereafter, the county record of eleven games fell. Then came the Mid-Central New York High School AA mark, which was only one game higher. Before I knew it, I awoke one Saturday morning to find my own face on the cover of the *Cooperstown Gazette*, proclaiming I was only five games away from the overall New York State High School Athletic Record!

Dad pushed the paper in my face, declaring that Wally Johnson had hit in twenty-one straight games in 1967, the longest streak in the history of New York State High School baseball since such records had been kept. The article also went on to mention near the end that if I could get to twenty-six, I would even eclipse the college record for the State of New York. The only unreachable mark that sat above that number, at least in New York, was the big record held by Joe DiMaggio in the Majors with a hit in fifty-six consecutive games. The article failed to mention semi-pro ball or Major League farm clubs. Maybe those records were lower than my high school mark had been. Too bad, dad joked, that we had moved to New York. In any other state I might have had a chance at knocking off a professional hitting streak.

The columnist for the *Gazette* outlined my chances against the upcoming opponents. Reynoldsville was a sure thing, he predicted, since I had collected six hits in nine at bats in a double header a month earlier on their field. The next time I faced them would be a home game to be played at Coops Field. Number seventeen and eighteen would be a challenge against a tough cross-county rival, the Mudcats of Morthaven who were heavily favored

145

to meet us in the state tournament. Luckily for me, the journalist noted, I would be facing the low end of their rotation. Admittedly, I was a bit incensed at that comment. Hits in games numbered twenty-two and twenty-three would come easily against Biglersville and Sydney Port, both teams who were near the bottom of the standings. And as my father read onward, the words faded into the buzz of revelation as I tabulated the remaining schedule I would face as I looked forward to my record-setting opportunity.

Dad's voice disappeared behind me as it came to full understanding that I would most certainly face Worcester in game number twenty-six. And, if my sequencing of their schedule put things in proper order, I would be facing not the nagging nemesis who had struck me out twice already that season, but my very best friend in the world. Kevin was scheduled to pitch game twenty-six. As it so happened, Kevin's prediction had been dead wrong. He would pitch against us.

Of all the lousy times to have fate intervene. Kevin had been having a terrible senior season, and needed as many strong outings as possible to get a fair glance from the scouts for college ball. And while I had experienced the best season I had ever known, here was my chance at a record that might stand for a long time to come. The conflict was too much.

Collecting the necessary hits to reach the record books came easily enough. The numbers passed me like exits on a highway. Each game came and went and I climbed toward my goal of a new record. I surpassed them all, chipping singles and doubles and home runs all over New York until I edged closer to game number twenty-six. I even hit a triple once, a rarity for me and the only base hit I had against Sydney Port for game number twenty-three. And, just as I had calculated, I was set to face Kevin in what could be my record-setting day. I was not as troubled by his lack of success that year as I might have been had he come in and pitched a normal game that day. Certainly, he would be aware of my streak and would challenge me for every pitch. All he had do was pitch solidly and I would find it difficult collecting a hit. He pitched better than solid. He pitched a gem.

The scouts knew what Kevin was capable of, of what he *could* do. Whether or not he ever got a fair chance at a minor or major league try-out depended on when he finally preformed as well as he could. That day, May 27, 1988, just so happened to be one of those days.

Newspapers from across the state and as far away as New Hampshire and northeastern Pennsylvania had sent correspondents to the field to see if I would collect a hit and etch my name into the high school record books. I was in such a groove that season that the pressure never got to me. If it had been mounting, I was somehow able to ignore it. I surprised myself by being nervous that day when the national anthem ended. It was the kind of streak a hitter gets on when he begins to expect hits. They just keep coming. How long it would ride out was not my concern – that was for the record keepers and athletic directors to follow. I had nine innings to worry about helping to get my team into a playoff tournament. We were 16-4 heading into that game, just close enough to the number of losses that might force some teams off the state schedule of playoff games. At that point, teams would be entered into a lottery pick to determine who gets the remaining six or seven playoff berths. This game was important to our team.

The contest was played on our home field and it seemed as if the number of Kevin's faithful fans equaled those hoping to witness my record. What friends he may have made were outnumbered only by the Worcester and Cooperstown loyalists who came out to root regardless of the game scenario. The talk had been floating that Kevin would get better as his senior year moved onward, and people wanted to see what he might accomplish. He hadn't been pitching badly to this point, not hardly. His record sat at five wins and six losses in thirteen starts. He had only struck out twenty-two hitters in those games, which was low for Kevin, and his walk numbers were higher than ever. He had unloaded thirty-seven free passes in just thirteen games, astronomical for any level.

Kevin was in the bullpen warming up when we came out of our locker room. I was the first one into the dugout and hurried across the field to see my old pal. Most of our team was ready to face their former teammate, most notably Jarrod McKenna who had lost a spot on the team to Kevin in our freshman year. Jarrod wanted to take Kevin deep at least twice, and he had the power to do it too. Others were happy to see him, though most were not phased about playing against him. He was just another opponent.

"Hey, Kev," I said, stopping by the bullpen area. "I sure hope that fastball is up today. I could use a hit."

He nodded between warm-up throws. "Augie," he said.

"How's the arm?" I asked. His catcher, not minding his own business, answered for him.

"It's good," he sneered. "What's it to ya?"

147

"Hey, Kevin and I go back a long way," I said. "This isn't your business." The catcher stood up and stretched his towering legs beneath him as he strode toward me. The kid was the size of a professional football player, not a high school catcher.

He stood a foot over me. "I think I might make it my business," he said.

"Snyder!" Kevin yelled. "Give me the ball. I need to warm up. And back off my friend, will ya?" Snyder the catcher glared at Kevin the pitcher and tossed him the ball underhanded. He shot me a quick glare before gathering himself behind home plate and squatting to catch.

"I forgot," Snyder said from behind the mask while hurling a pitch back to Kevin. "These boys are your old team. I sure hope you don't have any love between them and us winning today."

"Kev, I'll catch up with ya later," I told him, and headed back to the field where my teammates were also warming up.

The game got underway and we shut the Wildcats down in the top of the first. It was easy pickings. They had a weak line-up and relied on their middle three hitters to provide what little offense they could create when they happened upon a power surge. Three up, three down. Middle of the first, no score.

Kevin took to the mound for the bottom of the first with discipline and determination. He lobbed his last few warm-up tosses and gave Snyder the signal to throw the ball through to the second baseman. Kevin asked for the game ball from the home plate umpire and set to begin play once it was delivered. His shoulders stood square and high that afternoon. As the sun slid just passed noon, he kicked the dirt and wound into his first pitch. A dead-on, full heat solid strike. The first of what would be many on the day.

I wanted to get my first at bat over with. Kevin mowed through our first two batters like a new blade on a scythe – a strikeout to start the inning and a soft roller on the first pitch to Jarrod that was picked up by the third baseman and screeched across the infield for the out at first.

The on-deck circle seemed smaller that day. I took a few practice swings and watched Kevin zing several belly high fastballs into Snyder's glove. He was on target and his delivery was precise. Having to face my best friend for the first time, coupled with the looming record-setting opportunity, made me more nervous still. I rubbed some dirt into my bare hands and took a few hard practice cuts with the weighted bat. I hadn't been so nervous since the third grade dance when I had to dance with Cindy Eckler, the math teacher's daughter whose mother stood over us as the peering chaperone.

I dug in left-handed against Kevin the righty. No surprise. He knew I was a switch-hitter and could anticipate my positioning. He was obviously less nervous about our first encounter as opponents than I was. Maybe he was just more focused. He slid a sneaky slider onto the outside corner of the plate that I swung like a hurricane through a wind tunnel. Strike one.

My composure was startled, though not shattered. I stepped back and took a moment to concentrate before placing my feet back in the batter's box. The second pitch was a ton of heat behind a blazing fastball and I drilled it high and deep into right field where it sliced away into the stands behind the foul pole. Strike two.

The next pitch I took all the way and accepted as a ball. If I had to I would let him walk me. It would calm my nerves, and he was in such a zone that even early on it was evident that we would need to take whatever he offered to beat him. I was completely fooled by pitch number four. It came in high and slow like a lumbering helicopter and I teed up on that thing ready to knock it a mile. But, as I committed to my swing, the ball dropped out of mid-air and into Snyder's mitt like a clump of lead. Where had Kevin learned to throw a knuckle ball? I swung through it so dumfounded that I almost fell over trying to reach the descending pitch as it plopped past me. Strike three. End of one – no score.

In the top of the second, I handled an easy grounder that I almost launched over the first baseman's head. He snagged it down and made the out, tossing the ball right back to me as a relay to spin it around the infield, but he never heard my statement of thanks for correcting my blunder. The next two batters silently popped out to the outfield. Middle of two – no score.

The next inning saw our first batter face a worse fate than mine from the previous inning. He didn't even make contact with any of three pitches and struck out swinging. Our next batter popped up behind home plate and Snyder cradled the orb for out number two. The final out of the inning came on a lazy grounder to the first baseman who only had to scoop up the wayward ball and trot across first base to record the unassisted out. End of two – no score.

We continued to close down Worcester's scoring at a pace equal to Kevin's. We gave up a few scattered hits that were either turned into double plays or resulted in a stranded runner at the end of an inning. And at the end of five and a half innings there was still no score.

We went silently in our half of the sixth as an uncomfortable pattern was beginning to emerge. Kevin was working our hitters over like a detective cracking a key witness who turned out to be the number one suspect in a crime. He had us pinned from the start. For every adjustment our hitters made, he answered with a retaliation quicker and smarter. We thought he was leaning during his fastball, and hoped that might telegraph what pitch he was throwing. But when he leaned into a curveball, that hope went for naught. Our coach sent a sophomore up in the fourth and told him not to swing at anything no matter how good the offering appeared, hoping that Kevin would get uneasy and walk him. We needed offense and a free base on balls was as good as a hit. The sophomore struck out looking.

I stood outside the dugout for the bottom of the seventh inning and someone along the bench was trying to chatter up some enthusiasm. "Come on," he bellowed. "Let's get a hit off this guy. Bents never pitched this well when he was on our team. Let's get at him."

The comment struck me as odd, so I checked the scoreboard. Sure enough, we had not accomplished a single hit. Six innings of no-hit ball was over half the way home, and Kevin was in a concentrated focus so intent that I began to think we might be in trouble. I may have served my team better had I made this discovery *after* I had batted in the seventh. I put up a less than inspiring effort and grounded out to shortstop without even taking any look at what Kevin still had in the basket. End of seven – still, no score.

The Wildcats threatened in the eighth and finally worked our starting pitcher out of the game. He gave up a walk and two singles and would have given up a run had our right-fielder not made a targeted throw to the plate for the first out. The starter was lifted for a relief pitcher who barely finished the inning but did so without yielding a run. The usual chatter and goings on in the stands had given way to a silent murmur of excitement as Kevin inched his way toward a no-hitter.

While he busily buzzed through our lineup in the bottom of the eighth, I watched the action of the field and began to calculate just how well Kevin had been pitching.

"Mr. Philson," I asked the scorekeeper. "How many walks has Bentworth given up?" The scorekeeper was a guy who loved baseball as much as any of us. His son had graduated three years earlier and he had yet to relinquish his spot as the team's scorekeeper.

He sighed. "August," he said. "He ain't given us one runner all afternoon."

"You mean to tell me, he is taking a perfect freaking game into the eighth inning?"

A cheer rose up from the crowd when the final out of the eighth was recorded. Mr. Philson answered, "Nope. He's taking it to the ninth," he said.

No one on our bench made any mention of the fact that I had been held hitless thus far. For the first game in our last twenty-six times on the field, I was looking at posting an "0-for." As we made our way out to the field to defend our half of the ninth, the catcher, Mitch Underling, called me over.

He strapped on his shin pads. "Hey, Aug," he said. "Don't worry, bud. You'll get at least one more at bat. We'll shut them down this inning and either win this puppy in the bottom of the ninth or send it into extra frames so you can bat again." He made no other remark or comment, exuding absolute confidence in himself and his teammates. He flipped on his mask and trotted onto the field. "Let's go boys. One-two-three; easy as can be. It's a shut 'em down inning. Let's go." He was rallying the troops around me.

The Wildcats presented a mild threat to start the ninth by getting a lead-off double. Protecting the bag to hold the runner on at second, I was less concerned with my hitting streak than I was with winning the game. When a line drive sailed toward and above me, I reached as high into the air as I could pull myself against gravity and brought down out number one. I felt a slight tinge on my right side but no real pain.

The next two outs came easier, as our closer, Kevin Hughes, got out of the inning, though it took a while as he worked the fourth batter on a 3-2 count for several pitches until the hitter finally ignored a called third strike. Middle of nine – no score.

The better side of fortune seemed to be sitting on our bench now. As much as Kevin had pitched well, we knew we still had two opportunities to win the game. If we didn't score in the ninth, we would get to him in the tenth, the certainty of home field advantage on our side.

Our first hitter stroked a few foul balls into the stands before finally striking out. I checked with Mr. Philson and Kevin's count had reached sixteen strikeouts, accounting for more than half of his outs! By this point, a walk or a hit-by-pitch or a cheap single would be cause for celebration. All we wanted was a chance to score. We could beat these guys. They had had five hits and three walks with which to take the lead, and over nine innings they had yet to plate a run. If we could get a guy to first, it was our game to win.

The second hitter of the inning, Mitch, took the first two pitches looking and got himself ahead with a count of two balls and no strikes. Kevin was getting tired and a walk was right there, just out of Mitch's reach. Mitch let the third pitch slide by him for a crafty strike, Kevin still working the plate effectively. The next pitch was all Mitch's and he ripped a shot down the third base line for a sure base hit. Instant euphoria arose from our bench, only to be thwarted when the third baseman made a play on the ball the likes of which Brooks Robinson had done on the hot corner his whole career for the Baltimore Orioles. He snagged the ball just as it passed the bag, lifted with lightning speed to his knees and threw a streamline shot to first to beat the slow running Underling. Had it been a lefty at the plate with a quicker stride out of the box, maybe the no-hitter would have been busted apart.

Instead, there were two outs and the coach sent another pinch hitter, Thomas Welles, to the plate. Welles couldn't hit a beach ball on a string in zero wind. What the hell was the coach thinking? Welles was set down on four pitches and guess what? They were all strikes except for the first one that was zipped under his chin as a message from Kevin. "This is my game, no freshman is gonna break it up."

The nerves on the Wildcat bench were apparent. No one spoke to Kevin and their heads hung low between pitches. Here they had their starting pitcher riding a perfect game into extra innings and they hadn't been able to muster a single run all afternoon. Their composure on the field, however, was a uniquely contrasting matter. Once in position to defend Kevin's game, they were intent and focused. They concentrated to make the outs should we connect with the ball. No player on that team wanted his error to cost Kevin his perfect game. Technically, he had already accomplished the unimaginable. He had thrown nine innings of perfect pitch baseball. But no one would care about that if they lost the game in extra innings. They had to score to make it count. For him and for the record books. The perfect game was in the books, that much was certain. But no one wants a record that has a little asterisk next to it to denote that the feat came in a losing cause.

The game dragged on into the twelfth inning, and still no score. Snyder, the team's tiring but still huge catcher, made sure to help Kevin as quickly as he could. With one out in the top of the inning, Snyder spiraled a pitch into the bleachers for a home run. Now we were in serious trouble. Kevin had a lead, and with that lead on that day he was determined to shut it down. The next two Wildcats' batters faded quietly – the first on a pop fly that I hauled in myself and the last out on a squibber back to the mound that was covered by our pitcher. The Coopersmiths' bench lost its spirit. Middle of twelve – 1-0, their advantage.

I headed back toward the dugout knowing I would be up in the bottom frame. Kevin charged out to the mound like hell on fire. His intensity had grown with the possibility of victory and he knew he needed to be ready for the next half-inning. If it was to be won, and if it was to be a perfect game, Kevin was going to do it on his own terms.

He worked the frame like a magician. I was due up third, of course, and hoped that someone else would be on base by the time I stepped to the plate. If my hitting streak was to be in jeopardy, so be it. But I didn't want the final out of Kevin's no-hit perfect game to be on my shoulders. Let someone else blow it open and ruin his day. What a position I would be in. Do I let him shut me down, thus ending my streak and giving my friend the greater glory? Or do I reel in with every ounce of my talent and find a way to muscle a hit past him and his infield? I would be fair. Play for the hit. Make him beat you. Be competitive. That is why we play these games, to win. Was he even thinking these thoughts at all?

The first batter was a disappearing act. Three pitches, three fastballs, three looks, three strikes and he was out. The second was the work of an illusionist. Kevin danced the corners of the strike zone with alluring curveballs that the hitter, a senior, could have picked apart if he wasn't thinking so much. Kevin bewildered him into forcing a 1 ball, 2 strike count before mastering a hidden trick ball up to the plate. He swung with power but pumped the ball dully into the air, a simple floater right at the shortstop who only had to raise his glove for the out.

Dammit! It would be me against him after all. After such a long day of almost hits and could have been walks, I was striding to the plate after having unsuccessfully batted in three previous

153

attempts against my best friend and former teammate who happened to be pitching the absolute best game of his life.

He stood next to the mound and stared into home. He knew how to pitch me better than anyone and I could read his delivery like a comic book with no surprises. I stood outside the batter's box and we locked eyes on each other. The crowd swelled behind us in a round of applause and both benches chattered up for their respective teammates. Neither he nor I so much as flinched. It was a contest of will. Whoever first broke the stare and said, *Let's play this thing out* would be the loser. The other would have had his number. We stood straight and zoned in on each other, eye to eye for a minute, maybe longer, before the umpire hollered the command. "Let's play some ball, boys."

We simultaneously broke our stare and set to our positions. Kevin hung his right arm to the side, tired and searching for reserve energy. All I needed was a hit. I could not win the game here but I could win this one contest and extend my hitting streak for one more game.

The first pitch was delivered empty the promise of any excitement. It was a far-away offering that skipped off the dirt. Ball one. Was Kevin losing his stuff this late in the game? He gathered the ball from Snyder. The second pitch came harsh and relentless. I don't think I ever saw it. Strike one. I shook off my surprise and backed out, asking for time. It was granted and in that one moment I scanned the stands briefly. Mr. Bentworth was standing far atop the bleachers with a goofy looking hat shielding his eyes as if he would rather not have been recognized. Mom and dad sat together behind our dugout holding hands in what looked like prayer. I cleared my head, raised my bat before my eyes and puffed out a hard sigh. It is a superstitious thing, but maybe it blows the curse out of a bat. Who knows?

I took the third pitch low for a ball. Kevin was in fact growing tired. He retrieved the ball from Snyder and rubbed it hard between his fingers, taking a moment for his own timeout to remove his glove and smooth off the ball.

We both dug in for the next pitch. Kevin read the signs from Snyder, who had been orchestrating this game like a conductor of a symphony. Not enough credit goes to the catcher who calls a no-hitter. While accolades are leaped upon a pitcher's credentials, only the most ardent fans of the game commend the catcher. Snyder caught a smart game that day.

Kevin set to deliver and he brought me a pitch that to this day slows down in my mind every time I think of it. It was coming in so sweet and so right that all I needed to do was meet up with it and it was a one swing destroyer of all things glorious: perfect game, no-hitter and shut out gone at once. I replay the moment so often, but do so with an ending different from what really happened. I imagine that I have hit the ball out of the park a thousand times. Each time I connected on a line-drive homer that set a record with my name on it. I see that outcome every time...except for the time that it counted the most, the actual and only time it happened. It was the best pitch I had seen all day and perhaps the best any of us had been offered, and it should have been the one I clobbered. I swung too hard, enthused by the opportunity and set asunder by the intensity of the day. I over-swung and barely connected with the ball, chopping a check-swing foul into the third base bleachers. Two balls, two strikes. Game on the line.

As quickly as Kevin had built up the intensity of the day, it would disappear in a flash. That fourth pitch had been my chance. The absolute best chance we had to take that game. There was no way he'd give me anything hittable again. But, still, a 2 and 2 count is a hitter's pitch. I could take the ball and force a full count if it seemed a bit outside, or I could swing away and not risk striking out if the ball was fouled off again.

Kevin looked exhausted on the mound. He set into his wind up with what might have been the last of his energy and wielded around to throw the best pitch he had left. It too came in where I could reach it but it was much lower and had off-set my timing. I could have gone ahead and let it slide passed for a ball but I knew Kevin was dying out there. One more pitch might be the game. I could have slapped a lousy single into right field for an easy hit but I was thinking too much about the streak. I swung right through it like some dumb kid lifting a bat for the first time. I missed it clearly. Strike three. Kevin had his perfect game and my streak was over.

The celebration broke lose instantaneously in a berserk outpouring of excitement in front of me. Even my teammates came sprawling onto the field to congratulate Kevin and join in the banter. In the mayhem that transpired, I did not see my friend during his most glorious moment. The last I saw was the bright white number twenty across his back disappearing above a sea of fans as he was carried off the field. I made my way to the dugout to

155

gather my things and was greeted with a small showering of appreciation from the Coopersmith faithful. My manager patted me on the shoulder and said I had had a good run during the hitting streak, that I should be proud.

I wasn't bitter. I had had my chance and I blew it. Either way, coach was right, my run had been exciting. I had tied a state record and still held the Cooperstown High School record by a sizable margin. Someday, someone will come along and break my record, and that's okay. The spirit of competition demands it. If they aren't to be chased after, what is the sense of keeping track of records in the first place?

What made the situation worse is that most of the school, including Brian, Sissy and Lisa, had finally come to watch a game, only to see me choke. Afterwards, Lisa asked for the phone number of my catcher. Another strike out.

My only regret that summer and onward in through college was that Kevin and I never once discussed that game. What he did after being carried off the field, I have no idea. I don't know if he tried to lob me up an easy target on that fateful fourth pitch or if he hoped he would strike me out. Regardless, it was done, in the past and never to be discussed.

The next day in the papers, Kevin got all the acclaim. Headlines pronounced his amazing feat and cheered his stunning accomplishment. I was a repeated throw-away comment deep within each article. While the headline read, "Worcester Hurler Dazzles for Perfect Game" or "High School Pitcher Throws a Gem," I was mentioned as an afterthought. "Part of the drama included the end of Cooperstown High Schooler's August Monroe's 25-game hitting streak." Only one journalist offered an apology. Mid-way through an item from the *Gazette*, was written, "Bentworth's greatness arrived on an unfortunate day for the Coops' Monroe, who ended..." I needn't read the rest.

17 Unchartered

The only distraction I ever encountered that kept me from my focus on baseball was the ever-classic distraction of teenagerdom – girls. Try as I might to concentrate solely on my game, it was nearly impossible to avoid the lure of the young ladies in attendance, even if Lisa Russell had ignored me. Kevin had the knack. He was able to date any of a number of girls without ever getting distracted by their needs, their fights or the numerous "dates" when the weekly girlfriend watched him pitch. Maybe it was a gift or just a skill he mastered. I, on the other hand, was a bumbling tom foolery mishap of a mess.

The worst of it had come during the All-Star game during our junior year of high school. Lisa had showed up with Allison LaBlaine to watch the contest, and the minute I had learned that fact I was done for. What Lisa had in looks, Allison accompanied with a voice to challenge the angels. Where Allison was flirtatious and daring, Lisa was smart and sensitive. During one game in particular, I had tried my best to avoid eye contact with them in the student cheering section for only two innings. When I came to bat in the top of the third, they had let out a giggled cheer, and I spazzed-out. It was like a brain hemorrhage on hormones.

The pitcher, Dennis Brachman, was throwing absent-mindedly for the first two innings and on any other day I probably could have lit him up for two or three hits. But thanks to Lisa and Allison, it was a different story.

Shake it off, Monroe, I had told myself as I strode to the plate. *Ignore them.* Despite my forethought to erase their presence from my mind, visions of them both sprung up ahead of me as if they themselves were playing second base and shortstop in scantily clad uniforms. The pitcher stood on the mound, grimacing at me as if he knew the girls were rattling my concentration and proceeded to use it to his advantage. I can still see his wide cheeks smirking beneath a tiny, tiny nose as he looked in toward the catcher. He looked like Mr. Fucking Squirrel sizing up an easily obtainable nut. His first pitch was a slow, dumb off-speed breaking ball that I should have smacked for a double. Instead, I stood still, the bat frozen on my shoulder the same way I would stand around at a dance, lumbering and dull, afraid to ask a girl to accompany me onto the floor. Strike one.

157

The second pitch was worse. A mild, tailing fastball that even in fourth grade would have been a home run. I avowed to swing at anything Mr. Squirrel offered and swung through the pitch so hard that the thrusting wind from the bat must have pushed the ball backward an inch in mid-flight. Strike two.

Ah, hell, I had muttered to myself. *This is ridiculous.* "Give me the ball," I had told the catcher.

"What?" He had gazed at me like I was a lunatic and then pleaded with the ump for an answer. The ump, a pencil-nosed kid who looked like he had baseball smarts but lacked the ability athletically to play dodge ball, had shrugged complacently.

"Give me the ball," I had repeated. He did. I then proceeded to officiate my own strikeout. There was no way I was going to get a hit in my state of mind. So, in absolute sportsmanship, I tossed the ball into the air, purposefully swung and missed, and let the ball plop to the soft brown sand below my feet. "Strike three," I had told the ump. "I'm out."

The great roar of laughter from the hundred or so fans and players in attendance did nothing to ease the mood of our coach. He benched me and I never admitted what had taken hold of me to do such a hair-brained thing.

I hadn't yet had a serious relationship. I was afraid to kiss a girl and had yet to experience anything resembling a date. I was dumb and awkward and not exactly, but absolutely without a single clue as to how approach a girl for a kiss, or better to have her kiss me. That eventually changed, thanks to Melony.

I have always been a little put off by the comparisons between sex and baseball wherein advancing upon one another amorously is referred to as "getting to second base" or "scoring". And being turned away or rejected without satisfaction is labeled "striking out." It is as degrading to baseball as it is humiliating to sex. In the beauty of shared intimacy, there is somehow the need to defile that which is sacred. And if baseball is an American institution and the American family gets itself begotten through honest, caring sexual intimacy, then one should not represent the other. Besides, sex isn't a game and baseball doesn't allow you to survive when you outright fuck with your ability or opportunity. Enough from that pulpit.

Nevertheless, there are times in this amazing life when baseball does take a lower order of importance, and I find it harder to admit that than I do admitting just how seriously inexperienced I was with regards to the fairer sex. During my teenage years, I was just a stupid, bumbling and awkwardly backward goof ball.

Regardless, the need to push onward into adult maturities was of my doing and I one day came to share in that most beautiful experience of fornication with a young lady. Certainly I have delved back into that sea of tumultuous pleasure many times since, but somehow, and maybe this is really where men and women are different, the first occasion was, if not the best, at least the most memorable. After all, it is the culmination of expectation, an arrival after years of wondering.

I took refuse after my first forensic journey beyond foreplay in my favorite locale, Owls Stadium, and stared at the night sky wondering just how much I had learned that single night in 1989. The stadium was silent, sitting like late night reprieve against the summer heat. It was cooling pleasantly as night rolled into morning with a pace uncharted by humanity and absent the manner in which time impedes itself against progress. I strummed my fingers along the dugout railing in silent contemplation, unsure that anyone had any inkling as to my whereabouts or where I had been most of the evening. Mostly, I was certain that I didn't care. This was peace if it were to ever be found, and I intended to relish it. In a manner of speaking, a somber and present thud had been lifted from my spirit – a veritable pressure of youth removed from my back. The park was empty and shadowed; the field inactive and dissolving into darkness. The night itself distanced from the world entirely. The dugout was a stronghold. The bench upon which I sat detached yet whole for the first time in my life, inviting.

It had been a long and well-kept secret amongst the teenagers in town that all-hours access could be gained to the field at Owls Stadium via The Nest, provided one were willing to slink his or her way under the security station outside. The guard desk had been poorly devised, and what passed for a low-lying platform where security guards could gain a higher viewpoint of their surroundings, proved over time to be a six-foot deep by three-foot wide opening, a trench essentially. It opened to the west so far that any average sized person could crawl under and pull him or herself up on the inside of the bullpen behind the mesh netting that protected the fence from the pounding of pitches. Whether any players knew about it we didn't care. We'd rather not talk about it, or else they might call the grounds crew out to stuff the hole full of dirt. The irony of the ditch was such that many of the security patrons who had taken employment with the agency had themselves as teens slipped unseen into the park many times for carousing, havoc or the occasional solitude. In the tradition of a secret club, none of the guards went on to notify the team's management of the entryway once they took employment where they once prowled themselves. Of all the activities available once inside the park, the one I practiced most often was solitude.

Night stealths into the park were traditionally held around graduation each year when a game of Frisbee football under the moonlight might break out or perhaps even a full-scale softball game if the cloud coverage was nil and the moon full. But not this night, not for me. Not as I sat alone under a low ceiling of stars and contemplated the evening's events.

I had come many times for pondering, dreaming of a baseball career or for clearing of the mind when my young life seemed so troubled as to merit a clearing of thoughts. What could have possibly trifled an adolescent or early teen enough to seek solace is quite a mystery now that I'm older. Those thoughts at times seem so trivial now, but were so crucial at those moments when they defined me. They were, perhaps, the building block of consciousness. Considering the impact such events as a driver's test or a broken heart might weigh on the whole of humanity, it was silly to really need solace. From the mundane nostalgia brought on by the end of primary school to the exaggerated loss of sleep from having failed Algebra 2 (and facing what then must have seemed an intolerable, yes even insufferable, session at summer school), I had spent those and many other reflective moments under the silent welcoming hand of an empty stadium, an unyielding sky and many sleepless nights. They were the nights of youth, and who could blame any of us for passing on sleep when so many other things rattled around in the brain?

Whether awake with the infirmity of youth or too muddled with thought, there I went to reflect. So, too, it was that I sat this night, gazing up at a thin veil of clouds passing before a semi-circular moon, and smirked with delight, contemplating the loss of that most heralded and unwanted label – virginity.

Reviewing the evening's glee with a warm twitter in the belly and a heartiness of breath, I felt the assurance of having passed rightfully (and finally!) into manhood at the ripe age of eighteen, a little over a month shy of my nineteenth birthday. Had I known the outcome of that night's events, the night of June 6, 1989 (precisely at 11:42 PM), prior to setting out on what seemed a dismal excursion with friends, said evening would have proven disastrous. In short, had I thought about getting laid, I would have panicked, and the determinant interlude would not have occurred. Like I said, I had always been uncomfortable with the girls in general, though talking with them seemed easy enough. It was the physical events, the simplest clear through to the unimaginable, that were improbable and difficult for me to accomplish. So, I fumbled my way through three or four dances, never quite gaining the confidence to kiss a girl good night, or even ask for a real date. But tonight! Tonight's threshold was crossed with no young lady – most assuredly Mr. Monroe had met a woman.

I and Roger Finkweather, a classmate of unremarkable personality and a boy who would as soon drift into the past of memory as quickly as graduation day expired, had experienced enough of a party we were attending and sought better entertainment opportunities elsewhere.

Being lobbed with Roger more often than usual since Kevin's departure to Worcester, I made friendly, idle chatter with others and, as soon as the food was gone, suggested that we split. Finkweather was more than happy to oblige. We slipped out unnoticed and unaccounted. As Fortune would have it, Finkweather had other plans. I had planned to cruise in the car awhile, listen to some music and head home in time to catch the late scores on the news.

Finkweather pulled me aside in the street. "My brother says there is a party up at his school that we can go to," he said.

"I didn't know you had a brother," I answered.

"Yeah, he's a pol-sci major at U of B," he answered.

"Pol-sci? U of B? Fill me in here, Rog. Ya lost me at party."

"Political science, it's a major. U of B. A college. University of Buffalo! God, Monroe where have you been?" He tapped my forehead. I hated that. "Anyway," he continued, "my brother and some of his friends are hanging out my uncle's cabin up on Otters Lake and he invited us along if we got bored."

"I don't know. Do you think we should?"

"Hell, yes. There will be beer there," he answered. A greedy, hefty smile crept across his juvenile face. "And girls," he added, grinning wider. He climbed into my car with the apparent assumption that I had agreed and said yes I would go.

"I don't need beer," I bragged while opening the door and lowering myself into the driver seat. "My dad lets me have one every now and then with him out in the garage. Where is this Otters Creek?"

161

"Otter Lake," he corrected. "It's just up highway 86, east of Summitville. I know the way. Come on. I'll spot you the gas."

"All right. Let's go," I acquiesced, only half-motivated. I ignited the engine and spun the car around with an illegal U-turn to head for the highway, wondering just how much fun could be had with such company.

Melony. The name sprung out of vivid recall and into the air above the Owls' playing field. *As long as I live, I will remember that name. Even if never see her again.* The memory still lingered so sweetly and so powerfully that the mere mention of her name arose an embarrassed excitement, along with a virility I imagine someday I will look back on and miss dearly. From the quiet gray of the dugout I still yearned for her, imaging repeatedly sauntering with her subtle flesh in orgasmic revelry that nature is so kind to instill upon the youth.

The drive to Otter Lake took a little under an hour, much longer than I would have ventured had my colleague, who had afforded himself the luxury of a nap after giving me directions, been more specific of its whereabouts. It was creeping past 10 P.M. and my parents would soon wonder where their car was. Turning off the highway and onto a gravel road, the sounds of the party met us instantaneously as the cabin spread out ahead of the dashboard. Finks awoke with the enthusiasm of a horse out of the starting gate. A small bonfire rippled through the darkness, illuminating unknown faces still hunched around the make-shift camp of somebody's front yard. The night was far too hot for a fire but the rules of rugged out-doors-manship prevailed and a charred hearth was struck in a once homely barbecue pit.

Before I had shifted the car into park, young Finkweather was out of the car and headed straight for a night of consumption, soaked in beer and later left to pass out in the cabin's master bedroom. Having lost my compatriot so quickly, I wandered the grounds with caution, so as to not set the ever-sensitive "you aren't invited" alarm that such gatherings often promote. To my surprise, it was a welcome bunch who raised eyes and heads in reaction to my various greetings.

I nodded to a few guys, declined a beer and set to guzzle a Pepsi on the back porch, where unbeknownst to me sat a laughing, wonderful young lady named Melony.

The lake stretched beneath the moon with an ink-stained glimmer of blackish silver and a rippling wind caressing the surface. Distorted images of the moon reflected every which direction. I leaned against a porch railing and positioned myself to view the party inside, glance across the porch or stare out to the lake. Half-inclined to depart mid-way through the warming soda, I drained the remainder of the can onto a garden that was dying from neglect and headed for the door.

"Are you going in for another round?" a voice clamored from amidst a group of six students on the corner of the porch. They were discussing either German literature or cars – I could not tell which from the muted conversation that rose up between spurts of laughter. They could have been laughing at me for all I knew.

"Me?" I asked the mob.

"Yeah," a voice ushered from within the cluster. "Could you grab me a Budweiser? They're in the fridge." I won't exaggerate by claiming the voice was sexy, passionate or pumping with romance, but there was something beautiful hidden beneath the tone and composure, an alluring mystery, inviting and warm. On the edge of raspiness, it wavered on the vowels and shyly hit stress points in each sentence. It was almost like the warble of the ocean that can be heard from blocks behind the boardwalk at high tide, definite and pronounced yet subtle and scarred with grace. Anyway, she was growing thirsty and I was busy straining my eyes against the darkness to spot her.

"Yeah, sure," I answered, "A Bud, right?" I still could not tell who had requested the beer between a glare cast from a lamp just inside the window and the darkness engulfing the porch. "In the fridge, inside?"

"Uh, huh."

I passed through the tiny cottage but it was no simple task. It appeared as if the entirety of the U of B Poli-Sci class was present, not to mention half the faculty judging by the age of several men engaged in a topical discussion near the hallway. I spotted the fridge but had to yank hard at the handle to open it, inside which I found not just a supply of beer but a veritable beer garden. Ensconced in shades of green, brown and clear glass bottles with all the rainbow labels adorning the fronts was a drinker's delight. I wasn't sure I could even distinguish a Budweiser from a Lowenbrau from a Miller from a Corona as they sat somewhere in camouflage amongst each other. Surely I had seen a commercial for Bud before, I figured, after all those years of watching games on TV! Not a drinker by habit, I was amazed just how much her presence, not even that, just her voice, had clouded my thought. My friends insisted on labeling me the oddity of our age, never quite accepting that I understood two things about booze: 1) it was not necessary for a good time; and 2) binge drinking hardly justified itself as a reason to enjoy a fine beer. Also, as the saying goes, Instant Asshole, just add beer. I hated assholes more than anything, still do.

Locating the hidden beer and another Pepsi, I caught a whiff of something pungent. Near the door stood an ice chest, and reaching for the lid I detected the distinct and foul odor of urine from a nearby oven. Drinking a warm soda became a rather appealing idea, just in case the odor had come from, or within, the ice chest and not the abused oven as I had hoped.

I returned to the porch, tempted to pop open the stranger's Budweiser, down it and hand an empty to the amassed voice within the multitude, salute good night with a hearty belch and disappear. Luckily, something silenced the cynicism inside. That little decision, I would later recall, proved the impetus that set me apart from the boys at the party, and welcomed me into the company of men.

Wow! A whisper ran up out of the dugout and into the abandoned stands as I thought about her still again. *I never imagined it could be that good.* The indecency of replaying the occasion over and over in my mind never occurred to me. There I was, safely near home yet far away enough that I would not be subjected to that humiliating question from mom about what was on my mind.

The cabin door lapped shut, not really banging but rather announcing the arrival of the screen to the frame just enough to arouse the mosquitoes into flight. The solitude of the porch was welcome as I saw at last the face of the beer-ordering voice which had clouded my thought.

I handed her the beer, just then realizing I had not opened it for her. "Where'd your friends go?" I asked. A blush rose up inside while I stared at her soft cheek line and tender smile, grateful for the darkness around us.

"They went around front. Something about a bonfire volleyball match," she answered. She leaned up to reach for the beer. "Thanks," she said. Our hands rubbed slightly.

"Sounds intriguing. I think I'll pass," I said.

She laughed. Not many people laugh at my jokes, yet alone the off-hand remarks. "You're funny," she said. She was probably drunk.

"Oh, I wouldn't say funny," I announced in a deep voice that came from I do not know where. "I'm August."

"Hi, August," she said. "That's a great name. I'm Melony."

"Hello, Melony. I suppose I could open that beer for ya."

"There was a bottle opener around here somewhere." She scrounged around in the dark behind her. As she lunged for the missing apparatus, she stretched upwards and bent around the chair without actually getting off the seat, revealing quite an open view of her braless torso and her ample breasts. Fixated upon that glorious wonderland into which I had not yet ventured, I felt no shame for avoiding the announcement that she was holding a can and not a bottle.

She spun back to a sitting position. "Here it is," she said. "Whoa! I guess I'm a little drunk." When she realized the bottle opener would be of no service, I chuckled willfully.

"Mind if I sit?" I asked.

"Sure. Pull up to the cabana and tell me a lie," she said. Her voice again resonated the tender warmth of the ocean's echo. I think it was a line from a movie, but I wasn't sure which one.

"A lie?" I asked.

"Just a joke, August."

"Right, a joke," I answered not so convincingly. "You go to U of B?"

"No. Toronto. My roommate dragged me to the bash. I hardly know anyone here."

"Yeah. Me too." I sipped a drink, checked the lake. "Kind of cool you didn't make a stupid joke about my name. Thanks."

"Only a jerk would pick on you for a name," she said. "That is so fifth grade. So, you don't know these guys?" She seemed to be surprised.

"Just Finks. And a few guys I think I recognize from his brother's high school class. I go to school with Roger. Their folks own this cabin I think, or their uncle. Whatever."

"Oh, what's your major?"

"Sorry?"

"Your major. You go to U of B?"

"No. In Cooperstown."

"Cooperstown, is that Ivy League?"

"Uh, no," I blushed, a little embarrassed and further amused. "Cooperstown High. I'm only a senior in high school."

165

"Oh. Man. I get it. Okay. That's cool. I was like, what? Cooperstown U. Never heard of it, but you meant high school. Got ya."

"Well, I guess I'll be going," I said. I downed the warm soda. "Nice to meet you, Melony."

"Wait. Where are you going?"

"Well, I was gonna leave," I answered stupidly. "Go home, I guess."

"Why so early? You just got here."

"Well, you're in college, and I'm not yet, so I figured you'd – well, you know." I was talking like a complete ass. My head hung low, my hands sat in my pockets, and my feet shifted at some imaginary rock on the porch.

"No," she claimed. She leaned toward me and touched my wrist. Electricity seethed through my desires. "You're nice," she continued and let go. "Hang with me a while. I am not into that whole I can't hang with a high school boy stuff. Besides, if I wanted such stimulating entertainment, I'd be out front with the rest of the college intellectuals." Her sarcasm increased the allure of the ocean that was her voice. I laughed.

"Is your boyfriend out there playing...What's it called?"

"Bonfire volleyball," she said, sitting back. "And, no."

"What, he goes for a more serious game of volleyball?"

"No," she answered through another laugh. "I do not have a boyfriend. The last guy I dated was a jerk. He would have called you Mr. Month."

The next moments passed as such moments do, in awkward silence with shared knowing giggles and playful glances. I feigned the macho indifference so ingrained in man's ability not to swoon, searching my vocabulary for something else funny to say or at least something interesting. Instead, I pretended to sip at the empty soda. She meanwhile played not the coy school girl nor the confident collegiate co-ed. Rather, she remained simmering in her buzz and wondered, she later confessed, just how daring she had become.

Phew – finally! Reliving the moment as if before me on a television screen, I thanked the stars above Cooperstown for the step into manhood I had taken that night. It was all so natural. The self-introductions polluted by no one else's hand nor the uneasiness of expectation, followed by polite and lasting conversation wherein at least a sense of security was built, and then finally on into physical connection that led to the conjugal joining of two selves.

"Your boyfriend. He was a jerk, huh?" I stammered.

"Oh, you wouldn't believe how much he was – is a jerk." Her vengeance was a bit unsettling. After all, I am part of the male species she seemed eager to shred. "A real asshole. But he's just one guy. Not all guys are assholes. You seem nice."

I played my hand. "Come on, it couldn't be that bad." I had to make an attempt, however feeble, at drawing her attention. Had I even the slightest notion that I wanted to wind up in bed with her at that moment, it would have been a complete disaster, ending immediately in misery as I bumbled through half-sentences. But I really did like the girl and at that moment, despite the wandering imagination, I thought I could get to know her and have a good time. "Hey, if you don't want to talk about him, that is fine with me."

She asked the question I may not have been waiting for but found as a welcome distraction to the unnamed jackass. "What about you?" she said. "Do you have a girl back at Cooperstown High?"

"Well," I took a chance. "What do you think? Do I appear the kind of guy who would go out on a Saturday and hand out free beers to pretty college students if I had a steady girl back home playing scrabble with her parents?"

She considered that a moment. "No," she said. "I don't think you would. You seem too nice."

"I think I have you fooled," I gazed away momentarily. "No. I do not have a girlfriend. In fact. I guess I never had. I've had a few chances. You know, prom and stuff. That's about all. I guess I am too busy playing ball."

"You play ball?" She had lost interest in me. Dangerous waters here. *What if she hates jocks?*

"Yeah. You?"

"No. I can't stand basketball," she answered. "That has got to be the dumbest sport!"

"I don't play basketball. In fact, I suck at it. Now, baseball, there's another story."

"Oh! I was confused." she exclaimed, as if it should have been obvious. "Most guys call basketball 'hoops,' including the ex-jerk."

"So...we're back to him again. You must really be hung up on this whole break-up thing." The joke bomb exploded over

167

Otters Lake and fizzled into embers on the water's shimmering surface. "That was a joke," I added as quickly as possible.

"Not funny. Anyway, you play baseball, huh?"

"Yes, baseball." Glad to have survived, I remained quiet.

"Well, baseball I can handle," she answered with a slightly embarrassed look. "I enjoy going to the games. In fact, my brother is a big fan of the, oh what are they called, the Socks?"

"Red or White?" I asked on auto-reply.

"I don't know, they're from Boston I think," she decided, though I am not convinced she really knew or cared. If she is not *really* a fan and only continued the conversation, that meant she either liked me or was drunker than I could gauge.

"Red Sox," I answered a little too strongly. "If it's Boston, that is. The White Sox play in Chicago. Your brother, he's a good man if he likes the Red Sox." I hedged another bet. Maybe, her brother was a good guy.

"Yeah," she said in a contemplative way. She pulled her knees up under her chin and clasped her hands around her shins, locking herself into a mid-sitting position. "He's sweet. You'd like him; he's funny, like you are. He's a Financial Analyst for a Manhattan Brokerage Firm. You wouldn't think he's funny by his job, would you?"

"Sure," I lied, though I had no idea what a financial analyst was or did. "Anyone can be funny. Enough about that and your brother, no offense. You know how pathetic my dating life has been, and I know you just dumped a jerk."

"Hey! Who says I dumped him?" She was adamant about this point. *Damn*, I thought, *why can't I just say the right thing once and stay on her good side?* I was so uncool.

"Any guy," I treaded slowly upon dangerous ground, "who would let you go and make the choice himself is a loser. You dumped him. It's obvious."

"That's really sweet of you to say. And yes I did dump him. After I realized how much of a jerk he was."

"Right, a jerk. Got it. Okay, then. Enough about him. Enough about me and enough about him. What about you?"

"What about me?"

"God. Everyone says that. I don't know, just anything about you. There are a thousand things about everyone. Okay, your major. Do you study political science, too?"

"No. Way too dull for my tastes. Biology, life sciences."

"Hey, cool. My dad is a scientist. I can so respect that. What field?"

"Well, I hope to be a botanist but that, as well, gets to be boring after a while." She was beginning to sober up and became more and more enthralling as the buzz wore off and her natural enthusiasm took over. "So I am thinking," she continued, then paused. "No. You'll laugh."

"No, I won't laugh," I promised. I wondered what scientific field could be so laughable when they are all by nature rather boring. "I'm the comedian here, remember? Comedians don't laugh."

"What?" She smiled playfully.

"No, I'm serious. Comedians do not laugh. It's a rule. Have you ever seen one laugh?"

"No, not that I recall." She actually seemed to be logging through her memory to think of a time when she may or may not have witnessed a comedian engaged in laughter.

"See," I emphasized. "You just proved it. Comedians do not laugh. And if you think I'm funny I must be a comedian. I will not laugh. So, come on now. Tell me what it is." I had forgotten what we were even talking about. I made every attempt not to blow this. She looked at me for a good solid minute, her head tilted just sideways to the right and her lower lip curled into a scowl. After a moment, she plopped backwards and announced her decision.

"No, you'll laugh," she interrupted my denial with a hand gesture of *stop!* "Yes, you will. You'll laugh. Everyone laughs and asks, 'You need a degree for that?' "

This had truly gotten to be ridiculous. How bad can any career be? I raced through the possibilities from sailor to laundry maiden, from car saleswoman to librarian and back and forth again through donut shop owner, lobbyist, medical examiner and even public relations director for a baseball team, coming up with nothing that I found amusing.

"Now ya gotta tell me." I dropped to my knees. "Come on now, I am begging you here. Out with it."

"Sea World."

That surprised me. "Huh?" I hadn't thought of it...but I didn't laugh either.

"I want to work at Sea World." How could I not laugh? Envisioning everyone laughing at her caused the first ripple of laughter. Then the sheer epitome of that stupid whale leaping to and fro after a beach ball intensified the humor. I stood, suppressing a laugh but only momentarily as spurts of an uncontrollable giggle rose up from my chest and into my throat where muscles tensed and released automatically. I could do nothing but laugh, and the not-so convincing attempt to cover it with a cough did not help the situation any. She plopped back in her seat and let out a frustrated sigh.

"I'm sorry. I thought you were pulling my leg," I said. The rippling giggle subsided. "You're serious, aren't you?"

"I knew you would laugh," she said, hurt. "Screw you. Everyone laughs." This really bothered her.

Again, I acted quickly. I sat at her side and became very serious. Inside I was wiping the floor with a miscellany of ridicule I *could have* lobbed at her – about "going to school" or "studying on porpoise"; all the lame jokes she had probably already endured.

"No, I am really sorry. I can see why you would need a degree for that. It must be a very serious investment on part of the," the sentence compiled in my head as I searched for the correct ending, hoping not to burst wide with sarcasm, "investors, the animal trainers, and whoever owns the whole park. What would you like to do," I paused, which was not helpful, "at Sea World?"

"Listen, it is a very exciting career," she assured me (and maybe herself). I should have warned her that while a comedian might not laugh, he most always has to go for the joke when it was there.

"I really didn't mean to laugh," I said. "What do ya say we take a walk along the lake?"

The silence between the question and her reply lingered longer than the light from the stars.

"Do you know the trails?" she asked.

"Uh, yeah. Of course," I fibbed. "I've been hiking around this lake for years. Finks and me practically grew up here."

She jumped to her feet excitedly. "Cool. Let's go," she said.

Okay, let me just check with Finks to see if he and his girlfriend wanna go." I had no other choice. Without Finks, who was to be our guide?

"No," she answered, "just us." And that was when I saw them up close for the first time –not her breasts again, though they were certainly lovely and brushed me slightly as she stopped my progress toward the door – but those unbelievable brown eyes that radiated as she rose and turned toward the light. Depth. That was all I could think to describe the beauty of her warm, brown amber-tinted eyes. It was the first time I had ever felt moved by a girl for something other than looks of the outer body alone. If the warmth of fire was held in color, it might be red and perhaps it is true that the eyes are the mirror to the soul, but security, blanketed serenity, was layered in the brown iris of those eyes. The trance was unmistakable.

"Okay," I agreed. I was grateful she wanted us to be alone. "But I'm his ride, so let me tell him where I'll be or else he'll notice in about an hour that I'm gone and completely freak out. I'll be right back."

I made my way inside, scanned the smoke-filled room and, climbing over torsos, knees bent towards the ceiling and several small circles of people in conversation on the floor, I reached Roger leaning hard against the wall near the fireplace. He was speaking with, or through, a girl with very pink hair and a tattooed arm who appeared not to be interested and may have been ignoring him all together. He didn't seem to notice. He looked seven sheets beyond oblivion. I approached but couldn't tell whether Finks was entirely in the room, he may have even been stoned. Most assuredly, he did not recognize me whatsoever.

"Hey, Rog. Rog! It's me, August. Can ya hear me?" He turned slightly, not letting go his balance against the mantle.

"Ya, man. I hear ya," he stammered. "I'm right here, ain't I? Hey, are ya gonna score tonight, buddy?" he asked very loudly. "I think I might!" He pointed behind him to the newly vacant spot where the pink-haired girl had been standing. She slipped into the kitchen and whispered *Thank You* in my direction. "What do ya need?" Finks asked.

I spoke quietly. "I met a girl, and I want to walk around the lake."

"All right," he hollered. A lot of faces turned around. "Augie's gonna score! Here, man, hold my beer a minute." He, handed me the plastic (empty) cup while reaching into his back pocket. "You might need this later." He held out a single condom wrapped in a creased package impressed with the thickened **O.** It had obviously been in Roger's pocket far too long.

"Put that away," I warned, a little too embarrassed. "I won't need it. I ain't that lucky."

"Wouldn't bet on it," he slurred with confidence. "That lake is pretty romantic, been known to turn many a walk into an interlude." His giggle was of greater embarrassment than was the red package clasped between his fingers.

"No thanks. I'll take my odds," I said.

He returned the condom to its rightful spot. "Good for you either way, my man," he muttered. "Who is she?"

"Doesn't matter. Listen, I need a quick route around the lake. I told her I knew the lake but if I go out there I'll get us both lost."

"Okay. Where do you want to go?"

"I don't care," I uttered impatiently. "I just need a route. Help me out, man. You know the lake, don't you?"

"Yeah. Yeah," he answered in a half-effected tone. "I got ya. Okay, head to the pier, go dead right. No, wait. Left. Yeah, left. When you get to a make-shift lifeguard station, hang right and follow that trail. It stays near the lake and then circles back at the boathouse of a doctor's house about two miles down the shore. You can either turn back there and come straight here or follow the trail and be back in about double the time. It will be dark but it's straight and you can follow it well enough with the moonlight."

"Are you sure? I don't want to get us lost," I stressed, as if this point needed calcification.

He gazed at the ceiling and contemplated a moment. I was sure I would return to the porch to find it vacant, an empty beer bottle where I had sat, and no sight of Melony anywhere. He finally made up his mind.

"Yeah, that's it. I'm positive. Left, then right; Doctor's house; home or around. Yep. That's it."

I wasn't convinced. "Great," I said. "Thanks. Listen, we'll take off when I get back."

"Sure. You want a beer?" He picked a bottle off the mantle. At least he had the presence of mind to realize his plastic cup had been empty.

In the spirit of the party and the revelry I was feeling, I accepted the offer, downing a Schlitz in two gulps. The warm sauce pierced my gullet. "That is awful. Why'd you give me a warm one?"

"Didn't know it was warm. It isn't mine."

"All right, Man. See ya." I set the empty bottle in an ashtray near the mantle and turned to leave.

"August!"

"What?" I expected yet another delay before our walk could begin.

"Make sure you wait for me when you get back. I might be, you know, busy." He pointed a thumb toward where the disappearing girl had been. When he turned to find the spot vacated, I turned to leave, allowing myself to imagine how dumbfounded he was while searching the cabin for her.

Skipping stones. I uttered the phrase to an unhearing field and sky, trying to recall an old tune that had been running through my head since the moment we had first hit the waterline to start out into the night. Melony had bent down to pick up a flat rock and skipped it neatly across the black surface of the lake. She followed its path with quick-eyed precision as the tiny chunk of slate skirmished the surface for twelve or so feet then sank independently down to an unseen fate. *Why would a girl skip a stone?* She surveyed the widening lake for the last and longest ripple.

"Do you always skip stones?" I asked after her gaze broke from the dull water beyond.

"Only when I'm near water," she said. She added a spirited skip towards another small pile of stones along the coastline.

"Very funny," I responded. "I meant, do you skip stones often? Most girls don't."

She stared out to the lake, as if begging the stone to resurface. "Well, you, Sir, do not know much about us ladies, as you admitted yourself!"

"What? But I...How so?" I asked. I was offended.

"I'm kidding, August. Relax."

"Oh, kidding, of course."

She tapped my forehead. "You think too much, don't you?"

"No. No I don't think too much. I don't think I do. I mean, I think a lot. About, you know, things. Things like why this lake was man-made –"

My rambling sentence was interrupted by a quick and subtle kiss that sent bolts of sensation into every extremity, tickling muscles I hardly knew existed beneath my skin. The kiss lasted only a short half-minute and it was with embarrassed shame that I broke our lips from one another with an exasperated gulp. My embarrassment rested in the immediate realization that I had never kissed a girl before, and here my first kiss was initiated by her. It was sudden. Like an attack. Sure, I liked it but I was (maybe still am) a guy who liked things planned out before action is taken. I would have choreographed the first kiss down to a precise movement if and when I had was ready to kiss her on the next date. It's obvious why I never had many dates. She was right. I did think too much, even if I wasn't just a bit chauvinistic.

173

The moment after was not shy and silly as I had always envisioned, full of the bumbling childish act of venturing out into new emotions. A first kiss, regardless of age, is a reach into the realms of emotionality for both parties. And every subsequent first kiss, as new lips meet for the first time, signals the start of something. The mind filters through a state of equilibrium, of warmth. While it certainly did not disappoint, it was surprising and not at all as I had expected. In short, it was no big deal, really. Yeah, it was nice, great even. But hardly earth-shattering. The worst part about it was what it produced. And that was an urge for further exploration. But I checked my resolve and remained the gentleman.

"What do you think about that?" she asked. She smiled and turned her back to me. The lake was in front of us, doused with possibility. She pressed hard against my chest in a back step and allowed me to wrap my arms around her. The erection which had risen in my pants at the moment our lips locked did not seem to bother her, nor did it tantalize her either. This I found peculiar. I always figured girls would react one of three ways: become embarrassed themselves, be turned on entirely (which I was sort of hoping for), or be grossed out beyond further contact. But, just as naturally as the rock had moments before slipped across the lake and downward disappeared beneath the surface, she expected, perhaps even anticipated, the pulsating urge in my loins which itself dissipated. Its relaxation, brought on by her casual acceptance (Surely she had felt it! God, I hoped so; if not I was doomed for a celibate life.) soothed me, and the taut grip I held to her waist melted away into a comforting embrace as the admittedly minimal erection subsided.

"I skip stones for my father," she whispered.

I was aching for her, moments away from suggesting we sneak back to the cottage to an empty room, and she brought up her father! Humor would be my only hope.

"Could we not talk about your parents, please? I can't even think about that kiss." The desired effect worked. She laughed. This time, heavily. After our laughter subsided, she explained.

"When my dad was a boy, he often skipped stones across a lake near his parents' cabin, hoping to send a message to the wizards he dreamt about."

"Wizards?" I pretended to care while more arduous visions than wizards danced in my mind.

174

"Yes," she answered, She gazed up into my eyes and beyond to the sky and the stars behind and above me. "He had a dream. His earliest memory was of a dream he had where a great wizard promised to rise up out of the lake if he would skip a stone across an entryway from the waters below. So, the rest of his life my father skipped a stone on any lake he came across, partially to hope he might happen across the wizard's secret cove. And, I think, partially in remembrance of his childhood." She paused. "He was a happy man."

"Was?" I fumbled through the words. "Sorry, was..."

"Thanks. It's okay now. He died six years ago, heart attack. I have good memories of him, so I see no reason to be sad any longer. You get over the sadness, eventually and somehow the happiness survives, ya know?"

"Yeah," I said. "I lost my grandfather around that time. He was my best friend."

Letting loose the hold I had on her, I bent down and scooped up a handful of debris. Sifting through gravel, wet dark sand, scattered remnants of glass and other grit, I found a smooth shale stone. I lifted it into the crock between the right thumb and adjoining index finger like a good two seem fastball. I exercised a perfect grip on the stone and displayed to her the proper grip.

"Close your eyes," I whispered. I slid back into position behind her and took her right hand, caressed her arm as its limp form melded into place alongside my own. I contoured her backhand into my palm and set both our index fingers and thumbs in place alongside one another. I rocked her in a dance-like flow, left to right: one, two, three, then a fourth time, and in prefect coalition, pulled the enjoined arms backward, slid into the delivery and sent the rock sailing out into the brisk air where it sliced the surface and rebounded outward across the lake, skipping once, twice, thrice and more...six times it sauntered across the veil of water until it spun one last gyration in mid-air then floated cool and articulate into the enveloping blackness beneath. Neither eye moved on the shore, neither body twitched. Neither person needed to see where the rock had landed or in what particular course it had flown. We knew in a vision that the fabled wizard had sprung forth above, granting wish and happiness to the once-boy father long since gone from the Earth. Neither stirred. Rather, our arms locked. I fell back into a squeeze around her firm middle and our faces touched ever-so-gently. My head rested on her shoulder–the perfect precipice from which to watch the lake, sense the night and perhaps fall in love.

Unlike the moment after the kiss, this one passed as a threshold upon sensations of adulthood. No longer kids, we shared the intimate moment and smiled, warmly embracing the night together.

"Where'd you learn to skip rocks like that?" she asked, a tone of cautious jealousy crept into her words.

"It wasn't so good, really," I objected modestly. "Its texture ran off to the left a bit."

"You watched it? Cheater," she accused. "My eyes were closed. I thought yours were too." Her mouth let out a tiny huffing mutter, either signaling that this was the single most important thing in the world or that she had casually passed it off as nothing. Women are so difficult to read. The answer wasn't long in coming. "How can a girl trust a guy when he doesn't keep his eyes shut?"

"They were closed," I said, though not sure how much trust could really be counted, considering I had not actually promised to keep the allegedly open eyes (which were not open) shut. "Honest, I wouldn't lie to you."

"Then how—"

I turned her around before allowing the question into the records. I kissed her deeply. It lasted longer and created deeper sensations. She pulled away, and the brown in her eyes dissolved into the night like slumber. She began to walk away. She walked slowly at first to see if I'd follow. I did, and she picked up the pace.

"Are you brave?" she asked. She sped up in front of my path, walking backwards.

"Careful, you might hit a root and trip, or something," I warned.

"I'm all right," she declared. "I may be a city girl but there's a little backwoods adventure inside."

"Uh," I mumbled, "just be careful."

"So are you?"

"Am I what?" I asked, checking the trail ahead of me and behind her.

"Are you brave?"

"Listen, just turn around, would ya? I don't want you to trip."

She stopped walking. I, however, still too busy watching the trail ahead of me (and behind her) for signs of danger, plopped

176

right into her chest. I knocked her from her feet and landed on top of her rather heavily. She wasn't laughing, but she smiled. I lifted my weight from her and attempted to stand, but she grabbed the collar of my shirt and pulled me close to her side. We kissed deeply again.

"No, I'm not very brave," I finally answered after the warm kiss had ended. I rolled to her side. "But I may need to find better ways to protect you."

She leaned her head onto her hand and stared at me for a moment.

"Do you pitch?" she asked.

"A little, mostly second base."

"You probably pitch to get extra attention or a source of pride from the control."

I realized I may not have been dealing with an amateur. "How much, exactly, do you know about baseball?"

"I know enough," she answered. "Enough to get by and enough to figure things out. Are you any good?"

"Yes," I answered quickly. This was an issue of pride. I was not being conceited. Conceit is a mask to hide behind when proof is not there.

"Are you bragging?"

"No," I reasoned. "I mean, I think I'm good. Don't get me wrong. I don't like to boast. I just have confidence. Is there anything wrong with that?"

"Not at all. But you still haven't explained why your eyes were open." How we had gotten back to that point is an illogical trail I will not pursue. However, the question remained.

"But, hey," I clamored. "You must have opened your eyes at some time."

"Not a bit."

"You said it was a good throw. How could you have known if you had your eyes closed?"

"For your information," her sarcasm was as thick as muck, "having skipped so many stones happens to teach a girl a few things. The rocks make a sound when they hit the water."

I pulled her to her feet. "Come on," I said "There's a lot of lake to cover and it's getting chilly."

We walked down the path which Fink had mapped out, dividing the time between idle chatter and occasional attempts at resurfacing the wizard (though perhaps not thinking of that in the same way). It seemed we both inwardly yearned with that passionate ember that sets the heart alight each time love is introduced.

We arrived at the lifeguard stand. I let out a chuckle upon recalling Finks' advice and felt a little mollified for having not accepted his offer of the condom.

"What's funny?" she asked. She spun around as if she thought she had been followed.

"Nothing. Just–" I almost said too much. "Nothing. It's nothing."

"Come on tell me. I promise not to laugh." Her wanting to share things was a bit unnerving. She hadn't known me for two hours and already she was pressing. Immature perhaps though it was, it made me uneasy. "Since no one laughs at your jokes, that is," she added. "I was being silly. Come on, what did ya laugh at?"

"Oh, just a, uh, a memory from when me and my cousin used to play on the lake," I lied a rather solid lie, one she could not confirm. "This was our check point for war." I included a detail to enhance the story. She must have thought I was an idiot geek with dweeb syndrome. "Just a nice memory, that's all." I layered it on. Besides, it enhanced the believability that I knew the lake well enough to be escorting a young lady out into the night along its shore. That was when the real kiss came. And it wasn't her doing. To either shut myself up or get her mind off why and what I was laughing at, I moved into her. She looked up at me, still probably uncertain whether I was telling the truth. I planted a solid kiss onto her cool, drying lips. I thought it was solid, and it certainly electrified me. I assumed she approved.

Autumn was hanging frosted over the lake air, but the searing skin beneath my clothing was wanton for release, pent up with lust or infatuation, or perhaps just over assertive latent exploration.

We kissed for a lengthy time, tugging first softly and then increasingly more powerfully at each other's clothes. One by one garments became less a barrier and more penetrable. A button popped from one shirt. A shoe was kicked from someone's foot. Blouses slid open and jeans fell silently undone. Before long, we were one flashlight away from a misdemeanor should a security officer pass by to catch semi-naked kids at play in the open fields of nature. The cool waterfront hastened our passion as the only heat to be felt was the energy pulsating through our ribs and against each other's beating hearts. In tiny pants our breath exceeded the lung's capacity to hold whispered moans within.

178

Gradually, subtly the pelvises grazed one another and the heightened static maneuvering escalated to a frenzied aura of sensation. The titillation and ecstasy rose higher and warmer, urging us forward. Then the contact, barely skin enough to even notice at first, but gradually more and more, certainly it was flesh upon flesh, youth to youth, passion against passion. My hands caressed every inch of her body in repeated rhythms like a crazed piano player deeply in tuned to a maddening melody and searching feverishly every nook and cranny of the piano for a perfect note. Each tiny vibration from her sensuous form was a sky-reaching note, a tempo racing to the crescendo that awaited my presence inside of her. With the heat burning between us and the pressured cool against our naked backs, we fell into the Earth. Her long hair draped over my shoulders as the gravel dug into my back. Her adjustments were ample as penetration simplified far beyond the difficulty my wild imaginations had predicted for years before. And silky, the entry warm and tender, the symphony went on and on as she conducted her orchestration in sauntering, rhythmic melodies. I never wished that song to end. My teeth grimaced and bit into my lip. I felt the first trickling pulsation of her control over me and then let slide the most natural exhausted release to ever be sighed along any lake anywhere in the world by any two strangers who had dared love at the risk of unbelievable pleasure.

After long, the evening grew cooler still and, sorting out the clothing that lay strewn along the tiny beach, we dressed, not embarrassed but awakened by new sensory experiences. Damn, it was cold! What the hell possesses human beings to subject themselves to this, I asked, needing to remind myself of the energy such pleasure had enlightened. Eventually, clothed and clinging closely and wearing a telling smile, we made our way back along the lakefront in the direction Finks had guided.

Back at the cabin, the party was still going, though it had quieted greatly. The revelers, I assumed, had either left or had grown tired. As for the many imbibers, they had passed out. A few lights remained aglow as we reached the steps, and inside a conversation filtered through the screen. She turned to me on the porch.

"I had a really nice time," she said. "Thanks for the, uh," she stopped as a shy smile crept across her lips. "The walk," she decided.

"Walks are free," I quipped. "Tis your company I thank." I lowered myself at the waist in a mock bow. "Thy lady's grace is much obliged." I held a laugh behind my own embarrassed stupidity.

"Wow," she said, laughing along with me, "funny and corny. I like that."

"Seriously," I straightened, "I did have a nice time. Wow. That seemed lame. I mean, incredible, lovely time. Any chance I can see you again some time?"

"I don't know," she winced with a note of jest. "I could really get to like you. I'm not used to being with nice guys, ya know."

"Well, this was like a first date. Surely even the jerk was nice on the first date."

"No, not exactly nice for a first date. Let's see," she recalled a memory from somewhere deep in her mind. "Oh yes, I remember. He got drunk at a tractor pull and I had to find a cab home when he passed out behind the wheel after forgetting he had left the keys somewhere in the arena."

"And you called him again?" I speculated.

"Yeah, guess I was pretty desperate in those days. And yes, I would very much like it if we saw each other again. Though, maybe not quite seeing as *much* of each other."

"Great," I added. "Then this must be good night."

"Sure. Yeah. I think I'd like that. Yes."

"You sound unsure, Melony."

"No. I'm certain. You live in Cooperstown, right?"

"Yeah. That's right."

"And I'm in Buffalo a lot during school, and Toronto is close. So, when school lets out. Who knows?"

"Yeah. Who knows?" I said. "Maybe summers."

"I'm in the Hamptons all summer with my folks. It's a drag but it beats working.

We can write, talk on the phone and see each other in the summer."

"Great. Maybe we can visit on weekends. I can drive to Buffalo in a few hours."

"Sure," she grinned. And there are holidays, breaks."

Melony. The whisper floated off into the stars again. I felt like a love sick puppy. Hell, what is a love sick puppy anyway? I would see her again, that much was certain. It would be different, no doubt. Either way, the experience had left me changed and not only just a little like a man. Besides, she was only two years ahead in school, so who knew? I would not force the issue. If there is anything I had learned by that point, it was how to completely botch a date, yet alone anything as serious as we had shared. Perhaps a scholarship to Buffalo University to play ball? *Forget it, Aug. Take it easy. See her when you can get together and stay cool.* I reminded myself.

The night had grown deep into morning as Cooperstown began to rise from a summer slumber. I climbed over the outfield fence and took the long way home to avoid being seen. I followed the road that led from the stadium and out of the valley, alone under the stars, contemplating the sheer wonder of the world.

18 The First Ride

The road through Morton County that leads to Roth College off Interstate 83 is just shy of fifteen miles in length and stretched through a wooded area of old sycamores, daring young maples and field upon field of the local crop. The college we had decided to attend sat along the northeastern edge of town, nestled solemnly above a seldom used graveyard and a creek that carried about as much water as it did the memories of the lives who filled the tombs above. The gravestones ranged in years from 1750 - 1850, marking a chapter in history of forgotten names whose families had merged and moved onward into the great western plains years before the college was founded.

Roth College itself was established on staunch Presbyterian values and had only slowly warmed to the changing times of the twentieth century. The school had opened its doors to women in 1954, years after many equal and lesser colleges had admitted co-eds. Likewise, the tradition of sport had long been entrenched in the classical individual contests of running, javelin, discus and other field events. Over the years, the pious deans had seen the American landscape of entertainment pass for sport and felt it long inappropriate to allow their boys to partake of football or baseball or basketball. When the austere administration finally acquiesced it was only under the pressure of an aggressive student body that launched what was dubbed the Sports Manifesto, a declaration of rights concerning the students' preference to choose for themselves in which sports they should compete. And though it was successful, the protest brought slow and little change. At first, soccer and cricket were admitted. Four years later, bowling, bocce and archery.

Finally with the opening of the fall semester in 1972, football, baseball, field hockey, basketball and even the daring and controversial lacrosse were granted entry into the once proud school of sub-Ivy League credentials. Likewise, it was not until 1974 that women were allowed to compete, some twenty years after their mothers and aunts had fought just to attend the school.

By the late 1980's when Kevin and I began our college years, the baseball program had taken on a life all its own. Under the guidance of Eric Culpepper, the Roth College Roosters ran through opponents for the better part of two decades, claiming something in the area of a half-dozen National Titles and two unbeaten seasons. This was only Division III, but it was darn good baseball. And while dreams of making the Majors still danced in our heads, our choice to pass on larger schools such as LSU, UCLA, Northwestern, Miami University and the like, came down to one simple reality – neither of us could foresee sitting on a bench in Division I. As proud and determined as we were, we both realized that being amongst the top players in New York was, in comparison to the players in California, the Carolinas and all points South, a far cry from greatness. The simple reality of season often benefitted the boys who played high school ball in warmer climates based solely on the extra experience they gained by playing more frequently. More games, longer seasons and a greater amount of outdoor training equated to better ballplayers. Whereas in the north, players spent many a cold March and April just waiting to hit the filed for the first practice.

The logic, however, was not lost on our parents, and they agreed to let us follow our own paths, though separately divided in many ways, into what we hoped would become pro careers. We could either play ball for four years at Roth, the winningest school in Division III history, or ride the bench for two years at a larger school and then only hope for an outside chance of making the team as juniors, and perhaps starting as seniors. *No thanks*, that was our motto, and the answer given to recruiters one after the other with lucrative scholarship offers that were hard to pass up, *I've decided on Roth*. "Good choice," was the usual response as the phone on the other end went quiet, followed by a reminder to call coach so and so should either of us happen to change our mind. This preceded a dull, distant thump of the receiver into its cradle, leading, I can imagine, to a scratch of the head as the manager of Oklahoma State or Southern Cal sat perplexed, wondering if they could recall when anyone had turned them down before.

After a long senior season when both of our high school teams made it to the play-offs and lost early, Kevin and I looked forward to our first visit to Roth College as a breaking point. Our college careers began, but we were still entrenched in the machismo of teenage boyhood, driving in a second-hand car along a sleek highway with the road rolling under our feet and the wind whipping out sounds of Rush, Led Zeppelin, Boston or The Who as we rocked to our favorite bands. It was hardly a grueling ride but one that felt like our first American freedom. Each turn along the blacktop removed us further from the near-suburbia of childhood. And soon, the small town where we would spend the next four years loomed on the crest of a hill, as if its own distant castle. It rained there a lot and the town's center dominated the foggy and cloud-drenched skyline. One would not walk from Cooperstown to Roth College, yet somehow each ride seemed to grow shorter though the distance from point a, home, to the school in point b, Shadesville, remained constant.

Just south of Shadesville, the radio stations from Albany and other major metros began to fade and disappear in a crackled mumble of broken voices and fading rhythms. It was at a point exactly 6.1 miles from the west end of Shadesville, across from a row of upcoming evergreens that the radio began to fade. "Break Silent Point," we called it because when we rode with parents the ride usually continued in silence. Whereas together and absent parental presence, it moved us forward into discussions we seldom shared with others. This facilitated conversation in a way few are accustomed to with today's plethora of music opportunities, a refreshing silence in the uncrowded universe now dappled with satellites. After an hour and more of rock tunes, we could use a break anyway.

How silly fate is at times. If I got anything out of college, it was a prolonged revisit to the art of conversation. Between us, it was easy to discuss on any topic. Anything from the most obvious, baseball and girls, to the common, movies, music and food, and sometimes out to the far obscure, theoretical discussions about ice or the reminiscence of underground novels both had read, were sure to be the subject on any given ride. Our favorite, a rather clandestine commentary of Kevin's concerning what it might have felt like to have been Marconi at the very first moment the radio faded out. And how consumed he must have been with the dread that such a sound might never emanate from his rustic, crate-box speakers again, was recounted on occasion with a sort of nostalgia. Regardless of weather, storm or sun, and time, night, day or bleary morning, neither slept, and as soon as K100 Rock faded mystically into the car's rearview mirror, a conversation always began.

One month prior to actually moving in for the start of our freshman year, we were required to attend a baseball mini-camp and made the trip together in Kevin's movable yet undesirable old Chevy pick-up. Accustomed more to my Volkswagen GTI, which we were leery of, the truck soon rolled into and beyond Morton. The radio dove into its expected disappearance and I asked the question I had pondered and hinted at for years but had never the nerve to come out and just ask.

"Kev," I said. "Mind if I ask you a question?"

"You just did."

"Funny." I paused. "What happened to your mom?" I stared ahead into the roadway.

Met with silence, as expected, I allowed the moment to pass, not wanting to press the issue. I counted the trees and memorized patches of the scenery, stared out the passenger window...gave Kevin time to gather his thoughts and feelings.

"I mean," I added dumbly after what seemed an appropriate pause, "if you don't want to discuss it, I understand. Sorry for asking."

"She died," he said, plainly. "When I was young."

The pain in his face belied the hurt in his voice, as if somewhere his heart beat on a different level all together.

"Yeah, I sort of figured that," I concluded, not knowing what to say.

"What's that supposed to mean?" His tone was not belligerent exactly, though a hint of distrust was evident. Something had risen up in him, a defense, perhaps sadness.

"Well, I just assumed it wasn't like a divorce or anything," I went on. "You know, I just kind of thought that she must have died since she's never around and you never talk about her, that's all. I didn't mean anything."

"It's all right," he said, though a crack in his voice suggested it really wasn't. He considered my commentary a moment and then continued. "Yeah. That sounds logical, I guess. Listen," he said, releasing a sigh, "it's hard. I don't talk about it much."

"That's cool. I understand."

More scenery sped by as Kevin focused with grave intensity on the road. His grip was not frightening upon the wheel but its pressure dug into me with the awareness of just how hard it must be for him to discuss such a matter. A slight rain sputtered across the roof and beads of water rolled down the window. I looked for anything on the horizon worth counting.

"I'm sorry, man," I added. "Really, I shouldn't have said anything." I just couldn't shut up. I knew he needed to discuss it and I needed (okay, really wanted) to know. Still, I did not know myself what the apology was supposed to mean. "I mean," I stuttered, attempting to define my comments. "I am sorry she died and sorry I brought it up."

"No, it is okay," he said. His eyes remained fixed on the road ahead. "I should talk to you of all people about it. You've been my best friend for so long." His voice trailed off, whether into a memory or a realization I could not ascertain. Finally, after a solid minute of dead silence, just as the roadway dwindled from two lanes into a shallow, single lane, he asked me a question that seemed so illogical, but in the end made the most sense. "Do you ever wonder why I pitch?"

"No," I said, his direction lost to me. "You're good at it, I suppose."

"Maybe," he answered with a contemplative shrug. "But that's not it. It's the same reason I wear number twenty."

"You lost me, pal. What are ya getting at?" I stated honestly. "Listen, if you don't want to talk about it."

"What? Why'd you say that?" Again, his voice was not angered, though distant, lacking conviction.

"It sounds, you know," I stammered further, "like maybe you're trying to change the subject or something. And I just wanted ya to know that it's cool with me either way."

"I'm not changing the subject," he demanded. He drew his eyes away from the road to make momentary contact with mine, and then turned his attention, safely I might add, to the road. He added, "This is the story if you'd just listen."

"Oh, okay. Got it. Go on," I rambled as usual.

"It is a number, one-twenty."

"What is?" I was lost.

"Pitcher and my jersey," he answered without further explanation. None was needed.

"Oh," I declared, "you mean, scoring field position number one for the pitcher, and uniform number twenty?"

"Yeah. I do that as a sort of, I don't know, a tribute I guess." His eyes drifted away momentarily once more. "A remembrance," he half-whispered. "It's weird, I know." His voice pushed forward through the window and out into the open road with an emphasis that sent it sailing onward, as if he searched the future knowing that it would always be a part of him and may never be explained. "My mom," he continued, upon the edge of tears, "She, she died in a plane crash. And numbers may not mean a whole lot to many people but January 20th was the day the plane went down."

"Oh my God, Kevin!" The realization was peculiar, yet defining; one of those little secrets we somehow never share and to some level never understand without explanation. There are secrets we may never know. "One-twenty," I proclaimed. "That's your birthday, man. Oh, I am so... Oh, God. I never knew."

"Hold on, don't get riled yet. It gets even stranger," Kevin said, letting out all that he could of a laugh when faced with the absurdity of it all. "She was in Denver on business and promised to be home on my birthday, even though we told her that if she made it to the party two days later it would be fine. But she grabbed an earlier flight, and made it to the airport just in time to catch the midnight flight from Denver to Cincy, on flight one-twenty."

The pall of silence crashed through the window as if I myself had died. Neither of us had before reached such a moment with anyone in our lives. I had expected such intimacy to occur only once in life and that to be with a future wife. In the passage that slowly pushed us both toward our shared manhood and growing friendship that would someday grow beyond matters such as music and baseball, a bridge was reached where upon we etched an unspoken bond, a promise. *I trust you,* he had decreed, *with the most cherished and deepest parts of me as a friend.* I in turn could only think that someday, perhaps, I too would have something to share with him of such relevance. That promise was never found during our waking shared lives together; and to him I now offer this remembrance as a promise, as a wish fulfilled.

"How, uh. How," I sputtered yet again in an attempt to break that silence. "How old were you?"

"I turned nine," he stated proudly. "I guess I grew up a lot that year, too. Dad did his best to take care of us, but things were never the same, of course. I mean we ate and had a house and all, and moved to Cooperstown a year or so later, but it's just tough to have such sadness. Dad had his own fears and losses before mom died but things just magnified I guess. He was hurting."

"I'm sorry, man. I mean that. I truly am sorry. I never imagined that." I felt so stupid for having stated the obvious, of course no one imagines such horror. "She'd be proud of you, ya know that, don't you?" It was the first really certain thing I had said all day, maybe in my entire life. Whoever she was, the woman I had never met, would certainly have been very proud.

"Who, mom?" Kevin asked.

"Yeah. Definitely."

A smile edged the extreme inner points of his face. "You really think so?"

"Hell, yes. Here you are, on your way to college, a great ball player and the best friend a guy could have."

"Stop, you're making me weep," he exaggerated. "I could just hug you." He rolled into a good laugh that we both were able to share.

"Oooh, Kevin," I jibed back. "That is so sweet, you hunk. You are just the sweetest boy alive." My voice rang higher than the laughter that soon filled the car, severing the tension. The seriousness that had hovered within the car graciously raced out into the night as Kevin rolled the window down to let in the fresh country air. Against the pelt of rain, he raised his hand high into the thrashing air outside the car and waved it freely in the wake of the car's motion.

"Damn, this ride is long," he added. He reached across me and opened the glove box where he grasped at a pack of cigarettes. "You want a smoke?"

"A what? Are you kidding me?" I scoffed. "Hell, no. When did you start smoking?"

"Relax. I don't smoke. I mean, it's not like I am a smoker like those losers in school. I just have one now and then to calm down. You should try it. I picked up the ritual at Worcester."

"Ritual?" I was incensed. "Smoking isn't a ritual! It's a terrible habit."

"God, you sound like a teacher."

"Do you realize what those things will do to you?"

"Chill out, man. I just thought you might like it. It gets you a bit of a buzz. It's cool. And like I said, it relaxes me."

"Thanks," I finished with a sneer. "I'll pass."

"Suit yourself," he answered. The warm flare of the burned paper punched a sulfurous smell into the air. It lingered and dissipated as fast as the air outside the window could clear it.

"The coach know about that?" I asked, reminding him of his responsibilities to others than himself.

"What, my mom dying?" he asked. "No, why would the coach know anything about that?"

"I mean the smoking. Does Coach Culpepper know that you smoke?"

"Why would I tell him anything? No, Eric doesn't need to know."

"Who the hell is Eric?"

"Eric. Coach Culpepper, Eric Culpepper," he said.

"Coach lets you call him by his first name?"

"That is how I was introduced to him."

"So!"

188

"So nothing. We're college students now, adults. Not high school boys. Until I am told otherwise I intend to call each person by their names, as if we are peers, which we are."

"Man, you should be smoking something a bit harder than those Kent 100's," I warned him. "If you call just one professor by his or her first name, that teacher will bury you."

"No way," he tried to claim. "They want you to call them by their first names in college. It is part of the experience. The same with trips to the restroom."

"What, they go with you?"

"No, ya jerk. Piss off. My cousin went to Penn State and told me that you don't have to ask to go to the bathroom anymore. You just get up and leave whenever you need to go." He added an off-handed wave as if a trip to the can is the most important freedom life has to offer.

"Nuh-uh!" I blurted sarcastically, though he missed the insult.

"Yeah, uh-huh."

"Really? No shitting me?"

"Seriously," he stressed. "I am not shitting you."

"No hall pass or nothing?" I was laying it on and he was totally buying it.

"Nope," he answered. "Ya just get up and go. You don't even have to come back if you don't want to. Hell, you don't even have to really go to class most of the time."

"I wonder if I can catch a smoke when I get up to go to the bathroom."

"I guess," he answered off-handedly. "I don't see why not."

"That is a cool idea. I think I'll have a smoke with my professor on the first day of class." My laughter was intended for insult and it landed so with a heavy thud of exaggeration. "I just better not let Eric catch me because when he sees me dragging during sprints and finds out that I've been smoking he will tar my ass worse than those smokes will tar your lungs," I concluded.

The truck seemed to roll on absent of direction and the motivation of pressure required from Kevin's foot upon the accelerator as the trip wound down. Rolling into the gravel lot of the visitor's entrance and picking a spot, we ended the trip in veritable silence and passed from the Chevy pick-up into the warming summer air of the now dissipated rain. We both stretched and without speaking another word headed in the direction of the coach's office to report for the mini-camp where we were assigned a dorm for a quick night's rest.

The following day was to be a scrimmage between two teams comprised of the existing team and the incoming freshmen. The team was divided fairly, each getting six freshmen and twelve upperclassmen. The team's starters had been into their third week of practice and primed to play solid ball. The young recruits were fresh as well, save the lethargy they felt having just completed a full season and the fatigue from the long ride to campus the previous night.

We awoke to a fresh sunrise over a cool air as fog burned off slowly. The field was sparkled with drops of tiny dew glinting in the slanting sun as it crept its way into the sky.

I hit the field with wonderment, something the likes of which I had never seen or felt, only dreamt of in the days of my youth. Despite the numerous appearances on the field the Owls call home, neither Kevin nor I had ever worn the jersey of a team that played on a real baseball field. While Roth College was far removed from Wrigley Field or even Milwaukee County Stadium, it was a paradise all its own. In the tradition that winning had brought Roth College, so too was its pride in baseball enlarged. Since the years had been good to the team, the college returned the favor, having built a park equal to the finest to be found in minor league cities across the country. It was, of course, sanctioned by the NCAA to limit facilities and luxuries, so it was not Dodger Stadium, but its feel was real and its character charming.

We crossed the white line into the playing field and Kevin looked heavenward, probably wondering for the first time since he was nine when either God had abandoned him or he had abandoned God, whether or not his mom was staring down at him. Or, perhaps, he was just checking the weather. He strode to the mound a proud young man, swayed by encouragement the previous night to remember that his mom was proud of him, no matter where her unearthed soul rested.

The teams had been idly split into squads by chance and not by any systematic means to pit the best against the better. The coach simply went down the line and pointed: you, home; you, visitor, he proclaimed. I watched as Kevin slid silently to a spot two away from me. He must want to play on the same team, I had reasoned. After a senior season as opponents, the return as teammates was a welcome reunion. But it was not to be. As the coach barked out a pattern of back and forth for the better half of

190

the starters, he sized up the freshmen and evened out his tone, making it easier for himself. "You first three, you're up. You other three, take the field."

So we were set on separate teams again. I was slated to bat eighth, another new experience as I had always batted higher in the order. I was an aggressive hitter with good instinct. Get a guy on base and I could knock in a run. The temporary change to the eighth spot was fine with me. I welcomed the chance to show our new coach how well I adjusted.

Coach Culpepper called a quick meeting near the dugout as the players assembled, chatting idly and exchanging greetings. "Listen up!" He blasted through the morning like a gunshot. "Here's how this works. We play a full-length game with a rotation. Each team will send three pitchers to the mound. If you get in a jam, you're on your own. No pressure, just a way to keep the rotation intact. Got me?" His question was answered with a series of nodding heads, half still asleep.

"Coach?" an unshaved, untucked player asked, probably a senior I reasoned.

"Yeah," he answered. "What is it Williams?"

"Who pitches first?"

"We'll flip a coin. Regular starters will pitch the middle third so that leaves just a few to start." He scanned a roster and announced, "Bentworth and McAndrews, the first toss is between you." Kevin's reaction was as if he had felt a bolt of shock shiver through his veins. "Bentworth, call it in the air."

"I'll take my chances," Kevin said. "Let McAndrews call it and I'll see what happens."

"Fair enough. McAndrews, it's your call." The thin, wiry man lifted a quarter from his pocket, rolled it aimlessly in a palm, and set it atop the thumbnail so quickly that it was as if it had gotten there on its own. With the quickness of a fastball up and away, he flung the coin into the air where it tumbled heads over tails in rotations too many to be counted. The group heard a definitive, "Heads!" from McAndrews. The coin reached the maximum height to which it could stretch, paused at the apex, rotated once more. The glimmering sun reflected from its surface before it fled downward end over end toward the coach's outstretched palm where it landed docile and without shudder. His fist closed instantaneously around the coin, hiding it from view lest anyone sneak an early glimpse. He glanced temptingly to the team and shifted the hand open and over, implanting the quarter with its

191

final turnabout onto the outer side of his left hand. There it sat, covered, as we (or at least myself and Kevin and McAndrews) anticipated the call. I wondered whether McAndrews really cared at all how the quarter had landed but I dared not look up should anyone notice my anticipation.

The coach moved his hand and revealed the shiny quarter atop his tanned and liver-spotted hand.

"Tails," he proclaimed. He may have had more fun with the coin toss than the players could have. "Your call, Bentworth. Are you starting or relieving?"

"I'll start," he said, as always trusting in his confidence.

"Good," the Skipper said. "Always take the ball. Good attitude. I like that. McAndrews, you'll pitch the seventh through the ninth and Henratty will fill in the middle. Got it?" Again, a series of heads bobbed in unison.

"Coach?" McAndrews offered, "I would have chosen to start, too." He shaded his eyes from the sun.

"I'm sure you would have," the manager answered. "But thanks for letting me know. Take D'Onco to the bullpen and toss some warm-up to keep your arm loose. But don't overthrow. I want to see ya pitch fresh out there."

The young pitcher, thwarted in his attempt to impress, headed to the bullpen. The same coin was tossed in similar fashion to decide the other squad's pitching rotation, ending in a decision to start a returning sophomore who had had some arm problems the previous year. The players took the field behind Kevin, a few wishing him well on their way past the mound. At third was an especially chatty field general in his third year, Rod Pendry. Pendry's constant chatter comforted Kevin, setting a tone of camaraderie that lessened his nerve and strengthened his resolve. It felt like a real ball game, and that was what Kevin needed, to feel as if he belonged.

"Okay, men," the third base coach hollered, "let's play ball. If Pendry can shut his mouth!" A ripple of laughter spilled slowly across the infield.

"Give 'em hell, Bents," I shouted from the dugout. I leaned on the fence as my fingers gripped the tiny diamonds of wire links. "Let's see some of your smoke!"

The details of that single scrimmage matter little, except to say that Kevin did in fact smoke us all. In fact, he outright wowed us. His pitches were crisp and his decisions keen. Communicating with his new catcher, he captained the quick game like it was his most important. When Kevin walked off the mound, both sides applauded. We all realized just how good our chances might be when the next season started. Kevin had pitched a solid game, yielding just two base runners he walked in his first inning, and surrendering just one base hit. The early walks were attributed to the jitters. As for the hit, it was a cleanly-roped single delivered by a good hitter. After that, he hummed with great control. Kevin Bentworth had announced himself to our new team; and he had done so with absolute authority.

19 Try-outs

Within the whirl of life, two years had passed. Kevin and I had graduated from high school, gone on to begin college at Roth and had finished a freshman year that tucked under our widening bellies like an experienced weight-gainer bent on consuming record quantities of pizza and wings. Melony and I had dated pretty regularly since that magic evening when we met and looked forward to her graduating from college, the beginning of her career and the prospect of myself completing college a few years later. All the while, baseball moved right along with us and the Owls had built themselves into a contender.

As if Cooperstown didn't have enough to keep itself immersed in baseball each year, there was still another unique excitement about living in the town that fired our imaginations. Open try-outs may not have been the primary focus of the Owls' calendar, but it was important in its own right considering that the Owls knew the chance might one day arise of finding a gem within the Cooperstown streets.

Open try-outs was a day of hope where dreams and expectations aligned. Fans and families from states throughout the northeast and New England flocked to Owls Field, hoping to see the next rising star. The chance that a boy, a son, father or brother might make the team caused a ripple of sensation to billow through the northeast.

Try-outs for 1991 were somewhat special, the likes of which occur maybe once a decade. This year, a local boy was trying out for the team. He had done well playing high school ball for Cooperstown High and another local school, and he was hoping for a shot at the pros. Rumors had arisen that he was being scouted by the Astros and the Blue Jays. Yet, as draft day passed no one had called, so he and all of town looked toward Try-out Day for his hope at playing pro ball.

His name was Kevin Bentworth, and he could hurl a curve ball like no one Cooperstown had seen in recent memory. His fastball and his ability to work with the catcher to control a game were both solid skills. He had a tendency to be wild at times and let up on his concentration in the later innings. His coach had feared that discipline would keep him out of the Majors. With a little cultivation he could be a starter or perhaps a long relief man in The Show, but the jump from college ball seemed unlikely.

194

Kevin would not go far from The Owls even if he didn't make the team. That summer, after try-outs, make or break it, he would be out on the field, donning an Owls' cap and making sure that fly balls from batting practice steered clear of knocking him out. Kevin would remain as an assistant to his dad as long as he was in college. He had worked as assistant groundskeeper since his sophomore year in high school and saw no reason to quit even if the Owls did not offer him a contract. As for my take on his chances, I hoped he would make the team not for his own shot at the Big Leagues, though certainly I would have been proud to tell folks I knew him, but for my own chance at landing his job.

After all the introductions were through, try-outs got underway. A late chilly afternoon in March was leaving like the proverbial lion, and the cold had loitered for a number of days. It was still winter, technically, though our thoughts had already turned to spring. The last snap of winter had dampened our streets and our spirits. A light snow fell during the try-outs. The vendors sold coffee and hot chocolate in place of soda. The stadium parking lot and two hotels in town were full of cars with plates reading Pennsylvania, Maryland, New Hampshire, Rhode Island, New Jersey and even one from South Dakota. A handful of pro scouts from nearby New York, Philadelphia, Cleveland and Pittsburgh showed up, in the hope that maybe a young athlete would rise up out of the field of contenders and be ready for The Show.

The first to take the field were the defenders, the infielders and outfielders who shagged fly balls, chased down grounders and attempted to throw out speedy runners from deep in the outfield. All fared well and the crowd watched with eager impatience as they waited for Kevin's big chance. He would have to wait most of the day, though, and the waiting grew on his patience. As the fielders finished their performances, the hitters took to the cage. In single file, all thirty-two young men took ten pitches each to show their ability. While the long ball was always a crowd pleaser, The Owls (and many of the pro scouts) were, as a general rule, not overly impressed with home run hitters. The home run is an exciting moment during a baseball game, but not many players make a career out of just hitting balls over the fence. What was typically sought after was the all-around player, someone a team could bank on for solid defensive skills and ability at the plate. Most enticing would have been a smart hitter who could make contact and had a little pop to provide the long ball when needed or to bring the crowd to its feet. Kevin watched as balls sprayed all over the field, some launched into the seats as expected and others plopped shy of the infield's limits.

One by one, players from around the area and neighboring states lofted heavy bats upon their shoulders and took their shot at proving themselves worthy to play professional baseball. Scouts and coaches non-committedly jotted notes, took calculations and bobbed their heads up and down. Those who hit well and showed agile defensive skills left confident they might receive a phone call in the ensuing days. Others were stopped on their way off the field, their hands shook and business cards slid into their gloves with a reassuring pat on the back. It was evident in the slumped shoulders and disappointed gait of some that they would be heading back to warehouses and grocery stores or classrooms and offices, hoping maybe next year they would be better.

Finally it was my turn amongst the pitchers. Though I had been improving as a fielder and liked what I could do with my bat, I was arrogant enough to want the control of the game, much as Melony had questioned two years earlier. I still wanted to pitch, and it drove Coach Culpepper nuts thinking I might get beaned in some dumb try-out and risk losing his second baseman for the season. But I had to know whether or not I could actually pitch. That's where it's all at, on the mound, moving the tempo of the game, setting everything in motion. And this would be for me the deciding factor. If I could do it, I would; if not I would concentrate on honing my skills at second. Give it a shot, I figured. What could be lost? I watched ten guys hurl their best at the Owls' hitters and then took my opportunity to see just what I could do with the old fastball.

My pitching style required a sort of resilience. If I lobbed up a softy that was belted into the bleachers, I could usually dust it off and gear down to face the next batter. After giving up only one big hit against five hitters, those in attendance began to take notice. My fastball was clipping and the change-up was baffling every hitter. Maybe I could do this pitching thing after all! Batter six changed that, and the groove that I had been having began to fall apart. The one advantage I had over all other contestants at the try-out session was that I had been studying The Owl's hitters for so long it was more like a hobby than a challenge. Plus, I had three full seasons of experience watching the guys hit in every possible scenario, and all of that information, their tendencies, their reactions, their weaknesses and strengths, was all filed away in my mind.

While a small group of players had come and gone, the bulk of the lineup was stable for all three seasons. I knew Rogers liked a fastball in the wheel house, so I would keep pitches to the burly left-hander down and away. Matthews took a pitcher deep into the count and was susceptible to fastballs on a full count. The way they played out a try-out, however, favored Lance Matthews since only swinging strikes counted against the batter. After five pitches, each batter had to sit. I struck Matthews out swinging on three of four pitches. The other two were easy, one popped up and Steve Collins laced a single that the entire staff knew would have been caught had a shortstop been planted in position. But Denkinger was a different story. The bulky switch-hitter challenged me head-on and strode to the plate on the right side for hitting as opposed to the traditional left-plated position a switch hitter would take against a righty like me on the mound.

This shook me, though only momentarily. I stepped off the rubber and ran through in computer-like fashion just how to pitch the experienced power hitter. If the information I had logged as an internal database to this hitter was to serve any means, it had better not me fail me at that particular juncture. Had Denkinger not been such a slow runner and a merely adequate glove, he would surely be in the heart of any major league lineup. So it was he stood before me as a formidable foe, and I uncertain how to pitch to him.

Stay calm, I told myself. I slipped into game mode concentration. I envisioned a veteran catcher crouched behind Denkinger to counsel me through the at bat. Had Carlton Fisk been available I would have readily called upon his services. *Okay, kid, I coached myself, he likes the curve ball.* The guy had the eyes of Sherlock Holmes on an eagle and could read rotation like a preacher scans a sermon each Sunday. Typically, if the first pitch is his, he will take it. Toss him soft stuff and he will hold off, I reasoned. He likes to show his muscle on first pitches, and if he swings at a first pitch he only does so when he knows he can jack it out of the park. *Okay, work this one pitch at a time.*

I returned to the crest of the mound and ground the ball into my hip. I may have looked silly but that was my style. I played out the whole wind-up like it was a real game scenario. Imaging a runner on second, I heard a ripple of laughter through the crowd and the scouts who could read that I was taking it way too seriously. *Screw them*, I thought. *This is about you and Denk. Play it as if it were real.* I lunged into my delivery, letting up just enough at the point of release to fool Denkinger with a screwball that trailed off as it approached the plate.

It worked. Denks read the rotation and committed to an assault on the tiny white orb before it slowed down and broke away. He swung a big guffaw of a miss into the chilly March air. The laughter was silenced as the more serious baseball onlookers realized my demeanor had paid off on that pitch.

I retrieved the ball from the neutral, unemotional catcher who lobbed it back to me, rotated the mound again and calculated how to proceed. I heard the catcher chide his teammate from behind home plate but paid little attention to the commentary.

Okay you gave him what he wanted, now whirl something fancy by him. He hated to look bad. *This guy is a competitor. He wants this pitch.* I ascended the mound again and this time went to work with greater precision. Confidence seethed through my mind. Digging the leather-bound Spalding into my hip again, and checking the imaginary runner, I strapped two fingers firmly across the baseball's seams and wound-up. The ball lumbered in and again Denkinger read its rotation as it drifted away from the strike zone. This time he held off. Ball. We were even.

The ball was returned with a greater zip this time as the catcher, anonymous as an assailant, was getting juiced by the confrontation.

He read ya, Monroe. That was too good for him. He passed it up like an alcoholic forgoes a soda at a party. Now what? *A change-up he would be expecting after that trash you just showed him.* I could bring my best power to challenge him, but man he could knock that into the stands in a flash. *Okay,* I reasoned. *Give him all you got. Mano-a-mano, you against him. Give him your heat. You've gone easy on him. You can ride this guy outta here. This is your pitch, kid.*

Denkinger dug in for the next pitch with harder purpose than the previous two. I continued my routine and circled the mound, rubbing the ball firmly as I stared at Denkinger. The game was on the line and the runner at second would be going with the pitch if this were a game during real play, so I ignored the phantom runner, glancing back just once before setting for the wind-up. It was here that I realized my flaw. With a man on second, I would have been working from the stretch, not the wind-up. My concentration wavered.

198

Shake it off, Kid. No one took notice. It is only a scouting report they are working from. I took one long and deep breath and wound-up. The grip was wrong, my head had been jammed, perhaps my feet weren't planted. Whatever the reason, I tossed up a lollipop and it sailed into Denkinger's carnival like a hot-air balloon – so slow and open that Denks envisioned it landing out in the left field bleachers before he even swung. And swing he did. The ball reverberated off the bat with a sharp pang that sounded more like an aluminum bat used in high school or college. It was that soft and just fast enough to be launched forcefully opposite the direction from whence it had come.

I remained poised and circled the mound, watching with respect as the ball soared into the stands. The irony of the home run came crashing upon me. It is great to watch the solid object of white sail out over the fence, yet how bitter it drips inside your memory as the pitch you should never have thrown. Inside I was seething but on the surface, a consummate professional. I scanned the bench to find Murray, the Owls' coach. The signal went up. One more batter and my turn was through.

It went by so quickly, that I swear it felt like I had never tossed the next pitch. It was to Oliver, the free-swinging pull hitter who hit for average, had minimal power and could not see a pitch if it was played on a movie screen to discern between a curve or a slider. Still, he jumped on my first offering and wounded a would-be triple into the corner.

The crowd resumed its chatter and I strode off the mound, certain of failure. *Well, Kid, you rode it awhile then lost composure when you offered up junk.* Either way, they had seen what I was made of and they knew I had some serious stuff. I would probably be offered an invite next spring and be given the suggestion to work on technique. More likely, I'd be told to stick to second base.

I searched the crowd and I saw no sign of Kevin. How could he have blown this off? Here I had a legitimate chance, as much as anyone, to land a contract with the Owls and my best friend was nowhere to be found.

"Tough break, kid," a man whom I had never seen before but assumed was a scout, offered as condolences.

"Thanks, mister. Maybe next time, huh?"

"Hey, you got some stuff in that arm. Keep at it and you'll be there."

I hadn't the energy or the mind set to fantasize that I had just been promised a trip to the Big Leagues someday. I had work to do. There were still athletic skills trials involving throwing, catching and base-running that I needed to prepare for.

"Hey! Augie!" A familiar voice called to me as I was half-way to the bench. I turned to see Denkinger on the dugout steps. "Good pitching out there."

"Ya think so?"

"Hell, yes. You fooled me with the slow-up shit to start. Sorry I had to blast one on you."

"No worry, man. A game's a game."

"Yeah, business is business, hey?"

"Yep." I dropped my glove on the bench. Dejected, though focused, I tried keeping it all in perspective, but that was difficult. I kept my head high and unlaced the glove with defiance, staring out onto the field as another victim took the mound. "Hey, Denks?"

"Yeah, Kid. What is it?"

"Why'd ya come up on the right side of the plate?"

"Because you're that good."

"Not really. You crushed me."

Denkinger spun his bulky frame around and bounded down the steps, sliding in next to me. I admit I was a little bewildered. "Listen, kid. You are a decent pitcher, but with your brain and the conditioning you've done you can go beyond Cooperstown. Sure, I might have slowed ya down a step by wailing one outta here today. But this was all about show. If I had gone up there left-handed, as any batter would in a game situation, you would have railed through me like a freight train. Understand?"

"I think so. But –"

"But nothing. Getting on the Owls right now is too much too soon. I know you don't want to hear that from me, a washed up has-been who can't make the jump to the Big Leagues. But believe me, you made those guys take notice of you out there. They saw the way you approached a tough situation. Everyone out there knows I should have been up there swinging lefty. But you came at me anyway. And you threw good, real good."

The point lingered, somewhat lost on old August here. I swam under a muddled mixture of confusion and anger as the big dumb Irish face looked in at me from under his ball cap pulled down too far over his eyes.

"Listen. If you go out there today and land a spot on the Owls, you lose a winter and half of next spring to fully develop. I've seen it so many times, kid. And I like you. You're a great guy with a huge heart and you will play pro ball. I guarantee it. But you don't even know yet just how young you are. What are you, nineteen?" I responded with only a nod. "Hell, Monroe. By the time I was seventeen, my career was over. I got invited to spring training with the Twins and never made the cut. Wanna know why? Because they pushed me so fast that I never matured, as a player or as a man. Development, that is what separates the pros from us yahoos. I tell you, I was the cockiest son-of-a bitch to ever pull on a spring training warm-up suit. I was so blindsided when they cut me, I just reeled for a year. I had no idea what to do. I loafed through school, had nothing for an education. I joined the Owls because no one else would take me. I owe my life to Murray over there. Sure, I enjoy it and I play pretty well, earn a living and all. But it ain't nothing compared to what I could have been. With your potential and one, maybe two more years of learning, watching the game the way you do, you'll make it. I promise you and your whole family you will be a major leaguer, some day. No doubt in my mind."

"So you're saying you did me a favor tonight?"

"Yeah, I did, kid. I really did. Think about it. You're smart. You know this game better than anyone I have ever played with. Hell, you're smarter than some managers I've played for. Just hang in there, you'll make it." His lunging face didn't appear so dumb anymore as the wisdom of experience registered. "Listen, bud. I gotta go. I'll catch ya around the park, okay pard'ner?"

"Yeah, Denks. Sure." I heard the clatter of Denkinger's spikes fade off down the concrete walkway to the locker room and, while gazing out upon the greens and browns and whites that make up a baseball diamond, I considered just how wise Denks might have been.

I crossed to the water fountain and lapped up some refreshment. Taped to the wall above the fountain was the evening's schedule of events, listing each player and when or where his try-out would be held. Running a finger along the list for fielding events I located a name. And without so much as a hesitation, I lifted the grease pencil that hung on a string beside the schedule and ran a thick solid line of black through one name on the roster: Monroe, August.

I replaced the pencil slowly, such that gravity did not even bounce it once on its tethered string, where it hung motionless without rotation, like a solid knuckleball. I backed away from the fountain and the roster, turned toward the steps and up out of the dugout.

20 Above Ourselves

Coming off the field, I spotted my friend, Jeff Anderson, high in the upper bleachers, sitting woefully unmoving against the gray and green aluminum that surrounded him. His outing had not been much better than mine. He struck out only one hitter and gave up an array of base hits as if he was handing out free water to runners at a marathon. None of us had good performances that night, not even Kevin. While the try-out was not Kevin's best outing, he had room for error as a pitcher whereas Jeff and I had none. The scouts had seen Kevin pitch previously in high school games all across the county, and they knew his precision was tight and his understanding of the game intimate. Me, they hardly knew. Jeff, they didn't even consider. He was just having fun, but it seemed that at only eighteen years of age he had resigned himself to a life as a businessman or a carpenter and not a ballplayer. Kevin, though, would land on his feet; he would always be a pitcher.

I climbed to the top row of bleachers in the grandstand behind home plate to sit with Anderson. It wasn't so far that I was in another stratosphere but removed enough that solace was our companion. The smell of hot dogs still lingered somewhere in the air and the hum of the high-energy lights buzzed to a dull faded murmur. The fans had treated the event as if a real ball game had been played, the excitement just as intense. To me, it felt like failure.

I wanted to be as far away from the pitcher's mound as one could get without climbing onto the roof and disappearing over the stars. If I was not to be a pitcher, I would still play ball. But at that moment, the reality that I wasn't good enough set in like a frying egg...you only have a few seconds to get it just right, and my seconds had passed.

My legs ached as I reached the top, muscles straining for fresh blood as tendons confessed a lack of physical endurance. Maybe I wasn't cut out to be a ballplayer after all. Legging out a triple would tax my energy. I made a mental note to improve my sprinting. Luckily, I wasn't projected as an outfielder. The infield with its short strides, quick reactions and hard pivots was better than beating the grass in fast pursuit of long outs.

Cooperstown twinkled beyond the short outfield seats ahead of me, and I took the perspective of Argus, the Greek god who oversaw all things far and near. From my vantage point I could see my future as close as I could see the parking lot. Beneath me lay hope and dreams, and above the wide stretch of the universe encompassing all the countless possibilities of what might become of my life. Below was the baseball park, not just the field but the entire park, the very canvas on which I would map out my life and career. Would it be as a Picasso, turning daring angular feats of athleticism at second base? Possibly. Or would Bach be my guide, as I concisely honed note upon note in pitching concertos that would bring audiences to their feet while I intricately weaved my way through an opponent's line-up? Probably not after the evening's outcome. Perhaps Christopher Wren would be my nickname as I managed a team with structure and discipline all the while the architect of a masterful line-up utilized to bring out the best in the internal elements of each cornice and foundation of the team. Maybe someday. I'd like that, it has a nice ring to it: August Wilson Monroe, Manager. Yeah. That's good. Perhaps Walter Cronkite, a classic orator of the spoken tradition parlaying the sights and sounds of the game to a faceless audience spread out across the globe with ears tuned to radio stations as I called game seven of the ill-fated 1994 World Series. From where did that thought arise? If I had anything to do with the 1994 World Series, surely I had better be playing in it! I harkened back to that baseball dream I had had as a kid, and to the baseballs in the tent. So much life had passed, yet nothing connected those childhood hopes to reality.

And what of Kevin? He had become an enigma. While we were on one level best friends, we were growing further from friendship with each passing day. He was at once moody and brooding and at the next withdrawn and serious. Perhaps he was beginning to take strength in focusing toward his major league aspirations and wanted nothing in the way to dwarf his plans. I knew with greater conviction than my own hopes that he was bound for the Majors, and telling him such never seemed to matter to him. Besides, we still hadn't seen much of him. I had hoped to speak with him after try-outs, but as of yet he had not said much.

I stared across the field as fans and players and scouts dispersed into the waning evening. They disappeared below me in huddled, chattering masses, their conversations unheard amidst the milieu of fading activity. Out beyond the left field wall, a trail of brake lights and truncated headlight beams inched along the parking lot as weary drivers made their way home. The sweepers were busy with their cleaning duty and soon the ushers would be asking that we move along.

"From way up here, it hardly resembles a game," I said.

"Yeah, it is just a game, I guess," Jeff answered.

"Hey, you did alright, man," I said. The encouragement did little to raise his daunted spirit. "You gave it your best."

The response was null. The night levitated before us in a hesitant gap between altitude and groundswell. My head felt woozy, somewhere in limbo between a dizzy fall and restful plodding. Integral to the unnatural mixture of steep stairs and solid steel that makes a ballpark rise in its majestic glamour into the skyline, is the imbalance inherent in structure. A sway drags it along in playful, daring (even a tad nerve wracking) vertigo as it holds upon its shoulders the soft human creatures supported above the Earth and into the sky. The silence fell away as a voice shot through the air.

"Game's in the sixth inning. Two runners on and the pitcher is up. You're on the road with the score tied. Do you yank your starting pitcher for a pinch hitter?" The voice came from beneath us and reached my ears with surprise. Both Jeff and I flinched at the sudden sound. It sounded like Kevin, but neither of us had seen him for two days or more. I looked behind us to find the voice. We sat in the very last row of the stadium but the voice had come from somewhere behind, from somewhere up out beyond the sky. I recognized the trick.

"Bentworth. He's throwing his voice," I declared. "It's got to be him. He always does that. It's a trick I've seen before. He's around here somewhere."

He appeared below and stepped onto the landing at the entry way to the vending areas. His long black coat, an ambivalent shawl strikingly out of place against the surrounding light that welcomed the fans, swooshed at his heels. He locked his thumbs onto his belt like a cowboy en route to a showdown.

"What's up, boys?" he asked with a Cockney swagger. "What's a couple of young 'ens like you doing way up here? You aren't pouting, are ya?"

"Kevin," Jeff said. "Where have you been, man? We were beginning to wonder if you hadn't offed yourself."

"Well, after tonight's performance, I just might consider that option."

I asked, "What gives? We were worried when we hadn't heard from you."

204

"Luke, my fine friend, you ought to know me better. A true Han Solo rides alone but never in despair. Let's just say I was casing the joint."

"What joint?" Jeff asked.

"Why the old ballpark, my good man." He strode down to the lower section of seats and leaned against the outer most rail of the top level, speaking more to the mass emptiness around him than to us his friends. "The old ballpark," he repeated sardonically. "The Panorama of America. A practical landscape of idealism where each spring every hope is filled with youth and every chance is sprung anew. A true warrior never strays far from home, boys. Yes, I've been here. You just haven't had the skill."

"The skill to what?" asked an irritated Jeff.

"The skill to find me. I watched it all. Young August there hurling such bravado at Denkinger and showing such poise in the face of defeat. Disappointing and lackluster Jeff, absent the creativity to wow an audience, out there tossing absolutely lousy stuff."

"Hey, why don't you cool it, hot-shot?" Jeff argued.

Kevin shrugged. "Me? Cool it. Cool what? I didn't go out there and blow the biggest opportunity of my life, Jeffery."

Jeff lunged down the steps at him and threw a heavy shoulder across the unsuspecting defender's upper chest. Kevin bent backwards over the railing, where he gasped for air.

"Who's the hot-shot now, Kevin?" Jeff threatened.

"Stop it. Come on, let him up," I begged.

"Han Solo ain't so tough, is he August?" Jeff argued.

"I don't know and I don't care. Just let him up," I pleaded.

Kevin shifted his head left and right, still upside down, as if he searched the ground hoping that someone would look up and tell us to stop before someone (obviously Kevin) got hurt. His head bobbed against gravity and his legs planted hard to the concrete floor. A hand swung violently reaching for the railing. Jeff released his hold and pulled him dizzyingly into an upright position.

Kevin gained his balance. "What the fuck is your problem, jerk-off!" He screamed.

"Me?" Jeff threatened. "No, pal. You got some nerve. Disappearing just before your friend needs you around, someone who might have gone over scenarios with him or coach him just once more on the basics. But no, you take off like some child."

"Hey, it's cool," I offered in a vain attempt to calm the heated argument.

205

"No. It's not cool, Monroe," Jeff answered. "It's not cool at all."

"What's your problem?" Kevin yelled. "You could have killed me, you pompous jack-ass." Kevin stood still a moment and then ran a hand through his hair. "Fuck it," he said. He stated to walk off and then paused. "You know," he added, turning around. "Yeah, I could have helped out but I was outta here for a reason. August didn't need me around to screw him up, just like I did to my old man. I am a curse, man. Anytime something good happens to someone around me, they lose it in the end and it's always my fault. My mom did, my dad did, and I wasn't gonna stick around to see if Augie did, too."

A rage boiled inside of me. "Is that what this is about?" I said. "You think this is about you? And some made up curse in your mind? Man, you are wrong. Dead wrong. I blew it, okay? I got myself here and I am the one who threw the wrong pitches. I made those decisions. Not you. And even if you were here or in another corner of the globe, the result would have been the same."

We cut into expressions and emotions we had never felt. It was filled with the adrenaline of youth wherein anger, misguided as it may have been, ruled the mind and directed our actions. We had never fought before, and while Kevin and I had been friends the longest, it was not easy to side against Jeff. This was each man for himself. An entire year of frustrations came boiling over all at once and the three of us hashed and hammered our feelings into words we would someday regret.

"Kevin," I told him, "If you don't get it together, you will never be a pro ball player."

"Screw, you, Monroe. What do you know?"

"I'll tell ya what I know. I know you are good enough to make the Majors and damn good enough to stay there. But you gotta keep your head on. It ain't gonna happen with you treating people the way you do."

"Listen, Monroe!" Kevin hollered. "You don't know shit, okay? You've got it all down pat, don't you? Your life is just fucking perfect, isn't it? Mommy and daddy love you and you can do no wrong. Well not everyone has it so good. So just give up trying to solve problems for the rest of us, okay? Nobody gives a damn about your little hitting streak anymore or your little games of 'I wanna be manager someday so I am gonna kiss Murray's ass.' And, most of all, quit digging around in other people's past, okay! You're nothing but a bother, a regular nuisance. Do you have any idea what you did to my dad? Not to mention the fact that I am trying to get a few things done to make it in this lousy game, asshole."

Jeff interjected comments intended to slow us down, but which only stirred our anger. Why he had suddenly become the voice of reason only moments after nearly killing Kevin was beyond my ability to analyze.

"Guys, come on. It's just a freaking game. Relax, okay."

"No," I insisted, "this isn't about a game. This is about friendship. And I see where it stands between myself and Kevin. So, what's it gonna be, Kev? Huh? We've got some things to iron out here. Let's hear an excuse or a famous one-liner. Come on. You're the king of comedy. Make me laugh. Ease the tension, smart ass."

In an action I never saw coming, Kevin reeled back and unleashed a solid thump right across my jaw, sending me spinning slightly to my right. He punched me! What the hell was that all about? We had never raised a hand in anger toward anyone, yet alone each other. I had only a moment to consider what my response would be, but I knew in my heart it had already been decided. I have never been a fighter, and I wasn't about to become one then. I straightened up and rubbed my jaw. I stared Kevin deep in the eyes to see if I could make some sense of his anger, and then strode silently and angrily away.

Jeff restrained him from pursuing me further. I heard Kevin say behind me, "Augie, come on. I didn't mean to do that. Come back, will ya? We can talk. I don't know what I'm doing. I just..." Had he apologized, I may have stopped and turned around. The word "sorry" was not heard, if it was uttered I was too far away to hear it.

I headed out of the park, climbed into my car and made the worst decision of my life.

21 The Last Ride

The timeliness came together with striking jurisprudence. Three months after Grandpa's funeral, on the same day that Granmah-ma and Grandpa would have celebrated their 50th wedding anniversary, I went on a hunting trip and killed a deer. Exactly six months later, I took a ride in my car. It has come to be, quite simply, the ride that changed everything, unequivocally, from what I had known before.

I sped off to cool down after the argument with Kevin. Rather than take the direct route through town and home in less than ten minutes to a warm dinner and a quiet evening, I opted to go for a ride. A ride that would intersect with more destiny than I could steer through, and a short voyage into the very definition of my life.

The evening approached with a heavy chill that late winter day, and the hefty blue-yellow sky balanced either a storm in the offing or a stretch into calmer climes. It was difficult to judge which way the weather would shift, and it seemed as if the clouds rolled toward the former in dark and heavy spirals just as I turned left onto Route 210. Had I turned right, I wonder how different my life would have been.

At the junction of Route 210 and Museum Drive sits a "T" intersection, and making the right provides a direct path homeward. Taking a left sends one off via a circuitous journey through the great countryside. A blueish-gold light bounced through the last of the early evening sky, and I figured I had time to loop around Lormay State Park before heading home for the night. Without so much as a hesitation of forethought, I accelerated into the road and turned west by northwest onto Route 210, bypassed Creek Road, and into Cotter County. Had I heard the specter of fate whispering to me from the backseat, I might have flipped a U-Turn immediately and returned home to safety. But not that evening.

Two miles inside Lormay State Park, I headed toward Roth College; it was only an extra half-hour, one full hour longer considering the round trip, so I cut through the mid-section of the park and headed for campus. That part of the lake houses the lesser side of those who use the lake for society's events. Across the lake, between the peninsula and the dam, sits lofty summer homes of doctors and professors, a few lawyers and independent businessmen who always seemed to have beautiful, chatty women on their piers; women who waved with a sauntering gyration of the hips each summer as I or any other stranger slid by on a speed boat or pontoon. Little did they know that by blowing our whistles in greeting, we were mocking their superior society, their summers at ease, and perhaps, just a little, enjoying harmless flirtation. Maybe they enjoyed the attention. But that was the other side of the lake.

My side, where I drove and where we rented or borrowed cottage space for weekends, is a different sort of world. To the left are the bungalows and shanties that would occupy much of the summer activities. Every weekend there would be cookouts and family gatherings, volleyball and sunburn, water skiing and general summer lounging. But not that day. On that day, boarded up and isolated for winter's hibernation, the cottages appeared to be asleep. No life bustled in nor around the shacks, and not a person was near.

To my right, the great expanse of Lormay Lake, a manmade body far too large for the small communities that surround it and a rather audacious testimony to man's progress. The lake is quite remote and stands as the primary water supply between two counties, yet far away from the prime fishing resorts of Poughkeepsie, Chincoteague and others. Still, it's a peaceful place, and the well-kept, quiet lake is often an escape for families who live in the city or out on Long Island. Their summer retreats, vanquished and clapboarded, were my only company as I sped through the causeway and viewed the lake opening up on both sides west of the short row of modest summer homes.

Had I been more alert, I might have noticed how far the water had risen upon the causeway. Even for late March, the road surface was yielding ground to the waterway. All along the brim of the blacktop, two-lane road, a spritz of water glistened in the waning day. The lake had thawed considerably after a warm month and the sun had melted the surface of the lake – just enough for water to spill onto the roadway, en route to its ceaseless direction toward a sea-level home.

There were warnings. The empty stretch of gravel and cinder, loose asphalt and soft dirt, where orange rope was lined up to warn drivers of the missing stretch of guardrail. The miniscule spurts of water jetting out onto the roadway. The swirling ripples of water pushing back and forth, undulating under the stiff breeze. The clouds hanging leery over the lake, promising snow, harder winds and a chilly night. The simple hum of the tires as they alerted to the element of chance ever present in the roadway. The rubber skidding gently off and back onto dry pavement as I ascended north by northwestward along the high end of the lake, a mere ten miles from Roth College.

I don't even know what I was planning to do once I got to Roth. No one I knew would be on the campus. It was just a destination, the ride its greater purpose.

I arrived at Roth yet had no real reason to be there. Maybe my *reason* for going was not in arriving, but in what would occur upon returning. If so, then it all becomes perfectly clear. As clear as the fabled black ice that was forming along the lakeshore when I ended my walk around campus and climbed into my car, turning back onto the same road I had just left.

The campus disappeared into and beyond my rearview mirror moments after leaving Carter Hall. The road was primarily isolated for the entire trip except for one blue, two-tone Dodge pick-up truck that headed north by northwest on the direction I had just been traveling as I was heading toward home, traversing south by southeast. I recall that pick-up so clearly now, perhaps as an omen or just another reminder of how simply I was overlooking everything obvious. As the truck approached, its headlights were turned on by an unseen driver, then flicked off and on again in quick repetition. The night was overtaking the horizon, and with clouds sprawled across the sky the addition of headlights was not an illogical choice. I only paused a moment to consider why the driver had flicked the lights off and then on again, only to repeat the same once more for the briefest moment. In that moment I made up about 200 feet of blacktop and was already approaching the entrance to the causeway.

On land, a few feet back from the road and just before the causeway assumed the shore, where dead grass had hidden all winter, a pack of deer nibbled at the tiny strains of leftover grass or wheat or dandelion stems in their hopeful scavenge. They certainly did not look hungry for want of food. They were solid, grazing silently in the creeping evening where little noise disturbed them and even fewer intrusions interrupted their peaceful, daily feeding. As the thought of the truck's peculiar headlight actions wore away, I approached a determined, though hardly sharp, bend in the road that swung back along the edge of the causeway, just minutes from the row of homes sitting vacant and cold in their winter stillness.

How often I have relived these tiny moments in my consciousness. The slow motion effect of aftershock has planted

210

this vision into my mind like a film reel that is always cued precisely at that moment when I looked into the eye of the largest deer.

It suddenly occurred to me that the Dodge driver was reminding me that my headlights should be on. Of course! What a fool I was. It was growing dark. The causeway and ensuing loop through the park would be unlit. The courteous driver was offering aide: *Turn your lights on, buddy!* She or he seemed to offer. Though it wasn't just a reminder, it was a warning.

I approached the bend in the road and eased up on the gas, barely noticeable but enough to slow the tires as I reached for the headlights. I pulled the knob out and the dashboard lighted in a soft green glow. The headlights ignited like lightning, a vision that is reduced to an electrifying crawl when I play it over and over again, and caught the eyesight of the middle- sized of the three deer to the right, near the orange barricade. The deer froze, solid and sure, as did the fawn nearby. But their counterpart, the largest of the three, sensed danger and bolted in front of them both. In a stance of defiance, of protection, he stood. There wasn't enough land between the edge of grass and the start of gravel for the deer to stand, nor for me to steer the car out of the way. His front legs held the bed of the roadway, gravel beneath his hooves. As quickly as the deer sprung into the road, I looked away from its vision-locked partner and saw that he was about to be hit head on by my speeding vehicle. That was when I instantaneously forgot everything they tell you in driver's education class, as well as everything Grandpa and dad had gone over time and time again.

I hit the brakes hard and cut the wheel sharply. In that flashing instant, I hadn't the wherewithal to consider that the deer had no further intention of moving; nor that it would remain still to protect its family and offspring, even if it meant taking the brunt of my hood into its bare chest. What I should have done is obvious. I should have simply swerved and cut the wheel slightly while easing off the accelerator. In that case I would have missed the deer entirely. Instead, I jerked the car hard and spiked the brakes. I squealed into a fishtail spin. I struggled to maintain control of my whirly-gig vehicle and heard a distinct thump.

I clipped the deer with my back end, despite my best effort to avoid the beast. I tried to straighten out but cut the wheel the other way and caught a solid slab of ice. The car spun one quarter of a turn back toward the road before it slid along the patch of ice

211

that only an hour earlier had been tiny ripples along a thawed shoreline.

The plunge was not the worst part. It was the immediate silence beforehand that haunts me still. For what must have been three to five seconds, the car slid across the lake's semi-frozen surface. The tires lost their grip as the icy vector glided me some twenty feet into the emptiness where I slid to a stop above the barely frozen water.

The sound of crystals cracking and strained ice splintering echoed through the air. I have walked on the middle of a frozen lake, and it feels like utter isolation, of peace, of clarity. It is as if being on the surface of a distant world, so calm, so chillingly unfamiliar. Yet there is no fear. In January, a lake is solid – not so come late March. And in that last moment, as I sat, unable to move, merely stunned and waiting, levitated between frozen lake and sheer oblivion, suspended only by a fragile veil of ice, I understood so clearly how I had missed all the signs that might have turned me away from the fate I was enduring. I fumbled to undo my seatbelt, and the cracking grew louder, more defiant as it reached into the empty sky. Shivers vibrated along the crest of all things living. I unhooked the belt and reached for the door just as the ice gave way beneath the weight of the car.

The force pushed downward. Pressure seized my body. My right leg wedged against the steering wheel and I heard another solid, frenzied crack. I plummeted along with the car, a piercing freeze stinging every ounce of bone and flesh in one stunning and exhilarating loss of oxygen and sense. I gasped one last heavy breath of bitterly chilled air. The car dissolved into the icy water.

The car broke through the ice. It was no match at all for the strength which winter freezes the lake surface. Had the water been shallower, had a drought crippled our land that previous summer, had I been going even five miles an hour slower... I would have brought the car to a complete stop and walked away. Had this, had that, had anything. Nothing was different. It was as it was and those circumstances brought about my near death.

I thought I was going to drown. I gave up at one moment, ensconced in the warm, pale envelope of sleepy death that lured me inward. It was a comfort I have never felt under any blanket nor with any woman. It was the lulling, breathless sensation of nothingness. The water warmed around me as my body drew numbness from the shock. My mind danced with visions of eternity in a pale blue frame of solitude. And memory evaporated through moments and milestones. Mid-way into death, between the lull of surrender and the grip of fear that had escaped me, it was the physical world that brought me back to my senses. Something scraped a pain into my leg. Endorphins awakened, or adrenaline or hormones or whatever the hell it was, reminded me that I was still alive.

I screamed a merciless yawp of agony into the blistering, unforgiving water. I can only assume that it was a rock or a branch or a leftover piece of garbage someone had heaved into the lake, maybe an anchor. I don't know. But moments before succumbing to silvery death, I was jolted alive by a sharp pain running the gauntlet through my pierced leg and up my spine, into the brain. The surge of feeling enlightened my soul and warned my senses that death was imminent if action was not taken.

The scream evaporated into the sheltering water. My throat and lungs swallowed icy crisp water that seethed into the roots of my teeth, burned the linings of my lungs desperate for air and tickled the depths of my stomach. All of this resounded with the declaration. *Push!* It was like an unborn baby leaving the womb, so ready to taste life. I thrust my tired, weary self upward for I knew that upward was home. I could still see a faint, fading swirl of starlight cascading upon the water above. How deep? I had no idea. How long would I have to push and swim? *Just go!* I told myself. *Swim! Goddamnit, swim!* I clamored up the ladder of murky blue and stinging freeze into a new, breath-filled air of survival.

Bursting through the surface, from my voice could be heard a mixed scream of agony and one solid word, *Help!*

The buoying back into the water was frightening, but it gave me resolve to swim onward, to live. I turned in an agonizing swirl to find the shoreline, and there it was. In sight! As close as third base to home. I must stretch the base paths and leave no runner stranded. I swam, never my strongest skill, into the sluicing wind, against the freezing current and found life earlier than had been surmised. There, not twenty feet, but less than five, was solid surface. It was ice, but it was life all the same.

I crawled out of my encompassing tomb and heard the whispered grunts and disappointments of death bidding farewell as it lost a would-be victim to the ever growing human spirit of survival.

I pleaded to the heavens in gratitude and hope for I was not out of danger yet. I slid, in what could not be considered even a crawl, across the slippery surface, so jagged and surreal when face-down upon its hard surface. I gathered scrapes and bleeding bruises as I inched my way along. The hindering weight of one leg broken behind me fought the useless fury of the other, unable to perform without its counterpart. But it too pushed and crawled as best it could, absent leverage, absent its customary upright strength. The knees and hips slithered my torso and head across the icy tarmac and finally my right hand reached out and touched home base, solid Earth. Frozen like dead winter and unyielding to the touch, but terra firma all the same.

22 Recovery

The accident left me pretty torn up. I was not to play baseball, that much was obvious. This thought alone might have shattered my spirit had not more pressing issues arisen. According to the doctors, walking itself may have been a future impossibility. There was no way I was going to lose the ability to walk.

While I lay at home, recovering, my right leg was in a cast and right arm in traction, supported above me to reduce swelling. I looked like one of those eighties rock stars who had smashed up a Ferrari while high on cocaine and whiskey. What a mess. A plum of a bruise swelled above my left eye and my left wrist was screwed together in two places. Fortunately, no internal organs had been damaged, otherwise I may never have been able to swim to my safety. What adrenaline pushed me through the water and forced unknowing muscles and bones to work in lifesaving harmony I may never know. But somehow I had enough parts working and suffered minimal enough pain, probably because the water was so damn cold, to swim to safety.

Besides recovering and contemplating the thought of whether or not I would walk again, I had school to consider. My grades were good enough that I could forego a semester without losing my registration status, though I would be graduating late, at least a semester behind Kevin and our classmates. The big problem came when I learned that my scholarship could not be honored. Under Roth College's guidelines, any athlete who did not continuously play his sport due to matters of personal nature, academic ineligibility or (and this is what killed my chances) an injury sustained while *not* playing the sport for which the scholarship had been granted, would thereby surrender his or her rights to said scholarship. I filed a petition, leaning on the mercy of the college. It was rejected and suddenly my college career was in jeopardy. Mom and dad could hardly afford to send me to college. But still, in light of the lingering doubt concerning my education, other matters came first.

Not being able to walk scared me unlike anything I had encountered in the darkest recesses of nightmare. Like all of my peers and the majority of the people on the planet, I took mobility for granted. Sure, I had seen amputees in church or disabled men and women hobbling through the mall, but it never occurred to me to think about their situation. That is the selfishness of having it good, I guess.

Rehabilitative therapy was to begin the day I could stand on the leg, which was two and a half months after the accident. Melony had shown me a true message of love and support when she moved to town to help me train and strengthen my leg. We had dated non-committedly but had promised to always be there for each other if something major had come up. What we faced that summer was something entirely new. Truth be told, she upheld that promise in a way in which I don't know if I could have at that time. She may have been my saving grace.

I did not want to be a burden to my mom and dad, they had their own lives to worry about. Certainly, they could not lose work if I expected them to help finance what remained of college. Melony was working for a bank in Buffalo and applied to be transferred to the Cooperstown branch. Her dream of working at Sea World wound up being nothing better than an internship wherein she was disheartened by the humiliation of feeding fish to dolphins while crowds laughed at the porpoises' antics. Humbled but happy, she fell back on her credentials as an accountant and took employment at the bank. When I heard news of her transfer being granted, I saw the light of recovery for the first time. Maybe things would work out okay.

Diligently, she worked each day at the bank and came to the house to help me get dinner together. Never did she waver in her ability to remain positive, and the sources from which she drew her energy were neither exhaustive nor apparent. It somehow just sprung from within her, very much the way I envision a mother deeply loving the fetus within her womb long before a name is given or a personality explored. It was that sincere and constant. I was able to get around in a wheel chair after about six weeks and we had a combined task and fun maneuvering that clump of steel around the house – a house that had suddenly become a lot smaller. We even tried making love in the wheelchair. Not a good idea. Melony bruised her knees trying to find the right way to climb atop me and the idea was scrapped quickly.

At seven PM each night, we headed to the rehabilitation institute near the high school. There I tripped and stumbled, cringed and ached, first on walking parallel bars above a mat and then slowly and stiffly upon two wobbling crutches dug tightly into my armpits. Each day I felt a little stronger, but each night a lot more tired. The soreness spread across my body like a farmer overtaking a yielding meadow with a bulldozing tractor. Every time I reached exhaustion, Melony brought me back to the rehab rooms, pushed me a little further than I had gone the day before and found within me the strength to persevere.

Medically speaking, the thing that aided me in my recovery most was that I had not developed an infection in any of the wounded areas. This facilitated the rebuilding of muscle tissue faster and more naturally. Spiritually, what kept me going was Melony. Even though I told myself I would walk again, I often wavered between absolute resolve and dejected surrender. She refused to tolerate that. The greatest gift she gave me, along with an occasional kick in the ass of motivation, was her love and support. Five weeks into recovery she gave me a more tangible gift that still inspires and is a single reminder of what it took to get me through.

Melony was not one for sappy metaphor or highly charged "up with life" anthems. She was practical and somewhat stern in her ability to inspire. Determined and earthy, she saw reality for what it was, and typically would not get caught up in lilty praise, happy speculation or overstuffed hype. It was a song that she had found that kept us both going. That was the gift I received. She played the song for me the day after I had broken a crutch in frustration while trying to walk.

I had gotten to the point where I could walk five or six steps on the crutches, and each step was a grueling, pulsating reverberation of agony. The pain rebounded down the leg, ran through the ankle and across the foot like a steady warm oil pouring into my shoe. The return flow of pain back up the leg was worse. Against gravity it struck at every nerve in a skipping, twitching, scratching roll upwards into the knee and headstrong lunge across the thigh where it died in a silent, lethargic thud. Of the six steps I could manage at that time, numbers four through six where intolerable, and I could no longer shuffle the limp and clogging leg further. When the second week in month five of my rehab had begun, I stated that I would get to step ten that week. Perhaps I pushed it too far, but it seemed so reachable. It was only four more steps! I had counted how effortlessly Melony strode in twenty, thirty steps back and forth to our bags or to the vending machines, that it seemed not only possible but obviously attainable. Hell, only five months before I was walking hundreds of steps without a twinge of discomfort, without even considering that the number of steps taken even mattered. And now, I was a listless, immobile threat to gravity. For surely after five excruciating paces I was certain to collapse into a floor-bound heap writhing in pain.

"I can't do this anymore," I had screamed aloud across the busy rehab center. Eyes of patients, some with less severe inconveniences and some who could barely lift their eyes to see a dot on a color wheel, turned in my direction. I leaned against the heavy railing of the parallel walker and an anger rose up from within me in an almost uncontrollable rage. I pulled the crutch from under my right arm and got off two or three solid whacks at the railing before an assistant and Melony got to my side to stop the tirade. I had splintered the crutch into three pieces.

The aide remained calm. "Sir, you'd better watch that hand of yours. It isn't fully healed yet," he reminded me. I turned my left hand over and gazed at it sheepishly and quickly realized I could have separated the bone again, or worse, could have severed a tendon in the frail and healing hand.

"Oh, who gives a shit," I yelled. I thrust my own hand away from my eyes. "I can't walk, what's the sense of ever being able to dial a phone again or scratch my god damn head again? These are just parts, I don't care about them." I struggled to regain composure, took in a short breath, and said, "Fuck it." I limped from the walker and fell into the wheelchair. "It's no use. Melony, get me out of here."

However many apologies I offered, she would accept none. It's not that she refused forgiveness. No, hardly. She wasn't even mad. In the face of my self-defeat, when I had given up on myself and was ready to walk away to allow frustration to have the best of me, she found simple wisdom in my ordeal. "You have the right to be angry," she said. "It's not my place to be angry. Just don't let your anger get in the way of determination."

The next day, she brought home a new CD she had just picked up. It was a greatest hits compilation from Stevie Nicks, the former singer from Fleetwood Mac; and what a gift it would come to be. As she unwrapped the tight cellophane packaging, I researched my memory to find what song she could possibly consider as appropriate for this time in my life or hers. I had always liked Stevie's music, but saw nothing from her anthology that could prove inspiring or forgiving. Perhaps it was a love song, a broken-hearted melody to remind me that Melony and I were in this together. After all, heartache was perhaps what Stevie Nicks knew best.

"It's a new song," Melony stated.

"How could a new song be on a greatest hits CD?"

"Just listen, would ya? I heard this song called, 'Sometimes it's a Bitch,' on the radio last night. The timing is perfect."

As the song began, a series of compelling and anthem-like feelings fluttered in my spirit. From the very first note, the song evoked a subtle yet forceful statement of perseverance. The music was driving, yet passionate; determined, yet pensive. And the beat, powerful without too much force, drove the song into its opening verse.

It was clear that Melony had found a message of hope to guide me in my determination to struggle through. And it wasn't a happy-go-lucky, get-back-on-your-feet-and-dance song that may have turned me away with a cynical sneer. It was a song of hard knocks, of a road traveled by harsh and enduring standards – standards I could only begin to appreciate in my new experiences. It was also a song of hope, an absolute demand that getting through the worst of things could and will make a person better, stronger. Stevie Nicks had felt the pain of a life filled with turmoil, mistakes and decisions that others may have regretted, but not her – not if that song was any indication. Instead, those regrets were turned full sideways into lessons and teachings she imparted to me through her aging voice, still pure and elusive, yet gripping in its confrontation with a harsh reality.

While full of the simple truth of seeing both sides of happiness and despair, the lines pronounced that we are better not for our experience but for our endurance. It has become a sort of personal creed, a litany that I turn to in wavering times in order that I might find strength and to keep my perspective properly focused.

While that certainly wasn't all it took to get me to walk, it brought me back into a mindset more positive than the day before. I had a lot of work to do. And the only thing that would ultimately decide for me whether or not I would ever walk again was myself. I hadn't within me the single determination to do it alone. I needed Melony and her inspiration, in ways directly by her presence and indirectly through that song. The will I had espoused when recovery began had run dry like an infertile drought, but love and trust and encouragement replenished a parched determination. I would get through this, with a little help from Melony and a woman I had never met who sang like a veteran songbird.

Slowly my confidence returned and my progress increased. I tried walking without the crutches and absent a mat that would catch my fall should I lose balance. It was May 18, 1991. Ten steps is a victory when you feel like your mobility will be gone forever. I swung my right leg under the weight of the crutches and skipped the first six bumbling steps across the floor with no padding beneath. I paused, searched the open floor beneath and stepped a seventh time. Then the eighth and ninth, which was tiring but not defeating. Ten was one step away – the first of what would be many slow and steady victories during the ensuing months. With my weight shifting left as numbness trickled down the right leg, I managed to sludge forward a full step. Ten! I had met my first goal. It was a good thing I had only set that initial goal at ten because my leg weakened and the eleventh step would have been a test to my endurance. Melony greeted me with a hug that sent me sprawling backwards.

"I think I'll stick to that mat for a while," I laughed while rubbing a tender bruise on my backside.

"Oh, my God. I am so sorry, honey."

"It's okay, really," I said. I pulled myself up and reset my weight again upon the crutches. We embraced. I said, "I love you."

"You do?" she asked, surprised.

"Yeah, of course. Why? Haven't I told you enough?"

"You haven't told me once," she said.

"What? No way," I countered. I tried to recall whether I had ever done so. "Yes, I have," I think I may have lied. "Or if I hadn't I always meant to."

"August, a woman knows when a man says he loves her for the first time. Believe me, this is the first time."

"Am I in trouble?" I pleaded.

"Nope. I still feel too sorry for you to be mad, but watch it," she warned, jokingly.

"What about you? Do you, uh, you know, uh, love me too?" I stammered through the sentence with less agility than my first steps off the crutches.

She backed away and walked off to gather our things. "I don't know," she winked. "I'll have to think about that a while."

I don't know about her, but I felt like the road back wouldn't be all that long. My physical therapist.

As a reward, the doctor gave me the rest of the week off from rehab. He said resting the leg for two days would be just as good as conditioning. Beware, though, I was told, it might be stiff again come Saturday morning's exercise. I liked the pool therapy. It was less strenuous and more enjoyable with equal if not better results. I've always loved the water and was a natural swimmer. Good thing, considering I may have drowned in that lake. Getting back into any water, especially warm water, after the accident was like getting back on the horse. Had I waited until the leg was recovered, a trip to a pool may have been terrifying.

On Thursday of that week, the first of two days to do what I wanted after Melony got home, she suggested we go to the Hall of Fame. I hadn't seen it in a while and perhaps it would boost my spirit to surround myself with the game for a while. Surprisingly, no one else was interested in going. All of our friends were either off at school or busy working. Melony took a vacation day and we headed off to what used to be my favorite place in all the world.

Somehow the Hall seemed smaller that day, less important than when I had seen it last. But the space itself seemed larger, more cumbersome with plenty of corners to navigate the crutches around and tight rooms to squeeze into and out of between rests. The bathroom was a near impossibility bordering on embarrassment as I lumbered in with what must have appeared as a drunken stumble, limping hard after a half day on my feet. While in line for lunch, I felt a tingle drip down the leg. Resting for a long bite to eat and a refreshing Pepsi eased the pressure and I was ready for the afternoon.

"What site do you want to see next?" Melony asked.

"Yeah know, I'd really like to see the baseball card exhibit. That was often one of my favorite wings."

A separate wing had been added to the Hall of Fame in 1989 to showcase a unique facet of the baseball world. The trading card. While all sports eventually adopted the practice of printing and distributing cards that pictured each game's athletes, it was baseball that originated the idea as early as the 1890s. And it was baseball and its cards that captured the fancy of many boys (and some pretty cool girls) of the twentieth century. The Hall of Fame had decided to present their own representation of the hobby in a collection unequal to any shoebox stuffed with 1970 Topps cards. It was here that the years of our time pass by in style and depiction unlike anywhere else. The showcase is a veritable time capsule of style and memory, a panorama of our modern history. One can witness the evolution of baseball as it reflects the world of economics, of haircuts, of social trends, of expansion, of development, of new stadiums, of new teams, of new faces, even fashion styles from well the before 1920's and on through to today. Each year, as the cards changed they reflected the slow, constant turnover of America. From baseball's early years when innocence seemed so masked behind a black and white snapshot and up through nearly five decades of corruption and greed. On its way through history into the conservative and lean forties and the prosperous, sophomoric fifties made bleak and sensitive from World War II yet hopeful and safe with an eye toward the future, society marched onward. To the mid-fifties and into the early sixties when blacks entered the game and went on to capture the spirit of the times as social change exploded across the nation. Across the turbulent sixties as uncertainty plagued the country and all along the seventies wherein an unbridled, hedonistic lifestyle rode rampant through the mainstream, evoking consciousness and change. Burgeoning through the eighties' success as players escalated into millionaires and the face of American economics grew forward and further as world boundaries tumbled. And finally spilling over into the nineteen-nineties when the hobby itself took on its own skill as a trade, a full blown industry that would challenge its future by compromising its past. Lastly, to the day I stood there, taking in all that that one room encompassed. Almost a century and more of baseball cards, a reflection and remembrance of history. A grand collection indeed.

I had always tried to remain grounded about the beloved Hall of Fame. As a boy growing up, it was my haven, a spot for reflection and dreaming. As a teenager, it became my mentor. A periscope from which to witness baseball's greatest talents and discern what separated the 120 or so who had been inducted from the thousands of others who had played the game with far less accolades. It was there, in the wing of the Baseball Card Exhibit at the National Baseball Hall of Fame and Museum in Cooperstown, New York, USA, that I first realized I would never play baseball again.

For as much as I had aspired toward greatness, I had never considered myself lucky enough or good enough to someday be welcome into the Hall of Fame as an enshrined member. Had I played into my forties and retired after an illustrious career, I doubt I would ever have worried whether the Hall of Fame was in my future. That was history's decision. Or would have been. But the baseball card, and the symbolism it presents, was another story. Every player who suits up on the roster of a team for a portion of a season is issued a baseball card. Every player has at least one.

From the print factories in Duryea, Pennsylvania, to the candy racks of America, each man who has played the game at the professional level has a card which bears his resemblance. Before me was laid out the names upon names of players who would otherwise have never found their way into the Hall of Fame. Their accomplishments were no less significant, their efforts no less rewarding, their stories no less personal. But they hardly equaled the legacy and lore that the Hall represents in the names of Roberto Clemente or Rod Carew or Lou Brock and others. But everyone who played the game had a baseball card. Someday even Kevin Bentworth would be on a baseball card to be found when some kid sorted through his first pack, "Need it, got, need it, need it..." just as Kevin and I had done so many years before.

But not me. And it was there, standing somewhere between the cards of Hector Monpotose and David Monrow, that I realized one name would never stand the chance of being printed on a lousy slab of cardboard and shipped off to be stored on a thin shelf in the baseball card wing at the Hall of Fame. And that name was August Wilson Monroe.

My opportunity was gone, and baseball was over for me as a player. I pressed my nose to the glass and frosted the surface with a sobbing breath as the realization swam over me. All the months of frustration and fear came crashing into the realization that what was to have been my career, was over. Regardless of my recovery and whatever I would accomplish, the one dream I had possessed since childhood had been erased in one slippery motion of skidding tires and icy danger. The thought hit me like the force that had separated my leg from itself. I cried on and on, leaning hard against the glass that segregated my new reality from my past illusion. I was not sure who (if anyone) was watching and most certainly it didn't matter. I would be able to walk again and there was no small shame in that single reality. I was still alive, unlike others lost to similar or lesser accidents. I would have the opportunity to lead a normal, healthy, perfectly able life. All in all, that mattered more than anything. But still, in a quiet corner of the Hall on a dreary Thursday in May of 1991, my dream was rendered dead.

Within months, I was free of crutches and walking with only a noticeable limp. I was a clumsy, silly plodding fellow, but they were my feet under my legs carrying me. I think back to the doctor who had told me I might never walk again and wonder if he knew the competitive fire that burned inside my spirit when he warned of permanent paralysis. What if he had in actuality believed all along that I would walk, but knew that it could only happen if I believed it myself? It must have been a bit of reverse psychology he used to ensure that I would find my way through, otherwise he's just a good old-fashioned pessimist rendered hopeless by the facts of science. I hope in some way that he too has learned from my story. I like to think that he either continues telling people they will not walk when he damn well knows they can if they persevere; or he has begun telling people it can be done if he thinks they won't. Either way, he did me a favor. Tell me I won't walk and darn it if I ain't gonna prove him wrong! He gave me something to fight for, and that was one thing I had never had before. Had he simply said, "This will heal and you'll be up and around in no time," I may have never pressed on for that first step. But instead, I stood convinced that I would walk again, if only to prove him wrong. And in the end, I grew from the experience. It's not so easy to take these legs for granted any longer.

My injuries were quite minor in the grand scheme of things, except for the area above my right knee where the break had occurred. It would always be a weakened spot and possessed the risk of severing again if too much pressure were placed upon it with direct force. Swinging a bat was how the doctor defined too much pressure; running down a fly ball in the outfield was too much pressure; legging out an attempted triple was too much pressure. In short, I would not be able to play the game I dreamed of playing more than anything else. Baseball was too much pressure.

23 A First Time Fan

As a "fan" of the game, I realized there is no vantage point that compares to playing. Nothing could replace the view from the field to which I had become accustomed. It had been like standing among friends, everyone sharing in the moment and surrounding ourselves with a unified purpose, relying on each other to make the play or call the right pitch. No longer. Lost was the insider's viewpoint. No more was I to see the game at its base level. Aside from an occasional softball game or future Wiffle ball with my kids there would be no more baseball games of which I would partake.

Gradually, I began to appreciate the things I had overlooked before. In life, yes, but in baseball too. I had never quite figured out that a spring day crept so mindfully upwards as the Earth settled into winter's slumber and the bright fantastic day eloped to the sky for a brief interlude of warmth and passion. And then it would be gone so suddenly, left to drag on a few moments longer the next day. Until finally one day without even noticing, there you are sitting in the bleachers on a warm June evening at 9:00 PM and it is still as warm as summer can be.

I had been so wrapped up in practice, in routine, in perfecting a swing or memorizing scenarios for so long that I had lost sight of all that was not baseball, of all that life had to offer outside my game. Before long, my perspective took a full trip around the bases and landed me safely in the growth of change. As I began to contemplate the finer things in life, the simple things that make it such a joyous trip from birth to death, I gained yet another insight into the game I had thought made so much sense to me. How off-base I had been. Other players, better players, Kevin, Denkinger, even Murray, had a sense, an inner kinship to the game that I never seemed to possess. Despite my knowledge of, and love for, the game, I was missing an insight that I could not see from second base, but could only see from the outside while looking in. Theirs was more than the working knowledge that I had relied upon. It was an intrinsic connection to the inner fiber of the game's being, an integral link to its history – as if they were in fact meant to play that game, born to be baseball itself.

I was an outsider, glimpsing the game that I had thought would be my inner sanctum. In truth, I had missed it for what it truly is, just a game. A complex and paradoxically simple contest wherein members of society oppose one another peaceably, purposefully and with a cause no greater than a scored victory. How sad that our world could not ascend to such ranks and settle grander, more worldly conquests in such terms. If racism itself could be emancipated from the game, leading to other sports ushering the same and ultimately higher still to society as a whole, with baseball leading the charge, why then could not hatred, bigotry, prejudice be wiped clean from the bases for our game of life? Had we the skill and insight to skid around the basepaths, past ignorance, avoiding close-mindedness and slide into acceptance and worldliness, then why not hope that the world's problems, issues far larger than our own country's, can one day be solved by the intricate, compelling workings of a simple game?

I could see the patterns of the game begin to emerge, and could for once witness the symmetry unfurl. Baseball, in its choreographed, disciplined flux, in which each moment begins with pause and either lets loose with action or slows in repetition, became a representation of life itself. We each start from home and go on a quest to defeat those hurtling objects life tosses at us. We take chances, swinging into the wind at destiny or patiently awaiting walking fate. From home we depart, make our rounds, suffer our setbacks, stride round the world to all points far and near in successes both grand and inconsequential. But we always return home, in victory to touch home plate or in defeat where retreat leads to shelter. We settle into buildings that harbor us and where our friends and family await with joy or mockery or conceit or envy, perhaps even laugher if they sense the foibles from our journey. Yet each time we spring forth to defend that which is ours, to express ourselves through our talents or our smarts.

Occasionally while in the field we stumble over erroneous blunders, shine in spectacular defense or just hang around and wait for something to happen. But we must, I suppose if we are to go on living, participate. And each time, as one success leads to another chance, we trot back and forth between the two, taking our strides or positioning our attacks in an effort to gain the advantage. This grand metaphor for life had never kissed me with its wisdom before, but finally I saw it all in a way I had never appreciated.

Likewise, the literal watching of the game became altered while I misjudged fastballs for sliders and stolen base signals for bunt gestures. I was able to understand the positioning of the outfield, the strategy of the double steal and the highly underrated freedom of being able to holler, "That was a terrible call!"

From the stands, a whole new angle appeared, and from the press box later, the most incredible view of all came into focus. I was seeing what Bob Costas could see and what Vin Scully and Bob Prince witnessed. I saw the game from Jack Buck's seat and Phil Rizzuto's perspective. And what an incredible difference it makes to see the game from up there, up in the chilling air or the sweltering sun, instead of down there in the milieu of the play. And to be able to talk baseball! Endless reams of baseball stats and history rolled out before me, and I just spilled the stuff over into the unquestioning microphone like alcohol desires to numb its consumer. It was what I seemed born to do. All those days I had spent chattering with fans and players had prepared me for the day when I would no longer play the game, but would somehow need to understand it all the more.

What made the transition most difficult after my playing days were over was the passing of time from one game to the next with little else to do but try to figure out my life, or at least what I was going to do next.

And that is what I was to do once I could no longer play baseball.

Besides the more metaphorical things, it was also time that I got on with being a student. How mundane. In the middle of a four year degree, I was so unaware of all that college had to offer that I found it shameful I had squandered nearly two years focused solely on baseball. Aside from classes that steered me towards a new career, I learned how to appreciate education for what it is worth, to study not just to pass but to really understand.

24 Intersections

Nearly a decade had passed between the time of these events and the clarity of their significance, and somewhere in between I gained insight and perspective. By the summer of 1990, Kevin was one pitch away from the Major Leagues and I had been one minute from death. But it was a mere summer ten years earlier, an American season of parades, swimming pools, baseball games and the excitement of being outdoors that had laid the path to such understanding. By the end of that summer of 1980, I had a biographer's knowledge of Mr. Bentworth's past, including the one-armed man, and had successfully unraveled the mysterious riddled list. As well, I had convinced myself that the fateful tent master and his prognostications of destiny were mere hogwash. In reality, I was just too young to understand what had transpired and too inexperienced to know that such events held greater significance than I could have imagined.

The passing of 1989 into 1990 heralded the end of a strange decade, personally, socially and throughout the world of baseball. Cooperstown had undergone monumental alterations in the relatively short span of ten years, not the least of which was the completion of a new ballpark for the Owls. On a larger scale, media spanned across the world, severing perhaps forever the gaps between cultures and societies. Newer and savvier satellites soared into orbits from every possible position, broadcasting games and athletes and teams we had never before known existed yet alone followed. Cable television, born in the 1970's, peaked, ultimately exploding into homes and practically covering every corner of the globe and giving rise to new exposure and tighter scrutiny of our games and our athletes, as well as our fans. Political and social change redefined what it meant to be European, Russian, Canadian, Japanese, even American. All the while the sleepy hamlet of Cooperstown housed the ideal of America's past and the hope for the world's future. International players emerged as legitimate stars with greater magnitude than at any other time in the game's existence. American players challenged on an international field for the first time in history.

I had been a boy during the 1980s, a kid en route to adulthood. In my eyes, baseball players could do no wrong. In the short time between 1988 and 1994, I would come to realize that there are things more important than baseball, that there are men and women wiser, more revered, more respectable than ballplayers. Ultimately, I would learn that despite its deterioration baseball would survive itself.

The town I had come to know as home spun circles around itself trying to keep up with the era of progress. From the mundane when Main Street was widened to add a turning lane, to the monumental when Pete Rose was banned for life from the game, Cooperstown evolved, if only by its own little ripple. At the Museum, wings were added and rooms renovated.

Businesses boomed, opportunities emerged, advertising took off in daring new directions; MTV, HBO and a thousand cable offerings were created, launched and soared higher than the satellites that beamed their broadcast over the globe; the computer came to be a household word, a household item, and eventually a household divider. The world still had wars in remote places most Americans knew nothing of. Smaller empires came and went with greater frequency than in previous decades. The economy dipped and soared and fell again. And, yet, by the end of the decade, everything was returned to normal. How much progress had been made during the 1980's is difficult to gauge, but its change and the impact left on society was evident in every walk of life. Flux had been the decade, stasis its result.

After a thrilling up and down summer of expectation, excitement and emotion, my beloved Pirates faced off against Kevin's equally adored Reds for the right to play in the 1990 Fall Classic, the World Series. Here I was again, once more upon the doorstep of ultimate fandom. My team was winning and had reached the penultimate prize. Only now I was much older and much more a student of the game. I was a mere kid in 1979. By 1990, I was really into this stuff. We both followed the season with a newly revived sense of hope, and faced the prospect of the play-offs with both collegiate competitiveness and motherly distress. How could either of us hope that our own team would defeat the other's? It was like the Civil War, pitting brothers of northern allegiance against siblings of southern descent. While we welcomed the notion of our teams squaring off against one another, we dreaded the fact that one of us would celebrate while the other commiserated.

Throughout the summer of 1990, we bragged and bally-hooed about each team's separate progress. The Pirates had a stronger starting rotation, I would testify. But the Reds had depth in the bullpen along with a stunning closer, Kevin would counter.

Pittsburgh had a powerful double threat in an outfield that could hit and play amazing defense, I would launch in offensive. But Cincinnati had the best shortstop in the game and an infield to match, Kevin would defend. The battles went on and on, wearing down the line between friend and fan. To wit, the 1990 All-Star Game was held in Cincinnati, with a number of Pirates and Reds playing alongside one another. This only added to our determination to root each other's favorite team into defeat.

To ease the intensity fired by our Major League rivalry, there remained our own Cooperstown Owls, who were well on their way to regaining the form that had pushed them within one victory of the Championship Series two seasons earlier in 1988. The 1989 season had been a complete collapse as the team lost twenty-five games more than it had the year before, the result of injury and over-confidence by certain players. But 1990 was going to be different. It had to be. It was declared a pivotal year in the history of the club. Had they finished even one game off the pace, there would have been a complete tearing apart of the franchise. The ownership would restructure the entire organization. From the best player to the least known scout, no one would be secure. There was but one purpose and one purpose only – an International League Championship.

The owners had the money to make the ball club better, and they were not against spending it. More so, they were not afraid to let the press and the fans know what their plans were. After all, the system in place was not working. Without success, rebuilding would be the only option.

By the time the baseball season of 1990 was winding down for both the Major Leagues and the International League, Kevin and I had experienced significant changes as we grew into young adults. As well, those events from 1980 would prove to foretell events yet to be experienced.

It was our junior year in college and we returned to Roth College like frat boys to a keg. We were thrilled to be back on campus, one year closer to becoming seniors, two mere months from ending phenomenal baseball summers, though I was only a fan. Kevin's summer had been much more eventful than mine. While I was busy assisting Mr. Bentworth with landscaping duties at the ball park and continuing the same, less-interesting and lower-paying chores at both Mrs. Denton's' yard and the church, Kevin was on the cusp of becoming a professional pitcher.

In late May, just as school had let out, the Owls were on a trip to the southeast when their fourth man in the rotation, Edgar Smithon, took a bad fall chasing out a grounder and blew out his left knee. He joined the disabled list and Kevin got a phone call. Recounting the story to me, Murray explained his decision as it came to him in a Raleigh clubhouse on that cool night just before Memorial Day, 1990.

The Owls had just been beaten handedly by the Carolinians and were suffering the loss of Smithon. Murray sat hunched over the roster, examining his options. The flies were so big in the tiny office, buzzing about even in May, that he was mad as hell with indecision and was unable to concentrate. *Who can I call up?* he wondered. Then it occurred to him, "Bentworth..." he whispered to himself in simultaneous question and curiosity. *I wonder...*

"Hey, Shanks," he yelled to a passing player, the nearest ear he could find. "What do you think of that Bentworth kid?"

"Bentworth?" Shanks wondered out loud. "Never heard of him."

"Never heard of him? What good are ya?" Coach leapt from his chair and stuck his head into the locker room. "Hey, Rudy," he hollered, "Rudy, you ever heard of Bentworth?"

"Which, the kid or the dad?" the back-up third baseman asked from across the clubhouse.

"The kid," Murray answered.

"Hell, sure, I heard of him. He's a local kid, playing in college now I think. He's got great control and I hear he's learned a change-up."

"See?" Murray chided Shanks. "Rudy's heard of him." He sprang back to his desk and jotted down notes. "Seems he's learned to throw the change-up."

"Say, coach," Rudy said. "Didn't we draft that kid or recruit him last year or something? I mean, he's an Owl by contract or something. Isn't he?"

"I am way ahead of ya," Murray answered.

The very next day, Kevin got the call.

"Dad and I were in the driveway, working on the car," Kevin told me later.

"What?" I asked. "You don't know anything about cars."

"You're missing the point, Augie. I was working on the car when my sister called to my dad, saying some guy named Murray was on the phone. Dad wondered what was up if Murray was calling from the road. That was unusual, see. It turns out, Murray actually asked dad permission for the Owls to call me up to the league. Isn't that cool?"

So much had happened that summer, so much that made it seem as if 1990 had been pre-destined as a transition away from all that I held true as a youth and into all that I would cherish, know, realize, contemplate forever as an adult. The summer did not so much unravel as it came undone. I stood not a victim at its end, but rather a changed person.

It began in early June a few days after Kevin got the call. A heavy storm had pounded the state for close to a week with little sign of letting up when suddenly the storm just disappeared. The clouds rolled away and the sheer epitome of summer emblazoned itself upon the refreshed greenery and yellow of early rebirth, and summer resumed. But the winds had left their mark. The storm caused minor damage, reminding us that we are part of nature's whims.

I was cleaning Mrs. Denton's yard and clearing away debris that had scattered the driveway from the high winds after they spent the week seething throughout our borough. After completing my duties, I headed in to ask Mrs. Denton if there was anything else that needed to be done. The house was silent as the soft evening sauntered away in the trailing mist of the departing storm, and the shadows of night lay mysteriously sideways throughout the house. The sky felt tired and the sun could barely hold onto the disappearing daylight.

Mrs. Denton had a habit of turning on nearly every light in the house as evening crept inward, her fear of darkness comforted by light. But on this evening, she had seemingly felt inclined to allow the storm to pass in quiet solemnity as she cooled the air inside, absent the heat of the multiple hundred-watt bulbs that always burned throughout her home.

I climbed the stairs to the upper floor and called my neighbor's name but received no reply. At the top of the stairs, I saw through the door to her bedroom, cracked ever so-slightly, that she was fast asleep. She too had had a hard day. Mrs. Denton was an active, healthy woman of 76, and had insisted that aiding me with the tulips and a few weeds was surely no task for an elderly lady who had spent her life tending to a house the size of hers. She had overworked herself, and lay sound asleep in the fleeting evening. I crept as silently as the old house would allow and headed back down the stairs. I left a note promising I'd stop by

232

early the next afternoon for her evaluation, and locked the house up behind me.

The next morning she was dead.

I had risen sore and stiff and clipped languidly through my chores at the ball park with repetitious boredom. Tuesdays were always our least active day. I headed back to 16 Rushmore Street to learn whether Mrs. Denton had approved of my previous day's efforts.

I knocked four times and let myself in after hearing no reply. She must have risen early and taken a taxi up to Syracuse as she had mentioned she might do some shopping, I reasoned.

I headed to the table and expected to find a direct, though courteous, reply to my note from the previous day, written in her classically flowing pen-woman-ship. I stopped short. My note had remained. I figured I had the day off, and that she had found my work satisfactory, so I turned to exit. I noticed her keys remained where I had seen them the previous night, laid in the same position where she had tossed them onto the counter.

"Mrs. Denton?" I instinctively called to the quiet house. No reply. "Mrs. Denton?" I echoed, "Is everything all right?" I raised my voice louder and called to her a third time. I walked slowly toward the steps. I glanced through the same soft shadows that had enveloped the house the night before, but which had now slanted in an eastward counter stance as the day grew steadily forward. An unsettled feeling overtook me as I slowly canvassed the stairs. I stopped half way up to listen for a sound from outside. *Was that a voice?* I asked myself. *No, just a passing car.* The view from the last time I stood on the stairs and peered through the railing into Mrs. Denton's room had not changed. There she lay, still asleep, still in the same position.

"Mrs. Denton," I repeated in a quiet so soft as to be all but inaudible. "Is everything all right?" I stepped to the foot of her bed. She lay clasping a picture of her long-dead husband, with a look of complete satisfaction chiseled across a warm smile.

I called home. "Mom?" I jumped before she could say hello.

"No, it's your father," dad answered.

"Yeah, dad," I whispered. "It's me. Listen, uh, something has happened."

A police officer and the coroner arrived only moments after mom and dad had made it into the bedroom of the house on Rushmore Street.

Mrs. Denton's passing would have been enough to ensure that 1990 would engrave itself upon my soul forever, but much more was set to occur and her death was only the beginning.

With Kevin called up to the Owls and me out of work, Mr. Bentworth offered me Kevin's position as assistant groundskeeper. I jumped at the opportunity. The pay was much higher, the hours more regular and there was the added perk of being at the park all day, every day. A wise man once told me that if you're doing what you love you will never work a day in your life. While I have gone on to other duties in life, that summer was the best job, period. Unfortunately, I also inherited the duties of tending to Mrs. Denton's former neighbor, Miss Winthrop, when Mrs. Denton recommended that I would be a welcome replacement should I ever become unemployed from her own services. Not everything Mrs. Denton did for me was for my direct benefit.

As Kevin began play as an Owl, the whole town rallied around the team. It had not been since 1946 that a local boy had started for the Owls. And even then, no one had actually been born true blood and American blue Cooperstown bred and raised. Kevin was from Cincinnati, a far cry from being a true Cooper. Still, he became something of a town hero.

His first game was the stuff of movies. It was two weeks into June and a perfect summer night had been ordered and delivered. The freshly mowed grass lingered in the nostrils like a soft sneeze too weak to emerge and too persistent to be ignored. The lights seemed brighter that night as they began to glow across the field. And the sun appeared to set herself slower, more serenely and with finer grace than she had ever set herself upon the horizon before. This was what we had both lived for, a chance to play professional baseball, never mind the level. And Kevin had the first glimpse of how it really felt. Just like a first kiss is never really as rewarding as all the later, more experienced kisses, it is the most memorable.

I stopped by the Nest where Kevin was warming up. I could see that his focus was intent, his concentration stern, much the same as on his other great days – the perfect game, the scrimmage at Roth.

"Hey, Kev," I said. He acknowledged me with the customary flick of his glove and a quick nod of the head as he moved into his wind-up. He delivered a sharp fastball into the catcher's mitt. "Hey take it easy on Stebbings, will ya? He's only the back-up," I said.

"But at least I get a paycheck, Monroe. Not to mention the ladies." We shared a few laughs.

"Well," I added. "You need that heat for the game, Bents," I warned my friend.

"Yeah, yeah." He brushed me off with another flick of the glove. His next pitch was even harder, probably just to show me up.

The Owls park only housed 6,500 but that night the attendance topped off at 8,200! It was standing room only along the bleachers, the railings, even into the concourse. It seemed like everyone in town and three surrounding counties wanted to see Kevin's debut as an Owl. This was the kid that everyone would tell their grandchildren about. "I saw Kevin Bentworth pitch his first professional game. He played in the International League..."And no one could have been prouder than me, except maybe Kevin's father, though he was one not to let on. Somewhere between them a bitterness still lingered of things unresolved.

The seats were filled thirty minutes prior to the first pitch. Before I left the field to grab my seat, I made one final check of the chalk lines, kicked at the bases to ensure they were good and tight, and did a final inspection of the necessary equipment. Everything was in its proper place should a rain stir up or the field need resurfaced during the game. No. Not tonight. Nothing could have gone wrong that night. This was the stuff of movies.

I unlatched the gate that separated the field from the grounds storage area and had the unnerving sense that something was amiss. It was eerie, the same feeling I had waiting in that big, empty old house myself with the deceased Mrs. Denton. A few rakes had been knocked over along the wall, and two cans of white chalk paint has been spilled open. The paint seeped silently into the unyielding clay. A footprint, or rather the heel of one, disappeared from the farthest side of the spill area, as if someone hadn't noticed the great glob of white on the ground. A faint trail of left heels faded off toward a storage shed some twenty feet way.

I hesitated to speak out loud in fear that a group of kids might be up to some prank. I would have rather caught them in the act than later make accusations on speculation alone. I heard no sound but the reassuring chatter from the grandstands above. I stepped around the puddle of paint and toward the shed. I rounded the slight corner of the outfield fence and I saw him there, laid out on his chest like a wounded man shot in the back.

"Mr. Bentworth!" I yelled, leaping to his side. "Mr. Bentworth, are you all right? Can you hear me?"

I quickly reached for the walkie-talkie on my hip and called security, asking that they get help immediately.

"Mr. Bentworth," I repeated. I felt for a pulse and found it to be rhythmic and regular, though a bit labored. He was definitely alive. I found a flashlight and checked the area for signs of blood. I breathed a sigh that none could be seen. Two good signs – no blood and a noticeable pulse.

The paramedics arrived quickly, and while they worked on Mr. Bentworth I told them how I had found him. I urged them to get him to a hospital.

"I don't think that will be necessary," the shorter of the two medics answered. "What'd you say your name was?"

"August. August Monroe. Shouldn't we get him to a hospital?"

"No, that won't be necessary," the woman answered. "He's had these spells before."

"You mean you know him?" I exclaimed.

"Yeah, sure. I've known Ridley years. He'll be fine." She addressed her partner, "Let's get him seated." The man skipped over the paint puddle and commandeered a nearby chair. "Have a seat," she said to Mr. Bentworth. "Don't worry, August. Ridley is seeing his physician regularly and will report to him on Monday. We made sure of it after the second one of these last year."

"What?" I demanded. "How long has this been going on?"

"About two years," the male medic replied. "But, please, don't worry. He is fine. He has spells and passes out sometimes, mostly when he gets stressed or too worked up. Chances are he is excited about Kevin's debut and forgot to do his breathing exercises. He'll be fine."

While the two medics administered to Mr. Bentworth, checking his pulse, blood pressure, temperature and whatever else they do, I slid out of their way. Through the fencing, I could see into the Owls' bullpen where Kevin was talking and laughing with a teammate. With a glance back to my right, I could see his father in distress, strengthening each minute and coming to his senses, but fragile none the less. Kevin's name was announced over the loudspeaker as the starting pitcher, and a simultaneous roar went up from the crowd. The person who should have been most proud, should have screamed the loudest, should have risen in accord to usher the crowd onto their feet, sat limp and tired, exhausted.

And the most peculiar thing of all happened. As Kevin doffed his hat toward the crowd in acknowledgment of their support, he simply replaced the black cap emblazoned with the orange label of "C/O" upon his head and trotted toward the dugout for our National Anthem. He never so much as raised an eyebrow searching for his father.

The male medic tapped me on the shoulder. "August," he said.

"Yeah," I answered, a little startled while turning around.

"Mr. Bentworth is going to be fine. Just make sure you stay with him awhile. Maybe an inning or two so that he has his wits about him. Okay?" He listened to the crowd a second or two. "But," he added, "Make sure he sees Kevin pitch. It will be a good step if he sees his son out there doing what he loves."

"And if you could," added the other medic, "make it out that the Owls win, okay?"

"Sure," I promised. "I'll sneak into the control room and alter the scoreboard when no one is watching. Chances are good that the umpires might not even notice."

The laughter eased my nerves and the medics went on their way. From atop the stadium, the announcement of the first batter for the visiting Maryland Crabs ushered the game in with another howling roar.

I inched forward toward the screened opening in the fence from where Mr. Bentworth himself usually watched the game. From there I could witness Kevin's first pitch and spring toward his father's side should anything happen. The visiting batter lollygagged his way to the plate, kicking mud from his cleats. *What mud?* I recall thinking. *He's stalling.* Surely the Crabs knew this was Kevin's first game. They would use any advantage they could to beat him. If slowing down the start heightened Kevin's nerves, he made no show of it; for when the batter finally did step in to take his at bat, Kevin whaled into his wind-up and delivered a flat, solid strike. The crowd cheered, the tension receded and the game was underway.

The crowd soon lost the sole excitement of Kevin's debut and turned their attention toward the runners on base, the score on the board and the situation being played out on the field. They came and went in the fashion of a mid-summer baseball game, some chomping down their late dinners or extra snacks, some chatting over the latest news, some zipping back and forth to the restrooms and souvenir stands, and some just there to be a part of it all. Above me in the bleachers, the customary jeers were hurled to the visiting outfielders. Things said about their wives or their mothers, or sophomoric humor about their last names or their batting averages being the only thing lower than their IQs. Kids, both teenagers and younger, ran amuck to find friends, to steal kisses and to revel in summer.

"August, is that you?" I heard Mr. Bentworth's ask from behind me. The light from the field was sparse, but bright enough for me to see that his face was a bit discolored.

"Hey, Mr. Bentworth. How are ya feeling?"

"I guess I'll be okay," he answered.

"Could I get you some water or some ice or something?"

"Any chance for a beer?" he asked with a sheepish smile.

"I don't think so, Sir. Besides, they wouldn't serve me anyway."

I filled a cup with water and flicked on the single lightbulb that cast a small but sufficient glare into the room. Mr. Bentworth drank the chilled liquid slowly in tiny sips as he sat quietly a few moments.

"Did the game get underway yet?" he asked.

"Yeah, it's probably the bottom of the first inning by now."

"How'd Kevin do?"

"Real well. He got the first batter out on a ground ball, struck out the second on five pitches and forced the third to pop-up on his first pitch."

"Wow, that's a hell of a debut."

"Sure is. They gave him a good round of applause at the end of the inning."

"I heard that. Good," he whispered proudly. "That's real good."

Mr. Bentworth worked on a second glass of water while I positioned two high back stools into place so that we could watch the rest of the game together through the fence. He ambled over with a ginger step and I had to take most of his weight to lift him onto his chair. His strength slowly returned and he later asked for something to eat. I ran and got us both hot dogs and Cokes, along with a bag of popcorn to share. They weren't the best seats, but it was our own private spot, one that few others could claim.

Kevin worked well into the fifth inning, only yielding a walk and two hits, the second a monstrous home run in the third inning. No matter though, the Owls had tattooed the Maryland starter for six runs in the second and had run him off the mound in the fourth before the reliever quieted the Owls' bats, retiring the side with the bases loaded. So it stood 6-1 and Kevin was a few outs from an officially scored game. He would earn the win if the Owls could finish it off! When he mowed the side down in the sixth on two strikeouts and a long fly to deep left, he had amassed only twelve pitches all inning, a low enough total that might allow for him to hurl for the seventh.

In the bullpen, Sid Nikoski began warming up. He was a long closer who could pitch from the fifth on and finish a game if needed, though his specialty was fancy pitching and making hitters guess.

The Owls went down in order in the bottom half, giving Nikoski little time to warm up. Kevin took the mound for the top of the seventh and became the lollygagger himself. It was his turn to stall. The new kid wasn't so new after all. He asked the ump for a few tosses before the inning, probably claiming a stiffened shoulder. He was granted three pitches. Then he kicked the dirt on the mound, scraped at the rubber strip and cleaned his own cleats. It was a mastery of procrastination and the true patient fans of the game chuckled at the bravado. He timed himself perfectly. As the ump made his way to the mound for a warning, Kevin stopped him in his tracks, ushering with a hand that he was ready. By this time, Nikoski has gotten twenty or more pitches in and was ready to throw at game tempo. Kevin walked the one batter he faced.

Coach Murray called for time. Nikoski made his way to the field and Kevin stood in triumph on the mound. Though fleeting, that moment was the first milestone towards his ultimate goal – to pitch in the Majors. Murray sauntered toward the mound under a strengthening hum of applause. The crowd rose to their collective feet, clapping and cheering for their new hero. For a slow, sole moment, it was just Kevin on the mound. The opposing batter leaned his bat against a hip; the catcher stood with his glove pressed into his; and the umpire rested both hands firmly upon his own. Murray's step slowed to a pace and all the players on the field stood in silent approval as the ovation increased. This was his moment.

Just before Murray reached the mound, Kevin raised his right hand to his lips and thrust his index finger toward the sky. It was for his mother, his biggest fan and the only person who had not witnessed this moment with him. He handed the ball to

239

Murray, patted Nikoski on the shoulder and stepped from the mound. On way across the grass, he reverently doffed his cap to the crowd. Before he reached the dugout, he stopped and turned himself back towards the mound. Either Murray or Nikoski had said something that had stopped him short. Kevin turned to face them and Nikoski lobbed the ball in a slow, loping arch toward him. Kevin caught it bare-handed and shook the ball in appreciation to the fans. Not a bad memento.

These two events occurred within a few weeks of each other and divided what I had known of life into quadrants: there was a boy crossing into manhood, a child mourning the death of a respected elder, a friend witnessing the accomplishments of a peer, and a fan celebrating a new start. My recovery was going along well enough. I had regained much of the strength in my leg and had lost any fear of driving, though I walked with a noticeable limp, one that would remain persistent throughout my life.

One main concern lingered. Without baseball, how would I continue college? My grades had been solid enough that the school had no intention of releasing me as a student, but I was lacked the money to pay tuition. An academic scholarship was not entirely out the question, though it was much more difficult to get one as a junior than as an incoming freshman. Mom and dad had some money, though not a lot. We had bought the new house when I was guaranteed a scholarship to play baseball and the little money they had left over was for their retirement. Mom and dad had me relatively late in their lives. Mom had been thirty-eight and dad forty-two, now closing in on their retirement plans. If I was to remain in college it would be on my own, somehow. And with Kevin playing for Cooperstown, most of my friends on the team had already graduated. It was a new team, and I wasn't a part of it. I couldn't play, what use was I to the team?

Coach Culpepper tried to reason with the administration that I could manage, score and travel with the team as an upper-class coach / mentor / chaperone. But they would have nothing of it. Rules were rules, and if I could not play, then another student athlete deserved the financial assistance I had lost. Even so, I argued, with Kevin gone for the semester, that still leaves a half a scholarship on the books. "Maybe at a larger school," Coach apologized, "you could have kept your scholarship. But not at a Division III school. Sorry, Monroe."

July disappeared into a frenzy and August rolled along into the nothingness of memory. As the new school year approached I still had no idea what I would be doing after Labor Day when classes would resume. Then, a beacon alighted to reveal the answer.

Shortly after Mrs. Denton's funeral, I had returned to her house to lend a hand if anything needed to be done. Her two nieces and their children packed up boxes and made the necessary arrangements with surprisingly high spirits. There would be an estate sale.

I arrived and was welcomed with genuine sincerity, as if I were one of their own. Someone from the neighborhood, one of the unnamed, resourceful many who come to the aid of families in such times, had provided tea and snacks. Mrs. Denton's nieces invited me to share in the discussion about their grand aunt, to which I declined. Instead, I took a seat in the far end of the dining room where I could listen to the memories those closest to her had of the sweet, dear lady. The stories they shared were hardly spectacular. In fact, they were something like any of us might share about our own deceased grandmothers – remembrances of the little things done to brighten our days: the extra cookie, the longer hugs, or the walk in the park at a slow enough pace to accommodate our tiny legs (though perhaps grateful for grandchildren who walked at her pace). She was a generous woman with steadfast goodness. She had aided the elderly Winthrops when they were both struck suddenly ill and unable to work prior to retirement. She had given excessively to the church mission that would offer relief across the globe. It is in that spirit that I recall the most serious and most admirable expression of generosity I have received in my life. And, not surprisingly in the whole scope of life, though an undeniable shock at that time, it came from Mrs. Denton.

By mid-afternoon, the neighbors and extended family had left, and her youngest niece, Cynthia, approached me. I recall having had a crush on her when we had met ten years earlier. She was then a buxom teenaged baton twirler using her aunt's open back yard as practice space for her techniques and tricks. How many days I had spent mowing the lawn or clipping the hedges, reflecting back to the times I would sneak outside to watch her twirl that baton, especially when she added pyrotechnics and lit the thing aflame. She and I were both much older when Mrs. Denton died. She, her husband Dave and their family lived in Buffalo or Cleveland, I could never recall which.

She tapped my shoulder as I was eating a snack in the kitchen where I had shared so many iced teas with her aunt. We exchanged hellos and expressed condolences. Then, she got serious.

"Auntie Rose," Cynthia said, "was always very appreciative your work, August."

"Thanks, but it was nothing," I said, a little embarrassed. "I enjoyed her company. Your aunt was very kind."

"Dave said you found her in her bed after she passed." A smile defied the tear that appeared on her cheek.

"Yes," I answered. "I sensed something was wrong when the lights were still on. That's why I went upstairs."

"Aunt Rose loved to light this place up. I cannot imagine the electric bill she must have paid over the years."

We both chuckled, me a bit too long probably. "This old house probably hasn't been run through with new wire either," I added. "Must have cost a heavy dime."

"It doesn't matter," she surmised. "It made her happy."

"Well, maybe sometimes money can buy happiness; at least in little bits."

Her gentle laughter filled the kitchen with the same simple joy her aunt had possessed. It was then that I realized the she had more resembled Mrs. Denton than had her sister, Veronica.

"I don't know if you are aware," she continued, "but Auntie had made certain provisions for use of her estate."

"Hold on, Cindy, that is really none of my business. I mean, I appreciate your sharing but I'd rather not kno – "

"Please," she whispered. "Let me finish."

I attempted several times to ask that I be excused. Each time, she told me to wait. She called Veronica into the kitchen. Veronica greeted me with a clumsy hug, the type overly affectionate people give at such times, perhaps in a way to remain connected with the living.

Veronica withdrew the hug. She wasn't as pretty as her sister but had a sincerity that would attract many men. She said, "We cannot tell you how much Aunt Rose adored you, August. You were so kind to her."

Embarrassment swept across my face. "It was nothing," I mumbled.

"Well, the thing is," Cindy continued. "The estate cannot be settled just now. It may take a few months. Will you still be in town when summer ends or be able to get back should we need to contact you for anything?"

"Yeah, but, contact me? I don't see why you would need to. Do you need a statement on what happened the day she died?"

"No, it's nothing like that," Veronica said. "Just make sure we have your phone number at home and at school so we can reach you when we are ready to settle the estate. Okay?"

"Sure, suites me," I added dumbly. No matter what I did, I could not talk sensibly to a woman if I had ever once found her to be attractive. I left my phone numbers as well as an address at school and reminded them that I may not be in school at that time anyway.

Cynthia nodded with a smile and said, "We'll see."

I continued normal life of my new reality as best I could for the rest of summer. And in my own immature way, never considered what lie ahead for me. It's a good thing opportunity truly knocks because I was so unaware of it lingering before me that I would have tripped over it had it been in the way.

On a mid-week day, maybe a Tuesday or Wednesday, the Owls were on another road trip and Cindy called me late in the morning, asking if I could stop by her aunt's house later in the afternoon. We set two o'clock as our meeting time. Little did I know, this would be one of the most important days of my life.

I arrived at the house and it felt like returning to an old school. I felt welcome while still no longer a part of that life and community. The hedges were trimmed, though not to Mrs. Denton's style. Her nieces had hired a local company and they had shortened them below her preferred sixteen inches in height. Some upstairs windows had had the drapery removed and the swing was gone from the porch. Her old blue Buick sat in its same spot in the driveway, a "For Sale" sign eclipsing its privacy.

I rang the bell and waited a moment before the door was opened. Veronica greeted me, forcing another awkward hug over my shoulders.

"August, it's good to see you. How are you? Please come in."

"I'm well, Veronica. How are you?"

"Good. I'm good. We're all good. Thanks for asking. We've been busy getting the house ready for sale."

"Yeah," I muttered. "It sure will be strange knowing other people will be living here."

"Well, you know what they say, the living must go on living," she said.

"Yep," I added, "if not a little changed by it all."

Cynthia appeared in the hall and welcomed with her own hug, one that melted the part of me that still wondered if we could have dated.

The stillness of the house was a bit creepy, absent its lively source of memory and sensitivity. I accepted another iced tea, though one not nearly as sweet nor as cool as Mrs. Denton served. We talked idly for a few moments about the house, the impending sale and how the baseball team was fairing. They were not baseball fans, I could tell. I think they were being nice.

Finally, the talk turned to the reason they wanted to see me. Apparently, the promised information concerning the estate was to be revealed and I had to be there with them.

"Are we waiting for a lawyer?" I asked.

"No," Veronica stated. "We took care of all that with the lawyers yesterday. We want to let you know where you stand in all of this."

"Ladies, please," I attempted to excuse myself. "I appreciate your willingness to share this with me, but it's really none of my business."

"August," Veronica said, "actually, this is all about you. Auntie loved you like her own grandson and wanted to do something special for you." She pulled a manila enveloped from a nearby shelf. "A few months ago, shortly after your accident, Aunt Rose asked Veronica and I to look closely at her accounts. Uncle's magazine had left her a great deal of money, and she wanted to have it all prepared when this time finally came." She choked back a tear.

Cynthia took over. "She asked that Vera and I to put together a will for her. It's all pretty simple, legal stuff and all of that. She didn't have all that much, but she wanted you to have a little something."

"No," I objected. "With all due respect to your aunt's wishes, I really must insist that... No. I cannot even consider taking anything."

"Please, August." Veronica said. "You have to believe us when we tell you this was entirely her idea."

"But, I — I just can't. It wouldn't be right. I should go."

My parents had raised me to do the right thing, but I had no idea what I was trying to turn down. Honor is one thing, but common sense is quite another. How was I to know what riches (or maybe even precious heirlooms) awaited me? It could have been a chair for all I knew, and what damage would that have done? Or, if she and her late husband had really made as much money as the townsfolk had rumored, I may have been standing on the threshold of a serious windfall. I would like to think I was humbly rejecting a kind offer, that in the face of temptation I was being righteous. In truth, I was just naive and had no real idea that money could help me in so many ways. "Listen," I added. "Please. I just can't."

"August!" Cindy stated a little too firmly, as if scolding me. "At least hear us through. I think, we both think, that when you hear what we have for you that you will be very happy and accept Auntie's offer."

"This offer comes with stipulations, of course," Veronica said.

"Stipulations?" I inquired. "I don't understand. What does...sorry. What did she want me to have?"

"Your education," Cynthia answered. A vague smile returned to her lips as I passed a confused glance her way.

I was so dense, that this scene should really be read as a comedy. Here were these two kind, young ladies offering to hand me a lot of money, *and I was refusing*. Then, when it should have been blatantly obvious what it was for, I was still unclear and stammered through that stupid one word question with a fog as thick as my skull. "Education?" I uttered.

"Yes," Veronica explained. "Your education. Auntie wants us to fund the remainder of college for you through her estate. She felt terrible when you lost your scholarship after the accident, and decided that this was how she could leave you something that would really benefit you and all of us."

"And the stipulation?" I inquired.

"That's simple," Cynthia replied. "Just keep a B average and the tuition, including room and board, is on us."

"At any school I want?"

"Well, no," Cynthia clarified. "You're already enrolled at Roth, right?"

"Yeah. I mean, I would have been had I not lost the scholarship. I guess I still am. I don't know. Maybe."

"Well, then, it makes sense for you to finish up at Roth."

In her infinite generosity, the likes of which had stretched far across the world and right across Cooperstown, Mrs. Denton had ended the worst year of fear and given me a very real and serious chance at completing my education. I talked it over with my folks, and they agreed that it was a fair and appropriate arrangement. After all, dad reminded me, Mrs. Denton had encouraged my learning from early on, and neither of my parents had ever allowed me to take a dollar for the work I had done.

As for maintaining the B average, that wasn't so difficult. Roth College is no Harvard. Its academic rigor was certainly fair, but I had only chosen the small private school for its baseball tradition. The chance to play on a team certain to win plenty of games weighed greater importance than academic standards. But now things were much different. Of the three scholarships I had been offered out of high school, only Roth had a winning standard in its past. The others were mediocre at best, and while the education may or may not have been equivalent to Roth's, the baseball opportunities would have been less. Still, college would prove a fair challenge and Mrs. Denton's funds were spent well and with honest intentions.

Still, I cannot help but reason that for some purpose other than I will ever fully understand (or acknowledge when it becomes obvious) I was just not supposed to play professional ball. The oddity of fate, the conundrums of the gods or the mere happenstance of chance had so designed that I was to be a professional broadcaster of baseball games, not a challenger within its boundaries but a knowing observer just off the fringe.

Ultimately, those events of 1990 make perfect sense. As I sit here in 2001, waiting for the Owls to return home for game seven of the International League Championship Series – a game I will be broadcasting on national radio as the voice of the Owls, a game I may have played in had fate not intervened, and a game I would not be qualified to broadcast and write about had Mrs. Denton's generous spirit not found wisdom in my suffering – I further understand the point of a life well-lived. It isn't about always getting what you want, but it is about being grateful for what you get. To Mrs. Denton, I am eternally grateful, and to her husband, whose life had expired long before mine had begun and whose very fortune paid my way to an excellent education, even on into graduate school at Columbia University's MA program in journalism, I give thanks wherever he is. It is in part for his memory and her friendship that I write this tale.

But that summer of 1990 was amazing. Kevin had begun his trip toward playing professional ball. I witnessed the laying to rest of Grandpa and Mrs. Denton. And I myself had been the victim of a terrible accident that I could have avoided. Yet, all the while I was unaware that these events were pushing me in the direction of my proper place in life.

25 The Distance

College whirled into a blur. I became a fan, a baseball fan. I was no longer a player. I wasn't much of a student either. That took some getting used to. If a more contradictory statement than the "student athlete" existed in late twentieth century America, I doubt I have ever heard the phrase. I had to adjust to a new life in college. What was there to do? The few friends I had in classes were more of passing acquaintances, and the friends I thought I had on the team dropped me like a bad error at third. Nice to know one is still appreciated after one no longer has an immediate dividend to offer. I had to do something! Luckily, an opportunity arose in a rather crossing fashion.

While Coach Culpepper could not get my scholarship reinstated, he was able to arrange through the Dean of Students (who was an Atlanta Braves fan – but that's another story) that I would work as a faculty assistant in the Literature and Drama Department. This I looked forward to about as much prostate surgery.

On my first day at my "new job," I scaled the four floors of a building tucked deep on the northern end of campus and breathed heavy, silent complaints wondering why there was no elevator in the hundred-year-old building. I looked like a freshman again with a tiny hand-scribbled note opened across my palm as I wandered the fourth floor with a catatonic gaze trying to locate my new place of employment. Two-thirds down the hall, a cackle of laughter, many voices combined, echoed from a short hallway to my right. I followed the only signs of life present in the stretching tower and stopped short to witness both a sight and a sound. Seven people stood in the hall. They formed two rows and peered over each other's shoulder at a billboard-scale poster on the wall. The sound was a question all too familiar to me and strongly out of place; or, rather, the answer was all too familiar and the question oddly misplaced. I am not sure whether it was a girl or a guy who had asked it, but the question rang so clearly that I blurted out the answer without considering my intrusion or my manners.

"Sanguillen," I said automatically, as if I was expected to answer a question I was not actually asked. "Manny Sanguillen."

The group shot surprising eyes and head twists my way and the laughter ceased momentarily, though a warmth glowed from within the entourage, a welcoming openness that could be sensed almost immediately.

"How'd you know that?" asked a short brunette with eyes that looked like pancakes. She wore muted mascara, or whatever it is that girls use. "The clue is so vague," she added before repeating the original question to which I had blurted my answer. "'Ten letter Dominican catching for a Lumber Company?' What does that even mean?"

"Many Sanguillen," I answered. "He played catcher for the Pittsburgh Pirates in the 1970's, their nickname was the Lumber Company because they had so many power hitters who swung heavy bats. Stargell, Al Oliver, Dave Parker, Sanguillen. Wooden bats, lumber. Get it?"

A man who must have been a professor eyed the poster up and down, and said, "I think he's right. It fits with 117 down. Well done, young man."

"No problem," I added. "Could you tell me where I could find a," I paused while consulting my note again, "a Doctor Witherspoon, please?"

The professor penciled in the answer. *He could have used ink,* I thought. *It's correct!* "That wouldn't be that pompous, self-righteous David Witherspoon, would it?" he asked.

"I can't say, Sir," I answered. "I haven't met the man yet. Do you know where his office is?"

"Oh, yes, I do," the man answered while continually eyeing the poster. The group giggled playfully. "You won't find him stationed there just now, that much I am certain."

"Do you know when he'll be back?" I was getting annoyed at the giggling. "I need to meet with him."

"Oh, then you must be Mr. Monroe," he stated to my surprise. "That explains your knowledge of baseball. I am Dr. Witherspoon." He advanced towards me with a hand extended as greeting. "Please take no offense. Just a little fun, hey?"

"None taken, Sir," I stuttered.

"It's August, correct?" he asked.

"Yes, Sir. I'm the new faculty assistant."

"So you are," he affirmed. He turned to the small crowd who had taken considerable interest in my presence. "Students, this is August Monroe, he will be our new assistant this semester, and apparently knows quite a lot about baseball."

Roth College is not big enough that I didn't recognize some of the faces of the students waving at me and nodding heads,

249

including one guy whose name I think was Danny but I couldn't remember. I only hoped they weren't all assessing me as the former jock who had lost a free ride and suddenly needed a job. That's what I was, but they didn't need to condescend about the matter.

After a few hellos, Dr. Witherspoon excused himself, saying he'd need a few minutes before being able to meet with me. It was okay I told him, I was early.

"So you are," he agreed. He slid passed the brunette and into his office in the far corner of the narrow hall. His door closed behind him but remained open a crack. I waited for one of the students to say something. Finally, the girl, Tracie, did.

"Don't mind Doc Witherspoon," she said. "He tends to be tough on new people when he first meets them. He made me cry my freshman year."

"I think I can handle it," I said. I pointed to the poster that had been the object of attention. "What are you working on?"

"This," Danny answered, not realizing the question wasn't directed to him, "is the world's largest crossword puzzle, or one of them at least. Dr. Jasinski ordered it from a catalogue, and it is all baseball questions. I guess you can order other topics, too, football or history, biology or religion, whatever subject you choose. Jasinski chose baseball. I'm not much of a fan myself. I would have preferred literature or maybe movies, but I am learning and it has proven quite fun."

"Right," a noble Tracie interrupted, stopping Danny's ensuing river of babble. "The whole Literature and Drama department is working together to fill in all the squares by year's end. It has a thousand questions across and a thousand down."

"Geeze," I uttered. "That's insane. Cool."

"So, you know baseball?" Tracie asked.

"Uh, yeah. That is definitely my strongest subject," I answered. I stepped closer to evaluate the elaborate puzzle. "In fact, I would major in it if I could."

While she smiled a warm laugh, Danny injected information unsolicited. "Well, interestingly enough, The University of Pittsburgh is introducing a program in baseball history. It's a cross discipline between the history department and the media communications department. Ken Burns, the filmmaker who is working on the PBS Series *Baseball*, helped to spearhead the program through an affiliation with the university. The series is due to air in 1994, I think. I actually thought his mini-series on the

Civil War was spectacular, and will probably prove to be a better piece, much more informative, historically speaking, of course. Baseball is not nearly as important to American history as the war was. Are you familiar with Burns?" he asked.

I wasn't sure that he was actually done speaking. He had said more words in three minutes than I had said all day. I looked at him blankly "Burns?" I lied. "Yeah, loved his Civil War piece. Very well done." I blocked any possible rebuttal or questions that might catch me in a lie. "So, what's the next clue?"

Tracie said, "We've been stuck on this one all week. Witherspoon thought he had it figured out but the amount of letters didn't match. It reads, 'Evans, not of Fenway Fame.' Doc was certain it was Dwight, and the "D" matches, but there are too many missing letters. We are stumped."

"It's Darryl," I answered. "Darryl Evans played for the Tigers and Rangers. Dwight was a member of the Red Sox, thus it's Evans not playing for Boston."

"Hey, he's right," Danny gasped. "And it matches the second "R" on three-hundred-thirty-eight down." He turned to me with his arm extended upward. "High five!"

I slapped a non-committed five and read the next clue. Doctor Witherspoon interrupted when he called me into his office.

"We expect a lot of our students, Mr. Monroe," he said. He offered a seat. "And more of our assistants."

"Yes, sir," I said. "I'm dedicated to every job I take on."

"Athletes and students don't always make good bed fellows, you know." His accusatory tone was less insulting than it was embarrassing. He was judging me based on what I had done in the past, hardly offering an opportunity to show myself.

"I'm not an athlete anymore," I stated coldly. I fixed a stare upon him.

"No, you're not, are you?" He flipped through some papers. "I have been looking over your grades and while I am not overly impressed, I say you have done quite well, considering."

"Considering what, Sir?" He flinched. I guessed he wanted to say, *Considering you are a jock,* but he refrained.

"Considering the amount of time that extracurricular activities take away from study," he answered. He peered over spectacles which he removed before speaking again. "I would say you've done quite well, and I see you've carried at least sixteen credits each semester. That is rare for an athlete. We usually see the twelve credit minimum from most student athletes."

"I played baseball as a way to get an education, Sir. Not the other way around." My lie went undetected. "As much as I would have loved to have spent all my energies improving my game, it would not have been fair to the college to spend important funds too lightly."

"Well put," he said. He gazed out the window, reflectively. He leaned back in his chair and twirled his glasses absently. "You know, August," he continued. "I too once had fantasies of playing baseball myself. Fresh out of high school I thought I'd be an outfielder for the Yankees, but time grew that idea to a steady departure." *The Yankees?* I thought. *Why me? Why again?* "Of course," he elaborated, "I've never been a fan of the Yankees. I respect their tradition and their history, but at the time when I was starting college, they were the most impressive team there was. What boy in America didn't grow up wanting to be a Yankee, even if they loathed them personally?" He reset the glasses on his face. "At any rate, we're glad to have you aboard."

We discussed mundane directions about duties, hours, responsibilities and expectations. The money was hardly enough to justify my time, but it was the only spending money I would be getting, and it would put gas in the car or pizza in the stomach. All of Mrs. Denton's contributions were strictly for tuition, room and board. Doctor Witherspoon was likable and had an air of dignity behind his arrogance. He really seemed to know what being a college professor was all about, and in turn imparted upon students what it meant to be under such tutelage. I was surprised if a little pleased to learn that most of the professors were themselves baseball fans, and not unlike the old Owls teams, had an array of teams to which they swore allegiance. They too, like the Owls, came from varying points in America and Canada, had studied, traveled and grown-up in all corners east and west, and had adopted favorite teams of their own along the way. It wasn't such a bad gig after all.

I tried to find a way to inform the professor that I had a class to attend. He went on about a sundry of ideas and talked at length about each separate topic, offering countless opinions without requesting my input. Long after my afternoon history class had gotten underway without me, he touched on a topic that stayed with me throughout college. In his fluid voice I heard the far away echo of Mrs. Denton who had encouraged education all along.

"I'm going to like working with you. You're smart," he said. "I can see that. I want to challenge you, though. I want to see you go the distance. That is a popular sports analogy, is it not? Go the distance. Take it all, win big. An education is a fine and wondrous gift, August. Take it for what it is, develop it for yourself and be absolutely the best student you can become. An education can open many, many doors for a young student with the right focus and a little ambition. Do not spoil this opportunity."

Finally, he dismissed me from his heavily one-sided conversation, invited me back at any time to chip away at the crossword puzzle, and wished me well for the semester. I left with a sense of having understood someone for the first time in a long time. I passed through the hallway and stopped at the giant poster/puzzle. I could see from the vast white spaces on the board that they had not progressed very far in their quest to complete the crossword. Amateurs! Likewise, I could see from the clues that I could easily have stood there and penciled in some forty words without so much as raising a struggle to figure out the first batch of answers. I opted to hold off the flourish of pen that would have "chipped away" at the puzzle, and decided instead to save my answers for another day, a day perhaps when I could spend the time better by getting to know other students.

I descended the four flights of stairs, exited the tower and cut across campus. I felt a new sense of place, as if this college thing might be okay. I felt akin to people who studied and enjoyed Literature. I had read plenty, but had never considered that one's enjoyment in reading could be transformed into an education. College, I had always thought, was for mathematicians and physicists, future politicians and lawyers. I reached the lowest step outside the lofty building and began my trek across the sidewalk's grassy edge where I came across Kevin.

"Hey, Bents," I said in a friendly tone. "Rumor has it your best friend goes to school here."

"Augie," he said. He seemed to be caught off guard, as if he had been preparing an encounter but was not ready for when it occurred. "Yeah, I hear your best friend is the worst student on campus, too."

"No," I joked, "just the worst pitcher. There are plenty of students as dumb as he is."

We shared a laugh and exchanged *What's up?* comments, as well as an incongruous and awkwardly forced left-handed shake, as if he felt obligated to a decade-old pact. It was a subtle gesture, the kind we had shared many times before, but it seemed larger and out of place with people on campus witnessing the peculiar embrace.

"What brings you back to school?" I asked.

"Season's over," he said. I had all but forgotten that the Owls' season had ended. The International League does not play into October.

"How are your classes?" he asked.

"They're good," I answered. "How's the team look this year?"

"Solid, real solid, man. I think we'll go far in the conference tournament. Not the same without you, though."

"Yeah, I sure miss the game. But I'm getting used to this college thing."

"I've been wondering about you when it came to that. What's up with your scholarship and paying for school, and all that?"

I recounted for him all that had transpired since the accident. I wasn't about to admit the glaring omission between us since that winter evening a few months earlier, nor was I going to lure him into discussing the matter. That, of course, being his absence throughout my ordeal.

"So, uh, what gives then?" he asked with increasing discomfort. "What are you going to do? Coach told us at the start of summer practice that you wouldn't be on the team again."

"Yeah," I sighed. I jogged my head a little to the right. "It looks like I have to figure out what all these other students already know – just what the hell I'm gonna do with my life. Luckily, there are opportunities outside of baseball since I can't do that."

"Man, I'm sorry," he offered. "I had heard that, but didn't want to bring it up."

"No big deal, really. I pretty much accepted it back in the hospital. Traction gives you a lot of time to think, ya know?"

"Yeah, about that, uh, I meant to you know, get over and visit you in the hospital or during your rehab, ya know, but I was playing summer ball down in Syracuse and wasn't home much. I wanted to call, but, well you know..."

"No," I said. I confronted him eye-to-eye. "I don't know how it is. I have no idea how it would be to not see my best friend in the hospital when he's really banged up."

"Well, like I said, I meant to – "

"Meant to, Kevin? Meant to what?" I asked. "I almost died, man. Would you have meant to see my parents or go to the funeral if I had died?"

"Man, don't do this to me. I'm sorry, okay. I'm sorry that this happened to you. I am sorry you can't play ball anymore. And..."

"Never mind," I interrupted. I could feel the boiling up of a bad scene. There was no sense rehashing the past. Besides, he still had never apologized for slugging me in the stands at Owls Stadium. It wasn't his fault that the accident occurred. But if he had just acknowledged that he had played a role, then perhaps I would have felt differently. "Listen, I need to be getting to class. Do you wanna hang out sometime soon, maybe catch a movie or something?"

"Sure, that'd be great," he cowered. "I don't have a lot of free time with practice and all, but that would be cool. The coach has us on heavy winter conditioning so we'll be in shape for spring. Maybe some weekend when we aren't working out."

I shrugged. "There's a party tomorrow at one of the frat houses. I was thinking of going. You wanna hook up beforehand?"

"Uh, no, actually, tomorrow isn't good," he said. "Got lots to do."

"How about we rent a movie with the girls on Friday? Melony is coming up, maybe we can introduce her and Katie. I think they'll get along."

"Oh, shit. Friday's bad, man. I mean..."

"Jesus, Kevin," I cut him off. "If you don't want to hang out, just say so."

"No, it's not that. It's just that, well, I tell ya what. I'll give you a call soon, okay? We'll get together."

"Yeah, whatever," I answered. He backed away, blaming lateness to "this thing" as a reason for departure. He disappeared around Larner Hall and slid away behind a veritable ivy cluster of excuses, most probably lies.

Maybe we had grown apart. The accident was one thing, but the world we were exploring and the landscapes we would challenge individually were separate and not at all equal. He had his goal still set on the Majors, and I of all people could hardly blame him for that. Mine would be the same if my leg hadn't decided it was not prepared to carry me through a professional baseball career.

The distance between us grew vast and wide, a chasm across which neither could span. It was from one side of a cliff to the other, the separation between our new-found places in life. And still, I felt sorry for him. He had his own demons to confront, echoes of sadness he had grown up with and memories too painful and lasting to erase. He really only had his one shot. Kevin had something to prove, whereas I had only fate to deal with. Fate, and the ever-developing life ahead of me. Kevin, however, had to prove it to himself and to his dad that he could and would play professional baseball.

I decided to attend the frat party on my own, thinking I could visit with a few guys and girls I had gotten to know who were in my classes. I entered the frat house, not at all surprised to see Kevin already there. He socialized and partied like there was no reason to stay alive. And then I saw him do the unthinkable, and it leveled me. He didn't even know I was in the room. In fact, I didn't even say hello. Instead, I left angrily when I saw Kevin and a group of ballplayers snorting cocaine from the smooth surface of a fading mirror.

That semester went on and soon the puzzle looked more and more like a knowledgeable tapestry where sporting geniuses inscribed baseball's lore upon literature's anthology. I saw less and less of Kevin and heard only of his doings through Katie, whom I barely knew but ran into occasionally between classes or at various social gatherings. She was a popular girl and seemed to be well-liked. Her devotion to Kevin was sufficient for his attention and they dated exclusively throughout college. She was an amiable woman with many connections that would lead her into a successful career. I never knew what her major was, though.

I made friends with students in the English department as well as a few guys in the dorm. They partied a bit too much for my daily consumption but proved to be a lot of fun on weekends when I chose to knock back a six pack with them. We often watched football games together and I began to appreciate that game to a finer degree, understanding the nuances and intricacies of the sport when I had found little enjoyment in it previously. I hardly realized that spring was on its way when Katie asked if I'd want to attend a game with her in which Kevin would be pitching. I mean, I knew spring was approaching as I looked forward, very forward, to spring break, but had not quite calculated that baseball was preparing for its return – the first year I can recall not anticipating baseball's resurrection.

The Roosters were the furthest thing from my mind as I delved into my studies. Furthermore, the fall from grace that my former teammates took as I began to see the players for who they truly were, just another group of students getting their way through college, was a separation I was shocked to encounter. But Kevin took an approach opposite anything I had seen in him before, and one I had never expected. Getting Kevin to college was like letting loose a kleptomaniac at a petty thieves convention. He took all that had been bred in him and threw it at large into the sea. Okay, maybe I was being a prude, again. Kevin was hardly the first person to throw caution to the wind and party college away, but most of the people I had encountered who had done so before were just wasting their time on campus anyway. They never had a real shot at success and used college as an answer for the separation fear that kept them from striking out on their own. But Kevin had a real chance to turn the corner from college into a successful career. The Owls had even offered to return him to the roster when school ended each year. He went to the first practice so hung over in January 1991 that he couldn't even stand the dull sunrise that hid behind the stadium.

How could I meet up with him after he had done irrevocable harm to himself as well as taken the risk of killing himself, yet alone his chance at the pros? Not to mention the legal implications. Anyway, these decisions were put on hold as Katie convinced me to go to the game.

"I don't know, Katie," I answered when she invited me to attend. "I think being away from the team is best for me. I have other things to focus on now, you know?"

"It would do you good, August," she advised. I suddenly remembered that she was a Psychology major, and if she hadn't been one she probably should have. "Confronting the game as a fan and watching your former teammates succeed will do you wonders in getting over this." She paused, reached for my wrist. "Kevin told me that baseball has been a part of your entire life. You have a right to grieve. It is like a loss, really. A part of you is gone."

"It's not that big of a deal," I excused.

"Seriously? Are you even hearing yourself?" She had a strong personality. "You had a dream that was crushed. That has to hurt. Most of us experience the loss of our dreams by our own failures, we get a shot but come up short. Your shot was cut off for you."

I held back tears only Melony had seen before. "Damn, girl," I said. "You might as well get a job tomorrow because you certainly don't need a piece of paper to determine that you're qualified for this stuff."

I ignored the quaking rumble in the pit of fear that had become my stomach and scheduled a "date" with my best friend's girl. We would attend a game when the Roth College Roosters took on a team from, fittingly enough, Western Pennsylvania. Our opponent that day would be the Thiel College Tomcats, a similar Division III team who hadn't seen a winning season on this side of the Viet Nam War. It was to be a home and home series wherein Thiel would visit Roth again for one game and then we would travel to some place called Greenville, Pennsylvania, for a second game.

The contest was scheduled for a chilly March in 1991, and the Tomcats put up a good fight, packing their pride back to Thiel College with the knowledge they had given a nationally ranked top-five baseball team a good game. Kevin pitched well enough not to lose but was lifted in the sixth with the score tied. Thiel took a late but slim lead with a home run in the seventh, only to lose 5 - 4 on a two-out double and a throwing error in the bottom of that frame which led to two Rooster runs.

After the game, we met Kevin at a local pizza shop and the conversation was light and amicable. It had been several months since our confrontation on the school grounds when Kevin all but blew me off. I wasn't interested in talking about classes or grades or what was going on in the world. I was also not willing to discuss the past. Rather, I had hoped to catch up on how Kevin had been, including the status of Mr. Bentworth who I had also not spoken with in months. Unfortunately, that didn't happen.

Mid-way through a total man's meal of an extra-large meat lover's pizza, Katie only having sampled one piece and opting for a fresh salad, Kevin and I inadvertently tapped into an oil reserve of undiscussed topics. And it really wasn't either one's fault. It just came up, almost as if it had to be a subject we broached somewhere along life's path.

"What are the Pirates gonna do this year?" Kevin asked. He gestured toward the waitress for a new pitcher of soda.

"Well, after losing to your Reds in the play-offs, they'd better at least contend until the All-Star break."

The Pirates had finished 1988 with eighty wins and eighty-two losses. Having suffered losing seasons from 1982 through

258

1989, that one almost even year in 1988 would have been welcome reprieve from the desert. Despite a dismal collapse in 1989, and a play-off loss in 1990, they had the nucleus of a good ball club, and hope often runs high in spring training. 1991 was a year for optimism.

"I don't know," Kevin said. "I'm beginning to think playing a whole season just to finish out of contention is ludicrous. I wonder if they shouldn't cut the league in half every July and play out the remainder of two pennant races. I mean, if you can't win, why play?"

The comment was innocent enough, but one to which I took umbrage.

"I'll tell ya what I do know," I said. "That scenario sounds better than any I will ever experience. I'd rather play out a season in last place than the alternative I'm faced with, which is never playing at all. Hell, I'd rather finish in last place ten years in a row than never play at all. Oh, but I don't get that choice, do I?" I finished with heavy sarcasm.

"Man, you make it sound so tragic," Kevin argued. "It's just a game."

"Just a game? Are you kidding me!?" The waitress delivered our Pepsi and departed quickly. "What the hell does that even mean? It's easy for you to say, you're well on your way to a career, buddy. If it's just a game, then what have we done spending our whole lives perfecting our skill? You think it's a... God, I can't believe you! You have no idea how lucky you are."

"Relax, will ya?" he demanded. "I didn't mean anything by it."

"I doubt you mean anything you ever say," I countered-punched.

"Boys," Katie interjected. "Come on. This isn't fun. Let's cool it, okay?"

"No, Katie," I answered. "I'm sorry but I won't cool it. Kevin has no idea what he is talking about." I caught him in a death-eye lock and continued. "I know that I will never get to play baseball again, okay? How does that sit with you, smart ass? I won't ever get to slide into home for the winning run of a championship. I know I'll never pad around with my best buddies on road trips, and I'll never stand on the mound at Fenway Park. Got it, asshole?"

"Augie, calm down," Kevin insisted.

259

"No. I'm sick of being calm. I won't calm down. I've lost my chance, Kevin. And you expect me to stand around here and watch you blow yours like some dumb loser at a craps table who keeps betting sixes when the dice are loaded to roll sevens all night long? You just don't get it, do you? You have absolutely no idea." I leaned onto the table and shouted. "Listen to me. I love this game. Above all else, I want to see the best players in the world excel and keep this game alive and exciting for the fans, for their parents, for the kids for Christ's sake. But mostly for myself. What do you think about that? Huh? I'm a fan now, Kevin. That's all I will ever be. A fan. I can't play the game I love at the level I once knew and because of that I will never doff my cap to a cheering crowd on a warm summer evening when I belt homer number forty. I won't ever sprint out into the chilly afternoon air to start at second base for opening day in Pittsburgh. But I know you can and you will. You owe it to the game. The game is bigger than we are, Kevin. We make up its history. It has broken hearts of Dodgers fans, Giants fans, Indians fans and so on long before we ever breathed. And it elated the hearts of the Yankees fans, the Reds, the Pirates, the Cardinals and every other team that ever won the World Series. And it will continue to do so long after we can barely scuff at the dirt on the mound with our aging feet. The game needs to go on. Baseball needs players to play their best. So, your dad tried to keep you from playing, big deal. He only thought he was doing what was best for you. How dare you remain angry with him for that! He cared, and for that you should be thankful. He could have halted it a long time ago, told you, 'No way, uh-uh, no son of mine is gonna play baseball.' But he didn't. He saw something in you or maybe he just figured hell if you enjoyed the game, then what harm was there in that.

"I know more about your life than you realize, Kevin. Your dad has reasons why he didn't want you playing this stupid game as you dare call it. He sacrificed more for you by letting you play when it was killing him to know that at any moment it could all disappear. On a single pitch your career and your chances could end. In that very act alone, he showed more love for you and respect for you than half the guys in this world ever see from their parents. And if you can't see that, then maybe you aren't good enough to carry his name on your jersey when you stride out to that mound."

The silence resumed with a thunderous emptiness. Kevin stared at a plate, his arms perched angrily in a lock across his chest. His lower lip stretched red across the upper teeth that mashed into it. Katie scratched up the last bites of a salad. In my best imitation of Kevin Bentworth, I rose from the table, dropped my share of the estimated bill on the decorative tablecloth and walked out of the restaurant without a word.

26 The College Try

That spring of 1991 rolled into promise and excitement. It was the perfect marriage for a splendid summer, a winning baseball team and a town in need of a champion.

Before long, the school year had ended and I found myself at home with the Owls in the midst of a pennant race. The shear expectation of victory, the constant pulse of impending success, the crowds re-alighted with pride and the town awash in thoughts of championship runs triggered a sense of wonder, unquenchable in my wild ambition. If I had made any strides in agreeing with fate that I was to be a non-player, it was wiped away like thin fog on a windshield. That summer, as wins were amassed in droves and teams feared playing in Cooperstown, there awakened in me the passion to play the game again. It was not at all a dead passion, but rather a dormant one, having been prematurely put to rest by science and recovery. But now, with summer ablaze and victories abundant, thoughts turned toward possibility. The dangerous thought of *What if?* careened in and around my mind. What I had "accepted" a year earlier when I resigned myself to a permanent spot on the sidelines, suddenly became the driving conviction that I still had something left.

Had the Owls gone quietly along the early summer with more losses than wins, I may have walked into my future without ever again considering that baseball was still available to me. But with the wins doubling the losses and the Owls perched atop first place in the standings, my resolve weakened. To add to the difficulty, the Pirates were winners again for the second season in a row. Between both the Owls and the Pirates winning game upon game, I confronted daily the reminder of just how good it can be to play baseball.

Stubbornness took over and I began to wonder if old Augie didn't still have a little something to offer the game, at least on the level at which the Owls competed. I was, after all, still a young man, could still pound the bat pretty well (if batting practice was any indication) and had kept in shape after rehab had ended. "In shape" being the point to which I could jog without gasping for breath and could do sit-ups into the hundreds without being exhausted. So, I figured, why not?

August Monroe was ready to make his comeback.

It was late summer, 1991, and I returned to Roth College as a new student, a new human being entirely. I looked forward to working for the school newspaper, the only foreseeable benefit after the accident. I had dabbled in journalism off and on during my first two years and had often considered it my best option for *after* my baseball career. I had not considered it the alternative to a career as it turned out to be. Alas, my baseball career failed long before it even became a career. Journalism was supposed to be my major. In truth, I majored in baseball and took classes in writing and news reporting to fill the required course load. I had also made arrangements to try my hand at broadcasting after returning for the new semester. The senior, Dale Elinger, famous for his high-pitched cackle of a call shouting, somewhat overstated considering we were not on CBS Radio, "The Roth College crow is heard across the land as the Roosters do it again," after every school victory, had graduated and no one seemed to be interested in filling the position. Although football and basketball would take up much of the radio airspace, there were to be fifteen baseball games broadcast on the college radio station. It wasn't much of a radio station, maybe 500 or 750 watts that reached only to the outskirts of town, but it was a chance to put my voice in front of a microphone and see what I could accomplish.

That was all fair and well as I set my sights toward new goals and a new identity. It all changed when Coach Culpepper posted a sign in the student union building that triggered the continuation of my *What if?* thinking. It was a sign he had posted every year of his sixteen seasons as Roth's coach, and a sign I had passed idly by in both my freshman and sophomore years. It read, quite simply, that the team was looking for players to try-out for baseball. Nothing fancy, just a white poster board announcing try-outs on Saturday, August 31st. Seeing that sign was the point at which my resolve broke. I marked the calendar.

I decided not to tell mom or dad. They might have objected and yanked me out of college all together, replacing my living quarters with a rubber-padded room. Upon further review, I would have served my needs better had I told them, and not Melony.

Her voice grew agitated over the phone. "You're doing what?"

"I'm serious," I told her. "I'm going to try a comeback, play for the Roosters again."

"August Monroe, don't you dare make me come down there and break that leg of yours again. Because that's what I'll do if I

263

have to. I might as well do it now and save you the anguish. Don't so this!" she demanded.

"What? Why not?" I begged. "The leg feels great. I feel strong, and you yourself said my daily running has progressed my recovery further than the doctors probably thought possible."

"But August," she cried. A long pause followed into and through the phone line between us. I think she was crying. She continued. "Dammit. Why do you have to do this? What if you get hurt again?"

"Melony," I said. "I have to know. I can't sit by the rest of my life wondering if I could have been able to play again. I am young enough that if I tear up the leg again, it will heal in time. What if it is already healed well enough to play? The doctors said I shouldn't even be walking. Maybe this is a sign, like a miracle or a message or something. I don't know. I just know the timing feels right, this feels right."

"But, it's just a game. Give it up."

"No, I can't. It's just a game to you. To me it is a lot more. It is everything I know and the only thing I love doing. I'm not going to let a little adversity stay in the way."

"Fine," she said. Her voice dropped to a nearly mute octave. "Do what you want."

The line went dead, and I considered the finality of the phone call as a sign that we were through dating. While that would not prove to be true, the thought at that moment only furthered my resolve. *Fine*, I thought, *I'll do this on my own, on my terms.*

The first leg of my attempted come back would prove easier than convincing Melony that it was a good idea. I would have to gain approval from Coach Culpepper. I caught up with him just as he was leaving his office for the weekend.

"A comeback, hey?" he asked after I told him of my intentions.

"Yep, I think I can do it."

"What do your parents think about the idea?"

"Oh, they're all for it," I lied...again. What could they really do anyway? I was over eighteen and they weren't even paying for college. "They said if I keep my grades up and protect the weak leg and still be able to play, then they see no harm in it."

"Well, I can't give you back a scholarship," he reminded me.

"Understandable," I said. "I have tuition covered."

264

He patted me on the back. "Well, then," he said. "I guess I'll see you on Saturday. Just be careful."

"I will," I promised.

"And good luck."

So it was set. Just five days back on campus and I was ready to give it a try. I was nervous. I hadn't stepped on a baseball diamond since the try-out with the Owls on the day of the accident. With any notions of pitching erased entirely from my dreams, I could concentrate solely on second base, my old home. Playing second was a concern, however. The dexterity required to pivot and bounce, react and throw at second is much greater than that of an outfield position.

I spent the week in the gym relentlessly pushing the physical limitations of exercise. I focused on conditioning drills and took extra sprints in an effort to convince myself that the leg was strong enough to support my return. By Thursday, I had seen all I wanted of the inside of the gym. I awoke the next day to a drizzle-filled morning that would push us indoors for the first work-out – straight back into the gym.

I downed a moderate breakfast and jogged through the mild spatter of rain. I stopped alongside the entry way of the aging gym and peered inside. A mass of recruits anxiously awaited their first try at college ball. Beside them stood my former teammates. I pressed my back firmly against the damp, soft-toned yellow brick facade of the building and let out a heavy sigh. In that, my first moment of indecision about the comeback, I pondered the reality of my experiment.

Okay, Monroe, give it your best. Just do this and either make it or break it. Either way, you've gotta go in there and try. Besides, this was only to be a work-out, the try-outs were still a day away.

With my resolve recommitted and my face getting soaked, I pushed away from the wall and entered the gymnasium. I meandered into the open space of the gym through a narrow, dank hallway that opened up to a bright, static, artificial atmosphere of hardwood basketball flooring and high-reaching, steel-spanning girders. The presence of echoes filled my head with thoughts of competition and perseverance.

My former shortstop and double-play companion, Matt Pera, saw me enter. "Monroe, what are you doing here?"

"Hey, Scoop." I addressed him using the nickname I had come up with. "I'm here to give it a try."

265

"Really? That's awesome." He crossed the gym and greeted me with the manly half-hug and pat on the back that athletes so often share. "Hey, everyone," he addressed loudly to the twenty or so guys in the room, "Bags is gonna give it another try." I smiled through mild accolades.

Hearing Scoop share our dual nickname was all I needed to know that maybe giving it a shot was worthwhile, regardless of the outcome.

Coach skipped any formal introductions and lined us up in rows opposite each other where we were partnered with a catching mate. We tossed soft catch and stretched out our arms that had either sat dormant all summer or had never been used by those few players making their first try on a real baseball team. The stiffness lingered through ten or more throws and slowly worked its way out into a steady flow of loose and cozy tosses. Scoop fielded my awkward throws like the pinpoint shortstop he was, including the few error-laden lobs I dealt that skipped hard at him off the unyielding wooden surface. Somewhere, the Roth College hoops coach was turning in his sleep, knowing that his court was being scuffed.

Coach Culpepper wove in and out of the tiny tandems and delivered instructions on how to throw better, catch softer or step into a pitch more accurately. It was like being a soldier who had long been deprived the regimen of duty and discipline, and I could not have been happier.

Coach watched a few Scoop-to-Bags exchanges. "How ya feeling, kid?" he asked.

"Good, Coach. Real good," I answered. "Say, where are the pitchers?" I asked. I feigned mild curiosity while deep inside pissed not to have shocked Kevin with my return.

"They're lazy," Coach stated. "They sleep late and ruin my work-outs. I get them in the end, though. In a few weeks when the rest of you guys are all toned up and ready to play, I will have them logging extra miles around the track."

The two hour work-out of soft drills and routine fundamentals passed uneventfully, and by the time the clouds had cleared enough to take bats and balls out onto the baseball diamond, I was certain I had made the right decision. Being back with the guys was a welcome reprieve to the dull life I had experienced away from baseball.

Outside, the field was damp but inviting as we spread out in random formation to begin real practice. I hesitantly tapped the soft grass with my healed leg. It felt like my bed. I tested the bounce and resistance of the muscles that had not supported such endurance in months. While the step was a bit pensive at first, it felt strong and agile, ready for play. I calmly strode out to the second base area and eyed my former position like a guard dog crossing his domain. As the infield grass ceased ahead of me, the ginger give of drying sand reverberated ever-so-slightly under my weight. The transition was subtle but noticeable. I paused, wondering if anyone had noticed. Around me continued the chattering and the throwing that is baseball practice. I walked across the sand and again tested the leg's resolve. There too it felt sure-footed, grounded with muscular certainty.

We took to our stations on the field, and it was then that I met my would-be successor, a freshman named Jake Bellefield who would replace me after graduation if I made the team, or steal my spot outright with a better performance. He was taller than me, too tall to be vouching for a job at second base, I thought. Known from his high school play to have a good pivot and a stronger arm than mine, I knew I could out hit him but may not have bested him defensively. If there were to be a competition, it would be in the field.

I offered a nod of greeting. "You're Bellefield?" I asked. "How ya doing?"

"Yeah, Jake," he answered in half-breaths. "Didn't you play last year?"

"Two years ago," I told him. "I tore my leg up in a car accident, though."

"Can you play on the leg?" he asked. His question seemed sincere enough, as if he was really curious rather than staking out his chances at my position.

"Well," I answered, "we'll have to see."

"Hey, good luck. I hope the leg holds up for you. A lot of the guys say good things about you. I hope you're on the team."

"Even if it means sitting a scholarship player?" I pressed. I was being more defensive than the situation called for. The kid was, after all, being fair and pretty cool.

"Who me? No. Not a scholarship here," he added.

No scholarship? I wondered. My dig had gone for not.

Coach sent another freshman to the plate who sprayed grounders and fly balls in our direction, and soon the pattern of a practice emerged from the assembled stations. At first I was timid and allowed would-be hits to skip past me in lackadaisical effort to avoid really pushing myself. After fielding a few solid grounders, though, my confidence returned and I was chasing down harder shots hit my way. Between myself and Jake we only fielded twenty or so hits but we fought each other hard. A few fast ones got by me, which he snagged while backing me up. His glove was quick to gather in what I could not catch. Only once did I beat him, on a sharp drive up the middle that he had over-pursued and which I was able to backpedal into and collect. There was no clear indication as to who might take the starting position based on that one outing. Still, it was obvious I would have to work hard to take the spot from him. He was a good fielder and made minimal mistakes in judgment. He pushed me to excel.

As quickly as the two hours inside the gym had squirreled away, so too passed the hour on the field. Coach dismissed us to our classes, and I told him I was grateful for the opportunity to practice that morning. I was elated to have performed well without a tinge of discomfort.

That evening, I prepared for an early wake-up to get back on the field and give it a go again. I had polished off my studying for the day, had put in my hours at the English department (including several answers logged into the crossword puzzle), and went to sleep feeling absolutely certain that the leg would hold up and I would be playing baseball again.

I fell asleep easily. A dream resurfaced that I had been having since I was eleven years old. Time and time again it recurred as Kevin and I toasted a dreamscape victory in the 1994 World Series, champions of the Montreal Expos. How we had worked out a joint draft or contract never reasoned into the dreams, but always we were teammates. And the celebration as World Series victors became larger and grander every time I had that crazy dream. It had occurred sporadically over the years, presenting itself in no particular pattern of consistency. But it always returned and we always won.

Another morning greeted the campus with a shadow of rain-drenched skies, the second harder and heavier than the day before. The resilient energy I had fallen asleep with awoke to a rigid soreness throughout my tired torso and twitching back. As much as I had exercised and kept up with conditioning the previous weeks, nothing could replicate the heavy work-out of a day on the field. I pulled myself upward and stretched into the calm, dripping morning. I reached high to the ceiling and then bent forward to loosen the back. A twinge shimmied across the lower portion of

268

the repaired knee, just above the heaviest scar where bone had once protruded. A quick moment of panic shot through my hope-filled heart. Maybe the leg was beyond heavy use. I gave the leg a good shake and the twinge disappeared entirely. I told myself it was just a cramp from sleeping crooked.

Preparing for the second day, while slower and less energetic, was an exercise itself in perseverance. My mind and soul wished to race out to the field and turn laser quick precision double plays while my head reasoned solemnly that patience was in order. The heavier rains would keep us indoors again.

I consumed breakfast slowly. I crossed campus with a steady trot. I arrived at the gym. The foggy numbness that had sauntered in my brain seemed to exist equally in the faces and actions of my teammates. Some who had only the day before been jumping in place or tossing phantom baskets with over-expanded energy, sat slumped and weary along the bleachers. Jake lay down long across the second row of seats and engaged in a slow conversation with another kid who teetered on the brink of sleep a row above him. This was not the looks of a college team ready to win the title. It looked like the remnants of a party in the bleary hours of morning.

Coach Culpepper started us with light calisthenics and increased the regimen to striding sprints, eventually he had us taking lap after lap of jogging. Whatever the mayhem in the man's practices was, it worked. We soon resembled the lively, youth-driven pack of boys we were, hungry and energetic and charged for the task at hand.

I paid little attention to the soreness that was fleeing my muscles with each passing lap. Further from my mind was the tiny spurt of discomfort I had felt earlier from the knee. Soon, I was at full sprint, keeping pace with the other players.

Coach set up orange pylons on the court to mark the bases of an indoor field, a makeshift diamond. As the rain intensified outside and the chatter arose inside, we began to simulate outdoor play in unison on the hardwood floor. Playing the bounce of the hard leather ball as it reacted with sharp intensity against the flooring made taking grounders especially difficult.

The warm thud of a baseball hitting the dirt was replaced by the plank and ping of balls skipping off the surface intended for a larger, softer, inflated basketball. The scuffle of spiked baseball shoes across cindered surfaces was supplanted with squeaks and chirps of tennis shoes on the waxed parquet topping. As a tandem, myself and Scoop fielded mock double plays with the resonant plank, squeak, skip and spring of an indoor game. Hardly anyone noticed the liquid, wrenching splosh that popped inside my cartilage, though they certainly reacted collectively to the thunderous gulp of a scream and the sinking clump of my body mashing relentlessly against that same hard flooring.

On a routine play where Scoop did his best to facilitate his name by gathering up a short bouncer to the imaginary area designated as shortstop between two traffic cones, I planted my right foot with my senses keen to simultaneously grasp the ball in mid-air, tag the thick, bold rubber base of the cone which stood symbolically as the alleged second base, and pivot at the waist to throw to a fake first base. My weight shifted from left to right and I felt the stretch and tear of ligaments rip inside my leg like a famished lion indulging on the fresh carcass of a newly killed gazelle. The ball I lobbed toward first skirmished away into the open space of nowhere and bounded off into a corner uncaught. I plummeted to the floor in instant agony. All that I had worked for was gone.

For the second time in my life, hell the second time in twelve months, I was deemed "fortunate" by the doctor who oversaw my trip to the emergency room. Culpepper, Scoop and a suddenly present Kevin Bentworth carried me across their lumbering arms into a nearby car and rushed me to the local hospital. The quiet morning of an emergency room in tiny Shadesville was mildly interrupted by my party's intrusion. The thrusting through steel-framed, glass-clad doors and the begging for a wheelchair or a stretcher as I lay like a basket of wet wheat laboriously lugged between two farmers, sent the hospital staff into frenzied action. Soon, the pain subsided under the heavy warmth of Percocet. Coach Culpepper told a doctor what had happened, and it sounded much more gruesome than I remembered, his tale an arabesque recounting of the events just passed. Before his version of the story reached its gory climax, I slipped into numb unconsciousness as the intravenous drug penetrated my brain and lulled to sleep my confused and agitated central nervous system.

When I came around again, Kevin and Scoop were not to be seen, and Coach sat slumped and sluggish in a chair across the room.

"Coach," I whispered, the drought in my throat enough to plague an entire county.

"August," he said with a start, "don't speak. If you need to rest, let it be. You're okay. No damage, just a severe strain."

What the words meant to me at that moment disappeared beyond me in a rolling daze as I drifted away again. My second awakening brought me into a room filled with Coach, along with a mother and a father and a girlfriend, who like magic had been whisked to the scene to stand admiringly at my side. I wiped away the veiling fog of somnambulant narcotics.

"Quit staring," I muttered in an attempted joke. "You'll make me piss myself."

"Oh, August," mom gaffed, "that is no way to talk."

"How long have I been asleep?" I asked.

"Only about three hours," Melony answered. "The doctor was afraid at first that you might need surgery so he hit you with a pretty hard painkiller. When the x-rays on your leg came back negative, they lessened the dosage. So, wake up will ya?"

"Son," dad said. I thought for certain I was dead to rights in trouble if he addressed me that way. "You gave us quite a scare. After last spring and how far you've come, we thought." He paused. "Well, we thought you might have done irreversible damage to that leg."

"But the leg's okay?" I hopefully searched.

"Yeah," dad answered, "the leg's fine. You'll have some swelling and discomfort but it should heal nicely. But..." His pause told me all I knew I didn't want to hear; not then, not ever.

"No baseball," I uttered.

"That's right," mom added. "No baseball. And you're lucky to be in pain, because I could just kill you for doing this to yourself. Honestly, August. What were you thinking?"

If I tried to explain to my mother that having suffered this little setback was worth the risk and the opportunity to possibly play again, it would have been wasted words. Quite simply, she probably would not have understood. A lot of people would not have understood. But at least I knew. Regardless of what I would ever go on to do, I knew with absolute certainty that my body would not allow me to play baseball ever again. Maybe I was fortunate. After all, had the rain not forced us inside that morning, the leg may have stood with greater resilience when pressured against the soft dirt of the baseball diamond. It may have been weeks or months or years before the strain had given way to the popping pain I had felt. And by then the tear may have been too much to achieve full recovery. As it was, the leg was banged up pretty badly, would require repeat conditioning but nothing impossible or different than the previous summer. Dad had told the classic "protect my kid" lie when I first woke up by saying the leg was fine. Had he told me there was damage, though reparable, I may have slipped into a depressed coma and disappeared entirely. Instead, he lied a good lie and gave me hope.

I was returned to school, worked out the kinks in the leg and polished up the puzzle. Then, I got back into studying. The memory I will always have of that day will not be the screech of activity from one moment in a baseball drill up to the news that I wouldn't be playing again. Nor will it be the soft lure of drugs or the crunching jabs of pain. No, what I remember most vividly about that day was the long, sweet smile I received from Melony. Lying there with the realization that my life in the game of baseball was definitely over, this time without a single doubt, Melony gazed at me and smiled. It was, on one level, her way of saying both, "I told you so" and "I'm sorry, but it will be okay" simultaneously. Beyond her smile, I envisioned one dream being finalized as another took promise.

27 "The Gods, The Heroes & The Children"

The first piece I had published was entitled, "The Gods, The Heroes & The Children" and it was, not surprisingly, about baseball. With the essay was published, I became, officially (though I had been grinding out unread stuff for years) a writer. The story it told, while being about baseball, was essentially about me.

The story had always been a part of me, as it told of critical events that were absolutely true. It was, in part, the story of my Grandpa as well, though some details were exaggerated and others left out entirely. I guess that's what writing is really about anyway. Grandpa and I had always shared a special bond that started with baseball and grew onto levels beyond. As I grew, so too did our relationship. With all due respect to my dad and to my paternal grandfather, for I was lucky enough to have good male role models everywhere in my life and enjoyed solid relationships with both, the relationship I had with Grandpa was special. From Literature to politics, or from terribly offensive jokes that we would not share with anyone else to competitive tennis matches where he usually won, we shared things together that others could not appreciate. But it always came back to baseball.

Whether playing catch, attending a game or grumbling in the off-season that football winters dragged on, it was baseball that sought us out, brought us together and held us in check for the sixteen years I was lucky enough to share my life with him.

The story began in 1936 when Grandpa took a young lady on a date. Little did either know that said lady would someday be better known to me as Gram-mah-ma. Grandpa was not bold enough to presume that the young lady accompanying him that day would take him up on what he considered to be the perfect entertainment, and what he would rather have been doing on a summer afternoon in Pittsburgh. He had planned ahead to postpone their first date for a Saturday when the Pirates would be playing out of town. The young couple embarked on their innocent rendezvous, hopping a trolley and heading toward Oakland, where in those days everything that was anything in Pittsburgh would have been going on for everybody. Much to Grandpa's surprise, Fate may have been lending a hand. He had remembered the schedule incorrectly.

They jumped from the trolley on Forbes and Fifth Avenues, and were greeted by an on-rushing crowd heading in ways each and every. There wasn't a panic about the actions of the mob, though there was a certain urgency to their stride. Grandpa nodded to his date and pointed with his index finger in the *Wait, I'll take care of this gesture* that might have been customary for a gentleman in 1936. He asked a passing gentleman what all the fuss was about. *Where was everyone off to?* Gram-mah-ma asked Grandpa as soon as the stranger had disappeared into the herding throng of humanity. *Why, to a baseball game, it appears*, Grandpa had answered. Not one to miss a game, Grandpa whisked the young Bernadette O'Toole off to the ball park.

To hear her tell it is actually the sweeter tale, and the story that echoes with stronger romance. For while Grandpa can tell you that the Pirates outlasted the Brooklyn Dodgers by a score of 4-1 that day, Gram-mah-ma will relay that she had never been so bored in all her life! *The game was silly*, I can hear her complain. *What are they doing now?* She continually asked. Her date had suddenly lost all interest in her, a disinterest that had lasted all afternoon. But, Gram-mah-ma claimed, she was determined to stick it out for the entire date, no matter how bored she became or how much she did not understand the "silly" game. She liked the young fellow and surely wasn't about to sacrifice a potential second date by complaining about having to spend a few hours lost to boredom.

I took a few liberties with the story, and expanded it to explore my relationship with Grandpa. I surmised that baseball was about the aforementioned Gods, Heroes and Children. The term "baseball gods" was one I had heard quite often over the years, as if the game had its own special consulate to govern and predict its history. I envisioned a group of stout, conscientious overseers who served as prognosticators of victory or defeat. They planned when teams would rise and fall and stood in strict observance of the game, heralding its truth. The heroes were the players themselves, the contestants who bring victory or defeat to the fans. Baseball perhaps represents the people of a township or city better than any politic or religion. Finally, the children, represented in the story by yours truly, who were so affected by the game we love, the heroes we follow and the gods we worship who bring us summer sun, baseball fun and long home runs, as it were. But the children were not bound by age, for those who witness and share the youthful joy with the game are in some ways always children.

The essay was a treatise as much as it was non-fiction. I spent more space between the margins blathering about the more profound philosophical ramifications of baseball than I did in actually telling a story. Still, the importance of the tale rang true and needed to be told.

The irony in the actual events contains more of the meat to the story than the essay itself does. As well, it was the part of the story that was not fabricated, while many of the events were totally fictitious. A large portion revolved around that night in 1976 when I attended my first Pirates game. It was against the LA Dodgers, the same Dodgers (of Brooklyn then) who lost to the Pirates 4-1 as my grandmother whittled away the dull hours she spent at a game on a hot Saturday afternoon forty years earlier. And, while Grandpa could not even tell you the day he was married without looking at the calendar, were you to ask Gram-mah-ma when their first date was, she would say in her usual, love-fond remembrance voice: *Oh, that's easy; it was July 30th, your grandfather's birthday, and yours, too.* She always took the time to remind me that my birthday was July 30th, as if I was not aware of the fact, and that July 30th was also a birthday I shared with her husband, my Grandpa (which I also knew).

In essence, "The Gods, The Heroes & The Children" were all in cohorts to bring me into the great arena that is life and its subpart, baseball. The serendipity within such a story and its players lends certain credence to the powers such events have on our lives. Had I not attended that particular game, would the events have occurred? Of course. But irony also sets itself apart as beauty, perhaps greater. Grandpa and I agree that while we both wish we could have played professional baseball, neither would change how things turned out in the least. From Grandpa's perspective, had he become a pro ball player, he may never have married and may never have sired a daughter who later became my mother. He would have lost the opportunity to teach and share baseball further with me, his grandson. Had I not had the accident, and perhaps may have gone on to the stellar career I desired, I may never have seen the game for what it is truly worth. Baseball has had its troublesome times through a much maligned and colorful history – it has been hated, adored, despised, and regretted by millions – but it really is all about us. It is democracy and hope, and that, I think, is the ideal America.

There is still a greater irony of that fated day in 1976 which needs to be considered. And it all comes down to pitching.

While Gram-mah-ma and Grandpa watched the game in 1936, a young pitcher from South Dakota did his best to settle the Pirates but came up empty while trying to figure out their hitters. To the best of his abilities, Grandpa recalled, he could not get the knack for pitching when the Pirates were just better, period. The outing was terrible for the young hurler. In short, the scoreboard (and the Dodgers defense behind him) did him greater justice than his individual performance merited. He struck out just one batter and walked eleven while scattering 16 hits. He did not assist himself either, committing two fielding blunders and striking out at the plate in his two at bats. To add higher insult, he was thumped clean in the arm by a pitch in the seventh inning. A fastball caught him right below the rotator cuff. He dropped to the ground in obvious anguish. The man's pain, Gram-mah-ma will tell, was the only thing she recalled from such an otherwise uneventful day.

Billy Wigel's fate as a losing pitcher in 1936 is not so important to the story. What matters, as was written in "The Gods, The Heroes & The Children," and the final clue that solidified the concept for me as its author, was that Wigel was also in attendance as I witnessed the Pirates topple the 1976 version of the Los Angeles Dodgers, as a third base coach and assistant manager, though absent his right arm. I asked Grandpa how a one-armed man could possibly play baseball and Grandpa informed me that he had both arms in 1936 until that fatal blow caused a hemorrhaging in his shoulder that never healed right. Now, to be clear, he did not lose the arm at that juncture. After several surgeries, the arm was terribly deformed though, and never quite the same again. He lost it, Grandpa went on to tell me, later as a semi-pro player trying to make a comeback when his bruised and battered shoulder met with the same fate it had in 1936. He was plunked in the same arm again in 1947, presumably by a much harder and faster pitch from a stronger pitcher, thus rendering his arm dead from the shoulder on down. That second and much harder-thrown fastball was hurled by Mr. Ridley Bentworth, who I would meet decades later in Cooperstown.

That Wigel stayed on in baseball as a coach, I always felt, was a testament to his love for the game. Perhaps, as I grew older, it became apparent that there wasn't much else he could do. What good is a one-armed man in a steel mill or on an assembly line? The job choices were slim back then, long before the Americans with Disabilities Act opened up the various tasks that any person with a disability, no matter how severe or mild, could accomplish.

But it was late in the game in 1976, with the Pirates tied 2-2 when I saw just how useful and practical a one-armed third-base coach could be. With runners on first and second, the Dodgers' catcher, Steve Yeager, lined a ball to short left-center. The Pirates' center fielder bobbled the ball and the runners broke for home. Eyeing the activities in the outfield, Wigel was able to wave the runner home, thus registering the Dodgers' winning runs on July 30, 1976. For a third base coach to get a clear view of the outfield, he would stand outside the white chalk line, facing the field, so that his right side would face toward home and his left would be directed toward the outfield. As a runner rounded third, the signal to keep advancing is the windmill motion made with the left arm, urging the runner to pass third and head for the plate. No one needs two arms for that job, and with his outstanding ability, knowledge of the game and keen perception, who better than a one-armed, left-handed coach!

As the runners rounded third, there was Wigel, waving, though slightly off balance, his left (and only) arm in a wild, sporadic gesturing windmill. He signaled to the runner, essentially telling him, *Move as fast as you can and beat the throw to the plate!* Meanwhile, a quarter mile above, unaware of how all this was intertwining, there I sat, chomping away at any portion of the classic baseball meal: a flat Coke, stale popcorn and cold hot dog.

Thus, my career as a baseball writer began in much the same way my first love had begun, by accident, of sorts. I was asked to prepare a speech for a seminar I was attending at the University of NY, Binghamton, and used the premise of the above story as a sample. I wrote that baseball was a game involving "The Gods, The Heroes & The Children." The speech was uneventful and put more than one graduate student to sleep, yet one member of the audience perceived it as more than just a presentation. Dalton Morrison, editor and critic, later recommended that I edit the speech into essay form and submit it for publication. To which I said, "Are you crazy?" He said, "Uhm, yes. Yes, I am. But that has nothing to do with it."

Somehow it got published! To add to the madness of it all, it actually gained "critical acclaim and recognition." How odd that a bunch of ramblings about who I am and where I come from could land me a career as a broadcaster and part-time writer. Seven months later, the story was published in a literary publication called, appropriately enough, *Serendipity.* And while the rest was far from history, it is all, fundamentally, about this same story.

28 The Chase

This was The Chase. The Owls were finally in the thick of a pennant race. By the end of summer, 1991, they were headed toward the play offs.

The Owls had burned through July and August, going 24-2 and 20-6, respectively. They were eight games atop Columbus in the Northeast Standings and looked to gain home field advantage for the play-offs. Kevin withdrew from classes in order to play and had maintained his solid outings. He held a 7-2 record after August, including two no decisions where the team's run support could not aide him enough in consecutive 4-3 setbacks. He had left the mound with leads in both games. Still, he was effective, and was gaining experience and confidence. The tutelage of the older players gave him an insider's perspective on how to play the game professionally, how to act, how to handle the small news corps of Cooperstown. Even the most serious fan became no match for his skill at answering critics and praises. His biggest test came when they played on the road in New York where even the International League team, the Long Island Seascrapers, amassed a media entourage not unlike those to which smaller major markets in Kansas City and Milwaukee were accustomed. He responded well to the questions fired at him after the Owls bested the lowly Seascrapers 8-1 on July 16th and seemed to be unintimidated, if not entirely unimpressed, by the aggressiveness of the reporters. In fact, he was pretty straight-forward with them.

Dad and I made the trip to Long Island to see the game and greeted Kevin in the locker room after he had taken the victory with a complete game, a rarity for him considering the velocity with which he threw.

A small crew of reporters gathered around him with the usual questions about how he felt on the mound, what his technique was, and whether he hoped to move up to the Majors soon. The questions were fair and balanced until one reporter from northern New Jersey threw a sucker punch at him in front of all those microphones.

"Is it true your dad used to pitch in the Majors?"

"What?" Scribble, scribble went the note pads.

"I didn't know that," went the murmurs.

"Did you know that?" asked reporters to each other.

"Where'd he get that scoop?" inquired those more skeptical.

"That's good news, makes a hell of a story," uttered someone.

Kevin blinked. "Say again?" He asked. He regained himself nicely.

All eyes fell on the reporter from New Jersey and all voices quieted as he repeated the question. "Didn't your dad play pro ball?"

"Yeah, he did. For a while," Kevin answered.

"When?" the local guy up from Cooperstown asked.

"Back in the 50's I guess it was," Kevin answered. "He pitched for Chicago for a while."

"And St. Louis," I chipped in. Twelve sets of eyes peered toward me.

"So, who are you?" asked some guy with a Yankees hat on. (Just my luck.)

"He's my best friend," Kevin retorted. They ignored me as more questions were lobbed at Kevin.

"What was his name?"

"Did he teach you to pitch? That'd be one hell of a story."

"Was he at the game tonight?"

"Does he coach you often?"

Then finally, the jerk from New Jersey raised the question that he knew he had to ask to sell papers. It did make for a good story. He must have done his homework.

"Your dad maimed a guy at the plate, didn't he?"

Stunned silence fell across the locker room. Kevin stared straight at the guy.

"Yeah," Kevin answered, after a long pause. He looked away and down like a puppy in trouble. "Yeah, I guess he did."

In that solid moment of silence, three other reporters had made their way over to Kevin's locker and had learned from their cohorts what all the noise had been about. As well, a few of the Owls stood on the outer circle, wanting to get a piece of whatever was going on.

"What do you have to say about that?" asked one of the new reporters to join the herd.

"What do I have to say?" Kevin repeated, paused. "I have nothing to say. It's old news. Dad was cleared of any wrongdoing, he went back to pitching and that was that. It was an accident."

They pushed further, and I could see that my dad was edging toward irritation. Dad had always been a calm man, not one to create unnecessary conflict, but this was becoming something different entirely.

"How did he maim him?" a reporter asked.

"Did he kill a guy, hit him in the head or something?"

"Was there a trial?"

Dad stepped in at that moment and broke up the flurry of questions.

"Gentlemen," he said loudly. "This interview is over. Mr. Bentworth has a right to his privacy. I suggest you go to your own archives if you want to find out more on the story."

"Are you his old man?" one reporter asked.

"Yeah, who the hell are you anyway?" another followed.

"No." Dad paused. "I am not his father." And then the man who taught me honesty and virtue, who had told me to always face accusations head on, lied right in front of me, and I could not have been more proud. It was beautiful. My only thought was, *Way to go, dad*! He looked the jerk from New Jersey straight in the eye and said, "I'm his lawyer."

A few reporters peeled away, but the majority stayed, hungry for a story. Life must be pretty dull around New York when the Yankees suck and the Mets are flailing around average. So dull, in fact, that the best piece of news they could conjure up was at least forty years old.

"Well, come on. At least give us his name. Who was he? Who was the batter?"

Dad remained calm, lifted Kevin's jersey from its hook and turned it around, showing the reporters the back with Kevin's number. Across the top was stitched his last name.

"You guys are real geniuses, aren't you?" Dad ridiculed them. "It must take a graduate from Harvard to figure out that there probably haven't been many Bentworths to play the game. Grab an encyclopedia, boys. Though I recommend you get one of the baseball variety. Now, please, I insist that you leave my client alone."

Miffed, the reporters backed off like jilted hounds denied the carcass of a pheasant. They stirred and paced, looking elsewhere for a story.

"Nice work, dad," I said, sliding him an open palm for a quick slap of five.

"Yeah, thanks, Mr. Monroe," Kevin added. "You really got me out of a jam there."

Dad huddled around us and looked over his shoulder. "No problem," he said. "Now let's get out of here before they catch onto me or I'll be in their papers tomorrow, listed as an accomplice or some crap they conjure up."

We snuck out of the clubhouse, and I couldn't help but think that at least one of them would dig into Mr. Bentworth's past and uncover the story. Surely their resources were deeper and better organized than what I had dug through many summers before. Hopefully by the time it surfaced Kevin and the Owls would be long gone. Luckily, it was their only New York City trip for that season. The Seascrapers had played in Cooperstown in early May and had no chance of making the play-offs for 1991. The story might find its way to press, but it would not bring Kevin any pressure. At no other time did I welcome the tiny confides of Cooperstown with as much respect for quiet, small town America as I did then. He didn't need any distractions, not when his concentration needed to be at its peak. No, it wouldn't come up.

Or, I could have been wrong.

Cooperstown isn't so far removed from New York City that an eager reporter would not think twice about driving two hours upstate to dig into a fleshy story if it promised results. Luckily, it was not the jerk from New Jersey. Instead, it was a fair-minded columnist who wrote for the *New York Daily News*, a man who wrote about sports as well as local interests and vacation spots. He was a good writer, whose stories always had a unique flare. He often combined personal elements to enlarge a smaller story. Rather than just point out details, he looked for connections. His tales tied life to fact and intertwined the two into a significance that may have gone overlooked by common viewers. His name was Dale Stergum.

He had been in town about two days before he called on the Bentworths, and I only learned of his presence when Mrs. Highsmith, still at the helm of the library, asked me how Kevin was doing.

"Fine," I told her. "Why do you ask?"

"Oh, no reason really. It's just that a stranger came around asking about him day before yesterday. I thought it was Dale Stergum, the columnist." She blushed and continued. "I asked him what he wanted of Kevin and he said he just wanted to learn a bit about who he was in high school, maybe see some old news stories about his days playing ball here as a boy. Do you find that peculiar, August? That a big time New York City writer would be up here asking about Kevin Bentworth?"

"Well. Ma'am. Kevin has become quite a story of late. He's pitching well and the team is winning. A lot of people are going to want to know more about him. Do you know if Stergum is still in town?"

"He said he'd be here a few days and that if I found anything of interest in the archives to contact him at the Holiday Inn up on Route 17."

"Thanks," I said. I made my way to the door. Something seemed peculiar all right. Maybe it was the fact that he had arrived at all. Or maybe that he had gone straight to the library for information and had not contacted Kevin or his family first.

What ensued was not a media storm per se, but a strong gale making waves off the coast. Kevin was interviewed over and over by Stergum, who hoped he could crack the young pitcher. Kevin the baseball player had become a story outside of the game and the constant nagging grew on him quickly.

Kevin began to unravel. At first, it was just a funk, a bad phase he should have been able to throw his way out off. Then, he began walking batters at an alarming rate and making poor decisions in tight spots against batters he had bamboozled just weeks before. He was psyching himself out and was losing his composure on the mound. It began with a game on the road against Nashville. He walked in a run with the bases loaded to lose a game in the bottom of the ninth. If he had never appeared so sloppy before, it was a game I had not witnessed. A week later against Maryland, he could not get out of a jam in the fifth inning and was pulled for a relief pitcher with a four run deficit, men on the corners and only one out. It would only get worse from there. His next start was at home against St. Paul when Kevin completely fell apart. He didn't even get out of the first inning. He gave up seven runs on nine hits and a walk before the engines in the parking lot had begun to cool. The only out came at the expense of an interference call at second base.

Murray had warned Kevin that they didn't want to use up the bullpen. In fact, he had considered resting Kevin due to his recent string of poor outings but had opted not to, hoping to get him back on track. His plan backfired. Instead of being relaxed and having fun, Kevin was tense.

He reminded me how serious a losing streak could be. "If I go out there and stink the joint up again," he said, "they'll run me out of town."

"They will not run you out of town. Did one, single fan boo when we blew the state championship on our own field in high school?"

"No, I suppose not."

"Did anyone kill you when you struck me out our senior year to end my hitting streak?"

"No, they didn't but that was different."

"No," I said, "Not different at all. These people love baseball and they love to watch you play it. Sure, they want you to win but you just worry about you. I'll take care of the fans. Listen, just pitch your way out of this slump and you'll be fine."

"What? You think I'm in a slump? Hey, listen," he warned me, "I am not in a slump." It seems that every baseball player since Cy Young has been afraid to admit when he is in a slump, as if admitting it will somehow make it worse. It seems to me (and it seemed very clear to me talking with Kevin then) that admitting being in a slump would help a player out of that slump by forcing a confrontation with the slump itself. But not ball players. They are too damn stubborn. Maybe they are just plain weird. And not Kevin. He is worse than stubborn. He's obstinate.

So, rather than going to the mound and having fun, Kevin Bentworth did in fact stink the joint up. A few fans did boo – after all, fans will be fans. Most were indifferent to the who and why of the situation and sat in quiet disgust as St. Paul romped the Owls 10-2.

But I like to think that the fifth inning stuck in their heads more than the outcome of the game. As the teams were switching sides between innings, after Kevin had pitched a terrible top of the fifth, I implemented a plan I had devised as a distraction. Mrs. Denton's neighbor, Miss Winthrop of the terrible lemonade fame, was out of town for a week visiting a sister somewhere, and I had the added displeasure of keeping her dogs, the same two dogs, Mopsy and Poppy, who hated each other more than any tandem perhaps in history. Despite their senior years, both the pesky Shih Tzu and the wimpy Bull Mastiff could still put on quite a tussle. In fact, Mopsy scared the heck out of the milder but larger Poppy.

From under the opening in the Nest, I let loose the funniest entertainment activity to be seen in Cooperstown. Employees of the team work year in and year out to come up with creative and clever promotions that will attract fans to a game they might otherwise not attend. This was an especially important job when the team was losing more games than they won, and even more crucial in the minor leagues. As a possible distraction to the play on the field, promotions would be presented ranging from free cash grabs to egg hunts and from sumo wrestling to kite flying contests. Whatever it took to entertain or to draw more people to the parks, they would do. All summer long, the promotions personnel would shamelessly send out circus freaks and motor airplane geeks to entertain the crowd.

That night I bested them all, and to this day no one knows I was the culprit of what has come to be known simply as Dog Day. I snuck the dogs into the field through the groundskeeper's entrance and threw a hot dog into centerfield. The dogs took the bait.

With fervor and violence, Mopsy chased poor Poppy all over the field, yelping and barking as she charged hard while nipping his heels. The crowd and the teams laughed and pointed, engrossed in the oddity of the smaller dog harassing the massive beast that ran in fear from its life-long nemesis. It really was cruel of me. Poppy, after all, was a great dog and Mopsy was nothing but a nasty little snot. But I had to save Kevin. And by the time Mopsy responded to my sharp whistle (the same Miss Winthrop used to call her dogs to dinner) the crowd on hand had forgotten Kevin's performance all together.

What was the onus of Kevin's debacle and ensuing slide from precision? Our dear comrade in pen, Mr. Dale Stergum. If I had admired his writing before, I now despised his ethics and found him distasteful. It was not a question of personal integrity. I just could not tolerate the thought that he had done what he had done to my friend, my town and my team.

On the front page of *The Daily News* sports page for Sunday, September 1, 1991, his column was printed with the headline: "Is Cooperstown Harboring a Fugitive In Its Roost?" A sub-head proclaimed: "Local Pitcher's Father Hides Mysterious Past in Baseball's Gloryland." Beside the eye-popping headline was a picture of Kevin that had been taken that day in Long Island, snapped just as he answered in a dejected downcast voice, "Yeah, I guess he did," to the question, "Didn't your old man maim a guy?" Next to it was a picture taken straight from the twilight zone. It was a fuzzy photo but it was easy to depict what had occurred.

The photo had been taken from somewhere behind the pitcher's mound. Mr. Bentworth stared in towards home plate, his baggy uniform brazing the number 6 across the width of his back. His arms, one adorned with a baseball mitt and the other bare at the hand, hung loose to his sides. In the background, the aim of the camera's focus, lay a man writhing in pain across home plate, clutching at his right shoulder as the catcher and umpire lean in to assist him. It must have been snapped moments before the actual medical crew had arrived. In all fairness, it captured the image of great photography. The wounded soldier lie wrapped in pain while the slaying victor stood brooding from afar, taking in his victory from atop the battlements. In reality, it was a terrible accident that Mr. Bentworth would suffer from for his remaining days.

Under each photo read a separate caption that united the moments. "Senior Bentworth watches 1947 incident as wild pitch shatters Billy Wigel's arm," ran under the older photo. Under Kevin's more recent, cleaner shot read, "Local hero, Bentworth Junior, recalls memory of hidden tragedy."

It was a disgrace. Its timing could not have been more unjustified. Just as Kevin faced adversity on the field for the first time, this story ran about how his father had broken the arm of Billy Wigel over forty years earlier. Wigel later had his arm amputated as a result of the injury and, of course, never played baseball again. The injury may not have been so tragic had it been just a fastball that had gotten away. Nor would it have created such a fervor in the papers at that time had it been a curve ball that slipped out and up. Likewise, its affect would not have cascaded down upon history to intrigue thousands decades later had it been just any old pitcher tossing any old pitch.

Throughout the game's history, men had shattered kneecaps, lost their vision, separated their jaws and their shoulders, and have even died during the season, off the field. The pitch that inspired the photo from 1947 was the famed Steamer that Mr. Bentworth himself had invented. And it was he who maimed a young man. Had it been any other pitcher hurling any other number of pitches, the event would have slid into history unnoticed. But that was not to be the case.

Bentworth had used the pitch sparingly according to most accounts covering baseball at the time. Since my initial discoveries about the Steamer during my boyhood I had come across seventeen other accounts concerning Mr. Bentworth's place in history. The pitch had been mentioned in papers found in San Francisco,

Philadelphia, Houston, and even in my beloved Pittsburgh. Always it was reported as a phenomenon, a wind-up and delivery that might one day change the game entirely. And its hurler was revered as a genius, a man to remember for the ages. Never had he or his pitch soiled the sport nor its connection with America. Never, that is, until 1947. Never until the article I myself had found years earlier but had never shared, in which Billy Wigel's fate collided with The Steamer in a most grotesque fashion.

It was only significant that he had thrown that particular pitch that resulted in the ball striking with great force that particular vein that ruptured in the shoulder of that particular player that would sound the end of both their careers. Mr. Bentworth was out of baseball by the end of the 1947 season, asked never to pitch again. He did face a criminal trial but it was thrown out when the courts had ruled that they had no precedent with which to file suit. After all, the pitch had been approved by the league and it did not appear as if Bentworth had intended malice against Wigel. And Wigel bounced around as a coach and bench manager throughout the minor leagues, having only reached the major league level once as third base coach for Los Angeles Dodgers.

Thus, my life in baseball had come full and absolute circle. The one-armed, wielding third base coach who shook my imagination and fascinated me in his humility was a direct descendent of the story I had no knowledge of in 1976. Furthermore, I had no inclination to even imagine that it was as much my story as it was Wigel's, Mr. Bentworth's or Kevin's.

While the story did little to help Kevin, it sent the town into an absolute frenzy. What all the hub-bub was about was beyond me. It was a story from the past and could easily have just remained there had it not been for the nose of journalism. It was then that I promised myself that my skills as a journalist would be used to help the world and not as a means to tear others down. Whether I have done that I do not know.

What Stergum's article failed to address (For how could the journalist be aware of any such truth?) was the fate of both Bentworth and Wigel *after* the incident. If I myself had previously held any inclinations to discover what had become of Mr. Bentworth or Billy Wigel in the years immediately following the maiming incident, I as well would never have formulated the facts as they really were. Unlike Mr. Stergum, however, I had been privy to information which filled in the missing pieces.

My thoughts often return to the summer of my youth when all of this information first bore itself to me through mysteries and stories. I had been pursued by the one-armed man through the Cooperstown Library, and had met him fearfully at Watson's Deli on that afternoon when my security, Mr. Dewey, had opted to attend a baseball game with Miss Hollencheck, thus leaving me alone in peril out front of his closed eatery. It was there that I met up with the one-armed man who had identified himself to me as Billy Wigel, and off we went to the town square where he felt certain he could provide pieces to the puzzle I was unraveling that summer. Of course, at that time, as I was so young, the point was lost to me. But as the years have progressed and I grew to be a young man, the details remained lodged in my memory as a constant reminder of what I was hoping to one day understand.

Myself and Wigel departed from in front of Watson's Deli and walked casually toward the center of town. If fear had been visibly present in my gait or manner, no one we passed took any notice of my peculiar position. For if they had, certainly they would have stopped the stranger and asked what it was he was doing scaring the minister's son. Or was he a stranger at all? Upon reflecting back to the moments of that day when I had fled from the library only to be ensnared into Wigel's presence out of curiosity, I recall how peculiar it was that a few people doffed their hats to Wigel with a "Good day" or a "How do ya do?" It seemed as if he was in fact known by the citizenry of Cooperstown. I myself had never seen him, not that I was aware.

We had reached the square and stood near a concrete bench. "Okay," I demanded. "We're here where everyone can see us. What do you want?"

He gazed into the gazebo and fountain that stood across the quadrangle. "Do you know, by chance," he asked, "what the word retribution means?"

"Retribution?" I asked.

"Yes, retribution. It is like revenge, only sweeter because it comes with a cost. You do know what revenge is, don't you?" A sinister glimmer formed in his distant eyes.

"Yeah," I answered. "It means to get back at someone, like if I stole a friend's bike, he might take mine but do worse to it by damaging it."

"Yes," he seethed. "Precisely. You are a keen young man. The difference between revenge and retribution is the length of time or the value of repayment that one must guarantee the payback. Let us say, in your brilliant scenario, that your bike was stolen and you learned that your friend had taken it. If it were revenge, you are correct, you would damage his bike further and that would be the end to the matter. But if you were seeking retribution, you would see to it that your friend never rode a bike again. Now do you understand?"

"Why would I want that? My friend already suffered by his bike being taken from him. That's it, the debt is even."

He spoke in an evil purity that frightened me. "Oh, my boy," he whispered. "So young, so naive. You haven't the experience to understand." He stood and paced, imbalanced by a lack of coordination. "Don't you see, if your friend makes the decision to willfully steal your bicycle, then he hasn't the right to ride a bike ever again. You didn't ask him to take your bike. But he took it anyway. He needs to pay a price."

Wigel raged through lunatic sentences for five minutes before he sat down again and informed me of his ultimate retribution, and how, not surprisingly, it had been levied against Mr. Bentworth.

He leaned in, as if to confide. "Your friend, Mr. Bentworth," he said, "stole that which was mine, what was to be my career. He injured me beyond repair. Now, I am nothing but a freak. He also deprived me of my livelihood. Baseball was all that I had, and he ripped it from me with his wild imaginings of a great new pitch, a 'delivery technique' he had called it. Damn that insipid pitch of his. It was a sin!"

His voice reached levels where the human throat nearly loses audibility, and his face wiggled in angry spasms. His tirade only subsided at the passing of another townsmen, James Fettier, who worked for the Owls security force and who addressed Billy Wigel by name.

"Mr. Wigel," he said. "How do you do? August," he nodded as a hello to me.

That Fettier recognized, nay even knew, Wigel registered the truth that had plagued my mind since Wigel had first addressed me on the street earlier that day. How did Wigel know who I was when I had no knowledge of his being in Cooperstown? Fettier answered a question he had never actually been asked.

"You work for the Owls?" I asked the suddenly calming Wigel.

"Oh, you seem surprised," he uttered. "Work? No, not quite. I am a consultant, so to speak. Perhaps you know my brother-in-law, Thurston Hettingbone?"

The recognition of the name resounded like an opponent's home run defeating the Owls. Hettingbone's name had been in the news quite often during the summers of my youth. He had owned the team for as long as anyone could recall.

"I can see by your eyes that it is starting to make sense to you," Wigel continued. "It's perfect, isn't it? The way I have gained my retribution. You wonder why Mr. Bentworth, that sinister Ridley Bentworth, has done nothing more for himself than linger about in dreary Cooperstown with no greater hopes than shoveling dirt across the pitcher's mound or raking the grass in the outfield? Why he never played baseball again? Why he wound up here? Well, let me tell you, young August, that you will someday learn in this life that everything that matters is power. Power changes the world, drives a man to do things he might never imagine he would do otherwise. I was powerless to stop Bentworth from lobbing his crazy notion of a pitch into my injured arm, but I have been certain to take power to ensure that he never forgets what he did to me."

The arrangement was simple. Within a matter of years after their paths had crossed via that fateful pitch, Bentworth was out of baseball and, with little experience or training elsewhere in life, he had very few opportunities for employment. Wigel managed to lure Bentworth to a job in Cooperstown as the Owls field hand in the early 1970's, Bentworth himself unaware that Hettingbone had sought him out at the request of Wigel. Having little else to hope for as employment, Bentworth relocated his young wife and himself to Cooperstown where he took on his present-day job. The one stipulation of his employment, while somewhat illogical to him, perhaps, at the time, appeared as a conflict of interest. He himself could not play for the Owls, but his children could if they chose.

"Why?" I asked Wigel, the day passing on like years under my tiring eyes.

"Retribution!" he declared. "The family is cursed, August. Don't you see it? Bentworth knows it and Kevin will learn some day. With my arrangement, Bentworth would have to stand idly by and watch his son fail miserably as he tried so hard to play baseball. I guarantee you that I have every intention of letting young Kevin play for the Owls. And if I could, I would insure

289

apparent success so that his downfall would be that much more tragic. My joy will be in watching his father suffer so vehemently when his son falls flat in the face of failure."

I puzzled my best sleuth mind at the time. "What makes you so sure Mr. Bentworth hasn't told all of this to Kevin?"

"Because," Wigel answered, "he loves his boy. If it takes him suffering the memory of what he did to ensure that his boy might be happier, then he will quietly work every day of his life to do so. And I assure you, his son will not be happier. He will wallow in his failure. Besides, Mr. Bentworth is afraid."

I looked at him dumbly, unsure what to ask.

He grimaced. "The old man still works at that stupid stadium, doesn't he?"

"Yeah, but –"

"But," he cut me off. "He isn't going anywhere, and has no intention of ever going anywhere. He is trapped. By me, by my power! Every time he crosses that mound, he thinks of me and my missing arm. Every time he collects a paycheck from my brother-in-law, he thinks of what he did to me. Every single day he lets his boy play baseball, he remembers how foolish he was to do this to me. Retribution!"

He clapped me hard on the back, then stood and walked away. Over his shoulder I could see him absorb the warmth of the afternoon's sun as he departed alone. "Retribution," he said, and walked out of the square with a satisfied, uneven gait.

I sat there a long hour or more trying to understand the reasons behind Wigel's cruelty. I was too young to comprehend the depths to which adults would harm one another. Overwhelmed with the complexity of it all, I returned home and lumbered about in attempts to understand, when all the while I was trying best to forget that evil man and his evil ways.

I had all but forgotten the particulars of Wigel's maniacal scheme by 1991. Wigel himself was long dead, as was his brother-in-law, Hettingbone though the family still owned the team. It was Dale Stergum's article and investigative reporting that brought all of this back to me as clear as the sun had shown that day in my amazing summer of 1980. I kept the information from Kevin all those years and had no intention of informing him after Stergum's article had appeared. There would be no point in telling him then – then when he was so close to the biggest game of his life.

29 The Stretch

Kevin weathered the first media storm of his career with rather sound moorings. He answered their questions with honesty and dodged their attacks with dexterity. A week after Stergum's article, Kevin held a press conference to clarify any curiosity that had arisen from the story. Surprisingly, the media's excitement blew over and Kevin went about his task of playing baseball. And he played pretty darn well afterwards. I don't know if it was a result of removing some hefty burden from his shoulders or the realization that his father's past just didn't matter all that much, but Kevin went off on an absolute tear through his opponents after that week of inquiries. It was as if he himself had wanted to clear the issue.

His return to fortune started at home when he piled up back-to-back eleven strikeout performances six days apart from each other, then went on the road to win two more games, including a no-decision that the Owls won against Peoria. His two wins were impressive, the first a nine-K performance yielding only two runs against Erie. The second a ground ball gem where only three balls were hit out of the infield all evening, and he struck out three hitters in a 6-0 crushing of Davenport. He was simply pitching on another level, and as the Owls headed down the stretch toward the play-offs it seemed as if he was really becoming the ace of the staff. After completing the road trip with a 9-2 record, the Owls headed home on September 4th with a five game lead over slumping Maryland, and it seemed likely they would be counting magic numbers shortly.

A team's magic number is the term given to the number of combined wins by the Owls plus losses by the team behind them in the standings that it would take to ensure the Owls a play-off spot. Those words had not been spoken around Cooperstown since anyone could remember, yet all of a sudden the definition was repeated and defined in every barber shop, cafe and gas station for fifty miles around.

The team's confidence was so high at that point that there was serious talk of the championship for the first time all season. I accompanied the team on its trip to Erie. On the bus ride home, Kevin landed a bomb in my noggin with his announcement to me that he had a special plan for his next start.

He interrupted my second reading of John Steinbeck's novel, *Of Mice and Men*. "Augie, put your book down," he said in a whisper. The bus was rolling silently along Interstate 80, and the majority of the players were fast asleep. Kevin looked around the bus and leaned toward me. He said in a deeper whisper, "I'm going to start off the top of the first with the Steamer."

My ears rung with wonder and memories from childhood. "What? Are you nuts?" I had never told him about Wigel's maniacal plan.

"Tomorrow night. Against Rhode Island. Yep. I've been working on it."

"Kevin, don't do that," I warned him. "You're on such a hot streak right now. The league may not allow it. Besides, it's a tricky pitch."

"I've been working on it all summer back in the tunnel during games between my starts. I can do it, Augie. I know I can."

"Kevin," I warned. "These games mean too much. And after that crap you went through last month with the press, they will eat you alive if you do that now."

"Not if it wins ball games, they won't." He jumped back into his own seat before I could say another word. The bus rolled along the otherwise empty interstate. Golden amber-tinted lights sporadically illuminated the interior of the bus, and the soft glow brightened the faces of the team and their boyhood dreams as they slept.

I couldn't sleep a wink. If Kevin threw the Steamer, I'd... what? Really, I mean, what could I do? It was out of my hands. We returned home around 3:00 in the morning and headed back to our various homes or apartments. I laid awake a good two hours mulling over the scenarios that might take place the next night. In one flash I saw him deliver the pitch with awe and precision, a cheer going up from the crowd, a doff of his father's hat in a simultaneous gesture of thanks and congratulations. But each time that image arose another surfaced, one wherein he failed miserably and was laughed out of the game, the son having become the father. I finally fell asleep with the hope, though dimly lit, that he was only joking, that he had no intention of actually using the pitch. These games *were* too important to be messing around. His delivery had been flawless for five consecutive starts and he was getting into a rhythm strong enough to set the tempo for the team's chance at a championship dance. Yet he seemed willing to risk it, and for what? An article in *The Sporting News* or *Baseball*

Weekly? A sick cry for attention? A trick to lure the younger female fans? I couldn't guess. Once again, my friend was proving to be my greatest enigma.

For the first time in my life I awoke on game day dreading a trip to the ballpark. There had been days after the accident when I felt miserable going over to the park knowing I might never play the game again. But I still had the love of baseball as my companion. It was early September and I really wished to be back on campus to begin a semester at Roth. The fall term did not begin, however, until the week after Labor Day, one of the perks of attending a small, private school and undoubtedly my newest curse. I had nowhere to hide. Because if Kevin Bentworth dared to try that pitch in a game so close to the play-offs, with a possible championship season on the line, he would be run out of town. And I would not want to be anywhere near him shortly after the pitch was thrown wild or, worse, killed someone.

I saw him doing early warm-ups and approached him in the bullpen. The Nest was pretty quiet, save the loose chatter of two girls leaning over the railing trying to get a glimpse of Andy Gathco, a sharp and chiseled catcher from Maine who was a fan favorite amongst the *Tiger Beat* clientele.

"Kevin," I demanded. My command went ignored. "Kevin, get over here."

"Augie," he answered in a cocky grin. "Where are the crutches, my boy?"

"I left them at home. I'd rather limp right now, thank you." He tossed a few more pitches softly into the unrelenting backstop, and I seethed with anger. "Bentworth!" He looked my way with depth in his eyes and shrugged his shoulder before scooping one last ball from the bucket of reserves. He tossed it gingerly into the fence that stood 60 feet 6 inches away. "Get over here," I repeated.

"Geeze, what's got you in a tizzy?"

"A tizzy? You know damn well why I'm mad. I hope you've reconsidered and are not going to use that pitch."

He avoided eye contact, instead staring at his shoelaces. "Relax, Augie," he said. "I've got it under control."

"Under control? How so? You have never used that pitch against a real hitter. And where exactly did you learn how to throw it anyway? You've only read about it. And have you even done that? Have you read up on your dad's story or only gone on what I've told you and what you assume? Because there is a lot more to it than thinking you have the pitch under control."

"My dad showed me," he said.

"That is bullshit and we both know it. Your dad said he would never teach anyone how to throw the Steamer."

"I had Randy help me."

"Randy?" I asked, a bit stunned. "Randy Lerango, a lifetime minor leaguer with no fastball? That Randy?"

"Hey, Randy's a great guy. You hardly know him."

"I do not care about his personality just now, Kevin. I'm sure he is a fabulous guy. But what does he know about throwing the Steamer?" I was incensed. "Has he ever tried it? Has he even heard of it?"

"His dad showed him."

"So?"

"His dad played semi-pro ball in the fifties and saw my dad pitch. Randy thinks my technique is pretty solid."

"That is absurd!" I declared. "How could he know your technique is solid when he has no idea what that pitch is about? Let me remind you, my friend, that your father severed a man's arm because of that pitch. It is not meant for this game. It was a great idea, a wonderful concept. But baseball is just not ready for it. Maybe someday, when players wear football pads, but not now. And certainly not from you. One wrong spin on the ball's rotation and your career could be over, pal. I warn you, do not do this! I, I..."

"You what?" he asked. It was a good thing he interrupted or I may have stammered on all night. I was at a loss.

"I forbid it!" I finally said. I chomped my teeth and folded my arms in defiance.

"You what? You forbid it?" he laughed. "Okay, Padre. I'll be sure to say confession afterwards as well. Thanks for the inquisition."

"This isn't funny," I finished.

"Listen, I need to warm up, so if you don't mind, this area is for players only." He spat into the ground. "Don't make me call security."

He climbed atop the bullpen mound and resumed throwing soft warm-up tosses into the fence. I walked away but spun around when he called my name. He stood on the mound with his throwing arm bent upward and his palm laid out flat to the sky, gesturing as if a train whistle, i.e. a steamer, pumping up and down into the air. "First at bat," he said, laughing. "First inning, first hitter."

Somewhere between anger and anticipation I got myself so worked up over the situation that I was both dizzy and convulsive. I felt like I was trapped in a Hitchcock movie, where everything spun in a whirl and a daze, a vertigo of anger. It was silly, considering that it was not my game to win or lose, nor my career to jeopardize. It was all in his own hands, literally. And if he chose to risk everything he had worked for, everything he had experienced that I no longer could, then it would be his own fault for failure. I was tempted to race into Murray's office to warn him of the impending doom by which Kevin was about to destroy the Owls' season, but thought wiser of it.

The common pleasure of watching batting practice was torturous that evening, and the joy of greeting friends as they filled the stadium was a tightrope walk of quiet insanity. People who knew me must have sensed that something was not right and I had to continually dodge questions about *Are you all right?* or *Is everything okay?* It was all I could do not to scream.

The National Anthem finished, and something of dread churned in my gut. The scorecards were exchanged, the plate wiped off and the umpire gave the command to play baseball. The first batter for the New York Kings, Cecil Morningside, strode to the plate. The ball circled one last time around the infield from third to short to second to first and on into Kevin's glove. He quickly toed the rubber, skipping his customary pre-game ritual of sauntering behind the mound until the batter was prepared and in place. That alone signaled to me his sincerity in approaching this game with a valor he had not before carried.

Kevin swung his arms into the delivery and stepped off the mound, asking for time out. The umpire granted it and I released a heavy, groaning sigh. Those seated around me must have thought I had lost a bet that the game would start before 7:04 PM because there was nothing much more to groan about. Kevin bent to one knee and feigned the removal of dirt from his cleats. He looked in my direction. He located me in the stands along the first base line in the first row and smiled a cunning grin, mouthing the words, "Here it comes." I almost vomited.

He replaced himself upon his peak of infamy and set the ball to his glove. The pause before the wind-up, the calm before the storm he was about to unleash. And then it happened so smoothly that I think half or more of the fans and players didn't even notice at all. But the home plate umpire surely must have noticed. He called timeout while the ball was soaring in his general direction. I am sure that in some dark comedy somewhere, in a world of cynicism and hilarity, the ball would have struck the umpire in the chest or on the skull, rendering him dead. But not in this real world. Instead, the pitch landed solid and square in the catcher's mitt for what would have been called a strike had the umpire not stopped play. As it was, the first Steamer thrown in a sanctioned league game in forty years did not count in the scoring. A time-out had been called. Momentarily, the same meeting that had taken place decades earlier in Chicago, as described to me in *Sport View* magazine which I had read as a child, was to occur again in a comical deja vu of history. It was as if meetings of baseball importance should always be held there, on the mound where everyone's attention rest.

The umpire and the catcher trotted toward the mound and were met half way by Murray who was steaming mad and cussing a litany of vulgarity on his way from the dugout. Not surprisingly, the cussing was aimed at his young pitcher. The conversation from the mound was not nearly as colorful but was so heated I could hear it where I sat.

"What in the hell was that, young man?" Murray asked in a controlled rage, his lips as tightly wound as his brow.

"Oh, come on, Murray. You know damn well what it was," Kevin bravely defended.

"I can't allow that," the Umpire stated. "Murray, what the hell was that?"

"That was one hell of a pitch," Gathco offered, not realizing that that was probably not what neither Murray nor the ump wanted to hear. "How'd you learn to pitch like that, kid?"

"Andy," Murray fumed. "Get the hell back behind the plate and let me coach this team, will ya?"

"Sure. Okay, boss," he answered humbly. He departed, though not before adding, "Great pitch, kid. A real zinger."

The conversation became muted after that as Murray animated his anger on the field. The umpire stood by, saying nothing as Kevin absorbed the wrath of Murray's displeasure. Cooler heads prevailed and the two non-pitchers removed themselves from the mound, allowing the game to go on as planned. Kevin supplied a duplicate cunning grin in my direction, warning me that he was going to throw the Steamer again. By now the crowd had grown intrigued. Those who had not noticed the original pitch had been filled in by those who had, and all were anxiously awaiting the next moment. There had been no ruling from the umpire after the conference on the mound, so there was no telling what would occur. Judging by his exaggerated response to Kevin's second pitch, again the Steamer, perfect and strong to the mitt, he was not a pleased umpire. His reactionary jump to stop play failed to include the necessity of calling time-out as he leapt forward in protest, nearly getting knocked in the head. The pitch was a legal strike, recorded on the monochrome yellow on black scoreboard above right field that kept tally of such things. But what ensued was mayhem.

Murray led the charge out of the dugout for a second meeting on the mound. Kevin turned in disgust as if to say, *What did I do?* The batter lobbed threats at Kevin, warning that if he threw that junk again, he would personally see to it that Kevin never walked again, yet alone pitched. This comment was apparently not seen as favorable by Gathco, a burly man with a loyalty unmatched in any gang. He leveled Cecil Morningside with a square chop to the jaw, sending the thin player sprawling onto his backside. The benches of both teams emptied onto the field and a skirmish continued for some five or seven minutes.

The crowd, of course, loved it. We are somehow so enamored toward violence, as long as we can stand back and watch others engaged in it, that it is no wonder boxing and "professional" wrestling are so popular. You would have thought the Owls had just climbed into the ranks of the Major Leagues and had beaten the 1972 Oakland A's in the World Series. Nothing this exciting had happened at an Owls' game since God knows when. Maybe since the light standard burned out in 1967 or the Coke machine exploded in 1984. Who knows? All in all, it wasn't much of a brawl but it would go on to be the talk of the town. Rhode Island's centerfielder clipped Gathco with a solid cross punch and the Owls' Baran landed a strong right jab to an unsuspecting member of the Kings. But otherwise the fray was a lot of shoving and grabbing and little else. Eventually, order returned, the players simmered down and left the field with nothing more than a few shirts wrinkled and a threat or two exchanged, along with a headache for Andy.

As for Kevin, it was announced that his pitch was not considered legal because it was not recognized by the league, and that he would not be throwing it again that night. This seemed to have risen a series of inquiries from the crowd. *Why? What was wrong with it? It got the ball over the plate, didn't it? Better than we could say for Childress.* Laughter, etc...

I sat there, comforted that Kevin had learned his lesson and graciously anticipated the continuation of what still amounted to a rather important game that the Owls needed to win to step closer to post-season play. My security, however, was short-lived as Kevin once again smiled cunningly in my direction, nodded yes and wound up to deliver his now routine Steamer. A second strike was called and by now the home plate umpire had had enough. Kevin was ejected from the game, as were Murray and the Owls' pitching coach. The Rhode Island manager just shook his head and laughed.

The excitement and confusion of the first inning only served to distract the Owls and their fans as the team went on to lose 6-2, thus keeping alive Rhode Island's diminishing chance of knocking Cooperstown out of first place.

The locker room afterwards was abuzz with anger and intensity. Some who loved the pitch supported Kevin fully. Those who hated it cursed at him, and blamed him for the team's loss. Those few who had no idea what the big deal was, were probably so out of tune with the game that they would be spending their winter looking for a new job away from baseball anyway. Kevin was in Murray's office, the door closed, and a slow but steady course of muted screams seeped through the wooden surface. The blind was pulled tightly so that we could see nothing. Ten minutes after the game had ended, Murray stepped from his office and addressed the crowd that had built in the locker room, which consisted of players, family and a few writers.

"All media and personnel not on the Owls team or staff are instructed to leave the room, please." He was dead serious, but somehow that didn't stop Stergum from invoking his press rights.

"But Coach," the dumpy unkempt writer declared, "the people are going to want to know what's going on. They have a right to know."

"Somebody get that waste of a typist out my locker room," Murray boomed. "And the rest of y'all just make your lives easier by doing the same. Family too – out! There is going to be a team meeting and it will be private."

The small group of player's wives and kids, press corps and a few stragglers made their way to the doors. I somehow forgot that I was not a part of the staff or the team and stood near Kevin's locker as if I was not to be included in the exodus. I had been accused of having overstretched my privileges once or twice and those accusations would have been fairly assessed, but I had no intention of leaving. I did not disperse, assuming I was welcome.

"August," Murray said. I looked up to meet his eyes face to face. His glare was steadfast. "You too." I buggered out of there as fast as I could.

The twenty-five players and seven coaches inside that locker room were a cohesive unit, a club to which I did not belong. Kevin and I had always covered the events and goings on of our lives like two wise confidants. But it was different now. I stood outside the locker room that night and realized that I was never going to be a part of that either.

Whatever had been said behind those doors must have been sworn to secrecy, or perhaps remanded to silence by Murray. Not a single player or coach muttered a word. It was as if it had never happened.

30 "This Year"

Kevin was not suspended from the team nor the league. In a ruling by league officials, the pitch was deemed to be legal for use in any game. Much like the same story that had unfolded in Mr. Bentworth's odyssey years before, the league had allowed Kevin to continue using the pitch with caution and discretion. Part of me wondered if maybe someone in the league offices hadn't considered that it might stir up a little controversy, gain some national attention. (Not to mention the possibility of increased ticket sales.) It would be good for the fledgling International League either way. Coupled with the fact that the Owls were bound for the play-offs, there was sure to be some fans across the country who could not resist finding a way to see the Owls play wherever they traveled.

In the interim, the Owls cleared any thoughts of a play-off run from the Rhode Island minds by winning the next two games and sending the team out of Cooperstown with nothing more than the hope of a miracle to continue their season. The Owls' magic number had been reduced to one, and whether they won the game themselves or if Rhode Island lost one mattered little. The team would be back in the play-offs for the first time in over twenty years.

The two wins against Rhode Island were an early predecessor to a giant pause. The Owls' next opponent, their old antagonist, the Rochester Americans, swept a three game series and kept the champagne corks from popping for at least a half of a week. The losses had some of the Owls' faithful talking collapse, somehow allowing themselves to imagine that the team would run through September without a single victory. Likewise, Maryland found a resurgence and took a three game series from Vermont. Their fans were now talking miracle. It was all a home stretch should be in baseball. Summer was fading, and the cool, crisp night air of autumn began to steal its way into the later innings. Trees began to change the color of the landscape to harvest shades of brown and red. Kids returned to extracurricular activities, begging moms and dads to let them skip band practice or cheerleading to watch the Owls. And right in the heart of it was a pennant chase coming down the home stretch.

Lingering there was that colossal number - One. The simplest digit in our numerical system, so pure, so perfect, so unencroached upon. So often the beginning, but in baseball, the end. A goal reached. All they had to do was win one single game and the pennant was theirs. By this point, relying upon Maryland to lose had become a non-option. There was no way this team was going to back into the play-offs. They had to win. Just one game.

The final loss to Rochester was heart wrenching. The game went fourteen innings and the lead changed hands six times before their crafty switch-hitting first basemen launched a solo home run into the dissipated outfield bleachers, sending the Owls home as losers of three straight. It came with a heavy price, the loss. The Owls lost a pitcher, Zeyer, to injury.

Fate may have been playing with cruel irony. For as much as the loss of the game was a stinger, the potential threat to a member of the pitching staff was terrifying. Murray would have to move Kevin up in the rotation and pitch him on four day's rest, something Murray was adamantly against and something the smaller International League frowned upon. But it was Kevin who reminded Murray of the situation they were in.

"Coach," he said in the locker room after the loss, "I'm well rested."

"Yeah," the coach replied, "but I hate using a pitcher on short rest, especially a young guy like yourself. Your arm just isn't ready for that kind of stress."

"Coach, are you forgetting something?"

Murray looked up from his desk to see myself, Gathco and Bentworth all raising the Steamer gesture into the air.

"I didn't pitch," Kevin reminded him. "I was tossed out in the first inning. I'm as fresh as a spring chicken."

Murray's eyes grew wide with delight. In his methodical approach to his profession, he somehow had forgotten to account for the unusual event that had happened less than one short week ago.

"Kid," he said, "you are going to give me a heart attack with the shenanigans you pull, but I tell ya. You're one lucky son of a gun. Give me five," he hooted. He slapped Kevin and me a quick series of fives as he stepped into the locker room. "Gentlemen," he said, gaining the attention of his team, "we need not worry about our season. The pennant will be ours. We have ourselves a starter for tomorrow night's game."

He placed a solid arm around Kevin's shoulder, sending a group of grown men chirping and cheering in support of their young teammate who had seemed to do so wrong but who may have done just the right thing.

Kevin's next start did not begin with the Steamer, and a capacity crowd sighed a collective let down as the first pitch swung out of the strike zone for a ball. Kevin walked the first batter on five pitches, and disappointment rippled up into the rafters of the grandstands. Murray quickly called for time and trotted (less angrily) than before out to the mound.

"You all right, Kev?"

"Yeah," Kevin explained. "Just a little tight."

"And a bit nervous," Murray reminded him. "Listen, just stay loose, keep your focus and have some fun out here. This is just a game, remember that. Hey, why don't you throw that Steamer? If the league approves, why the hell shouldn't we use it? Besides, it's what all these people came out here to see anyway."

Kevin shrugged. "I don't think so, Coach."

"You don't think so? You used it last week without clearing it with me and now you don't think so! Use the pitch, Kid. But do it when you're ready. You throw that thing better than your dad did. I think it was meant for you."

The crowd grew restless, chanting "Let's get on with it!" and "What's the hold up?" The home plate umpire began his slow trot to the mound to break up the two-man symposium. Murray descended the mound and headed back to the bench.

Kevin stepped from the mound, practiced his former ritual of pacing on the grass in front of second base and went back to work. He threw a nasty strike right past the hitter. No, it wasn't the Steamer, but it was a blazing fastball. He worked the inning well and had two outs with the runner still on first when he finally gave the people what they wanted. A smart and sophisticated hitter strode to the left hand side of the plate. I doubt whether Kevin had wondered if the pitch would be effective against lefties. His only game trial was against the right-handed Cecil Morningside, whose ego had remained bruised long after that game had ended. But the Rochester right fielder was a classic hitter's hitter. A thinking man with great ability to see the ball, know the strike zone and anticipate the next pitch. He too would go on to play Major League ball in Kansas City and Cleveland, but for now he was the challenge at hand against Kevin.

Kevin was a pretty bright fellow himself. When Murray returned to the bench I could hear him utter to his players, "I gave him the okay to use it." He said no more. One would think that

Kevin would jump at the opportunity to bring the crowd to their feet with the next batter to step into the box. But he had already run down the order, knowing who he would face that inning. Unless a ground ball turned into a double play, he would face a total of four hitters that inning. And he had to have known the Americans' right fielder, Billy Patterson, would be the perfect guy to fool with the Steamer. The other two hitters would have frozen easily, taken their strike before protesting to the ump. Not Patterson. He was already calculating what he would see. And when Kevin geared down and fired six sharp fastballs at the number two and three hitters, Patterson walked to the plate and had to be thinking change-up. *There is no way this kid is going to throw me heat after all those fastballs,* he was probably considering. He rubbed his bat with the pine tar rag and eyed Kevin up and down. Even as he turned his back to me in the batter's box, his demeanor suggested that he knew a change-up was coming first.

He held the bat lower than his shoulders, much lower than his usual stance wherein his bat is held high above his ears as he awaits a pitch. He had figured right, Kevin would not throw a traditional "fastball." But he had no way of guessing that he would throw a different and harder type of fastball.

Kevin set his motion, checked the runner at first and shook off two of Gathco's signs. Andy shrugged his shoulders as if to say, "Then throw it, Kid. I can catch anything you toss at me." And throw it he did.

In antithesis to the agony I felt a week earlier while dreading the arrival of the Steamer, I stood on crouched toes. Kevin brought the ball to his waist and paused. It was a long pause, a solid pause. He then brought his glove and ball to his torso, began the wind-up with the subtle leg kick, the turning of the mid-section, and the crooking of the elbow. The thrusting of the white orb into the open atmosphere of space, the leaning back and stretching of the right arm toward the outfield where typically a pitcher would hold the ball before aiming it homeward. A hush filtered across the stadium. Patterson gazed upward ever-so-slightly as if questioning what he was seeing. The ball heightened its ascent, paused and began its downward journey as expected, not spinning, not rolling, just falling weighted and direct toward nothing. And in the very beauty of the pitch, the sheer syncopation of the delivery, Kevin's open hand gripped the ball during its descent just as it reached the point where it might have fallen before him.

A week prior I was so up in arms about the Steamer, so much that I didn't even take the time to appreciate watching the actual thing happen. Here had been this mysterious piece of baseball lore, and I was one of only a handful of people alive who knew of its existence, yet I had rarely seen it delivered. When I did, I was sick from it. But that had changed. As the ball whizzed into Gathco's mitt, signaling a strike from the ump, I relished in the moment as if my own son had pitched a perfect no-hitter. I had actually witnessed Mr. Bentworth's Steamer brought back to life by his son.

What followed was a mere parody of what had occurred in 1947 and had repeated itself a week earlier. In fact, it was the same exchange of *What's* and *How's* that would go on to occur every time Kevin first threw the pitch against a new team until every manager had seen it against one of his players, had sprung from the bench in protest, and had been told to go back and have a seat because the league had okayed the pitch.

The crowd overwhelmingly voiced their approval. They had come to see the Steamer and Kevin had delivered. And there remained poor Billy Patterson, perhaps the smartest player on either bench, who was so dumbfounded by the bamboozlement he had endured that he simply stood by and watched two more pitches pass for strikes. The first was a slider and the second a Steamer to record the final out of the first inning.

The Owls' hitters fed from the frenzy of the first inning and scored quickly in the bottom half to gain a 2–0 lead, their first lead since beating Maryland four games earlier when their magic number had been reduced to one. It felt good to be winning again.

But winning doesn't always come easy. Kevin hummed along for six solid innings, mixing a nice array of sliders, the Steamer, and pure fastballs. The Rochester batters never knew when to expect the Steamer, and the two who had not had it thrown their way paced with angst in the dugout, just waiting for it. He must have had them all thinking through their guts and out of their minds. It was as much fun watching the mind game going on as it was seeing the Steamer.

The trick to the pitch, it seemed, and perhaps what Kevin's dad had figured but had not been able to work around, was altering it slightly for each individual hitter. I recalled having read that the senior Bentworth had found success against taller hitters with the pitch but had oddly lost control of it with men who stood closer to five feet ten or thereabouts. It didn't make much sense at first, and

304

in fact the idea of alterations was only suggested in one article, but it was a definite trend seen by the writers of that era. Was it his own inhibition working against a smaller target? Or perhaps a mechanical flaw wherein the pitch naturally soared a bit higher? It was impossible to judge since there wasn't much film from the three seasons Mr. Bentworth had played in the Majors. In order to justify any real complexities, the pitch had to be used in games in order to be truly gauged. Then it occurred to me, somewhere into the sixth inning of that momentous game on a deeply cold September night when I should have been at school studying.

Kevin's arms were longer! While he had the tight shoulders and heavy chest of his father that allowed him to accelerate his momentum, his arms were easily three to five inches longer than his dad's. They were more like his mother's arm as evidenced by pictures. And that was where the mechanics separated themselves from the pitch. With extra flexibility in a longer, lankier arm, Kevin could adjust the pitch at the very instant he gripped the ball as it descended into his awaiting hand. When facing a shorter hitter, he dropped his elbow level with his shoulders to deliver the pitch. And with the taller opponents, those roughly six feet or taller, he extended the arm, releasing the ball when his arm stood at a right angle away from his shoulders.

He had really studied and practiced the intricacies of his inherited pitch. And quite well it seemed. Not only had he understood the mechanics of making the pitch rotate to his benefit, but he also grasped the physics of the ball's approach toward home plate. During that sixth inning, something else finally occurred to me that made me laugh to myself full-heartedly. *Oh my God, of course!* I whispered in my internal voice. That's why he transferred to private school for our senior year. He had said it was for science classes so he could go on to study engineering in college, but it was for the pitch. While it was partially true that engineering was a good education for him, it also was a practical move by which he could study physics. It was like an extracurricular work in progress. Having the knowledge of physics, Kevin manipulated and mastered the pitch systematically and scientifically to make it works at its optimum performance. Brilliant!

As if that wasn't a loud enough resonation of awareness, the next piece of logic I assembled nearly sent me sprawling up the stairs in a fit of laugher unlike any seen in a comedy at the movies. He hadn't disappeared at all those weeks after confronting his dad

305

at the fair. He had begun practicing the pitch that very moment! The clarity was uncanny. How could I have missed it? There I was, brooding all summer over the alleged retreat of my friend, and he was already preparing himself for this moment, for these games. To etch his place in history.

By the top of the seventh, Kevin began to tire. The lead-off hitter, who had been fooled by two Steamers in his previous at bats, was expecting the pitch. Kevin did not throw it. Instead, he lobbed a nice, juicy pitch over the center of the plate that was lined for a double into left center. Next up was Patterson, the original victim of the first official league recognized strikeout at the hand of Bentworth's Steamer. He was still miffed when he reached the plate, and stood in defiance of Kevin's victory over him. His second at bat in the fourth inning was a walk surrendered on four pitches, a non-intentional intentional walk as if Kevin had said, *I respect you. Here, have a freebie.* All it did was stoke Patterson's fire.

Kevin's first pitch was a clear brushback, a reminder that Kevin was not afraid of Patterson. The tough veteran glared with disapproval, pointing his bat at Kevin not so much as a threat but in the unwritten language of baseball. Patterson stepped into the batter's box and rather than rest the bat on his shoulders, held it pointed out towards the mound. The novice fan would have seen it perhaps as a timing measurement used to judge the pitcher's wind-up. A baseball insider knew it to be a warning, a statement: *Don't push your luck!* But Kevin hardly flinched. He spun a pretty slider by Patterson for a strike. Patterson accepted the challenge and rested his bat back upon his shoulders, relenting that his warning had been heeded. The next two pitches were foul balls off of Kevin's hardest fastballs of the evening. The count stood in Kevin's favor, one ball and two strikes. The runner on second base was of no concern. The Owls were ready to concede the run to get Patterson out.

Kevin looked long into Gathco for the signal. For the first time in Gathco's life he called for something called "the Steamer," a rough signal they had only concocted prior to the fourth inning. The signal made sense, the three last fingers of the right hand pointed upwards while the thumb held the index in check. Kevin shook it off. Poor Gathco must have been going nuts. He finally suggested the pitch and the kid waved it off. He called for a slider. Kevin shook it off as well. Fine, Gathco must have reasoned, throw whatever you want, and gave the no call signal, leaving it up to Kevin to choose.

The pitch was a curve ball, not part of Kevin's repertoire of pitches and one he was unpracticed at delivering. But before he threw, he forced a time-out. He appeared to have stepped into the wind-up to deliver the Steamer, and as the ball descended, he stopped cold, called time out and grabbed the ball before it hit the ground. It had to have been a mind game against Patterson. Officially, it should have been scored a balk. Apparently, the umpire wasn't thinking that way and allowed the time-out to be taken. Now Patterson was probably thinking Steamer and increased in confidence after having seen the offering before. Surely, he could knock it a good solid whop if it came.

But instead Kevin threw the unpracticed curveball. Patterson hesitated just slightly in reaction but leaned into his swing with the hammer of a mauler and launched the ball into deep right field. Had he not hesitated, it surely would have cleared the fence, but in that instance he took enough off of his swing to land a solid safe hit into the deepest corner of right field. As Towleson chased after the ball, the runner scored easily and Patterson rounded second, sliding in safely at third for a triple. He grinned a venomous chuckle in Kevin's direction. Kevin ignored him.

Kevin forced the next batter into an infield ground out, thus not allowing Patterson to advance. With one out and a runner on third, every member of Rochester's team knew Kevin would not be bringing the Steamer. It would give Patterson all the time in the world needed to steal home. Hell, the pitch took so much time to deliver that it would not even have been stealing home. It would have simply been there for the taking. The cards were in their favor. The hitter, Rochester's catcher Davey Owens, came to the plate and chatted with Andy Gathco.

"Where'd that boy learn to pitch?" the catcher asked his counterpart.

"Hell," Gathco answered.

It was enough to shake the catcher. He stared oddly at Gathco, not sure what to make of the statement. Bravely, he shook off the implications of the comment and dug in to take his at bat. The result proved to be a good fight between pitcher and hitter. Kevin got him looking at the first pitch for a called strike and Owens watched a loose second pitch head away as a ball, holding off his swing and taking the pitch. Then Kevin reached into his reserve and blew a fast slider straight past him. Owens swung hard

307

and missed with a swooshing gulp of air that turned little spirals in the dirt. Kevin was nearing exhaustion and it was evident in his timing. After each pitch he hesitated and lollygagged behind the mound, digging for strength in his tiring arm. He worked the count to two balls and two strikes on a curve ball that was suddenly working for him. Then it was Owens' turn to take some time. He adjusted his cap, his gloves and his shoulders before stepping back in. Kevin gave him the high heat that Owens wanted and Owens fouled off three consecutive pitches, offering souvenirs to the chanting fans.

Kevin was out of gas and could throw no more heat, and Owens seemed to sense the fact. It was either a curve ball or a slider, which may not go for the long ball but could certainly bring in the runner from third to tie the game with a single. Kevin reared back again, lofted a hard slider into Owens' wheelhouse and it was drilled high into centerfield. Not high enough to score the run, though, and the ball landed in the mitt of Langston in straightaway center. But Patterson tagged unexpectedly and broke for home!

Gathco, already on his feet, tossed his mask aside and awaited the throw from the outfield. At that moment, I envisioned myself as the cut-off man at second base, where I may very well have been playing had I not had the accident. The second baseman yelled, "Runner!" signaling to the center fielder to prepare to come up throwing when he made the catch. It all happens so fast that it is a precision timepiece of activity. The second baseman watches the runner, sees he is tagging, turns to receive the cut-off throw and hollers the command. Had it been me, I would have loved nothing more than to receive the ball, pivot and launch a laser beam of a throw into Gathco's mitt to record the out.

But the throw never hit the cut-off man. Langston was gunning for the out all the way. He took the ball and heaved it directly into home plate. The ball in flight sent a momentary pause through the stadium as all eyes tensed with the anticipation of the exciting play at home plate. The ball bounced once just north of the pitcher's mound and skipped gingerly into Gathco's mitt. He had the plate blocked and was a solid catcher, but Patterson was larger and could have bowled him over. The tag was applied simultaneously with the thump of Patterson's body into Gathco's. The call would come down from the umpire, based on whether or not Andy could hold onto the ball. He rolled head over body away from the plate toward the Owls dugout and sprang to a full standing position, showing the umpire that the ball was lodged safely in his mitt.

"Yer ouutt!" was called.

A cascade of erupting thunder welcomed the unorthodox but nonetheless effective double play. The Owls held their lead, 2- 1, and maintained their chance at clinching the pennant.

The Owls' half of the seventh, as well as both sides of the eighth inning, ended silently with nothing more than an Owls' runner left stranded on first in the eighth. Kevin struck out two while retiring the side in the top of the eighth, the inning-ending-K a third called strike. Then came the top of the ninth and with the Owls ahead, a sheer electricity spread through the ballpark. To my surprise and to the fan's obvious approval, Kevin took the mound to pitch the ninth. It was a risky move by Murray but a solid one at that point. Remembering that his pitching staff was exhausted, and considering that this was not yet the end of the season, Murray gave Bentworth the chance to win the game outright. Kevin had not hurled a complete game yet as an Owl, and what better stage to announce his presence than that night when the Owls could claim their prize?

I counted six games remaining on the schedule. Surely, the Owls would win one or Maryland would lose another. And that was all it took at this point. The Marylanders stood seven games out. Thus, barring any so-called miracles, it was just a matter of time before the Owls would clinch the pennant.

The ninth began wildly out of control for Kevin. He sent the first pitch sailing beyond Gathco's reach and walked Jose Cordisca on five pitches. Murray called for time. He offered Kevin the casual advice to calm down, watch the strike zone and end this thing. Bentworth pushed the count against Riggins to two and two, a hitter's count. He would be taking all the way in case the ball sailed out of the zone. The pitch was low but hittable and Riggins got on top of it, bouncing a dull roller toward short. Mackenzie easily slid the ball over to Rakowski for the force out at second but could not turn the double play. Riggins was a sprinter and made it to first without a throw. One out, a runner on first. Kevin could work from the stretch.

Owens was up and drilled the first pitch deep but foul down the left-field line, sending a scream of panic through the crowd. Kevin knew he would not get that lucky a second time. He threw hard and low to Owens and dogged him into a lazy pop-up that landed quietly in Mackenzie's glove. Two outs.

Kevin's nemesis took his time getting to the plate, gesturing to the crowd that the fence for a home run ball was not out of his reach. "He's tired," he said, pointing at Kevin and grinning.

Kevin stepped from the mound again and rubbed the ball hard and serious. He told me later that he walked himself through the entire at bat before it happened. Start him with a slider, then bring heat until you get two strikes. Then see what happens. Sure enough, the first slider, which still had pretty good movement on it that late in the game and in cooling weather, caught Patterson by surprise. He swung heavily, missing the ball outside. Strike one. Kevin kicked up a swirl of dirt in self-adulation, then regained his composure, took the ball from Gathco and reset to pitch again. He brought the fastball and it too was drilled to deep left field just as Owens had done. It hung out there like a balloon above the ocean, not knowing where to go as the hopes of the team rested on its landing point. The third base umpire tipped down the foul line, watching the ball as it finally hooked and sailed into the stands. He signaled foul ball, and a second sigh of relief echoed throughout the park.

Kevin then toyed with Patterson and lobbed up a ball so soft that he had to take it. If he had swung, it would have been a weak grounder to the mound that Kevin could have fielded and recorded the out. In fact, he did it twice. The same helpless pitch that snuck into Gathco's glove just before it risked hitting the dirt. Kevin knew what he was doing. Patterson would be assuming that he was losing his speed and would hope for a walk or look for an easy pitch to render a single. But Kevin was better than that. He coughed up a ball so tight and inside that he forced Patterson to foul it off. Kevin wasn't smiling on the mound. His countenance was stored and reserved. But inside I know he was having the confrontation of his life.

For the first time all game, Kevin rested the ball on the tops of his knees, bending over as if winded before continuing. He checked the runner at first more for show than any real threat. The object of his concern was Patterson. After a quick set of position, he started into his delivery and returned the pose we had not seen for some four innings. He was bringing the Steamer, Patterson's own nemesis. The ball went up, Kevin gyrated and adjusted, the ball came down and met his hand as planned. The pitch was launched. Patterson swung so heavy at the pitch that a sound barrier somewhere must have been broken. But to no avail. He

310

swung right through the pitch, missing it completely to record the final out. The Owls had won the pennant!

Pandemonium let loose in the stands and on the field. I was one of many who leapt the railing and celebrated along with my team on the grass around the pitcher's mound. Kevin had done the improbable. He had led his new team to the International League Championship Series!

31 The Series

The town of Cooperstown was abuzz with glee and anticipation the week prior to the championship series. The Owls knocked Wheeling from the play-offs in a swift four-game sweep, and as Raleigh and Columbus battled to a seventh game, the Owls rested up and prepared for the series. The summer had been long and the schedule rough as the talent pool throughout the International League reached levels it had not seen since the era before World War II. Still, the pains of a long summer, stiffness from repeated injuries and the wear and tear of life on the road at a less than luxurious level could hardly keep the Cooperstown Boys of Summer from experiencing sheer excitement. Batting practices were light, pitching rotations reduced and condition training less than vigorous. All about the ball park levity and confidence filled the air. If ever there was hope throughout our tiny burg that a championship was within reach, 1991 was the year. This was our season. Endurance would be tested, nerves stressed and a champion crowned.

Rumors of a prematurely planned victory parade were quickly squashed by Murray. He marched right into the mayor's office and demanded that she please tell the citizens to stop that kind of talk, it was a jinx and could only hurt the Owls in their championship quest.

The series was to start on a Saturday, and it was the Thursday before when I made my way to Owls Stadium in mid-afternoon to watch batting practice. I gained a good perspective on the team's status if I could witness batting and fielding practice. Besides, it made me feel as if I were a part of the team, and also provided a means to ease my ever-mounting tensions. I was more nervous than the players.

My old mentor Denkinger was at the plate taking his practice swings. He swung his usually heavy bat that year and had carried the Owls upon his experience, if not his determination alone. He had been relegated to the role of a pinch-hitter and a Sunday catcher, having given his life and his knees to the game. He wanted to win a championship worse than anything he had ever wanted his entire life. He had, he told me, previously reconciled to the fact that this was as far as he would ever get in professional baseball. He was never going to The Show, and he felt certain the end of his semi-pro career was fast approaching. This would be his last chance at a championship. Not only was he living to enjoy each moment, he also had every intention to make the effort count.

He swatted baseballs over left field and into the parking lot as if he were tossing candy to kids three feet away. With each crack of his bat an echo resounded around the park and all eyes watched as the trailing orb disappeared time and time again. He had already hit three solid shots by the time I approached the dugout, and Murray sat smiling in awe of the veteran's prowess with the bat. Denkinger mashed pitch after pitch into the outfield, and Murray began counting the players on the field. His face took on a puzzled look as he finished his count.

"Monroe?" he asked me.

"Yeah, Skipper?"

"Remind me so I'm not crazy. How many players are we allowed to carry on a play-off roster?"

"Thirty-one," I assured him, paying little heed to his possible reasons for asking. "Forty in the Bigs."

"That's what I thought," he said. He counted again. "How many pitchers?"

"Ten," I answered.

"That leaves 21 others to take BP," he stated more than questioned.

"Yeah," I answered. "I guess it does, Coach. What's the point?"

Before he answered, I saw the logic of his question. I had heard him count to 24 both times. The number, including coaches, should have equaled 23, the 21 players and two coaches allowed on the field by league rules during batting practice.

In a simultaneous pause of such moments, a pitch was released from Coach Baylor's throwing hand, the ball sailed obediently into Denkinger's powerhouse. The batsman swung hard, lacing a solid line drive over the shortstop playing area. Murray sprinted up the steps, releasing a hollering warning to stop the activity on the field. But it was too late. Something Murray had seen and sensed was out of place. As Denkinger's whizzing line drive made its way toward the outfield wall, all eyes were on Murray, all eyes except for two. Emerging from the scenery in deep left field and ambling slowly toward my right, which was in the direction heading towards centerfield from left, was Matt Satnik, the young starter who had filled the Owls' need for a third strong hurler during the season. He did not respond to the coach's voice billowing the stop command. Nor did he notice the sudden

313

frozen hesitation of others on the field. Instead, he continued to walk, directly into the path of Denkinger's racing line drive.

The next movement on the field was sudden and spontaneous. Murray came to a halt atop the dugout steps, and the left fielder responsible for relaying balls into the infield during BP took to quick and momentary flight. He had surmised quickly enough what Murray's warning had meant. To say that he saved Satnik's young life is no overstatement. He ran four or five fleeting strides to his right, and leaped into the air, diving at Satnik's midsection in an effort to tackle him away from the baseball's locomotive-like path. Contact was made solid and sure as a murderous thump resonated in the air. The screeching ball mashed itself into the hardened cranium of the young man's skull. The momentary frozen stadium was instantly set alight as all legs rushed to their fallen comrade. Murray instructed me to call an ambulance, which I had already begun doing from the nearby dugout phone.

By the time I had arrived in the deep outfield where a small crowd had gathered, Satnik was no longer bleeding and the team's trainer ensured us he was unconscious though stable. He had not been killed. The ball had grazed just an inch north of his right ear, a blow which surely would have killed the man had the leather weapon made forceful contact with his temple.

The usual rushing to the hospital, calling to the young man's fiancée and parents ensued, along with numerous questions, a brief but serious league investigation, speculation and hearsay from press, the fans and our future opponents. In the end, Satnik would be fine if not humbled. Whether or not he would play ball again was yet to be seen. That he would never put himself at such risk again was obvious. Had he not been injured, Murray warned him, he would have been suspended from the Series regardless of his condition. It was the dumbest damn thing Murray had ever sworn to have witnessed in all his years around the game of baseball. And the young pitcher should count his lucky blessings to have been alive. In the rush to ensure he was okay and to save his threatened life, no one had thought to survey the crime scene for clues as to Satnik's error. But sometime during the confusion, the bat boy had picked up the accomplice to the crime. As it stands, Satnik himself was the perpetrator of his own ill will and brush with death. His partner in crime had been none other than his own stereo headphones.

That he was out of place was excusable. The entire team had been lax that week and had taken things lightly, though such light-heartedness was sure to disappear from practice after the accident had occurred. That he had not heard Murray's scream to halt all activities was mysterious. That he had been wearing a set of stereo headphones and had the volume up so loud as to not hear Murray's warning, as well as hindering his own concentration, was absolutely inexcusable. As well, it was just plain stupid.

Despite the fans' and the team's misery at having witnessed the near-minded ballplayer's brush with death, there remained the not-so-small matter of winning a championship. Murray rallied the troops and put their concentration back to one thing, winning The Series. One game at a time, win four and they'd be champions. The one lingering doubt in everyone's mind (including mine) was simple: if the Owls had needed a good third man in the rotation so desperately, and had finally found him that summer of 1991 in the person of Matt Satnik, then how could they have been expected to advance to victory in the series without him?

After Columbus defeated Raleigh in the final game of their series, it was the Owls' turn to take on the experimental Columbus Empire. They were a temporary team made from the remnants of two defunct teams, one from Lansing, Michigan, and the other from Newark, New Jersey, who were to play in Columbus only one season while a stadium was being built in St. Petersburg, Florida, where they would join the Southern Atlantic League for play in 1992.

The series would be a best-of-seven event, wherein, following the professional ranks, whichever team won a fourth game first would be crowned the champion. Kevin's luck had run out with the conclusion of the play-off series against Wheeling. Or, so it had seemed. Being the fourth man on a roster meant he was the last man on the roster. And in championship series play, the team's best throwers often pitched on three day's rest, meaning the number one starter would pitch games one, four and seven if needed, and the number two guy would pitch games two and five. The last to pitch was starter number three who was guaranteed at least a start in game three and if the series went on would pitch game six.

Kevin was just rolling with fate. When Satnik went down, it was Kevin's move into the number three spot that ensured him at least one start in a championship series game. Even if the Owls were to be ousted in a four games consecutive loss sweep, Kevin would walk away from 1991 with the claim that he had started in game three of the International League Championship Series. Only his future accomplishments in the Majors would serve to outdo such a pinnacle.

The Owls had possessed the league's best overall record that year and would be rewarded with home field advantage, meaning games 1 and 2, and games 6 and 7 (if necessary), would be played in Cooperstown. Tickets sold out quicker than ice cream in a heat wave. Game one was electrifying and nervous, but the Owls prevailed 3-1 with a late inning rally after having entered the eighth down 1-0. Keith Potomak had cleared the bases with a double for all three runs and the Owls were up one game to none with only three wins standing between them and their championship.

Game two was another close contest as the Owls held a slight 4-3 lead through most of the game, only to lose in the top of the ninth on a two-run home run by David Wilkins, a sturdy swinger for Columbus. The Owls were disappointed but hardly despondent. They left the field defeated but upbeat and, heading on the road, faced the knowledge that they would have to win at least one game in order to bring the series back to Cooperstown.

Awaiting Kevin's debut for game three was a mastermind of impatient torture. I could not tolerate the days between the games. We travelled to Ohio for the game. When we checked into the hotel, Mr. Bentworth and Kevin turned in for a long night of restless sleep and heads full of anticipation while dad and I carried a conversation on long into the early hours. We discussed topics ranging from the game we had just seen to Kevin's chances against Columbus the next day, and from hopes for a good trip home to other matters, some trivial and some more important. We talked at length about his relationship with his own father, how having lost his father young had given my dad the courage to take responsibility for his life and to make something of himself. He had been quickly thrust into a role a "man of the house" and worked hard to maintain good grades in high school while working various jobs to help my grandmother get by. It was these lessons that abled him to excel in college and earn a prestigious degree in structural engineering where he went on to study greater ways to strengthen construction materials.

"How did Granddad Monroe die?" I asked.

"That's kind of a sad story." Dad revisited a long-ago pain. "He died on a job site while hanging steel."

316

"But he designed the work. Why would he be on site?"

"Usually, yes, he designed, but a lot of people did both back then," dad answered. The disappointment of haphazard death stole across his face a glint of indignation and regret. He then sort of just spoke to life in general, not precisely at me but rather just as a means to be talking. "It wasn't his design, even. Dad was filling in for another guy who had landed the job because somebody's uncle knew somebody who owned the company. That guy got the day off. The long of it is that your grandfather was killed when a support beam that should have been better reinforced in its initial design let loose on a building and fell free. He was in Massillon, Ohio, where he and three other workers fell five stories to their death."

I felt empty. "I'm sorry," I blatantly said. "Did Grandma sue or file a wrongful death claim?"

"No," he answered, placidly. "People didn't sue back then. The work force was different. People accepted their lot in life. Well, anyway. That's another story."

"Didn't Grandma go against you wanting to do the same thing?" I asked. "I mean, how could she support your following those footsteps when it killed her husband?"

"That's a brave question, son," Dad added with a kind of smirk edging on pride. "It takes a parent to understand the sacrifice one will make for their kid's happiness. Besides, I don't really do the same thing. Back then there was no division between the laborer and the designer – not as much as there is today at least. I won't even scale a building. But I was determined that no one would be lax in designing and building again."

He went on to explain how he hoped to someday work with OSHA (The Occupational Safety and Hazard Association) where he could ensure that young boys would not learn word that their hard-working dads had died because of someone else's incompetence.

I slept that night with a firmer understanding of my place than at any other night in my life. My dad could easily have persuaded me not to pursue baseball, to continue in the love of science that he and his father had followed. But he had seen in me early on a love for this intangible game, and he allowed that love to be cultivated. Kevin's dad, ironically, had played the game and wanted his son away from it, going so far as to hide his own past from his son to protect him if he could. What strange conundrums parenting must bring. So there we were, the four of us, slumbering in a hotel in Columbus, Ohio, awaiting Kevin's chance to pitch the biggest game of his life, the most recent in a series of big games that would continue to escalade throughout his career. One day, there would be his first outing in spring training for the Oakland A's, later his debut as a starter in a regular season contest. Ultimately, he would take the mound at the All-Star Game and finally, after being traded, in the World Series for my dad's favorite team, the Indians, in 1995. But at that time he had to worry about game three of the International League Championship.

It was a sight to behold on Tuesday morning when the sun radiated behind departing clouds. And what a strange event it would be. If Cooperstown is the Mecca of baseball, than Columbus must be its Wailing Wall. So far removed from baseball is Columbus that hardly a fan had shown up to witness their team, The Empire, take on the Owls. Perhaps it was the fact that the team was simply renting its fans for a year, but you would have thought it was a spring try-out. Or, perhaps, The Ohio State University so exhausts the town's wherewithal for sport that a minor league baseball team is simply overlooked. Had it been a Saturday and the Buckeyes were hosting Michigan or Iowa, I would have called the ambivalence to baseball fair. But even for an afternoon game in mid-week, the crowd was dismally unrepresentative of the occasion. There was less than a thousand people on hand as the Owls came to bat at the top of the first inning. What greater anti-climax to Kevin's Championship Series debut than a bleak and quiet stadium whose team meant nothing to the local fans, not that there actually appeared to be any fans.

Kevin won the game blissfully by commanding a tight strike zone all afternoon and mixing in timely fastballs against a lackluster opponent. That the crowd was a reflection of how the team felt about itself was obvious. They sauntered through nine uninspiring innings in a 6-0 loss.

Game four was even worse as the Owls ratcheted sixteen hits and pounded the Empire 13-1; their single tally coming on consecutive ground-rule doubles that snuck into an auspicious corner of right field where it seemed the stadium favored the home team with a missing portion of fence. At any rate, the Owls were ahead three games to one and appeared poised to finish the series in game five when either fortune or divine inspiration came to life. The Empire rallied themselves before a sparse crowd to win an exciting contest 6-4, thus sending the series back to Cooperstown with the Owls up 3 games to 2. And the game six first pitch would be in the hand of Kevin Bentworth with the possible series clinching in the offing.

Another trip across three states and a full night of anticipation ensued. A storm that had left Ohio a few days earlier rolled into New York and dumped gallons of teeming rain upon Cooperstown all day Saturday and into the evening, postponing the series by one day. The fans of Cooperstown braced for the arrival of game six as if it was the storm itself rolling in with threatening possibility.

Because of the delay, there was talk that Kevin would not pitch game six. Murray stunted that rumor faster than he would a bench clearing brawl. He would save his ace, Paul Spellminster (the same player I had met ten years earlier and who had returned to end his career as an Owl), for a possible seventh game. Murray decided to pitch Kevin and keep the rotation intact. He had seen enough of the Empire to feel certain that if they were lucky enough to win game six, they would be all out of luck for game seven.

"Why?" I, the broadcaster-in-training, asked.

"Because," Murray answered. "You can't coach to win game seven until you've won game six. Our worry is to win game six. Period."

"Coach," Spellminster said, "ya gotta let me pitch tonight. Let's win this thing right now."

"No way, Paul," Murray answered him. "Bentworth pitches. I want you on the mound if we need to play game seven. No offense to Kevin, but your experience will be more worthwhile if we *have* to win instead of when we should win. Got it, Ace?"

"Fair enough, Skipper," he added, but he wasn't happy with the coach's decision.

And so it was settled. Kevin would pitch game six. And when game six arrived, the town was divided between those either ready with hope or those eager with insanity. They had not seen their local boys play in close to a week and the waiting drove them rampant. They were as excited as the players who somehow remained focused and calm in the milieu of media and hype that surrounded the early fall contests.

Owls Stadium was more alive than the dreadful Empire had been two nights earlier. Game six could not have begun more perfectly. The Owls were ahead in the series, were certain to win this game, and the weather had cleared out after the storm like a refreshed and autumnal reprieve. Gone was the stale air of lingering summer, wiped away was the soppy moisture of mildew-soaked clouds. In their place rested the crystalline brilliance of a new blue sky, a comfortable evening breeze and air so breathable that it felt like pure oxygen.

Owls Stadium resounded with a louder hum than I had heard in my time as a fan there and have yet to hear again to this day. The murmurs had ascended into a whirling crunch of chatter and hope, a blitzing appendage of excitement. It was as if those in the stands were eager and ready to burst through the red, white and blue bunting that adorned the lower grandstands and take the field themselves. They were prepared to throw forty plus years of frustration at the Empire in homemade curveballs and schoolyard double plays. This town was as determined to win the game and the series as the Owls and Murray were. Enter Kevin, his determination evident in his stride and brazened across his concentrated sneer, who would go out there and pitch and pitch and pitch and pitch. Not the best game of his life, not the longest; just the absolute worst!

Poor Kevin. After all the hype and success in Columbus and the impending sense of victory, it looked as if the Empire had fed off the frenzied fans of Cooperstown for their own motivation. In place of triumph run amuck, a sloppy and frightening defeat arrived. Slap base hits turned into staggering triples as fielders misplayed easy hops. Crafty pitches turned their charm against their maker as tricky fastballs lit up the scoreboard in the thinning air as seven home runs ascended from the bats of the Empire. Standard and tested pitches went dumb in the face of a changing century as strikeouts turned into walks and walks became hit batsmen. Everything that could have gone wrong went unequivocally wrong. Even an intentional walk to load the bases plated a run for Columbus when Kevin threw wildly into the dirt to chase his catcher to the backstop as the runner on third trotted home in the fifth.

For six grueling innings, Kevin meandered in a wallowing display of baseball ineptitude. His control was so off that he could not even keep his hat on his head, which came dislodged during his wind-up three times. So bad was the outing that Kevin didn't even toss the ball into Murray's hand when he came to rescue his young and woe begotten starter with one down in the sixth. Kevin retrieved the ball from Denkinger with the score a searing 13-0. He plunked the ball in the dirt and walked off the field, not in the direction of the dugout nor the bullpen but right straight out to

320

centerfield where he hopped the fence, slid through the groundskeeper's area and disappeared out of sight.

I would not see my best friend again for seven years.

Sure, the Owls went on to claim victory in game seven as Spellminster pitched a hell of an effort, throwing a complete game and winning in grand fashion by striking out the side against the Empire in the ninth. The ensuing celebration eclipsed the 4-0 performance by Paul Spellminster. The tiny town north of nowhere partied into the wee hours of morning, giving toast to the next day's sunrise with championship champagne and a bleeding headache. A parade a few days later carried our beloved players through the town's usually mundane streets – not a long procession, but one nonetheless that inspired yet more revelry as the party from Sunday spilled over into Tuesday. All but two citizens from Cooperstown reeled and danced in gleeful celebration for the days following the victory. Nowhere to be found amongst the hoopla and insanity were the Bentworths. Neither Kevin nor his dad had been seen since game six.

32 No Regrets

The town of Coopers had their baseball championship. Not much else was theirs for the asking. All winter long they would stir the imbibing pride of victory, and for years to come they would reflect fondly on *The Year!* The Year the Owls Won it All! They would tell their grandchildren about it, brag to visiting fans and always look fondly upon that one final summer when childhood dreams mingled with civic pride. Isn't that a grand trick of history, a justification unto itself for why we play the games we play, why we meet the people we meet and why we live our lives? For, were it not for memory, what else would we reflect upon? What would we cherish?

The next seven years were a time dissolved, far from recollection. I spent my life watching Kevin Bentworth from afar. His career was played out in little spurts of information gathered from a variety of sources: an article in *Sports Illustrated* one month, a clip on the news a few weeks later, and on and on until he made his permanent stay in the Major Leagues. Little did I understand his reaction to the loss in game six, though certainly it was of no surprise. It was becoming evident that Kevin spent his life running from defeat rather than accepting his setbacks. Yet, still, he managed to silently and privately overcome that single loss and remain focused toward his primary goal.

Had he simply jumped that fence and disappeared from the landscape of baseball entirely, I might have dubbed his tale the new American tragedy, the undeveloped talent of a misunderstood genius, perhaps the under-appreciated artist lost in a world beneath his accomplishments. That is not the point to Kevin's story, however. His tale, while sad at times, is one of erstwhile perseverance, of obstacles met and confronted. Not always defeated, but addressed on his own terms. It offers the possibility that things beyond our view are what motivate those who are simply more driven than the common person. We might have expected him to hold court to explain away his game six debacle, as if justifying it to us his fans was a responsibility he carried. Not Kevin, his was the only reason he needed.

The first appearance of Kevin's whereabouts came in the spring of 1993 when he was invited to spring training with the Oakland Athletics. The A's had strung together three consecutive World Series appearances in the late 80s to early 90s but had only managed one championship title, that coming in 1989 during the famed Earthquake Series when the San Francisco / Oakland Bay Area was ripped wide open by a massive quake during game one of the series against the Giants. By 1993, the A's were ready to solidify an aging corps of superstars whose contracts were bulging and whose championship run was ending.

Kevin did not make the team in 1993 right out of spring training, but was called up periodically throughout the year to cover for injured pitchers or to be available for a double-header. It was good experience for him as he furthered his skills on the professional level. Whether or not anyone in the Majors realized that he was the kid who lobbed that goofy Steamer pitch was something I cannot ascertain. Had they known, it was never printed. If they cared, they made no bones about the fact. In the Majors, perhaps, the silly antics of the lesser pro leagues are ignored.

The years following the Owls' championship season passed through the early 1990's as fast as I had wished high school would have ended. Before I could forget the name of the Owls' third string catcher on the championship team, it was 1995 and the Owls were woefully inept once more. Murray was ready to retire, having tasted glory and having subsequently lost the passion to rebuild the team yet again. My old mentor, Denkinger, had finally called it quits, too. He played on through 1992, giving up on playing when his body finally reminded him that twelve years of baseball were enough. He opted to live part-time between his home in Minnesota and his new-found comfort in Cooperstown. I see him often and we watch a lot of baseball together.

By 1995, I had completed graduate school and stayed on as the Owls' full-time broadcaster. What else was I to do? I liked my station in life and found my job to be rewarding. And on long summer nights during an eight or nine game losing streak when frustration drives at my hopes for the team, I sit high above Owls Stadium during commercial breaks, still getting free hot dogs and Cokes (a perk for the media crew) and reminisce about that glorious summer when everything came into place for the championship run.

I had been offered a job for the White Sox from an old college buddy who worked in marketing for the South Side Chicagoans. Minus the aspirations of a greater radio wattage or a stronger Arbitron rating, I turned the offer down. Cooperstown was home. I just wanted to call games, raise my kids and spend my life in my adopted town. The only place I left room for an amendment to that stipulation was obvious. If the Pirates offered a job, I would leave Cooperstown as quickly as I recall being uprooted from Pittsburgh over twenty years earlier. Lanny Frattare still called a pretty good game and had a firm hold on that market. Besides, the line of people behind him who wanted his job was as long as the Allegheny River that flows through Pittsburgh itself. My chances of that gig were, and remain still, quite slim. Melony and I were married in June of 1993, a year after I completed college. She helped me though graduate school, mainly through her encouragement and by keeping me from bankruptcy as I fretted over theory and research. There was still plenty of money left in Mrs. Denton's coffers to meet the educational expenses incurred there. The generosities of the woman have spread as far across my life as one can imagine. I am indebted eternally.

With the news of Murray's retirement after thirty-four years as skipper of the Owls, people started talking about a reunion of the championship team. Why not? The timing was right. The summer of 1996 would mark the five year anniversary, and if Major League teams could bring back the stars from a championship squad on five-year repetitions, why not the Owls? As a potential bonus, some hoped that the current team would be inspired by the stories of the old guard and kick themselves into victory mode. No such luck. The Owls finished 1995 in dead last, a dismal nineteen games behind first place Rochester, their hated rivals who were on top again!

Kevin, not all too surprisingly, did not make it to the reunion. In fact, he didn't even respond to the invitation. More than one member of the team was put off by his arrogance. Of the members of the championship squad, only a handful of them even made it to the Show, and by 1995 Kevin Bentworth had become something of a household name throughout baseball. It appeared he had forgotten where he had come from.

Other than Chad McKenzie who had a relatively successful stint as a utility infielder for the Padres and Mariners, only Steve Collins made a lengthy stay in the Majors. He was taken by the Colorado Rockies in the 1993 expansion draft and dealt the same day to the Montreal Expos for two draft choices and a player to be named later. He hated that moniker. "I'd rather be named later myself than be the guy they trade to get someone later," he quipped. "Oh well, at least it's the Majors," he said. His days with the Expos, though, were the envy of many of the Owls former

324

players who packed the ball park for the reunion on that steamy summer day in July of 1996. The event was held was during the All-Star break to accommodate the availability of McKenzie and Collins, as well as Kevin had he opted to attend. It added fuel to his former team's ire that Kevin was not absent because of the All-Star game itself. Had he been pitching in the game, the old Owls would have excused him from the reunion with pride. He was not making an appearance in that year's game, though he would go on to start it in 1997.

Kevin's career began to take off in 1994. After a year of toiling between the Majors and the A's top farm club, he hurled an impressive spring to be listed on the roster for the 1994 season. The A's had shipped Dave Stewart off to Toronto, Dennis Eckersley was looking at retirement, and the staff that had won them their own championship was no longer together. So, when Kevin's shot arrived, he took full advantage of the opportunity. By late 1994, however, baseball was in turmoil. The players were locked out and the World Series canceled.

"Excuse me? Did I hear that correctly? They did what!?!" I ranted through the house when the news was announced.

The championship reunion of 1995 heard more complaints about baseball having canceled the World Series than it did reminiscing about the collected former Owls and their shared glory. Not even catching up on the proverbial old times could steer the conversation away from the maelstrom of baseball's injustice. Indignant as they were regarding the events taking place at the Major League level, they still adored their game. A few of the younger players who dotted the Owls' 1995 line-up had hoped baseball would fold entirely under its previously existing structure, thus leaving open their opportunity to eagerly fill the void of greedy, over-paid players.

"Don't be so quick to judge," McKenzie warned a guy named Provionk, a back-up shortstop and outfielder on the 1995 team. "You'd jump at the chance to make that kind of money playing the game you love."

"Yeah, I would," Provionk defended. "But you've got guys losing thirty-thousand dollars a day! And they are complaining about not being able to make it. Cut me a break! There are families in this country who do not even combine to bring in thirty-thousand during an entire year, and you expect me to care for a millionaire who is whining about it? I don't think so."

The conversations went on in a variety of avenues, but always came back to that which we all agreed – baseball is the same game, when you get between the lines and the first batter comes up, it is still and always will be a great game.

Where 1994 will stamp itself upon the history of baseball, and to a larger extent America as a whole, is a discussion for historians. While it went onward into a dismal summer, I was reminded of the strike in 1981. 1994 was different, though, because the owners now had more control over the matter. After season-long debates and threats over contracts, television deals, free agency, something called collective bargaining, and a host of other issues, baseball exercised the equivalent of professional suicide. When neither side, the owners nor the player's union, could come to agreement on these hot issues, the commissioner's office canceled the play-offs and World Series after a work stoppage that had begun in August trolled on through the waning summer. So much for that dream I had back when we were kids. The vision where I was at second base, Kevin was on the mound and the Expos were poised to win the 1994 World Series! What ironic fortune telling it was that I had possessed as a child.

Most unfortunate about the work stoppage, outside of the lost records and the assault on the integrity of the game, nor the millions of fans who missed out on their seasonal rite of the World Series, was the fact that two franchises, the Expos and the Indians, were finally close to baseball's promised land!

The Montreal Expos had toiled in obscurity since their inception in 1969, save their astonishing run of 1981 when they put together a play-off team bested by the Dodgers to end that strike-shortened season. But other than that one year when I was a kid, the Expos were often terrible, the laughingstock of baseball. Maybe it had something to do with Canada. Did our Northern neighbors understand our American game enough to support a team through losing ways? Did the ownership pay out in American salaries what they brought in with the lesser-valued Canadian dollar? Who knows? But either way they were awful. That was the case, until 1994. Likewise, the Indians had suffered even worse ignominy, having spun around as an also ran since the early 1950's. Granted, they had their World Series title in 1948 and an appearance in 1954, but they had not tasted the post-season since. This was forty years of frustration for a city devoted to its team. Things were so bad for baseball in Cleveland during the 1970's and 1980's the people checked the standings each day, afraid that if the Indians were to lose any more games they would fall out of last place in the American League East and into first place in the American League West! But all that changed in 1994.

In some cruel trick of fate, both teams headed their divisions with powerful, awe-inspiring seasons in 1994. The names and figures, statistics and reasons why are lost to me now, but both the Expos and the Indians had rightful claim to stake that had the season not been prematurely halted that year, either or both may have played in the never played 1994 World Series. The Expos, it seems, suffered the worst of the two fates, for while Cleveland rebounded to appear in the World Series in both 1995 and 1997, the Expos faded into mediocre obscurity.

While this and other talk dominated the reunion, one other potential drawback to the reunion was the fate of yours truly. After the reunion, Collins and I kept in touch as we rekindled an interest in the games back in Cooperstown and I began to follow his career more closely. It was a year after the reunion, just as baseball was beginning the slow process of rebuilding itself after having approached oblivion, that Collins called me with a tempting, frightening offer.

The phone rang in the den and Melony answered it on its first ring. Her jumpiness tested my resolve quite regularly, an alert quality I could have used the day of the accident all those years ago.

"Honey, it's for you," she hollered down the corridor of the house we were renting. "A guy saying he used to play for the Owls."

Kevin? I hoped. I picked up the phone. Hearing Collins on the other end was a good thing, but the disappointment that it was not Kevin must have sounded in my voice.

"Hello?" I asked, a bit enthused.

"August. Hey, it's your old pal Steve Collins. How are ya?"

"Oh," I muttered. "I'm okay. How about you?"

"Gee, don't sound so thrilled to hear from me, buddy," he said.

"No, sorry. Just a bit distracted. Hold on a minute, will ya?"

"Sure."

I saved the document to the computer that I had been working on and adjusted my disposition to sound more inviting. I shut the computer off entirely and picked up the phone again.

"So, to what do I owe the pleasure?" I said cheerfully. My ploy worked as Collins made no further mention of my initial reaction.

"Well, my man. I have a proposition for you."

"A proposition?" I asked. "You sound like a salesman."

"Maybe, but probably more of a dream-fulfiller."

"A what?" I asked with a scoff. "Cut the bullshit, what do you want?"

"Hear me out," he laughed, "and we'll go from there, okay?"

"Sure," I said. "I'm listening."

"You know I retired from playing last year, right?"

"No, I didn't actually. Congratulations, or maybe regrets are in order?"

"A little of both, really," Collins said. "I miss playing, but I still work in baseball."

"Oh, yeah?" I asked. "What are you doing now?"

"That, my friend," he answered with a salesman's approach, "is precisely why I am calling. As I said, I am still in baseball, hell, probably always will be. Anyway, the long and short of it is that I am now director of player personnel for the Iowa Farmcats, we play in Dubuque and have games against the Owls next season."

"Hey, good for you," I congratulated. "And I am not so old that I forget the Owls' schedule. I am very aware of the Farmcats. You've got that pitcher, Andreas Wilson, in your system, don't you? They are touting him for the Majors."

"Yeah, he's a good kid. But that's not why I'm calling. You might think I am crazy, but we want you to try-out for the team." A dead silence strung all the way through the phone line from New York to Iowa as Steve awaited my reply. I gave none. "August?"

"Yeah, I am here," I uttered.

"Listen, I cleared it with management. We'll pay to get you here and feed you. It would be a base contract with a very small chance at ever making the pros, but we'd love to have your knowledge of the game on our bench to help the younger guys. And you know as well as I do how unfair it was that you never got to play ball after the accident. So, what do ya say, man?"

The silence lengthened to a distant buzz of the phone's transmission, only the dry static of technology whispered between us. I reflected upon my thwarted effort to play my senior year for the Roosters in college. I had given it my all then, and left the hospital that day satisfied that baseball was not for me to play, but to study. I had nothing left to prove, and stirring up old dreams would only fizzle grander defeat in the end. I was approaching thirty, young yes, but too far along to be thinking about playing baseball. I had other things to worry about.

As the summer sun dipped behind the thin clouds of western Cooperstown, I told my friend, simply, "No, Steve. Thanks, but no. I am all right here."

We continued our conversation for an hour covering other topics and discussing how the Farmcats would be in 1995 and how the Owls might fair in the years after that. Sometimes that's all fans have, really, is the looking ahead to better days. He made no further push to lure me into a lucrative past filled with the dreams of a younger man, though he did hang up offering that if I changed my mind I could call him at any time. I told him I would keep that in mind, though I knew the call would not be placed. We said our farewells.

As I hung up, the long summer day had disappeared and I reflected long into the sunset about a decision that was surprisingly easy to make. Had it wracked my brain with indecision for days, I might still be out there every spring trying to convince myself that I could still play the old diamond pretty well. But with a swift decline, I accepted my position in life and that serenity sat fairly well.

There comes a time when one realizes that life has given pause to worry, that the poignant sliding away of days into autumn is not so much an aging as it is a revelation, a rite of passage. Or perhaps a series of passages. The seasons themselves reconcile that spirit, offering fresh reminders of how ill-fated constancy really is. So, too, it is that somewhere between attempting to understand and trying not to live down to the challenge of wisdom, one gains insight. It happens. Period. And while such a simplicity is grand understatement, the truth remains as deep and solid as the continents. With age comes wisdom, with experience understanding. For some there is a crossroads, a point of understanding due to an event or a moment when everything is clarified in crystalized formation. For others, it is a transgression, knowing well that each moment through a phase of deliverance is transit to another side of awareness. Still, there are those who just come to realize one day that they have reached where they always wanted to be, even if they know not how they arrived nor that they could even had described it beforehand if asked.

329

So it was that I, still so young and yet absent the fire that had consumed my being for so long, moved onto acceptance of life. Mr. Bentworth had taught me greatly without ever so much as dictating an ideal or lesson. And for that I was grateful. For surely, had I been told *August, this is what life is all about, etc...* I most assuredly would not have listened. Instead, I took it as a part of the game. Mr. Bentworth had stood on the brink of what would have been personal greatness and profound accomplishment, and having lost that, said farewell to a reality he need not to anguish over and went about his life in the quiet, unassuming way that was his.

While my father and mother stood by strongly, had seen me back to reasonable health and supported the anger swelling within, it was not overriding fear but ultimately acceptance that brought me to peace of mind. Had I pressed onward, obsessed by an idle dream, then I may have ended somewhere in tragedy, that dirty, mumbling guy at the bus stop who no one knows. He is looked at, scoffed on occasion and often ridiculed by the local kids. But he too has a past, a story from whence he comes, a series of events that led him from what? Marriage? A family? A decent job and a persuasive position in his community? And what led him to where he ends? Corporate cutbacks? Disease? Divorce? By his own hand at booze or drugs or gambling? Or maybe it was just good old fashioned bad luck. I didn't want to be that person. I had had enough bad luck and the hand I had been dealt was playable, still is really. It's very playable. The memory of August Monroe may not be aces high over a royal flush, but damn if a full house ain't hard to beat.

33 1998

There is some truth to a theory which states that death approaches in a pattern of threes. I have never known of a name for this phenomena, and if there is one I can't imagine that it verifies or denies the existence of such a mysterious pattern. I remember from early on in life when mom would comment, "death always comes in threes." I found it difficult to comprehend what she meant. Supposedly, we learn of the deaths of three similar people during a certain proximity of time. For instance, if a great TV actor from the 1950's was found dead in his hotel room, then certainly over the next few days to two weeks the news would surface, completely coincidental and unrelated to the first, that another Hollywood star or musician had passed silently in her sleep at her ranch home in Wherever, USA. And then, days later the third victim of the triple threat would be killed in an automobile accident. He or she as well had been famous in one form or another. Usually the fame itself is linked, be the deceased a politician or an actor or a singer. The next triple death might come in the form of an aging uncle, a distant cousin or a grandparent's sibling. Some would hit closer to home: a favorite cousin killed in military duty, followed by a grandmother's demise of old age, then completed by a friend or closer relative succumbing to disease. It is an eerie premonition, but as true as I can count all the way to three without aid, the occurrence has repeated itself throughout life.

Whimsically (and somewhat macabre) I like to joke that it's the same principle in life as in baseball: namely, three strikes and you're out; three deaths, end of an inning. As I grew, I sensed time and time again that mother was right about her bizarre, if not frightening, theory. Personally, I think of two such trios that exemplify the pattern: my mother's uncle Willie died of lung cancer in 1974, the first time I had heard the words "death" and "cancer." Two weeks later, Willie's cousin, Barbara, was killed in a skiing accident in Vail, Colorado. Ten days after Barb was buried, my father's second cousin (who had grown up in Ireland, though that really isn't significant to his death) passed in his sleep at the age of thirty-two, the victim of a massive brain aneurism. What connects them? I never knew a single one of them except for stories told by mom and dad, and their deaths occurred within a matter of weeks. Thus, they were connected to each other and died in a collective demise.

Then, in 1983, two guys and a girl from our school district were all killed during the summer. All three were unrelated and in different places, the last out of town on vacation, but all three were from Cooperstown Middle or Senior High and all three died that same summer.

So, while the argument may be the work of coincidence or mere happenstance, I have absolute conviction that it is a real phenomenon that occurs regularly in life, regardless if anyone else believes it. Maybe it has something to do with the Holy Trinity, who knows?

Yet, there remains one such triumvirate where the third person was not identified immediately, and remained unknown to me all these years. At the time, I figured that the third to be deceased had been someone I just didn't know, or that news of the death had not reached me if it had been made public. Maybe he or she had been part of someone else's group, and I just happened to have known persons one and two. Perhaps that person hadn't die that summer. If he or she had died, I did not know about it. It was the summer of 1990, and I had already lost my grandfather and a close, dear neighbor lady to death – both by natural causes and both within nine days of each other. I thought the dreaded curse of the triple play of death had finally been broken because on that occasion the third death toll had not instantly sounded. It was not until eight years later that the third party died, breaking the timeliness rule of the deaths, yes, but strengthening the shared position of the threesome, most assuredly.

I am troubled by it because the distance between the first two deaths and the third stretched so many years, almost a full decade. And in that time I had entirely lost interest in discovering who the third death had involved. In fact, days after Grandpa's funeral it had slipped my mind almost entirely, the specter of doom lifting from my awaiting heart only to creep back on future occasions when I heard that a third ballplayer had passed or a third in-law had slipped the surly bonds. It was as if I had lost all interest in learning of the third person who would complete that dying trio. Let me make it clear that the person was not dead those eight years – oh no, very much alive! – and was not discovered dead in 1998. No. The third member of my most revered triumvirate was initiated into the gruesome threesome in 1998, solo and apart from the others but very much the final piece to a complex and personal puzzle that has defined my life.

In hindsight it makes sense, almost *perfect and absolute* sense! If I were to define my life in 1980 based on those people who were of greatest significance to me then, I would not have seen the beauty for which these three departed souls offered me wisdom. I would have said mom, dad and perhaps a baseball hero I had admired, Mike Schmidt or Carl Yastrzemski. But after so many years, nearly a decade, I can see where the third death was not of such an issue of timeliness but rather that his final lesson had yet to be imparted upon me before his demise.

The third death, that of a close personal friend my own age, finally brought clarity to the events of the summer of 1980, and in effect brings clarity to each day of my life, my purpose and my own simple legacy. However dull that legacy may be.

1998 was a robust year of contradiction and consternation. And, perhaps, the most important year of my life.

The summer baseball season of 1998 was a joyous ride along the path toward baseball history. An entire nation, even those who were simply *not* fans of the game, followed the marvelous feats of two superb athletes who battled and challenged one another to accomplish the implausible. They were determined to set a baseball record that had stood for thirty-seven seasons. Now, thirty-seven years somehow seems an eternity to our American perspective of on-demand gratification and instant response, when in reality it isn't all that great a length of time. More years have passed since the conclusion of World War II, and nearly as many since JFK was assassinated, than between 1961 and 1998. But it is the gap between those years that had all of America following baseball at a fevered pace for the 1998 season. It was a good thing, really – for baseball and for the country, and it was a wonderful thing for my dying friend.

It was early in 1998 when I decided to call Kevin on February 18th when pitchers and catchers reported to spring training. He made no mention that he actually wasn't in Florida with the Indians for spring workouts. We had talked at length about recent signings, how we hoped (though knew better) that either of our favorite teams would capture the championship. We shared a few laughs over reminiscent memories and hung up promising to speak again on the first day of the regular season. When April 4th rolled around, no call. I checked the messages at the office, and there were none at all, not from anybody yet alone from Kevin. I was home all day and not a single jingle of the phone. Nothing. I asked Melony three times whether she thought the phone had gone on the blink and each time she answered: *The phone is fine, dear. Relax! He'll call.* But he didn't call. Not on the fourth, nor the fifth, and all the way through to the tenth and eleventh of April and I had still not received a phone call.

I checked the baseball standings in the paper. Despite a rain postponed game on April 6th, both his employers the Indians and his beloved Cincinnati Reds had begun the season. The Majors were in full swing! There had to have been a reason why the call had not been placed.

By the fifteenth, my resolve was shot. I had traipsed about for ten days plagued with worry, indecision and doubt. I tracked down his winter home number and dialed. The phone buzzed in the earpiece as it rang relentlessly at his home in Asheville, North Carolina. I was about to hang up, wondering why the answering machine hadn't picked up, when there arose from the other end a rattle and then that familiar voice of his, though sounding a bit groggy.

"Hello, who's there?" he asked into his end of the receiver. I was relieved to hear his voice. He wasn't dead at least. Though, perhaps, he was worse off.

"Kevin, it's me. August. How are you?"

"I'm fine, Augie. Just fine. A little tired today, but you know how that goes... Uh, say. What can I do for you, old buddy?"

"Old?" I said. "We're not even thirty yet."

"Uh-huh," he said. "Listen, Augie, I'm kind of tired. Was there something you needed? I'd like to get some rest if you don't mind."

"Been working extra?" He said nothing. I said, "I didn't hear from ya last week. I left a message. Did you get that? Is everything all right?"

"All right? What do you mean by all right?"

"Well, it's just that you didn't call last week. And I haven't seen you listed on the Indians' rosters. What's going on? Are you injured?"

A long silence followed. I heard him reaching for something between a series of clattering noises that rustled up from behind him. I could envision him at his home office desk, surrounded by papers and folders. The clatter ceased momentarily, resumed briefly and then faded away entirely as he breathed heavily into the phone piece.

"Well," he said. "It seems I did miss the start of the season this year. I'll be damned. See, I still have my calendar set for March."

"But what about the team?" I asked.

"Oh, yeah, the team," he answered. "I've, uh, taken a little time off, a bit of a, uh, leave of absence."

"Is that so?" I asked.

"Yeah, appears to be," was all he answered. A span of silence passed.

"Kevin?"

"Yeah, I'm here. Sure."

"Kev, is everything okay? You sound distant. Is there anything you want to talk about?"

"Uh, no. No, I'll call you again real soon, okay?"

"Okay, then. You take care and call if you need anything." And then he said the oddest thing, rather addressed the oddest person because it wasn't my name he uttered.

"Okay, bye, Paul."

"Wait!" I hollered. "What did you say? Did you just say Paul? Kev, it's me, August. August Monroe."

"Right, yeah sure. August. Sorry. Like I was saying, I'm really tired right now. Okay, pal. See ya."

The connection ceased. A gap of silence opened between the receivers. I hung up the phone and glanced at the nearest clock: 2:20 PM. Outside, the sky confirmed it was mid-day, a bright, spectacular spring afternoon in 1998. Surely, Asheville, NC, had not relocated to the other side of the Earth and remained steady and sure within the Eastern Time Zone where it too was only 2:20 PM. Something was amiss.

I spent the next day scrounging through national sports magazines and various newspapers in search of a hint for why Kevin wasn't with the team. There were no leads, not a single sentence pertaining to Kevin's unexplained absence.

Through the radio station I was able to order several newspapers from Cleveland, and still came up empty-handed in my search. Finally, I contacted the Indians directly. While they would not comment about Kevin's condition, the public relations woman I spoke with corroborated Kevin's comment that he was on a leave of absence, of sorts. He was still a Cleveland Indian.

Finding little information readily available, I set my mind to other matters. I had several games to broadcast over the next few days and would be going on the road with the Owls for a swing through the Midwest. I had a lot to do and it was the only thing that kept me from worrying endlessly about my friend in South Carolina. Besides, there was a season to concentrate upon.

1998 was indeed the rarest of seasons. The Milwaukee Brewers took roost in the NL Central the same year that Mark McGwire and Sammy Sosa sent themselves and fans everywhere on a thrill ride all summer, along the way to the seemingly before unreachable milestone of sixty-one home runs in a single season.

There are times when life is magnified behind the backdrop of history, when our common days give way to events that make humanity an amazing platform for spectacle. It is when soldiers rise to generals, students become presidents and a farm boy and a peasant kid from the sandlots become home run kings. Intermixed with our mundane existence sometimes arises the spectacular, the extraordinary, and we the commoners sit back and watch or take up arms in resistance. It is during these times that we acknowledge a true understanding of ourselves, as a people and as a nation. It is evident of glorious times and sad times, in time of war and in moments of beauty. It is a constant reminder of why we are a shared community. The greatness reflects that which we long for, that which we dread, that which, perhaps, we might even hope to become ourselves. Reflective of these times is often the happenstance of nature, the very tapestry of humanity against the forces that swell within and around our days.

1998 was such a year. On the playing fields of America, a great contest unfurled, while in the Earth's atmosphere there loomed a thunderous threat unlike anything we had known in recent years. In the sports pages loomed the possibility of number sixty-two, all the while a determined and brooding storm raged in the southern Atlantic Ocean.

As 1998 wore on into a brutish summer, Americans suddenly took notice of events that baseball fans and pundits alike may have predicted earlier. We were caught up in the maelstrom of history as another first and second-place record was threatened daily to be wrestled from the ranks of the Yankees. Mark McGwire, St. Louis Cardinal, and Sammy Sosa, Chicago Cub, were hot on the heels of history, pursuing each other's feat simultaneously. Equally, they pursued Roger Maris' mark of sixty-one homers in a single season. Separately, they pushed each other onward toward the record in a public display of sportsmanship. It was a testament to all that competition could be, fair-minded, friendly and challenging absent the swagger of braggadocio. I understand that Mr. Maris was a fine gentleman, though I cannot say from experience because I never had the chance to meet him. I sense that Mattingly is a true sportsman, as quite certainly many Yankees have been. And most of us worldwide either know of the Babe's numerous antics or at least recognize the name. It is not these gents whom I revel in to see their records fall, it is only because they wore the pinstripe cliché of the New York Yankees. But enough of this. A record was being sought.

McGwire and Sosa were simply awe-inspiring that summer. They dazzled the imaginations of children everywhere, reminded men why they fell in love with the game in the first place, and introduced a lot of ladies to what it is that their boys, their sons and their fathers had always been so crazy about. There is something to be said for spectacle, and as part of a generation overfed on the stuff, there was the magical upheaval from the summer of 1998.

The world was relatively peaceful, times were good. The economy was strong and, despite fears of collapsing markets abroad in Russia and Asia, the power of optimism stretched to nearly every corner of American society. And that foreboding storm continued to grow and grow off the great coastal eastern shore of America.

As the summer of hope moved forward, with one eye focused on a thrilling baseball climax and the other leery of the impending hurricane still amassed over the Atlantic, my focus shifted as quickly as gale force winds over Bermuda and with as much wrath as a McGwire home run. I was brought back to perspective upon learning that Kevin's absence from baseball was the result of cancer, the deadly deterrent to many a dream.

337

I had been too wrapped up in my own pursuits to notice how sick Kevin had become. The cancer first appeared sometime in 1995 or 1996, according to his doctor's best estimate, and from there spread to his kidneys quickly and approached his spine slowly as it corroded his life. How sad. I was busy going about life while a lifelong friend was clinging to what remained of his.

As the plane departed toward North Carolina, a litany of memories ran through my mind. I had known Kevin only eighteen years, several of which we in absentia, yet they were significant years. Together we had begun as young kids, unaware of a looming world around us where we could come and go and do all but nothing under the safe, uninhibited world of childhood. We grew to be young men who took an interest in the world, cared about our communities and even voted on issues that would help sculpt our children's future. We saw a larger picture of ourselves through those we affected, those we touched. At times it was the little girls giggling to watch us play ball, at others it was the high school class gathering to unite different social castes for the purpose of acceptance and understanding. On a larger scale, it was celebrating the common thread that wove a small town together when baseball brought joy to the citizens of Cooperstown. I will never forget the look on Mr. Dewey's face as he celebrated the Owls championship along with his new bride, my former teacher Miss Laurie Hollencheck, who had adored the man all along.

And now, as men, leading lives busy and separate, somewhat quiet and I like to think respectful, we were to close off a certain bond, say goodbye to youth and part ways with the bridge between adolescence and adulthood. Those ten years between eighteen and twenty-eight, so defined by independence and reaching out into the world for acceptance or rejection, of finding the self within that would leave our mark on the world, whatever it may have been. We were relatively young. Hell, what am I saying? We were just plain young. We were only twenty-eight for God's sake – a decade removed from being legally labeled adults and all of three or less removed from really knowing what the hell the world is really all about. Somewhere between eighteen and twenty-eight, maybe around the age of twenty-five, I started to figure it all out, what really matters that is. How responsibility compensates for angst. How settling down isn't settling at all, but accepting different roles and challenging one's self to receive that role with dignity and purpose, and to pass it on to others who need to have that role be a part of their lives. And somewhat, it is all about knowing that what you want to do with your life isn't necessarily as important as doing something that fits. In a more meaningful interpretation, doing something that lends itself to the betterment of society. Sure, there are doctors who cure people and scientists who invent the cures. There are firefighters who save lives and politicians to pay them. There are social workers who feed the poor. But each of us reaches into someone else's life in some way uniquely grand or minutely consequential. And we gather that reaching into a collective willingness to contribute to that which we believe upon, that by which we are a people.

I am a broadcaster. It's what I'm good at, and they pay me well to do it. What can I complain for? I wasn't cut out to be the next Pete Rose or Robin Yount. Big deal. Someone else will fill those roles. I only hope they appreciate how fortunate they are for having the chance to do so. Sara McKenzie, the woman who sells me a cup of coffee nearly every morning before work, has such a grand purpose to so many people. And it isn't the coffee, obviously (though she serves up a fine brew) but it is the way she greets every single customer with a smile and a heartfelt "Good Morning." After two or three days, she knows your order exactly. I have not had to request a cup of coffee in four years while working at WCPT. Since my fourth day on the job, she has known my order precisely. Coffee, one cream, two sugars. And the way she pats you when she delivers the cup into your welcoming hand, it's like home when mom makes soup. Tell me that isn't where life resides.

I was thinking about a lot of things on the plane down to North Carolina, and it struck me as intriguing that as much of a constant as Kevin was for part of my life, it was amazing just how short of a time span we had actually known each other. Relatively speaking, eighteen years is nothing. It's like driving a car. A kid cannot wait to get his license. He frets and worries and waits and grows impatient to be sixteen. And before he blinks, he's thirty-two, has had five speeding tickets, a couple of accidents (one pretty serious that scared him into driving a bit slower and more cautiously...) and then one day begins to wonder how it is that he has been driving as long as he waited to drive in the first place. That's how it feels to put my friendship with Kevin up to a time measurement. I have known people who have had friendships that lasted fifty years, and I wonder if they ever once took the time to say to each other, *Hey, you made a difference in my life. Did you know that?* I know I never told Kevin. I hoped, maybe, that this would be my chance. And it's hard to comprehend sometimes just how much one grows familiar with his or her place in life without ever really appreciating all that is surrounding it. Had I taken stock of it all, I would have stopped to think maybe something just needed to be said.

Making it to Kevin's side was easy, the flight was on time and the traffic average. Remaining there during the saddest, darkest days of his life was painful but something I do not regret. My visit was a way of saying, "Hey, you made a difference." Watching him slip slowly and drudgingly into death was sheer torture. I selfishly wished each day that when finally my day arrives I will die a more sudden, less painful death. His wife, Katie, and I spent the majority of our hours on the porch or at the table discussing what we should do to end his suffering. Neither could bring ourselves to admit that we just didn't have the strength required to extinguish his anguish at our own hands. It is a complexity all too shameful and compelling to understand. On one hand, there lies your loved one, a husband and a life-long friend, suffering beyond human toil, whose only wish is to ease the sudden and numbing pain that revolts against his own body. And on the other side lies what remains of a life, still fragile, still so magically filled with the spark of existence, the simply unexplained element that breathes life into our lungs, our hearts, our very souls. And it can't be extinguished, not until it has lived its fullest. Ending it prematurely somehow seems unjust, the arrogance of human strength. Between the two sides lies the mongrel of reason, of law, of right versus wrong, of empathy and sorrow. Of anger and confusion. Somewhere therein lies the answer we were searching for but could never find.

"He looks so peaceful this morning," Katie uttered over coffee. She stared back into the room where still lay sleeping the man she had loved and married. They had hoped for children, to raise a family. But that had never happened and now it was near the end.

I sipped a too-hot brew and imaged Sara McKenzie holding out a cup to me. "He slept well last night," I said.

"Who wouldn't?" she said. "With that much morphine, the world just disappears beyond some veil of numbness."

"The wonder drug," I bleakly intoned.

"Too bad he can't even enjoy it," she joked. The laughter, as always, was good. If Kevin required morphine to push back the demons of pain, we needed humor to abate our own suffering. Laughter is the opiate of the soul.

"What shall we do today?" she asked, attempting to regain cheer.

"Why don't you get out for a while? It seems nice outside. Go for a walk or a ride on the bike. I'll be fine here with him," I assured her.

"That would be nice, but I don't know. I am so used to being here for him."

"Katie," I demanded. "You need a break. Get out for a little while. Do some shopping. Buy something new. Replace that terrible dress you're wearing."

"Hey! What's wrong with this dress? It's sunny and comfy," she defended.

"I'm joking. I wouldn't know a good dress from an address. I just wanted to get you riled. When you're riled, you'll get antsy. Once you get antsy, you'll have to get out of here. Now go find those ugly blue shoes of yours and replace them too."

"August Monroe!" she warned. "I swear if your best friend weren't my husband, I would take you out to the malls and show you how to treat a woman."

I checked the clock. "Oh, look at that!" I evaded her. "It's time for Kevin to wake up."

Shared laughter filtered off in either direction as she headed upstairs and I entered the family room. Passing through the doorway into the room that had become his bedroom and nursing station all in one, I caught glimpse of the newspaper lying folded on the table in the hall. The storm that had rocked South Carolina was still making headway northward and would pound the coast in a matter of days. The Carolinas had been spared the brunt of the storm and only suffered minor damages. Heavy rains, resounding winds and blowing water were enough to keep this northern boy from ever buying ocean property, but it only strengthened the resolve of the coastal inhabitants who chocked the storm up to yet another they had survived. Still, the storm looked to be growing in intensity. And the fact that it did not slow down near the Carolinas bode poorly for the eastern seaboard.

Seaports all along Maine, Rhode Island and New Hampshire were bracing for the thrust of the storm, with Boston, Philadelphia and New York City warning of possible evacuations. It was an immense hurricane and it was throttled on full overdrive, ready to barrel down and reach land somewhere, sometime soon. Every town's hope was that it would pass them over for another town, along with a little prayer that probably got them through the worst parts.

Kevin lay on his back, his eyes a mere gaze of reality as the morphine drip slid him in and out of consciousness. Our summer had been something of a reunion and avoidance, like parents explaining to a kid that mommy and daddy were getting a divorce, but that it wasn't the kid's fault. Upon first arriving, there was tension, sharing the usual *How do ya do's?* and the awkward catching up of things which we should never have lost touch. There were *How is the golf game?* chats to cover as well as *How is work?* and then the inevitable *How are you?* question that I needed to ask to introduce the real subject we were dancing around. And, let's face it, the only real reason I had traveled to visit. It was evident from the moment he opened his door in early May of 1998 that he was sicker than I had imagined. His weight had not dropped yet and his step was pretty solid considering the progression of the cancer, but his face showed the effects of the disease worst of all. His classically warm smile was now a mere shadow of its former brightness, his sharp eyes dull reminders of the life sliding past him. Sallow cheek lines dropped from his face in lines longer than memory, and his hair, thin and brisk, fell sparingly upon his scalp.

I thought I had prepared myself for that moment when I would first see him. But it can't be done. Nothing prepares you to look at death through someone else's eyes. Preparations such as that are not taught in school or rehearsed on airplanes. In fact, they are never even quite complete because the next person I see nearing death will shock me further in some other way.

All in all, in early May he was doing rather well, and soon the discussion turned to baseball.

"How long are ya staying?" he asked.

"Well, I have as much time as I need," I answered gingerly, the inference of totality too sharp to dull.

"Who's going to call the games?"

"We got a kid on intern from Columbia. He's bright and sharp. He'll fill in well."

"Two week's vacation?" he asked.

"Well, I have a lot of time off, so I guess as long as..." and I couldn't answer. I think he may have been pulling me into one of his old jokes.

"As long as I live. Figures. Everyone is writing me off. Oh, well. No one lives forever. Say, how do the Owls look this year? We don't get much news about them in these parts."

From that moment forward there was little talk about his actual impending death. We talked about life, baseball, memories and everything else to fill the time. He knew I was there until the end, no matter the time frame. Besides, he and I both knew Katie could use the help and the company.

The summer went on its way, each day becoming a tightrope of emotion, one day filled with the fear of death, and the next reminded of the joy of life. Most days, though, were joyful. Kevin's spirit was a gleaming ray of hope in a house overridden with grief.

"Yeah know something, August?" Katie asked mid-way through June. "Kevin is more upbeat than we are. Isn't that terrible? I mean, here we are, you and I, alive and healthy, still ready to live the rest of our lives for years we cannot even count or imagine, and we're saddened. What right do we have when Kevin, who knows he is going to die and probably soon, is the one who keeps our spirits up? We're being so selfish."

I could offer little response, except for a subtle touch.

Kevin became as caught up as anyone and wished for nothing more than to live long enough to see McGwire hit number sixty-two. And then, when Sosa of the Chicago Cubs made a leapfrog turn into the headlines by amassing twenty homers in June alone, including three in one game against Milwaukee, there was talk of a new horse in the race to eclipse Maris' thirty-seven year old record. And consider this, when Babe Ruth hit the original watermark of sixty home runs in 1927, it took only thirty-four years for that record to be eclipsed. Maris's record stood longer by three years! In defense of Ruth, Maris hit his in 162 games, Ruth in 154.

The Fourth of July snuck up on us, and soon the All-Star break would send us into the second half of the season. The Pirates were a surprise contender fighting for first place despite playing average baseball. The Reds were barely above ground and nothing could save Kevin from chalking in the whole season. It was a lost cause. Except for Sammy and Mark. The Chase. What a story! What a year 1998 was for baseball.

The news brought Katie into the discussion. "What's all this hub-bub I hear people talking about with home runs all of a sudden?" Katie asked. "Women at work are discussing it, people in the lines at the store. What gives?"

"Katie, dear," Kevin, answered. "This is *why* we watch these silly games."

"And that means?" she asked. I took Kevin's silence as a cue for me to answer for us.

"It's all about possibility, Katie," I told her.

"Possibility?"

"Yep. See, there is this record that has stood since 1961..." and I proceeded to tell her all about Maris and his link to the present between McGwire and Sosa. To say she was enthralled would be an understatement. She was hooked! As quickly as the numbers escalated, it was Katie who suddenly calculated how many home runs either *could* finish with, as well as the statistical probability of either doing it first. Her usual glancing at the world news was replaced with first checking the sports page. Baseball fever had claimed another victim.

By mid-July, there was talk that McGwire would break Roger Maris' single-season home run record of sixty-one. The whole country became caught up in the fervor. People who had never before talked about baseball were discussing Mark McGwire around the water cooler as if they had been lifelong fans. *Did you hear, he hit two more last night against Houston?* Baseball was returning to its previous height as a favorite recreational activity for Americans. Young and old alike witnessed the rebirth of the game with an awe and wonderment that had not been seen since the likes of Reggie Jackson or Hank Aaron in the 1970's. And, when all of a sudden Sammy Sosa lit up the home run standings through June, it became a two-man race toward history in the most compelling spectacle in all of sports.

In a matter of days, McGwire cooled off and Sosa made up ground in the race.

"McGwire's been sitting on number thirty-seven since the end of June," Katie declared. "Sosa has thirty-five. He can catch him, you know. Do you realize what that means?" she asked.

"No, Katie, I don't. What does it mean?" Kevin humored her, but enjoyed seeing her so excited. In a very large way, it distracted us all from the matters at hand.

"McGwire's probability ratio is dropping exponentially!" she declared to unwitting ears. Our confounded stares sent her sprawling away with a frustrated sigh as she left the room scribbling numbers across a sheet of paper, re-calculating McGwire's ratio, whatever that meant.

"Oh, Katie!" I called to her through the slumbering house late that evening as Kevin dozed off during a Cardinals' game against Houston. "McGwire just went yard."

"Yard, went yard?" she asked from the stairwell, the voice of an obsessed woman needing further information raising up like a panic. "What does that mean? Is that good? Does that refer to an injury?"

"No, not an injury. It's very good," I assured her. "It means he has hit another home run."

"Well, that doesn't quite put him back on track, but..." Her sentence was lost as she continued on with her numbers once again. I enjoyed even further informing her the next day, July 12th I recall as that is my mother's birthday, that McGwire had hit not one, but two home runs in a single game. This threw her into fits of statistical prognostications only a mathematician could have understood. I failed to mention that both Sosa and McGwire always held the potential of connecting on *three* homers in a single game.

During the years immediately preceding 1998, fans and writers and players had speculated that if anyone could break the record it would have either been McGwire or Seattle's Ken Griffey Jr., a free-swinging left-handed hitter who was perhaps the greatest player of the decade. Year after year they would both set an early pace without quite reaching a consistency strong enough to initiate serious talk about breaking the record. Both were somewhat injury prone, and were getting older. It seemed at times that the record would indeed stand forever, as if no one would ever match Maris' stunning feat of sixty-one home runs in a single season. Griffey and McGwire had both hit fifty-eight once or twice but neither ever really challenged the mark by hurtling the first barrier of sixty in a season. Sixty-one was just too many, we had all pretty much decided.

What ensued was what baseball is all about – fun, sportsmanship, competition, excitement and the big show. It was an extravaganza unlike anyone had seen in baseball for close to twenty years. Yes, the most ardent fans could recount the numbers Greg Maddox had put up during the 1990's or the accomplishments of his team, the Atlanta Braves. And the fans of any given team could recall their fondest hometown memories. But for absolute national baseball attention, there may not have been anything this exciting since Denny McLain's 30 win season in 1968 or perhaps Reggie Jackson winning three World Series titles with the A's in the early seventies only to return to the Fall Classic as a Yankee to win two more championships in 1977 and 1978. The only event that nearly matched the Sosa / McGwire chase was Cal Ripken's climb toward baseball greatness as he himself knocked Lou Gehrig into second place on the baseball records as the player to have played in the most consecutive games. But that sweet evening in 1995 was somber and rewarding, a recognition of a long journey of persistence and perseverance. It was more about anticipation than about question. It wasn't *Will Cal do it, but when will he do it?* We all knew Ripken would get there, we just had to check the schedule, count up to 2,136, and wait.

All along we indoctrinated Katie to the marvelous feats and history that is baseball.

On a day when Kevin had been feeling especially strong and was in a very receptive mood, we talked baseball. "So," Katie asked. "McGwire or Sosa will be known as the greatest home run hitter of all time?"

I looked at Kevin with a humorous grin that suggested one of us had to field that question. He shrugged and explained.

"That, Katie," he began, "is a terminal debate. Our guest Augie here likes to think that one season does not crown a player as Home Run King. He thinks it's all about big numbers."

"Now, just wait a minute," I demanded. "This argument needs some elaboration for the sake of clarity."

"Be my guest," Kevin added.

"No," I insisted. "This is your sideways theory, and since all of the baseball world agrees with me perhaps hearing your defense would prove more interesting."

"Guys!" Katie exasperated. "Just get on with it. What is the debate?"

"Well," Kevin said. "There are some who agree with August here that the greater feat is the career mark for home runs held by Hank Aaron at 755. I seem to be the only intelligent baseball fan who views that the single season mark is of greater significance because it demands a longer stretch of consistency in a concentrated period of time. McGwire and Sosa are on absolute hot streaks, but they will have to maintain that pace all year to eclipse Maris' record. Aaron, with all due respect, had periods of hot and cold and could go twenty games at a stretch without a home run. Maris did not have that luxury, nor does McGwire or Sosa." He paused. "It's more compact."

"And," I countered, "it took longevity unheralded by other players to accomplish Aaron's numbers. It is a more significant mark because of the years. There is wear and tear on the body, the changes over time to the strike zone, the countless number of pitchers who threw against him, including those who figured out how to beat him. Year after year, Aaron made adjustments, kept a torrid pace and built the numbers upward. It all adds up to a greater accomplishment."

"Men!" Katie huffed before walking away. "You guys think way too much."

I left my argument with a shrug that was answered by Kevin's nod. It was a debate left to the ages. And as we watched a ball game that evening, I thought further about my side of the argument.

Hammering Hank must have been a joyride. And as much as Kevin's use of book-ending a record within one season was ancillary to the feat itself, Aaron's final moment of glory came a season after it had its crescendo. All summer long he inched higher and higher toward Babe Ruth's record, but winter interrupted the fury with Aaron sitting on 713 dingers to end the 1973 season. It took the absolute wind out of the sails of history as Hank and the world waited until spring of 1974 to witness the other once-thought improbable feat. Tantamount to Aaron's record is a two-fold complexity Kevin could not seem to appreciate. Considering that understanding anything historical must be reflected upon by its context in time, it is safe to say that Hank Aaron had two great specters to deal with in his march toward greatness. First, there was the racial issue. For a black man to hold the record as the greatest home run hitter of all time was not equality as the Civil Rights Movement had hoped. It was outright dominance. Aaron did not retire tied with Babe Ruth, but over forty home runs *better* than the "Sultan of Swat."

All along, Aaron battled the bigotry and ignorance of racism, having withstood threats to his safety should he break that record. All he did was persevere. He silenced critics and those who threatened him by setting the bar higher than ever. I wonder if there was a little of the other, more famous, August Wilson to be found in Hank Aaron.

Likewise, he dealt with the Icon of Babe Ruth, the man who had become a myth as big as Paul Bunyan and as important as

Uncle Sam. Ruth was a symbol for America, of Yankee greatness, of the best. And a lot of folks did not want to see that image tarnished at all, yet alone by an African-American. It was a similar fate suffered by Maris minus the racial implications. This was the equivalent of defacing a legend, a sad legacy Aaron and Maris shared.

After 1961, when Maris broke Ruth's first great record, the world accepted the fact that the Babe's accomplishments would and could be surpassed with time, inevitably falling one-by-one as the seasons rolled along. But they didn't get to that opinion easily. Finally, by 1998, all memories of Babe Ruth had been brought level to the playing field and his status as a god had been reconciled to a human being who happened to be a great ballplayer.

Hoping for sixty-two home runs in a single season meant dealing with nothing but timing. There would be no waiting until spring of 1999. It had to be done then or it may never happen again. All sixty-two runs for a new record had to come between April and September. And arrive they did, like meteor showers and shooting starts upon the firmament of the sky.

Sosa and McGwire. 1998. The Home Run watch. That was excitement to its very definition. There was no telling how far the run would stretch. There was always the threat that injury would slow one of the players down, and always the possibility of a slump. Each time either slowed into a three or four game drought the talk turned again to *That record will never be broken.* But one of them would have a two or three homer performance and all the buzz would return. What added to the competition were several other intangible elements that furthered national appeal. Somewhat notably, the Cardinals and Cubs played in the same division, the National League Central. Since the 1994 realignment of baseball into three divisions within both leagues, the NLC faired quite poorly and never produced a World Series champion from amongst its five teams. This was the NLC's chance to shine. Most notably, this was the Cardinals and the Cubs! This was history and tradition and rivalry. These teams had been entrenched in the lore and glory of Midwest America for the entire century, baseball's previous focal point. The Cardinals had won World Series titles over the years and the Cubs remained steadfast losers, breaking the hearts for generations of fans.

The spotlight of baseball was right there in the Midwest, focusing on those two teams. After all those years growing up when we heard about the big cities of Los Angeles and New York, people started talking again about Chicago and St. Louis. It must have been what the twenties and thirties were like when baseball was the undisputed national pastime and Chicago and St. Louis were the biggest draws. And don't let anyone ever suggest that civic pride was not a factor. Those cities cared. Each wanted the home run record to be felled by their own hero.

"How much could this really matter to the city?" Katie inquired, having overheard Kevin proclaiming that he hopes for Chicago's sake that Sosa gets there first. After years of futility, he reasoned, the Cubs fans, who were ardently some of the best fans of the game, deserved something to celebrate.

"It means a great deal," I answered. "On one level it is packing those stadiums each night, which means a lot of money for a lot of people. The owners, obviously, but also tee-shirt vendors, local bar and restaurant owners, marketing sales, you name it. And it's not just in St. Louis and Chicago, either. Every game they play, be it in New York or Philadelphia or San Diego, or wherever, draws a lot of commerce. A sensation like this, while great for the game and its history, serves the economy well, too. But even still, the fans feel pride connected to their team, and it's just as good as a championship. For a fan to say she roots for the team with the home run record holder on its roster is a kind of bragging right."

"I just don't get it," she added. Her enthusiasm, while swelling with anticipation to follow the record-setting events fell short of true fanaticism. "I guess you have to really follow the game to get into it that much. But, still, it is a lot of fun."

As we watched the race, neither Kevin nor I (nor the rest of the baseball viewing world) could predict what might become of the great race. I, at one time, even threw the towel in on the whole thing, surrendering to the often accepted and over quoted belief that the record would always stand at sixty-one. It was a magical number, after all. Maris hit sixty-one home runs in 1961. There was symmetry, it made sense. It represented a day long gone in America, a revered past. The fore-longing for those days was equally echoed throughout baseball as the game changed and the players became detached, less a part of the city for which they played than they had before.

But, still. That number. 61. It strikes an odd irony for me and perhaps a multitude of Pittsburgh Pirates fans both young and old. Historically speaking, of course, since I wasn't alive in 1961. Mom and dad hadn't even met by 1961. Yet it still stands as a tarnish of sorts. The underdog Pirates had triumphed just one year earlier in the 1960 World Series, stealing the spotlight and the thunder from the hated New York Yankees to claim a Pittsburgh championship. It must have been a grand time throughout the fall and winter of 1960 and into the summer of 1961 as the Pirates reminded everyone they were the champs! Before long, the 1961 season wound down and Roger Maris climbed higher than the immortal Babe Ruth. I often think history has a short memory. Our greatest heroes, Ruth, Ty Cobb, Lou Gehrig, Honus Wagner from the early, early days, and Mickey Mantle, Sandy Koufax, Ted Williams from the mid-century era, are all so revered. Yet they and so many unlisted teammates both winners and losers alike had their fair share of womanizers, drunkards, gamblers, racists, showmen extraordinaire. They were no better socially off the field than so many figures we chastise today, yet we elevate them to a status somewhat higher than what we expect of ourselves and it may be simply because we forget how they lived.

As 1961 reached its apex, the Yankees won the damn thing again anyway. And wouldn't Kevin have hated to remember that they bested the Cincinnati Reds eight years before his birth? But still, the 1960 championship stands, then, as the fall of a civilization, perhaps the last stab at the old guard. As the 1960's wore on, our president was assassinated right here on American soil, civil unrest erupted into violence fired by social inequality or rage against a war Americans did not want to partake of. Viet Nam tore asunder a nation that had stood undivided since the dying days of the Civil War some hundred years earlier. And sport remained. While men landed on the moon, Martin Luther King Jr.'s body was laid to rest, a drug culture undermined a conservative nation's view of itself, and a country so confident began to lose faith in its own leaders, sport continued to offer release. But it was never to be the same. And somehow, that year, 1960, stands tantamount as perhaps a closing of one era and the dawning of another. The Yankees, who represented the glitz and the glamour of fame and prosperity, had been bested by the rusting town of Pittsburgh. Behold, the glamour had chiseled.

For Maris' record to fall, a grand series of events would have to take place. And they did. Mark McGwire had been an Oakland Athletic his whole career and only moved to the National League via trade in 1997. McGwire had been a teammate of Kevin's since Bentworth broke into the Big Leagues. He had a special place for him, hoping Mark would break the record before

Sosa. I was pulling for Sammy. Wearing number twenty-one seemed to be an homage to Roberto Clemente, and being from the Dominican Republic, one could suggest that Sosa's hero was none other than Pittsburgh's favorite adopted immigrant, Clemente.

"That McGwire is all gentleman, ya know," Kevin told me as we watched a game against the Phillies in late June. "He was a force on that A's team, the one I came up with. He was great to be around." We shared stories of Kevin's days with Oakland for the entire evening.

Perhaps had McGwire remained in the American League, the events of 1998 may never have transpired. The thought that it may not have happened in the American League is supported by Sosa, also a National Leaguer. Was pitching just weaker in the NL? Perhaps. Were ballparks smaller? Or was it a result of expansion or the Designated Hitter rule? It's hard to say. Suffice it to argue that Maris himself set the sixty-one home run plateau as a new record in an expansion year as well when the American League added two teams, thus thinning the pitching staffs of his opponents, much the same as the National League had done in 1994. And again in 1998, McGwire and Sosa's NL only added one new team, the Arizona Diamondbacks, though the Milwaukee Brewers moved out of the American and into the National League that year as well, stretching out the value of the pitching commodity. The debates were exchanged in bars and stadiums all summer long and no one could answer unequivocally why it was finally happening. It gave pregnant pause to the argument that the AL is a hitter's league, a point fans of the National League had argued against for decades. With the designated hitter, the AL can score more runs, faithfuls would argue. But the NL has more strategy, traditionalists would counter. And their pitchers have to face the prospect of hitting. The great investment of taking sides goes on and on.

Whatever the cause, it was an awesome show of the most spectacular spectacle in pro sports. The Home Run. It is, perhaps, the most thrilling occurrence in competitive athletics. The touchdown is exciting, yet foreseen and anticipated. You know a team is getting close and that is always the goal. A slam dunk is thrilling, but borders on showmanship and anyone who can't dunk probably isn't playing basketball these days anyway. As for hockey, perhaps the penalty shot measures in intensity but it is as rare as the no-hitter and is an event of precision, the game slowed down, the clock not moving. Now a home run! That is the thrill of the moment. It is the unexpected. The same player who struck out the last two at bats may catch a high fastball and send a pitch oblong into the stands at any moment.

On August 8th, the two hitters were about as close as they would come to trotting into history as a tandem. McGwire's lead had dwindled down to just two homers ahead of Sosa. And then, as if this stuff was written for Hollywood and discarded as absolute trash, too unbelievable, nobody would buy it, they were deadlocked, completely tied. Number forty-eight had them wrapped tightly, but only for a matter of innings.

"The Cubbies are hosting the Cards at Wrigley tonight!" Katie excitedly informed us, as if we were not aware of the impending showdown. *Cubbies, Cards?* I wondered. Since when did she get to know the teams' nicknames? "Look," she added, shoving a schedule in our faces and pointing to August 19th on the calendar. "They are playing each other. Isn't this exciting?"

"Yes, dear, it is," Kevin's responded.

In the fifth inning of that game, Sosa connected on a pitch and sent home run number forty-eight sprawling through the Illinois sky. His feat at having tied McGwire was short-lived, however, as McGwire launched another towering home run himself in the eighth inning, along with yet another, his fiftieth on the season, in extra innings, helping the Cardinals win the game by a score of 8-6 in ten innings.

Sosa wouldn't get as close as he had been those three innings as McGwire opened up a commanding lead over the next few weeks. At first, his distance came with a stride and then a full length, ultimately pacing the race when he amassed four homers against Florida in two day's time between September first and second. This accomplishment, not surprisingly, sent Katie on another tirade of numbers and probabilities.

"Why doesn't she just enjoy it?" Kevin asked.

"I don't know," I answered. "You tell me. She's your wife!"

"Well, I don't care what number he gets to afterward," Kevin said. I just want him to hit sixty-two, hell, either of them can do it. Home runs are what baseball is all about. It's what people pay to see, it's what they want to see." He coughed hard, caught his breath, and remained silent.

McGwire had picked up home run number sixty-one that night, setting off a nationwide frenzy as he sat tied with Maris on the precipice of history.

His wish came true on a balmy September evening with the season fading down to its World Series climax. Only this year, in 1998, the attention was not on the surging Yankees who would go on to win an unprecedented 25th World Series Title! Nor was anyone paying much attention to the surprising San Diego Padres who would go on to lose the Series to New York, thus depriving the great Tony Gwynn of his last shot at a championship. That all took a back seat as the record appeared fallible more and more with each passing game.

Again, it was with Hollywood irony that the Cubs played in St. Louis on September 8, 1998. The night before, McGwire had drilled number sixty-one to tie Maris' record. The national television audience waited pitch by pitch to witness baseball history, and in a lot of ways, American history.

The anticipation was not long for the evening, however, and was far from anti-climactic. In the fourth inning, McGwire took his strides to the plate.

"Ooohhh!" Katie squealed. "I can't watch. This is just too much. Tell me what happens."

Kevin, barely a gaze behind the death mask to which his face had succumbed, watched as I narrated for Katie.

"Trachsel sets for his delivery, and... McGwire swings. That will be a line drive out," I told them. "Maybe a bloop base hit." The ball was a lumbering, quirky slice, not the power crunching, noise-barrier-breaking thumps McGwire had been hitting all summer long. As the ball sauntered its way toward left field, a heavy pause fell hushed upon the crowd on hand and the nation in front of their televisions.

Just as I had dropped a French fry years earlier while discovering Mr. Bentworth's legacy in Watson's Deli, a potato chip hit the floor beneath my feet as I slowly realized that the ball was on its way out.

I let out a yell. "Hold on!" I leaned forward in my chair. "That sucker might clear the fence. It's high enough, and..." just as the ball plopped heavily over the very pinnacle of the left field wall, the screams on the television echoed my disbelief. He had done it! Just like that, in a fashion unbecoming the slaying of a giant, McGwire had muscled his name into the record books, not with power but with poise.

Finally, he had reached number sixty-two, and all across this nation there let out a collective sigh of relief and a simultaneous gasp of joy as the events of a special summer culminated in grand fashion in St. Louis, Missouri. Mark Twain would have been proud. That Sammy Sosa moved up the all-time list a mere five days later was hardly an afterthought. We reveled with equal awe as Sosa supplanted Maris into third and stood all alone in second place.

The most chilling scenes came on that September night when McGwire reached the record. He embraced his son, lifting the boy high in the air. He greeted the Maris family, Roger long since deceased at the hand of cancer. McGwire was warmly met with a chest-bumping hug from Sosa, his opponent and friend. And he smiled as he doffed his cap to the cheering multitudes, all who allowed McGwire that magic moment while secretly wondering if the record would ever be broken again.

And wasn't the scene similar in many aspects to what we were doing in North Carolina? Kevin lay withering of cancer, awaiting his father's hand on his planned trip in a matter of days. I, the baseball fan and former player, celebrated along with my friend, the milestone he lived to witness. And Katie, the bridge between families, fulfilled her husband's dying wish of seeing his father one last time. While it wasn't perfect symmetry, it was balance with all of us secretly wondering how long Kevin had left.

35 Father and Son

The morning came bleak and surprisingly light as a soft mixture of cool cloud coverage limbered across the muted sky. The air was restless, pushing the storm northward and leaving a cutting chill behind. All that had been damp and humid had evaporated into the sauntering wind as it rushed out of Florida, leaving across the Carolinas the gray, streaky chill of a winter morning. Winter, if we had been in Pennsylvania or Ohio and most certainly in Maine and Vermont. But there it was, out of place, disjointed, a leftover straggler from some former winter that had fled too earnestly in pursuit of spring. In the chambered stillness of the house, I rose slowly and contemplated the day's events. It would be a sorrowful day, a day long remembered and often wished away. The heavy heart of those departed lay square on my shoulders as a reminder of what was to be faced, and I felt old at twenty-nine. Surely sadness lingers as perilous upon the aged and the infirmed as I felt that morning.

I busied myself quietly while getting washed and dressed. I chose not to shave, a custom I rarely forego. I headed downstairs and felt the pallor of endings reach up the stairwell and into the quiet recesses of the soon-to-be abandoned house. Katie would eventually sell the home and move back north to be with her family, leaving behind nothing that would signify to the new residents that anything had ever happened there, save the peculiar and always present feeling that something was amiss in the house, or the creepy sensation that someone had once died there.

Mr. Bentworth's plane was due in at 9:30 AM. I headed for the airport without saying good morning to Katie or to Kevin, even though the gesture would only have been a pat on the shoulder for the latter and an uncomfortable nod toward the former. Kevin could barely hear me at that point, and Katie was trapped in the silent place where waiting widows reside. Regardless, it was not my place. What right had I to be the first to say "Good morning" on what was sure to be his last day? His wife or his father deserved that opportunity. Even though they had been bitterly opposed for some ridiculous amount of years, it was just not right for me to intrude upon the fatherly right of a sad man and his dying son. Despite his stubbornness, Mr. Bentworth was a good man. He cared, and who could blame him for that? It was his son who could not seem to see just how much he was loved by his father. I guess I saw it as an outsider. Always aware of dad's love for me, I could see it in Mr. Bentworth. Kevin somehow missed it.

I pushed the car behind the fleeting storm and cruised along Interstate 40. It occurred to me that I hadn't had a moment to myself outside of sleeping in close to four months. If I was not Kevin's companion I had been Katie's friend. If I wasn't talking with her or cleaning up the dishes, I was at Kevin's side. Alone in the car and still twenty minutes from the airport, all that was about to end came at me full front, a paradox to the storm disappearing ahead of me along the road.

I bawled my eyes out. For the better part of three miles I cried as much rain as the storm above me carried across the state to be dumped onto Virginia and other points north. I wept like I had never wept before and the catharsis was a strengthened testament to a friendship I could no longer express in person. Kevin never heard the sobs or saw those tears but somehow, like during our countless road trips through Morton County to and from Roth College, I think he knew what I was saying.

The airplane was on time and Mr. Bentworth disembarked the aircraft a tired, soulless man in need of hope. He was not scraggly like a withered smoker appears, nor bent humbled like a wounded veteran. He was sad, just sad. The distance in his voice as he met me sounded like cannons of regret forging an apologetic knell of remorse. We embraced a forced, uneven hug and patted each other on the shoulders.

"How was your trip?" I asked, clearing loose the remaining emotion lodged in my throat.

"Oh, not too bad," he answered forcibly. "You know. Air travel's hard on these old bones."

"Did you run into any bad weather with the storms?"

"Ya know, I can't say that we did. Then again, it's likely we might have. Say, uh, how is he, August?"

I was startled by the jump from small talk right into the heart of our meeting, and queerly stumbled through a meager reply. "Good." I lied. A cringe in my gut tightened with apprehension. "He's good, Mr. B. Really, he's...He's doing okay."

His tired eyes stared at his shuffling feet. "August," he said. "You know, this is hard for; well, for both of us. Kevin and me. I doubt either of us has much time together. I need to know if he will be aware that I am there. So, you be honest with me. I can take it." He raised his head to meet my eyes and an immobilized tear hung on his warped cheek, caught between years of wear and regret. "How is my boy?"

The stare from deep within that man's soul was onyx, dark and as sad as it was colorless. With a hefty sigh, I squared my choking voice to hold back tears and answered with absolute honesty. "He's in bad shape, Mr. B." The words came in forms I could hardly think yet alone say, but still they had to be spoken. "It's pretty close to the end. He, uh, huh-hum. He could die today."

"Well, then," he added gruffly and with determination. "We should be getting along. I don't want to miss him before..."

The incomplete sentence wafted away somewhere into the airport as we began the slow, meaningful walk to the car in silence.

We fought the sparse business day crowd and got to the car. The highway again rolled out before us. Mr. Bentworth faded in and out of tiny naps, muttering half-sentences about a billboard with an inane message or about a passing car driving perilously close. I could not tell whether he was frightened or sad or slipping in and out of his own sanity. I let it be. After what must have been a solid nap of ten minutes, he arose fully aware and alert, regaining suddenly a personable quality I had missed as it lay dormant all the years I had known him.

He gazed at the dashboard like a man fixated. "August," he said. "You know what keeps getting me about all this?"

I wanted to suggest that if it was the wasted years or the senseless silence between them, I understood. Or perhaps that it had been the empty energy spent burning anger like an exhaustive fuel, he was forgiven. Or that... All the things that could have been said. I remained silent.

"What gets me the most," he answered after my silence, "Is that this isn't the way it's supposed to be."

"I know," I added. "Cancer is terrible. It..."

"No," he interrupted. "Not just the cancer. I mean, that's bad enough. It is a terrible thing, you are right in that. But this, this death of his. It's unnatural. It's out of synch, in the wrong order. Do you know what I mean? He is supposed to bury me. That's the order of things. You bring a kid into the world and you raise him and he supports you in your aging and takes and buries you when you're gone. That's just the way it is meant to be. But this..." He clapped his hands on his knees, "This is just wrong. It doesn't make sense. That's all."

"I see your point, Mr. B.," I said dumbly, a little moved by his sudden perspective. "I guess I never thought of it that way. This is hard on you, and I..." again, the sentence fell away from my emotional grasp of situations. If Kevin's father noticed, he gave no indication either way as to how I might have made him feel. He was letting go of his emotions and perhaps it was my time to just listen.

"When his mother died, God rest her soul," he continued. "I promised her I would always look after him. I thought I always did what was best for him. I wanted to raise him to be a good man, a citizen people would be proud to know. Hell, he didn't need me for that. He could have done that on his own. What he needed was a dad, not a supervisor. I guess I failed her in that." He slowly turned his head toward the window and gazed out at the empty fields passing by. "But worse I failed him. He had years left to live then. She, well, she was already gone."

The rest of the trip was a stilted silence. I searched my own soul for the words that would comfort this man in his misery, but none came. I was a silent arbitrator when the defendant required a boisterous attorney. As the street to Kevin and Katie's house approached, I felt relieved at the opportunity to break the silence.

"Here's their street," I stated, perhaps a bit too excitedly. "It's that red brick house, the third one on the right." I pointed out.

"My God," he said, surprising me.

"What? What is it?"

"I just realized. I have never even met my own daughter-in-law. She's been good to him. He said so in his letter."

"Oh, she's wonderful. Mr. B. You'll like her," I assured him. I spun into the driveway and leapt from the car as fast as I could. While I fought his oddly shaped, though impeccably weightless suitcase from the trunk, Mr. Bentworth came around to the back of the car.

"Aug," he said. He patted the fender as if to avoid saying what he was thinking. "We've known each other a long time, you and me. And I don't think you know how much it means to me to know that my son," he paused, continued, "always had a friend in this world." After the compliment, his attention to the fender waned and his eyes met mine. The tired, battered soul that had peered from behind the same eyes earlier had been transformed to a man of courage, a father willing to face any fear for his children. "That means a lot. Friendship," he added. "Friends are like an extension of your family. You can count on them, hope with them and always know where they stand. Not many people are lucky enough to have a friendship like you and Kevin have had. I guess what I'm trying to tell you is, well, thank you."

"In the future," I attempted to joke as the suitcase wedged itself free of my trunk with a few jolts and twists, "I will have to get friends with better suitcases."

For the better of my own embarrassment, Katie's voice arose from the porch.

"Hey, you're here. Great."

"Oh, this must be..." Mr. Bentworth said. He twirled around to meet his daughter-in-law. "Damn, Augie, you should have warned me," he uttered through half-closed mouth over a shoulder. "She's quite the looker."

"Yeah," I replied. "She has the personality to match. She's a great lady."

Katie stepped toward Mr. Bentworth and paused. It was the most awkward moment I have ever had to smooth over.

"Mr. Bentworth, this is Katie; Katie, Mr. Bentworth."

"Is it okay if I call you dad?" she asked. She swelled with tears and embraced the man.

In that single, heart-felt sentence, she had encapsulated everything I had been trying to say to Mr. Bentworth since I had met him at the airport gate. Her succinctness was a beautiful sentiment.

"Dad?" he wondered. "I like the sound of that."

"Here, August," she said, disembracing. "Let me help you with those." She took the smaller case and headed in before us. Mr. Bentworth gave me the signal to go ahead of him.

"Mr. B," I said, turning abruptly at the porch.

"Yeah, Aug. What is it?" He stared past me into the house. "Don't worry I can handle whatever it is," he added after a moment.

"No," I said. "I just wanted to thank you for what you said earlier."

"You're welcome," he said. He patted my arm and passed me into the house. "Now, let me see my boy. Say, Katie, do you have a dog? Kevin always loved a dog."

I scampered behind Mr. Bentworth and entered the house, thinking that I had never seen a dog near their house in Cooperstown. He and Katie had paused at the kitchen and were standing side-by-side, his right arm holding her left as she held his right hand. They were going to face the moment together.

359

"He has trouble hearing sometimes," she said. "It's the morphine. He made us promise last night that after you were here we'd let it wear off a bit so that he could be more alert. So, we'll have to slow down the dosage soon."

"Does he need to sleep?" Mr. Bentworth asked. "We could let him sleep if he needs his rest. I can see him later."

"No," I answered. "He may be weak but it would be the death of all four us if we let him sleep while you were here. He's been talking about you all week." A stifling silence plunged into the room. "Well, when he's been able to talk," I added morosely. *Just shut up, August*! I told myself.

"Well, then," Katie said. "Shall we?"

They stepped together through the thin veil of curtain between the dining room and the family room. I brushed aside the curtain and followed them. The ever-present and pungent smell of soiled linens drifted into the room. They stopped at his bedside and Mr. Bentworth patted Kevin's right arm ever-so-slightly.

"Looks like he could pitch a no-hitter," he laughed through mounting tears.

"Kevin," his wife whispered, tapping his triceps soundly. "Honey. Dad's here. Can you wake up?"

We stood in silence as the monitor pumped to the rhythm of his waning heartbeat and the oxygen compressor rose and fell with a hiss and a whirl.

"Kev," she said, a bit more loudly. "Can you hear us? Your dad is here to see you."

Slowly, like a witness to a bizarre motion beside him unsure of what he was to turn toward, Kevin's head pivoted in our direction. His eyes were glazed but inert. A wan smile creased his discolored lips. His right hand flexed as the three inner fingers edged upward in a wave.

"Save your energy, son," Mr. Bentworth said compassionately. "I'll be here a while and we can talk later. Get your rest if you need it."

Kevin shook his head slowly, two solid discreet no's, then closed his eyelids to fall off to sleep.

"When he wakes up again," his wife said. "He'll be more alert. The morphine usually takes an hour to ninety minutes to slip off."

"Will he be in pain with it off?" Mr. Bentworth asked.

"Not much," I offered, perhaps uninvited. "It remains in his system long enough to keep him comfortable. The dosage is really more for resting periods. He'll be less groggy, that's all."

"Good," he said. "I'd like to be able to talk with him. And if you don't mind, while he sleeps for a bit, if you could show me to my lodgings, I'd like to get out of these travel clothes."

While Mr. Bentworth disappeared upstairs, I checked the sports headlines. Mark McGwire sat on home run number sixty-eight. We were heading into the final week of the baseball season and there was talk that he might actually reach seventy. Too bad that Kevin could not share in the news. He would have loved the idea of the improbable being accomplished. I could hear the echoes of debates we had argued as teenagers. *There is no way anyone will ever beat Maris' record,* I had said. *Cal Ripken will not keep the streak going for that many games,* I had predicted. But Kevin always believed in the superiority of the human being over the can nots and the rules of the world. *Why not?* I heard him ask from a day so long ago. *If Hammering Hank could hit 715, then anyone can do anything.* Always the skeptic, I reminded him that *Hank wound up with 755. That is one record that will never be broken.* He took on his classic "Why not?" stance and answered, *Yes it will, someday.*

I stood in his living room, not really reading the paper, and I considered that notion. Why not? Maybe Kevin was right after all. That someone out there, just learning to play ball right now or someone not even born yet or a superstar of today, will come along and chase the fans along another magical summer, edging closer and closer to number 755 for a career. Why not?

There are days that I reflect upon that make perfect sense, days that seem to have just been right for all the right reasons. These are days like Christmas or the first memory of birthdays, the perfect early spring and the halting snow storm that temporarily immobilizes a city. Isn't that what we're all in search for, really? Memories, I mean. The ability to conjure up some recollection of how things were, of what we used to be, of where our lives were at one touching moment in the past. Not a perfect moment, those would be dull and lack the luster of interest. But of a moment that reminds us of life – filled with a bit of chaos, a touch of understanding, a little doubt and little wistfulness. It's a recipe for memories, I suppose. And isn't it grand that we can categorize them by the days on which they occur? Maybe that old calendar makes sense after all. It chronicles our memories for us.

The day Kevin died was just one such day. It wasn't the perfect day of departure in which choirs of angels greeted him in sun-drenched glory. Nor was it the bleak, reminiscent gloom of despair ushering him into the grave. It was a day of balance – at one moment an upheaval of tender proportions filled with sorrow and regret and hope and love, and at other moments it was acceptance, tolerance, forgiveness, storytelling and grace. And in the end, it was saying goodbye.

An hour or so after Kevin had drifted off to sleep, Mr. Bentworth returned from upstairs a changed man. Gone was the pleasant man humbly welcoming himself into their home and in his place was the irascible man I had known since childhood. It was as if the fatigue of travel had enlightened his spirit and had humbled him in turnabout, and the comfort of rest had invigorated his zeal and pessimism. Without so much as a *hello* to either myself or Katie, he lapsed into a tirade about coffee and needing something to eat.

"I've been traveling all day," he clamored. "You'd think the accommodations would be more comforting. Can't a fellow get a cup of coffee and a biscuit, maybe a bagel or something, without having to ask for it outright?"

If Katie was outraged, she did not let on. Her reaction to the behavior was either to be startled, or she felt it appropriate to act the dutiful hostess. I did not know her quite well enough to understand her true spirit but I was surprised to see her jump into action. To the shelf she went, to get the coffee and a biscuit, maybe a bagel. She dumped fresh coffee grounds into the filter and paused. I saw in her face a reflective glance. It too was puzzling. Was it bewilderment at herself for having attended to Bentworth so adroitly, or was it perhaps a fond recollection of having aided her own father with his morning cup? Who could tell?

"Hey, August," Mr. Bentworth addressed me. "How about getting up off that chair. I'd like to flip through the paper and the light seems better where you're sitting."

In a silent, though accurate calculation, I assessed that the lighting was equal at all points because of the circular and low-hanging chandelier that hung above the table. There were two windows, one at the head and one at the foot of the table and it was near mid-day. There were no trees outside to block either window's light. It was a strange request.

"Sure," I acquiesced and yielded my seat. I noticed the newspaper was not in his hand. It was probably still on the phone stand where I had read it earlier. He sat on my recently vacated chair, slid the placemat before him out of the way and smoothed both hands over the surface of the table, either looking to clear crumbs or hoping to buy the set. With his hands folded roundly in front of him, at rest on the tabletop, he glared at me with a quizzical grin.

"What?" I asked, defensively.

"My paper," he said. "Where is it?"

"It's not your pap –" I began to say but was interrupted by Katie sliding a plate with warm biscuits (and a bagel!) before Mr. Bentworth.

"The paper is in the hallway, August," she said, glancing pensively at me, "on the phone stand where we always keep it. Why don't you get it for dad?" She looked away from me. "Dad, would you like butter or jam for that bagel?"

"Butter," he ordered. "And cream only in that coffee. I don't take sugar. And none of that hazelnut or butter rum flavor. Say, that isn't decaffeinated, is it? I need coffee with flavor, ya know?"

I am not sure how long it took me to get the paper, but I was not swift by the standard of any man's age. How was this angry, bitter man able to boss us around that way? Who did he think he was to have a right to tell two other adults what to do? He was a guest and he acted like the proprietor of a run-down establishment bitter at the hired help for having lost him his fortune. Maybe it's just seeing his son, I reasoned. I should give him some space, let him release his frustration, even if it is aimed unfairly in my direction. After all, he was beginning the painful task of burying his only son. How level-headed could I expect the man to be?

I returned to the table and offered him the paper. He made a few terse remarks about its condition, that the sections had already been rifled through and that this town was hardly a journalistic treasure. He continued on about one or another complaint, sipping his coffee (which he surprisingly never said a word about, good or bad) and reading the paper. Katie and I sat idly by, waiting for something to say or hoping maybe Kevin would save us all one last time. He did.

When I had had enough coffee to sink a cruise liner and Katie had managed to nibble her way through six pieces of toast, we were anxious for something to do or say. Each tiny spurt of conversation either of us were inclined to begin was met by Mr. Bentworth with a stunting grunt or a short, harsh clearing of the throat as if we were interrupting him. And then the buzzer rang. Kevin!

"Hey, he's awake," Katie declared. She finished a sip of coffee and jumped at the chance to leave the table.

"What the hell is that infernal racket?" Mr. Bentworth asked, not taking his eyes from the business section. "Sounds like the doorbell has a short in it."

"Actually, it's Kevin's buzzer," I answered coldly. "I installed it so he could reach us anywhere in the house without straining his voice. He rings it as soon as he wakes or if he needs something."

"Oh, I see," the man responded. He looked beyond his newspaper into the room where Kevin was laying. "Well," he said. He neatly folded the paper back to its original rectangle, repositioned the sections in their correct order, twice checking that "B" followed "A" and so on, and took one, slow final sip of coffee. "Oooh, that's gotten a bit cold. You might want to warm that up for me a notch." He patted the table firmly before rising and took several small, slow steps across the kitchen floor and into the family room toward Kevin's side. He paused beyond the entryway and I could see his fist behind his back, hanging low near the seat of his pants and behind him. He flexed then stretched then rubbed each hand three times and then set them to a loud clap as he stepped forward into the room.

"Well, son," he said, a bit too loudly. "What have ya gone and gotten yourself into now?"

I could just see beyond Mr. Bentworth's frame that a smile arched across Kevin's upper lip. It was the slightest recognition, but it announced that Kevin knew it was his dad and that his dad was okay.

"Hey, dad," a brittle voice ushered from Kevin's throat. "How are you?"

"Oh, I'm just fine," he answered. He tapped his boy on the shoulder and pulled a chair alongside the bed. "Don't force yourself to talk. I don't want you risking your comfort." The compassionate man had returned at the moment he was most needed. His harsh, order barking tone was gone as he softly said that Kevin should rest and they spend some time together. "I'm not going anywhere. We got all the time we need to talk. Say, your family here is quite nice. Your wife has been an ideal host and August, well, August did all right by me, too."

Kevin nodded a thankful glance in my direction and smiled toward his wife. He seemed at peace with us there. I made my own way into the room to be with them. The dishes (and I hope Mr. Bentworth's coffee) could wait.

Shortly, Kevin's energy increased, either a result of the morphine wearing off or the presence of his family, or perhaps a combination of both. He was soon piecing together slow, full sentences that showed coherent thoughts. His breath remained short, but his conversation resonated of happiness.

They talked mostly about how things were in Cooperstown and how Kevin liked living in the South. They reminisced about Kevin's mom, filling in pieces to the puzzle of the woman I had never known. They shared favorite baseball moments and future hopes for the Cincinnati Reds. Kevin's responses came mostly in short, jerky phrases or comfortable smiles, with an occasional cough or sputter between. Laughter seemed to be his most easily attainable reaction. Mr. Bentworth did most of the talking and Kevin would smile at some memories, laugh at others, and allow others to pass without reaction. But his laugh was full and alive. A stark contradiction to the fading depth within his eyes.

When the idle chatter of memories and laughter transgressed into final farewells and tender moments, Kevin's wife stepped toward me and shrugged her head in the direction of the kitchen, urging me to join her.

"No," Kevin uttered as we stepped away from his bedside. "Please, stay." The words were barely audible.

It was Mr. Bentworth who completed his son's plea. "Stay, please," he said. "You are our only family here and anything we discuss is your business too. "Please," he added. He touched my left forearm and ushered us back to where we had been standing. "Stay with us. Talk with us."

I couldn't help but smile that Mr. Bentworth sounded so much like a priest. I wondered if my mother had not said those words a thousand times while she administered someone's death. It was strikingly comical coming from this disgruntled, sometimes sharp and unhappy man. I wiped my smile away, hoping it had passed for warm sincerity at the invitation, and stood at Kevin's side. This was, quite obviously, not a funny situation.

Kevin had a way about him that insisted upon finding the good in everything. He didn't want to die a sad, somber death. He wished that he be with those who loved him and that their burdens, our burdens, be somehow eased by his optimism. There the four of us were, alive and together for the first and only time, and as the conversation wavered in and out, I began to reflect on Kevin's passing years which had suddenly caught up with us.

I thought back to that day when Kevin and I had tossed fantastical wishes into a canvas tent on the opening day of the 1980 baseball season, in Cooperstown. How many days had come and gone between then, days after we first met, and now, when my friend was dying. I thought of the irony of youth, how it slips by us and we only realize how sweet it is after it is out of reach. And I thought of the bonds and boundaries of friendship, for both at times are as equally compelling. I had certain rights as a friend to be there at this passing, to have known him and to know his family. Yet I was still unwelcome in certain enclaves of his being. I never understood the depth to which he missed his mom, nor would I share with him the profound misgivings about his father. I could only enter so far, somewhere into his mind to learn of him what he wanted to share.

I remembered so vividly the look on Kevin's face on that day back in April of 1980, as he tossed the carnival baseball into that strange tent with its peculiar hawker standing guard. It was so clear, his glaze, so definite that Kevin knew exactly what to wish for. I may have wished to play in the World Series or maybe walk on the moon. Who knows, maybe I wished to be a sports journalist and had all this time never realized that my wish had come true. But somehow, the look in Kevin's eyes that day said he was determined then and always to know his wish and to see it come true. And there on his death bed, I saw that look again. Only now it was from the other side, the look of satisfaction, at having reached a goal. The look so few get to share, the look of a wish fulfilled. It wasn't that he was dying, that was not his goal. It was in something his father had said to him. And in searching through my memory of their conversation, I finally found the words that had brought Kevin his final happiness.

They were so simple, and were words I had heard time and time again as a boy and as a man. While they were words not difficult to hear, they were words sometimes difficult for their giver to speak. My mother and father had said them too often, perhaps. So much so that I lost in the repetition their true meaning and took for granted what they were saying.

"I'm proud of ya, son," Mr. Bentworth said. "And I love you."

And that was all it took to erase years of heartache, years of doubt and anger. Kevin needed the solemn recognition that who he was and what he had become was something his father could respect. In the contradiction that was Ridley Bentworth, he did not launch into a litany of Kevin's baseball accomplishments. No, when Mr. Bentworth finished his sentence to Kevin, it was not baseball that was on his mind.

"I'm proud of ya, son," he said. "And I love you." He pause. "You've always been a good person. You've got a nice family, and damn if you didn't stick by me all these years when I was not the easiest person to tolerate, yet alone love. I wasn't great at raising you and your sister without your mother around, God rest her soul. But we tried our best and we got through okay. Thank you, son." He whispered. "Of course, you could have given me grandchildren," he added. The warmth of the joke spread like compassion through the aftermath of a catastrophe. Katie and I let loose our tears at that moment and Kevin laughed a hearty, spitting laugh that convalesced into harsh, heavy coughing. He was having his last laugh.

The cough subsided into a silent hum of air passing finally through the frail lungs, and the heart pumped remorsefully through the diseased veins, carrying the diseased blood into the withering organs. Kevin opened his eyes and peered through a painful haze – he had been without the steady droll of morphine some four hours now – once at each of us, holding a steady gaze on each set of eyes.

His first and quickest gaze was to me. We had been friends for so long that there wasn't much to be said. We had spent our whole lives saying those things, and I would continue living mine wishing I had said more. That's what friends do. They say things from the heart by doing things together, by laughing, by supporting, by just being friends. Besides, he owed longer gazes to the others.

Then he stared long at his father, trying so hard to fill in one instant all the missing years of stupidity between them, to pass in a minute the many lost moments they could have shared. The memory flickered in his eye as a tear appeared and he blinked it away. They had said their peace, and his passing was not an atonement but rather a recognition of contentment.

The longest and final gaze was to his wife, a plea and an apology all at once. A plea to go on living, to find happiness, to maybe even remarry someday if it brought her joy. And an apology for having to leave. They had had a good marriage and she would find it difficult without him. But for now, she was at peace knowing his suffering was about to end. For despite the pain-numbing effects of the narcotics, it was his mental anguish that bothered her most. Seeing him possess the knowledge of what was happening had crippled her. He winked at her with his right eye and she fell into tears. It was his way of saying "I love you," as he mouthed the best effort of those words through his dry and starched lips.

Then he closed his eyes briefly. The murmur of the heart monitor crawled along a decreasing rhythm toward death. He took in a breath and reopened his eyes, looking collectively at the three of us. Would his final words sum up his life? Would he release a pent-up secret held quiet all these years? Would he attempt one last joke, "I told you I was sick, but no, you didn't believe me..." Or would he just wait?

He raised his left hand a half an inch from the bed and waved goodbye.

36 The Funeral

I have previously written that Kevin's funeral was a direct antithesis to his life, and that matter holds truer to my heart than the sentiments I expressed that morning of September 28, 1998. While he was charismatic and jovial at one turn and moody and complex at the next, Kevin was all about show. What separated him from the competition was that he could back his show with performance. He was like his former teammate and part-time friend, Mark McGwire, who had reached the improbable number of seventy home-runs in a single season to cap off the unbelievable feat we had all followed that summer. Kevin had lived long enough to witness that spectacular moment on September 5th when Maris' record finally fell, but he could not have imagined McGwire would go on to hit eight more before the season's final out. That Sosa as well had reached the sixty-second plateau of home run immortality was all the more reason to engulf ourselves in the clamor. Kevin was weak, barely awake, but still coherent as I told him Sosa had done it.

What a season! It was the stuff of legend, the kind of story they would have told about Kevin Bentworth had he lived longer, had he played further into his years, had death not taken him out of the game mid-way through the fourth inning.

His performance was so practiced that he barely resembled himself while in game mode. It was the personality of concentration that divided him from who he was on and off the playing field, a split personality not of mental health but rather keen awareness that pushed him away from those who could not understand him and drew him closer to those who loved him. He was revered for what he could do, but respected by those who knew him best. He maintained true to himself in the face of other's lack of appreciation. He was Kevin Bentworth, through and through, during greatness and defeat, in life and in death. There was no oscillation. On the mound, he would taunt and ridicule players as his confidence grew and when they bested them, he never apologized. Competition brought out the best in his ability but the absolute worst in his personality.

In his personal matters, he was more sincere than God. Nothing kept him distant from his wife, his responsibility to her was determined and righteous. It helped that she understood his career would take him on the road, across the country and away from home for weeks on end. Katie enjoyed traveling with him and loved to watch the game she had played during high school in its softball form. She told me they never fought longer than was necessary. When they did, all matters would be resolved before Kevin went to practice or started a game. It was as if neither wanted to be angry when away from each other. I guess he spent a lot of time respecting and admiring her to compensate for how much he had angered and hurt himself about his father, and for how deeply he needed and missed his mother.

A modest religious ceremony marked his departure. Those players from his team who came to offer their condolences were relatively few, a good friend he had played with for several seasons or a coach he had known since the minor leagues, and a few others who wanted to say farewell. The commissioner of Major League Baseball was there as well as a few dignitaries, owners and financiers of the game who appreciated what he did for his team and the game. The most striking representation at the funeral was from my employer, The Cooperstown Owls. Murray, long since retired, hobbled in on the shoulders of our old pal Denkinger. He was by then the third base coach for a Triple A team in Indianapolis and hoped to someday make it to the Majors as a coach. He had never played under those grand lights.

The funeral came after a smaller, private ceremony was held in Kevin's honor at the Methodist church he and Katie had attended. I was to speak at both occasions and struggled over what I should say. How does one encapsulate nearly twenty years of friendship into a ten minute eulogy or a five minute commentary at a chapel? In a way, this is my eulogy to Kevin, the extended version of what I wished I had had the time to say that day.

An hour before the funeral, a small group, including Denkinger and Murray, Mr. Bentworth, Kevin's sister Sylvia and her family, Katie of course, a minister whose name may have been Milton or Miller, my mom and my dad, Melony and I, met to bid farewell. I read the same poem there as I would later read at the gravesite. I thought a poem by another would best surmise the life that had disappeared before us these last days. It seemed an appropriate way to remember Kevin. I read A. E. Housman's, "To an Athlete Dying Young."

There are too many moments of sadness on the day of a funeral, I recall having thought. There is the quiet, solemn time before the funeral as loved ones gather around to ponder or reflect. It is a sharp contrast to the visitation the day before when countless and unmemorable faces surface from the past to bid farewell in a respectful, purposeful manner. It is all they can offer, as if they want somehow to say that someone's life mattered. We refer to it as "paying respects" and it is heartfelt in its sincerity, yet poignant in its misfortune. Had we ever said so much to that person when he was alive? Had we ever shown so much love while he breathed and listened and needed to know that he was noticed? What calamity! We slowly tumble in and out of each other's lives, never thinking to say those things that we later stand around at a funeral home wishing we had said. I wonder, does anyone of us live this life really knowing, really hearing, how other people feel about us?

Then there is the mournful progression of the casket into the church and its temporary resting as we pass through a litany of payer and remembrance, sending up hope that the soul we knew is somewhere close to an imagined heaven. Then comes the profound drive to the cemetery, filled with the knowledge of finality. A trip we'd rather not see end, a destination which would be best left unseen.

And then the ethereal, determined gravesite. Its gaping hole of entrenchment, its grounded humility, its dusty permanence. We lay rest the body that had held the spirit, the charisma, the soul of a man, and we return to visit the spot in hope of some connection to all that which we do not understand. The body is in there, somewhere beneath, but the soul lives on in our memories, or perhaps elsewhere.

These thoughts encompassed my soul as I waited my time to speak on Kevin's behalf. Finally, the minister ushered me forward where I spoke to the tiny congregation.

After awkwardly stumbling through words that were intended to encompass Kevin but which never rose to the level of truly portraying his spirit, we climbed in our cars as a funeral director sealed the casket and lifted Kevin's remains into a hearse; an event unseen and eerily omnipotent.

We crossed a bridge on the way to the cemetery. I could do no more than watch the shadows of the cars emblazoned upon the concrete barrier that separated the traffic on the bridge. How parallel and so even, our cars and the people inside appeared when shadowed by the great sun above. It was early morning and the sun's angle was low to the horizon, casting long, heavy shadows that only mirrored our hearts.

The short drive across town to the church was an unfortunate time for us all. What we needed was reflection, a

371

chance to focus and contemplate. Instead, we were whisked into the church and filed into the pews with speed greater than wind, and the funeral began.

The usual hymns were sung and the minister went about his greeting, expressing generalities about Kevin meant to comfort the attendees. I did not envy a minister that position. Having attended and served so many funerals for mom, it never occurred to me before just how precarious a situation it is to oversee a funeral. How well can a minister or priest be expected to truly indoctrinate herself to a person during a simple passing on Sundays or an occasional chat at a social gathering? It is hard work, a veritable tight rope walk, that profession. Teetering between sincerity while expressing grief, and hope in offering evidence of the afterlife, the minister travailed through comments that impressed upon those who barely knew Kevin that the minister had grown so close to the departed, and made those of us who knew Kevin best appreciate his effort. It is an inoffensive trespass into a family's memory, and a dangerous encroachment of the soul. The minister was likable and joked well enough. Fittingly, his jokes were most attuned to Kevin. They were lousy. He tried his best to work baseball into the affair but obviously knew nothing about the game. It was sincere but painful watching him. At last, his comments concluded and he yielded the pulpit to me.

I had never been a highly spiritual man, but I believed firmly in a God who comforted and healed in the collective presence of those who shared similar beliefs. Mother had impressed upon me the courage to find God in everything, and while I was not devoted to the level of her commitment, I was evidence of God's work. I paused before speaking and looked over the small congregation. I sensed the lack of God's presence. As if he had more important matters by which to attend. It was a practical sensation, one that would have made me laugh had the situation not been so morose. I was to be a messenger, perhaps relaying God's will. My habit had been as a messenger of baseball facts, of statistics and scores. This was parlaying into territory outside my realm of experience. I searched the congregation to find mom's eyes for reassurance that I was up to the task but she was looking downward, perhaps in prayer. I can't say I felt empowered, but rather prepared. It was my task to comfort those who knew Kevin best.

"Anyone know any bad jokes?" I started. A ripple of fond laughter circled the church. "Kevin? How about you, buddy?" I asked a silent, motionless coffin. "No. Speechless. For once."

Another small trickle of laughter faded away before I continued in a more serious tone. "I think Kevin would have preferred it this way. Us, together, laughing a little. That was his way. He loved the spotlight but never wanted individual attention, and somehow found ways to do that with his off-beat humor. He was a team player, and wanted to win. Today, he has won and we, sadly, have lost. But not the final loss. 'The season is long,' our old Coach Culpepper from Roth used to say after a poor outing by the team. The season is long. And so is life. While we are sad today and will miss our friend dearly, we all have so much life to live tomorrow and the next day and the next, that we serve him best by living. And if there is a lesson to be learned, it is just that. Let us live the life Kevin has lost. Live until you're eighty, ninety, even a hundred if you can, just because Kevin could not. He would have loved it. If he had lived to be eighty, the Reds would have at least won one more World Series. That alone would have kept him happy. But his family, his wife, his friends, his laugher. All would have kept him going and enjoying whatever came of what could have been his next sixty or so years on this earth.

"Twenty-nine. Whew. I can't comment too much on how short that really is. I can still remember running around the Owls' playing field up in Cooperstown as boys, or kicking around campus together hoping to meet some girls, but in his mind he was searching for someone as sweet as Katie, whom he actually met there. That was his style. If he had an idea in mind, he was going to do it. He knew he'd play baseball and pitch for a living. And he did. It was just that easy for him. He knew he'd be married, and he married an amazing woman. I wouldn't doubt it if he knew that he would not live to turn thirty.

"It's just not much time. And yet, isn't it sweet that he had just enough time to touch us all? In only twenty-nine years he was able to affect each of us sitting here today in such a way that we traveled from New York, from California, from Minnesota, just to show how much we cared for this man. He lived long enough to make a difference, even though we perceive that time to have been too short. I know he made a difference in my life. What more can a guy hope for than a best friend? And all of you, the way he has helped you, remembered you at the holidays, sent you tickets so the kids could see a ball game. And ultimately, how he sealed up the one wound that had held him down all these years. It does not need to be addressed specifically because those it touched are here today and know full well what it is that Kevin has been able to do."

373

I located Mr. Bentworth and we exchanged a knowing smile, to which Katie patted him supportively on the arm.

"I'd like to read a poem I wrote recently while thinking about Kevin:

> Here go those days,
> those days of summer we used to share;
> The grand charlatans, we once compared
> Ourselves to legend.
> And hoped to ascend to heights unending.
> Of days from youth we passed on through,
> Into these days of Spring anew;
> When ours is hope and dreams unfurl
> From where we stand upon the world.
> To days of glory, in September's passing,
> We found these days were everlasting.
>
> And so it is we've come to die,
> To pass beyond this mortal eye.
> To summer's gone and springs eternal
> We grant this wish for hope immortal—
> That still the years are held inside
> In memories within our pride,
> For we have come to consider thee
> A friend, a friend, a friend, indeed.
>
> And that is how we must depart,
> Hold truth to love and love to heart;
> As timeless as our childhood...
> together any mountain we could
> Have climbed upon the highest crest,
> I lay thee down my friend to rest."

The tears that choked back in my voice were betrayed by those streaming down my cheek.

The remainder of the ceremony passed in the manner in which such things do. The scent of incense rose into the air, the lofty organ resonated to the heavens above the sadness we shared, and the minister bid final parting to Kevin's soul.

The procession out of the church was uneventful and marked by the silent plodding of heavy hearts. The lengthy time of reflection we wished for an hour earlier came as we made the half hour journey to the graveyard. It was a time of quiet for those in the family limousine, of which I was invited. No doubt that those in the other cars in the procession were busy chatting about the weather or the beautiful ceremony or their return trips home, or perhaps remembering other funerals of people even dearer to them. I as well had these same talks before as the outside visitor to other funerals. Now was different. This was my first experience of having lost someone from my own generation, my own friend. The few congratulatory remarks I received on having given a nice eulogy could hardly remove the cloud of sorrow that danced about my mind. I had all along been steadfast in unflinching emotion. I had not wanted to let Kevin know I was going to miss him when he died, and I had not wanted his wife to be burdened by others who were grieving. I allowed myself to sob.

The events at the gravesite were customary and went a little long due to the weather scorching above. Maybe it wasn't God's lack of presence I felt in the church but the air conditioner, I considered. Now that was a joke Kevin would have laughed over. It was inappropriate but the internal laughter helped me through. I did not help the fellow funeral goers when I chose to read the A. E. Housman poem a second time when the minister asked if I'd like to add any words to my moving sentiment.

And that was it. The ceremonial clumps of dirt were lobbed onto the coffin and we departed in slumbering silence back to our cars. We had a dinner for a few choice relatives and friends, even smaller than the morning's moment of prayer before the funeral. After which, we departed, back to our homes or hotels or the open road toward home. I wondered how many of these people I would see again over the years, which would attend my funeral; whose funerals would I travel to join. It is odd to think that at one moment the people we share a special day with may never come to cross our lives again. We can only hope that how we treated them, how we interacted, how we touched them will leave a worthwhile mark on the spirit they bring to our lives.

I stayed on at Kevin and Katie's house a few more days, long enough to see Mr. Bentworth back to the airport and to help Katie with a few chores necessary to prepare the house for selling. We would keep in touch we promised. I had promised as well to Mr. Bentworth that I would not be a stranger once we both returned to Cooperstown. This was a promise I will keep.

I packed my things with the odd sensation that I had visited a European hostel, a place where you are neither a guest nor family but rather a welcome occupant somewhere between. Katie entered the room with a silent knock.

"No need to knock," I said. "This is your house."

"You can't trust a widow," she said. "You never know what she's up to." I chuckled an uncomfortable laugh but her smile told me it was her way of coping. "Widow," she added, reflectively. "I guess that will take some getting used to." She carried a neatly folded package that looked like old newspaper print. She handed it to me. "Kevin wanted you to have this," she said. "It may smell like moth balls. It's been in the cedar chest a long time."

"What is it?" I asked.

"Well, open it and see."

I unfolded a time-trip memory as fast as the original moment had passed years earlier. It was a baseball jersey too small for either Kevin or me to wear as adults, but just the perfect size for a teenage boy. Emblazoned across the chest was the word "Worcester." Its fading orange color reminded me clearly of the day when Kevin had pitched a no-hit perfect game, striking me out in the tenth inning and thus ending my hitting streak.

"There is also this card," his wife added. "He signed it about six months ago. He said you would understand what it means. It didn't make sense to me."

I laid the uniform gently across my suitcase and opened the card. The cover was an animated baseball saying, "Hey, Thanks!" in a cartoon balloon above its make-believe head. Of course, somehow, he had found a card with the baseball caricature waving left-handed. *Best friends for life.* A pact. Opening to the inside, I read Kevin's recognizable scribble. "Here's to a 2 and 2 count," it read, "and the best friend a guy could have." Even I had forgotten that the count was 2 balls and 2 strikes. I would have guessed 3 and 2, a pitcher's pitch. But at 2 and 2, the pitch was all mine to either ignore or belt into the stands. He lobbed up a pitch less than his best and I swung and missed. And he remembered it like it was yesterday.

"Thanks," I said to his wife. "This is real special. It means a lot. Thanks."

"What's it mean, though?" she asked.

"Oh, not much. Just a little score we had to settle."

37 Approaching Storm

Summer hung parched and withered atop the northeastern United States and into Canada for the betterment of three months. The raging heat pulverized the flow of humanity to a slow crawl. The drought which had ensued after months of little or no rain was threatening crops and livestock from as far as North Carolina and into Nova Scotia, stretching westward into New York state and out to parts of Ohio, barely relinquishing the Midwest in its hell. Fear ran silent but deep that farming setbacks might be so bad as to cause a food shortage. It was hearsay to some, to others trepidation. Quite simply the worst summer on record since the great Dust Bowl, it had all but paralyzed the territory unlike any in over a half century. And the hope of release was slow and fading.

Desperate at times for cool air or rain, human activity was reduced to either necessity or escape. Necessity in work, mail delivery, shopping, an occasional mowing of a lawn (though many stood dry and parched all summer, and offered only that satisfaction of having done something rather than actual landscaping). As for escape – escape was just that, a means to forget about the heat and feel free from nature's grip for a span of hours. Often, comfort was found in air-controlled interior climates or in bowling alleys, bars, shopping centers or any place with a Bryant or a Trane. But for those determined for fresh air, open skies and the outer life to which we are accustomed, natural despite its unrelenting heat, there was no grander salvation than that of the old ball park. Such salvation in exchange of sweat and stickiness seemed free entry onto Olympus. As long as a good game was on hand, cold beer available and the home team was giving it their best, what price of discomfort the fans would pay was incalculable.

That an unwavering torrent of heat and humidity and dryness coincided with such a year only increased a spreading paranoia of the coming century. As Americans and world citizens alike, we lived in unchartered fear as the year 2000 loomed on calendars and clocks, the fires of doomsayers, conspirators and the like only stoked by the blistering cruelty of the summer heatwave.

As August gave way to September, the relenting wall of parched and withered air promised little respite. But in the tropics, that sultry land of sunshine, the circling seas were rising up and pushing storm after storm northward to meet the sweltering agony with open fury. Each week a new threat rose up in the form of hurricanes off the Atlantic shore. Most died out and dissipated somewhere out in the Atlantic, a few spun inward and wreaked mild havoc along the great coastal shoreline. But none were so severe and threatening as Hurricane Bryce, setting harbor just 250 miles south-southwest of Cape Hatteras, SC, where it stalled and gyrated, for two weeks, baffling weather prognosticators at its unusual activity. There it sat, gaining energy, force and momentum for its striking plunge northward, ready to level catastrophic destruction.

The birthplace of hurricanes continued to push humid north-westward air into the opposing dry land as the last of such major threats spun toward the shoreline. In mid-September, the winds began to cool as the Arctic fronts north of Canada began their winter creep toward January. And in that year the cool air may just have been our worst enemy. Such an air mass provided a welcome relief as cooler air instilled a return to open windows, and set folks to walking outdoors again. Yet, it was small relief as the arid climate remained absent that ever-refreshing, life-giving and sanity stabilizing force of rain. The storm glided past Georgia, across the Carolinas and over into Virginia with little more than a threat of gray skies and sprinkled showers. It was building in intensity and catapulting itself northward along the sea, swallowing gallons of water with each turn of its cyclical patterns. All along its path, eyes watched the ensuing storm, leery of where or what or who might be trampled underfoot of its heavy shoulders, and appreciative to recognize the technology that warns of such storms. And then it turned. Just a week into its reprieve as we sat ready and waiting for the lower states along the seaboard to feel its wrath, Hurricane Bryce swung outward into the Atlantic and northward to stand parallel to South Carolina. It had loomed there an entire week. In its threatening menace, we were reminded of our frailty. Katie and I had watched the news like children awaiting a forgotten Christmas as Kevin drifted between haze and death.

The television was tuned ritualistically to CBS channel twelve. We had heard the reports that a real threat existed. The forthcoming storm might grow massively enough to move inland farther than any hurricane before. Towns all along its path were in serious threat of being hit by Bryce, the century's worst hurricane. Despite the faith in science that was instilled upon me by father's passionate career in such matters, I merely scoffed at the idea that such a storm could push high winds and torrential rains that far west. We had never experienced a hurricane. But Mother Nature is fickle, and toward home it came. While equally marveling at the possibility of such a tremendous storm, I cautiously disrespected it and ignored the warnings.

So it was, then, that the report being launched from a satellite a thousand miles above in the unknown sky and transmitted into the safe haven of Kevin and Katie's home had confirmed what I had known was a far more threatening reality. Luckily, I was on the road that fateful day. Many of my co-workers had suggested not to travel, and the status of their safety as well as that of my entire family remained unknown to me.

38 Chapter the Last

I drove back to New York after the funeral. No sense flying into a possible hurricane. The slow steady road would ease me of my many burdens, soften the altering landscape of my life and ultimately point me immediately homeward. As the great highways of America rolled under the churning, constant wheels of American labor driven by, well, Japanese technology actually as I rented a Honda, I thought again of the Housman poem that I had read at Kevin's grave. In its utter simplicity I had found comfort in my friend's premature passing, yet the poem so profoundly echoed the opposite of Kevin's life. He had never won a race for his town, and not a single person from Cooperstown carried him shoulder-high through their streets. This was, of course, a product of his own doing, spurned by his conspicuous absence, but still it was not all that the poem made victory out to be through Housman's poignant message.

I rolled into and through my birth state of Pennsylvania. The storm grew in intensity as the wind-wrecked seas of the Atlantic pushed inland. This was another reason why flying was less appealing. If I were to find a flight that got off the ground, there was no telling when or where or at what mangled angle it might touch the ground again if the storm chose to blow it out of the sky. Driving seemed a better choice. Tired, hungry, weary from the road, I stopped off at a Bed & Breakfast somewhere outside of Somerset in a town called Johnstown, ironically famous for its floods throughout history, and laid low to wait out the brunt of the storm. I would face high winds and heavy rains, nothing compared to those who lived along the coast. I would also learn the next day that my accommodations were far less than another demon that caught Cooperstown in its sleepy ambivalence mightily unaware.

It was in the silent loneliness of the warm hotel with adequate service and fair accommodations that I decided to record these events for sake of my own understanding, perhaps as a series of memories. I was, fittingly, on yet another trip, one of many that have defined my life. Safely nestled between the past buried in a funeral vigil and the future bracing for a walloping storm, I pivoted in emotional limbo while contemplating my life. Kevin's fate had been decided, Cooperstown's was hanging in the balance, and mine was still being explored. After many revisions and about a gallon of Pepsi (Hey, old habits die harder than a kidney stone!), I jotted down the beginnings of my memoir. Upon re-reading, and almost throwing the pages into the garbage, I realized that the beginning is really the end, for it's where we end up in life that matters most. What got us there and where we were before are just fragments of the complexity. But where we are, where we stand with our ideals and our dreams, defines us and helps us to know ourselves.

Life has been pretty good to me, despite what appeared to be setbacks along the way. I have come through my experiences a stronger person with better judgment and clarity of thought. I sometimes consider myself fortunate for all that I have been able to do and experience in my lifetime. But I also waver back to thinking that it was all a product of my own doing. *Do the right thing*, my father had often told me, *and good things will happen to you.* I think he was right. Still, I cannot help but wonder if maybe luck had something to do with it. After all, I played the game then and report it now the only way I knew how – with one eye on the future, one eye on the past and hands planted firmly in the present steering the imbalance between those two extremes. I will probably spend the rest of my days wondering whether life is about luck or planning. Who knows? There is plenty of life to be lived and maybe I'll have a definite answer some day. I know I still have a lot to learn. In fact, there is only one definite: of all that I have come to know, the only thing I know for absolute certain is that I do not know enough.

I have a family now. Melony gave birth to our twin sons in the fall of 2000. The oldest, Hank August, is much like his dad but smart as a whip, much like his mom. His brother, Kevin Roberto, is serious and determined. Neither dad nor Melony objected to baseball-inspired names, but dad understood something about the nod to equality in the naming rights of both of my sons. Fences and records can always be broken, but it takes baseball to bring down social barriers. Dad and I are closer now than ever and neither allows ourselves to regret a day of our time together. For that I am fortunate. He was never one for juniors anyway, or else I would have been Christopher William Monroe the Second. Or maybe the third. In some way, it lends credence to the fact that naming someone isn't always about who they will become but more so about who you hope they might best resemble.

I returned to Pittsburgh in the early spring of 2001 to watch the Pirates take the field in a way I had never thought possible. On real grass and playing at home. It was a dream come true and a hope fulfilled all in one solemn moment. With the opening of its baseball-only stadium in 2001, Pittsburgh christened PNC Park, a natural grass playing field designed in the tradition of old-fashioned ballparks, thus earmarking a new era of Major League Baseball to start the Pirates' third century of play in our changing hometown. I took my mom to the game and she quickly recognized the light scaffolds that had been designed as an homage to Pittsburgh's past, echoing the structure of Forbes Field where the Pirates had played from the 1920's to the early 1970's. Somehow taking mom was as appropriate as naming one of my sons Kevin. She was always a bigger fan of baseball than dad, and I think she liked being there in her own father's place. She was part of a legacy that Grandpa and I had shared. This was our way of ushering in a new generation with a resilient tradition.

And yet, the day had a unique sadness. That morning, the great Pirates player Willie Stargell had died. He was undoubtedly the leader of the 1979 Championship team which had so inspired my youth. It was somehow fitting that his passing came with the dawning of a brand new era, for the city of Pittsburgh, for the Pirates, and even for myself. It was as if childhood had finally been sealed shut permanently. Kevin was gone, Cooperstown was torn asunder, and my boyhood hero, whom I had attempted to emulate by teaching myself to bat left-handed at the age of ten, was gone. The future looked bright, but just a little glance to the past kept things in perspective.

Pittsburgh's people paused in a reverent moment of absolute stillness as memories of "Pops" lingered in the paradoxically balmy April afternoon. Then, the game began.

Overall, the experience of watching the Pirates play in a new ballpark was surreal. I expected to reach the end of the game, depart from that new stadium and drive home to Pittsburgh – as if I had been in another city's park watching the Pirates on the road. Twice during the game, I looked toward the scoreboard and found myself lost in a mild confusion and wondering why the Pirates were batting in the bottom half of the inning. I had to remind myself that this was our new ballpark, and not some other locale where the Pirates would be the visiting team. The whole scene, the whole experience, was out of place. After having seen the empty spaces that had swallowed the game at Three Rivers Stadium for so many seasons prior, watching the Pirates in PNC Park was like a fantasy come to life before my very eyes.

It was a day that stands out from all my days in baseball. The weather was not seasonal at all. All of the fans on hand wore shorts and tee-shirts as we checked out the Pirates' new home. The threat of rain had persisted all morning and held off all afternoon. The temperature hung just below seventy degrees with a slight wind so that comfort was possible under loose and passing clouds. It was early April and the Pirates opened the 2001 season against, who would have guessed it, the Cincinnati Reds! Despite a Pirates' 8–2 loss, the irony was again striking. Had the opponent been the Dodgers, I would simply have given up my questions about life and accepted that Fate predicts all of our motions. However, the fact that the Reds played made me wonder. If there is an afterlife, Kevin smiled.

What wonderment it is to have one's team back and ready to play ball after threats of departure to new cities with newer facilities. The construction of PNC Park ensured the Pirates would remain in Pittsburgh at least until my fading days. And who knows, maybe someday we'll see another World Series parade come marching down Grant Street.

In a way, it was the same as it had been in 1936 for Grammah-ma and Grandpa, as it was for me in 1976, and as it was that day for me and mom in 2001. Another generation of fans watching a new crop of players.

The park is all that a Pittsburgher could have hoped for. As teenagers, Kevin and I used to visit our respective cities to watch the teams play in either Three Rivers Stadium or Riverfront Stadium, mirror images of each other in architecture, design and boredom; both cisterns of baseball oblivion. On these visits, we often discussed how we might design new ball parks in both Cincinnati and Pittsburgh, what they would look like, where in town would they be constructed. One look at PNC Park assured me that the reality of the new park far outreached my wildest hopes. It is perfect. It has character and quirkiness, mass appeal and feelings of home. Its site lines are immaculate and its view of downtown Pittsburgh stunning. From any seat, one can envision the enchanting historical push through time that Pittsburgh represents. In a single panoramic view from inside PNC Park, one is witness to the rolling Allegheny River, muddy in its entrenchment through the centuries. One squints against the sun's bounding reflection from the high reaching glass of skyscrapers. One is taken aback by the composite of new and old, the weathered and the fresh. It is a skyline that represents the halcyon days that put Pittsburgh on the map as steel spurred our nation's growth. Its collective simplicity renders thoughts of nature, cyclical in its progress from east to west, buildings rising and falling, up and down, like time. Its strength rests on the flourish of development from the post-World War II era, the renovation toward cleanliness of the 1980's, and the steel expansiveness of the ever necessary rustic bridges that carry traffic across the rivers and in or out of downtown. Surrounded as I was by the newest initiate to the Pittsburgh skyline, PNC Park, I could not help but think of the irony of the passage through time which we call life. Of all the games played in that memorable city, of all the fans who attended, who booed, who hoped, who commiserated; of all the players who strutted across four fields in some twelve decades, sharing the team logo; of all the people who called Pittsburgh home and worked in the city who shared one common goal, rooting through good and bad and trial and glory for those damn Pirates!

There I was, a grown man, returning to the city of my earliest youth, in a ball park built just for fans such as myself, and before me sat the sprawling urbanite history that is Pittsburgh, Pennsylvania. On the fresh dirt and slender grass of the great outdoors that is baseball, young men and aged veterans alike began to pursue their dreams or complete their imperfect careers, and baseball had survived. It had survived the economic flux that had time and again driven it to the brink of oblivion. It had survived racism and social unrest that sought to separate it forever. It had survived wars which threatened the lives of its greatest athletes and surrendered the lives of so many of its sincerest fans. It had been passed on by generations now gone into the hands of women and men who would go on to birth its next great hitter or its next heartbreak pitcher. It had even survived itself! And in proximity closer to my own reality, it had indeed survived what had seemed a monumental storm – a tornado that had leveled Cooperstown just two and a half years before. Yet here they were, playing baseball still. Playing it again.

It all came back to me that afternoon. The realization that the tornado was just a part of the grand history that is our game, and the grander backdrop of life which the game represents. It was not the end of an era, but rather the turning point of one era that will remain as long as people come to watch the people who come to play the game. It was, in a way, the first step toward rebirth. For as much as baseball turns its eyes to Cooperstown, its heart is in the fans who watch the game and in the players who compete its contest.

Sometime during the seventh inning stretch, I relived the moments when Kevin and I first stepped on the street that once housed our beloved Hall of Fame. I was never a big fan of the singing of "Take Me out to the Ball Game" anyway, and the distraction passed the time. Sure, disliking the song contradicts everything I believe about baseball tradition, but I can't help wonder about its author. From all accounts that I have studied, the poor fellow never reaped a penny from his ditty that is such a part of America's fabric. In fact, he may have died completely broke. For all I know, maybe Francis Scott Key did as well and I should allow myself to drift into thought at the playing of our National Anthem as well. But I don't. I only lose myself in thought during that song about popcorn and crackerjacks. And on that April afternoon of 2001, I happened to be thinking about the storm that had annihilated my home in 1998, a few days after Kevin's funeral. And, not coincidentally, it seemed to me, shortly after the McGwire-Sosa extravaganza.

Two separate masses of cloud had split across the sky like a soul divided on that day. As the west relented, offering to abide, the east pushed onward, threatening storm. In reckless confrontation the sides entangled, and underneath the living masses slept. The division stood fast like a river of peace awaiting the final hour with hope as its only vestige. It too had a mission: coming forth to conquer the thwarting prowess of nature, a dimly lit cauldron of goodness. But still the storm was waged, and as its price the heavens tore apart the eternal peace accord, and relenting was impossible. A thick and heavy weight hung upon the sky as if black, saucy drips of night were falling from the stars. The air grew taut, holding back the deluge with the strength of history and the weight of the gods. But even that was to give, unable to hold and unable to withstand the unleashing fury that would pull the heavens in upon themselves. Daylight, in its last glimmering moment of surrender, disappeared behind the sky in fleeting fear. First blue, then sanguine, then purple, then fading, fading black, then gone. Night creased open and the storm squeezed through a crevice of pause. A wind rolled out from the clouds, slowly crossing the frontline in early attack, increasing in volition with each burst through the parallel opening. Colliding east into west, the night broke clean apart in a glorious, awe-inspiring tumult of energy encased in the cradle of God, embodied in the force of

385

nature and wrapped in the pulse of humanity. A searing blast of bitter rain leapt toward the ground as cloud after cloud hemorrhaged and ruptured, bleeding water unto the sky. And the masses awoke.

The air hesitated in its own stillness as the people below rose to a sound and a serenity they had never before imagined. Some fled to their knees, prostrate to the welcome end of the universe. Others scampered for shelter in corners of the man-made lodgings that hid them from the glare and deafened them from the din. Still, others stumbled into the madness, stricken with either fear or amazement or respect, and dove their hearts into the whirl of passion that was the storm. There are but a few souls alive who would recognize the end of time for its unmatched rampage upon the era, and there they gathered in a seemingly drawn network of togetherness as if high priestesses of the apocalypse had called them outward into the storm. It is not the devastation, nor the victory of the ages that draws them near, but rather the sheer adrenaline of witnessing such an event. If guaranteed survival, one might offer to stand head to toe against a tornado just for that glimpse of such raw, unrelenting poison. A power so grave, so thrashing and yet so alluring.

Even as the sirens wailed and families ran to save their own or to protect their neighbors, no one in the tiny village of Cooperstown quite knew what it was that was encircling their night. A day that had ended so quintessentially normal as to appear commonplace beyond routine, had lodged itself unequivocally into history as a crossroads with destiny.

To repeat the destruction in terms of numbers would do injustice to the human spirit that strode beyond the storm. The damage was awesome. To rebuild was their only notion. It was not just hope, not some afterthought of opinion. It was a way of life. To forge onward, to surrender nothing, save the lives lost to the storm and the energy spent to survive. The dignity of the community was brought to a perfect understanding that declared, *We will go on.*

Amidst the broken chaos, the rewards of history and the relics of a game were scattered like a plane wreckage across a field of aviation disaster. Strewn upon the ball field as a testament to their will – and thrown some fifteen hundred yards where it shook to a resting point upon what must have once been the infield (for nothing else resembled the light dust that once held runners aboard its shoulders) – lay the sign that had brought fame, recognition and civic pride to the community. Its steel frame bent just slightly, the plaque that had welcomed visitors to the National Baseball Hall of Fame and Museum lay askew upon the dirt, looking upwards to the now resilient sky.

That symbol, the tattered, surviving sign of the town's inner fabric was to become their rallying cry. What had built the city once, would build it again. Lost to the trees and the mountains were priceless, irreplaceable artifacts that would slip silently into legend, but what remained was a spirit, a belief in something greater than the whole and more significant than history. To lie would be to declare that the world wept. That was just untrue. Certain dignitaries took notice and patches of humanity joined in celebration or mourning or whatever cathartic reckoning they could muster up so as to feel part of something far from them. But as for worldwide declaration of grief? No. The tornado that tore Cooperstown at its heels was not a worldly event. It rocked the baseball world and terrified the most ardent fan, but it was not the death knoll of the twentieth century that some may have proclaimed it to be. In the greater story of existence it was merely a storm that spun up, levied rather awesome damage and went off into the fabled lore of time with a wisp and disappearing whirl back into the clouds.

But to those people and the millions around the world who share a sense that baseball is a seminal part of life, it was a devastation unlike any we had known.

I would love to suggest in poetic justice that the Hall had stood, that amidst all the shambles of our tiny hamlet stood the last bastion of greatness – as if Truth herself had declared it sacred ground and that all the pantheon and religious mystics of time had ascertained it right that such a place would resist the forces of nature. But that would be a lie. No Gods protected the Heroes for the Children. The Hall of Fame was tattered to every last shred of its glory. It was wrecked, solid and through to the core. Not even the foundation reminded me of much of anything that used to be something. It was a pile of rubble, some pieces tossed, all lost and an enormously hefty sum washed away to the wind.

There in PNC Park, on that nearly perfect Monday afternoon in early April of 2001, I remembered my first thought upon seeing Cooperstown devastated at the finger of the tornado. Tomorrow, we will begin to rebuild our town, I remembered thinking. And with it, the Hall of Fame will begin anew, enshrining what memories remained and hoping toward a new season to begin filling the chambered halls again. And if anything stood as a testament to what we were, to what we still may be, it was the knowledge that somewhere on baseball diamonds throughout America, young men and women alike were busy scooping up the leather bound object of fascination, tossing it into the air or to a nearby friend, and picking up where history had left off: top of the first, no score, no runners on base. Play ball!

About the Author

Dan J. Kirk lives in Pittsburgh where he follows the Pirates and raises three children with his wife, Michelle. He holds an MFA in Creative Writing from Chatham University, and an MA in Theatre Arts from Marquette University. When he isn't writing, he listens to the greatest rock and roll band of all time, Rush. Dan teaches composition and speech at Pittsburgh Technical College, and theatre for youth at Accent School of Performing Arts. He plans to publish his other novels (*Homestead Harvest* and *The Thorns of Life*) and various short stories and plays, and is working on his newest novel, *Twenty-One Funerals*. Kirk can be followed at www.danjkirk.com, or on Twitter (@DanKirk2112) and on Facebook.

About the Artist

Michelle Kirk is an artist of various media, though she specializes in jewelry and art parties in the home. She has a BS in Art Education from Edinboro University, and has taught classes at Michaels Craft stores for over ten years. Michelle teaches her three children as a home-school mom and also assists her husband, Dan J., in designing theatrical sets. She can be reached for cover art, parties or other freelance art projects via Facebook at Art & Crafts on the Go.

Made in the USA
Middletown, DE
19 September 2017